Lovestruck

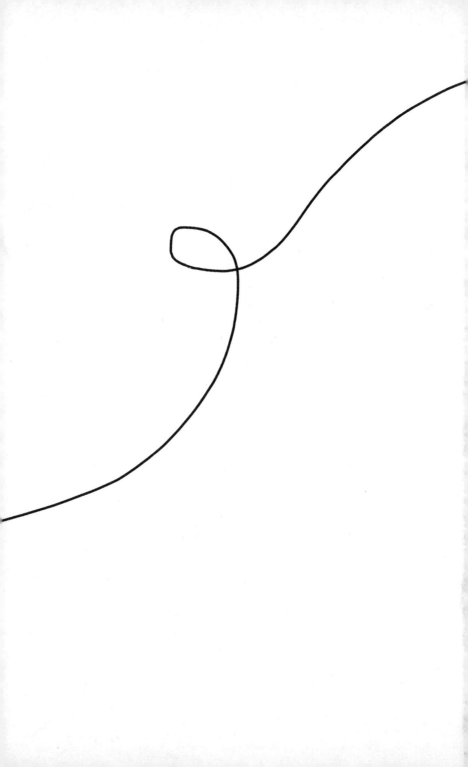

Lovestruck

Kate Watson

flux®

Mendota Heights, Minnesota

First Edition
First Printing, 2019

Book design by Sarah Taplin
Cover design by Sarah Taplin
Cover images by Pixabay

Flux, an imprint of North Star Editions, Inc.

Library of Congress Cataloging-in-Publication Data (pending)
978-1-63583-030-9

Flux
North Star Editions, Inc.
2297 Waters Drive
Mendota Heights, MN 55120
www.fluxnow.com

Printed in the United States of America

To Elsie, Hugo, and Archer,
who have given me three new hearts, a borderline
caffeinated-soda addiction, and immeasurable joy.

I love you more than everything.

Chapter One

Shooting an arrow into a crowd of people on the Copacabana in Rio de Janeiro is highly illegal.

Good thing I:

A) don't care, and

B) can't be seen.

I look at my target, a twenty-six-year-old beach rat who spends more time playing volleyball than he does even on his perfect hair. Then I glance past the vendors selling *camarão* and *água de coco* for potential matches.

Gaia, I hate this job.

Beach Rat is running his hands through his hair, wearing his speedo, like most of the Brazilians I see, and leering at the bikini-clad women who pass him. I've read the report on him: he was abandoned when he was six years old, and he was destined for life in the poorest *favelas* of Rio, begging, conning, and stealing to survive. Yet, somehow, mercifully, he was found only a few weeks later by his estranged grandparents. They took him in and raised him in a humble but loving home.

All of my assignments have stories like this. Olympus doesn't get involved in run-of-the-mill relationship problems. Only exceptional and difficult cases require divine intervention: the ones whose hearts have been damaged and who can't allow themselves to find real love because of their fears and personal demons. With a scope of billions of people covering most of the Western World, that means the Erote department is big and busy.

Beach Rat has had a string of one-night stands that is as long as the Copacabana shoreline, but he hates himself for it. When he gave a silent, desperate prayer for help one night last week, the job was processed by the Erote department and sent to a probie—me—because evidently the match is a simple enough one. For, you know, an exceptional and difficult case.

As if there is such a thing.

Months ago, I had a Thunderclap. *The* Thunderclap. The moment when everything became clear. Since then, I seem to be the only immortal on Olympus to see the truth behind matching. The reality is that I could spend days or weeks studying Beach Rat and the people around him. I could invest my heart and soul in his happiness—I could soulgaze, for Gaia's sake—and it would still all be for nothing. Because in the end, the Fates will decide what happens, no matter what I do.

I rub my stinging nose, swallow the lump in my throat, and turn back to my assignment. I've been here for an hour already, far longer than I need. It's time to match this *cara*.

Girl after girl passes him. He's a very attractive mortal, so the less-than-beautiful don't get a single glance. Seeing this, I know exactly what I'm going to do.

A pale, mousy girl in a dowdy one-piece walks by, and she looks at him longingly. Perfect.

I grab the bronze necklace I'm wearing over my bikini and pinch the arrow charm. My beautiful recurve bow twinkles into existence in my hands. I reach for my quiver and snag an arrow with a shimmering head—the mark of an Erote arrow—and nock it in one fluid motion.

The myths say that it takes two arrows to make a match, one arrow into both of your targets. Wrong. Of course, those same myths show my kind as chubby, cherubic, obnoxious, diaper-clad babies named "Cupid," because evidently the Romans weren't satisfied with causing the fall of Ancient Greece, they also had to steal and bastardize an entire pantheon of gods for their use, and . . . and . . .

Don't get me started on the Romans.

I have Beach Rat in my sights, waiting for him to make eye contact with the girl. If he isn't making eye contact with her at the precise moment of the arrow strike, he'll be matched with someone—or something—else. There's a reason Erotes spend twenty hours a week at the archery range: timing is everything.

And he's taking a lot of my time. If he would just look at her, already!

Ah, Styx. I'm going to have to suggest this.

I close my eyes and whisper to him with my mind to look at her. Suggesting isn't my strong suit. My dad says I'm too closed off for it, which is the same reason I can't communicate telepathically the way most fifth-years can. But don't underestimate how badly I want to get this job done and get back to Flagstaff for my other match.

Wait, where did that thought come from?

Concentrate, Kali. I put an image of the girl into my head and push it into Beach Rat's cluttered mind.

I fight through the sea of bikinis and workouts-of-the-day littering his mind until my suggestion clicks. My eyes fly open and I focus hard on Beach Rat. His eyebrows lift, and for a moment, I think he's going to make a rude comment to the girl, who glances away when his eyes meet hers.

Come on, he's finally looking at you. Look back at him. Look!

And she does!

Their eyes connect. I release my nocked arrow. It whizzes past tourists and vendors and sinks right into Beach Rat's heart. Slowly, the cocky grin on his face melts away, replaced by a look of reverence and devotion. A quick glance shows her wearing the same smile. They walk through the crowds to each other, and I have to steel myself to keep from getting sucked into the scene.

He thrusts out a hand and introduces himself. "*Oi, meu nome é João.*"

She grins and speaks slowly and loudly. "I'm sorry, I don't speak Portuguese. I'm Lana. I'm here with my parents." She points to a couple standing at a nearby booth, buying coconuts to drink.

So, obviously I don't care what happens. I don't. Unfortunately, my rapidly dropping stomach doesn't quite believe me. Because it just keeps getting worse.

This girl? She's here on vacation from North Dakota for her birthday.

Her fifteenth birthday.

Ferry me to Hades.

Chapter Two

I arrive at the Port on Mount Olympus moments later. Two dozen enormous, proud columns surround this expansive clearing, separating the Port from the forests and fields beyond. Transportation agents monitor the Port as hundreds of Olympians pop to and from their mortie jobs. Their clothes flash along with them, fashioning them in the style of immortals or mortals, depending on whether they're coming or going.

One impatient goddess stands out among the throng: my gorgeous, overachieving friend Deya. She glares at me with deep brown eyes, arching her immaculate eyebrows dangerously.

"Kali, have you lost your cursing mind?"

I stuff down my resentment as my mortal appearance fades. In its place is the simple white chiton all students wear. And my immortal glory. "What do you know?"

She's already striding away from the Port. "Everything. A high schooler? From North Dakota? What is wrong with you?"

"I didn't know!" I say, catching up.

"Then you should have taken the time to find out!"

Deya is in my year, but over the last few months, she's started acting like she's my de facto supervisor. Which I don't love. She worships my dad (figuratively, of course), and because she's the best in our year, he's given her unofficial license to watch over me. Considering that we're practically sisters, I think she's a little too eager to make her report.

Deya lectures me on every rule I once cared about, as if that will make me forget the Thunderclap. So as we walk from the Port to the Erote headquarters (where I'll soon receive a much scarier lecture from an Old-World God—a Big G), I distract myself with . . . anything else. The cloudless sky, the perfect, eternally seventy-five-degree weather, the gorgeous emerald-green grass and forests, the breathtaking flower gardens, the stables, the centaurs hitting on satyrs. Anything but another lecture.

After several minutes and thousands of upset words, Deya pushes me toward a building that makes the Parthenon look like a crude little barn: the sprawling Erote headquarters. Like most of the buildings, our headquarters are open air. When the weather is utterly perfect at all times, what's the point of blocking it out?

It takes a while to even get to the front steps of our building. There was a time when the marble and gold building with statues of famous, beautiful matches filled me with pride. Now the sight fills me with dread. Resentment.

But Deya isn't marching me inside. Wait . . .

"Deya," I say, "did my dad send you?" She doesn't answer. "You Gorgon turd! You were with Cosmo when he was monitoring me, weren't you? Has my match even been reported yet?"

"No, and you can thank me for that later."

"Why would I thank you?"

"Because this is mismatch number four, Kal! You know what happens if you get five."

I do know. I just don't care as much as everyone thinks I should.

We're coming up on our training grounds now, across from which stands the monolithic quartermaster vault, where our QM,

Cosmo, is on duty, along with thousands of other QMs. Cosmo is Hephaestus' grandson and utterly brilliant, just like the God of metallurgy, technology, and other genius stuff. Lucky for us, Cosmo has been assigned to the Erote department, something Deya happily takes advantage of.

We step up to the heavy, metal vault doors and Deya closes her eyes, a sure sign she's communicating telepathically. Moments later, the two-foot-thick door glides open, and Cosmo limps up with an aqua screen, an arrow, and a besotted grin.

Cosmo's adoration of Deya is an unfortunate birthright. His grandfather, Hephaestus, was once married to Deya's mom, who shattered his heart. It's sad, but no big surprise. Aphrodite leaves a trail of broken hearts wherever she goes.

The Goddess of beauty is kind of a jerk, even if she is Deya's mother. I can say this because she's also my grandmother. Like Aphrodite, Deya is the embodiment of beauty and desire. Her father is a gorgeous river god of the Amazon, and Deya shares his bronze coloring. Deya's is a kind of perfection even immortals don't see every day.

Meanwhile, Cosmo shares Hephaestus' shocking strength, dark features, clubbed foot, incomprehensible genius, and unrequited devotion.

Poor Cosmo.

"Cos," Deya says, "do you have the reversal arrow ready? I want to get Kali's assignment fixed before the day's reports are sent up." Before Cos can answer, Deya looks at me. "You know if you ever get your wings, this won't be an option, right? Reversals only work with training arrows."

"Gee, Professor, thanks for the totally new information," I say.

"Uh, Deya? The arrow's ready when you are," Cos interrupts.

He's wise not to address me, because he knows I don't care. Just like I didn't care the last three times I had a match reversed. "Deya, do you want me to go over how it works? You've never had a reversal," he says, not quite fawning.

As much as I hate my job, watching Deya flirt with Cos for her benefit is even worse. I glance across the training grounds to one of the few things I truly love about being an Erote: the archery range. But what I see isn't the orderly competitiveness of my typical training session; it's chaos, like a scene from the Trojan War. Arrows literally fly everywhere. People scream and cry and run for their lives. But instead of hotties like Achilles and Paris shooting, it's a bunch of puny first-years who don't know which end of the arrow is up.

Rather than yelling at the first-years for their abysmal aim like she usually does, the archery coach looks distracted. I narrow my eyes. I've never seen Artemis look so . . . so lost.

"Hey," a smooth, low voice says over my shoulder, and a swell of emotions rushes over me. I tamp them down and turn to see my best friend, Hector. He's the kindest and best immortal I know, not to mention the hottest. As the son of Apollo and the muse Calliope, he has his mom's black, wavy hair that reaches just below his ears, and his dad's piercing green eyes. He's also a muse, which just happens to be my dream job.

"Hey yourself," I say, holding back a smile that would set the fields ablaze. "What are you doing here?"

"I came to see my aunt." He gestures to Artemis but keeps his eyes on me in a way that makes the task of not marrying him on the spot positively Herculean.

I train my eyes on the field. "What for?"

A kid just shot an arrow into another kid's butt, and Artemis still hasn't yelled at anyone. What is going on with her? The commotion pulls Hector's attention, too. His eyes narrow. "I just need her help with one of my jobs. You know that reality TV producer I'm musing for?"

"Yeah, for the show where they hunt animals that terrorize villages and towns and stuff? What's it called, *Most Dangerous Game?*" He nods. "Nice job on the title, by the way."

"Thanks." A hint of a smile forms on his lips, but the flush on his cheeks tells me how much the compliment means to him. I'm not the only one medaling in restraint these days. "Anyway, I feel like I'm stalling with him. The network is pressuring him to go into monster hunting, you know, like Sasquatch."

"Why can't they leave that poor creature alone? He has a family, for Gaia's sake."

"I know. It's ridiculous. Anyway, the producer's vision for the show is good, and if he just sticks with it, it's going to be huge, even if he has to switch networks. But the 'talent' the network hired is this colossal tool, Stone Savage. He's a good hunter—great with a bow and arrow—but he's all about the monster crap. I just need a little advice on how to capitalize on the producer's vision."

It's a brilliant idea, going to Artemis. The Goddess of the hunt-slash-wilderness-slash-animals-slash-archery-slash-moon et cetera is the perfect person to ask for help. As if she senses his need, she raises her lovely, eternally youthful face and smiles at her favorite nephew across the field, waving him over.

Hector puts a hand on my elbow, shooting a frisson of hot energy through my arm straight to my heart. Pre-Thunderclap Kali would literally melt right now. Post-Thunderclap Hector knows this and is obviously not above using it against me. "I gotta run, but I'm going down the mountain later to take a cheesemaking class from the satyrs. Do you want to come?"

Hector doesn't care about Olympian politics and has no problem being friends with immortals nowhere near the peak. As if it's not hard enough to resist the guy.

I cock an eyebrow. "Are water nymphs going to crash this party just to worship at your feet again like they did during the watercolor class? That was not fun."

"Hey," he says, looking mock offended. "Can I help it if water nymphs are the most discerning of all nymphs?"

I purse my lips until all of the flirtatious remarks that spring to mind have been stuffed into the back of my head. "Regardless, I can't come. But if you need a taste tester, I'm your girl." My ears get hot. Stupid, treacherous lips.

"Always," he says with a smile he seems to have made just for me. "I'll see you later."

I watch him cross the field, the back of his chiton both a relief and a regret. Artemis catches my eye and winks. She's my favorite teacher—by far—and she's always dreamed of something happening between Hector and me.

Get with the times, Artemis. Not gonna happen.

Cosmo calls me over to the aqua screen to review the particulars of my mismatch. I take the reversal arrow from him and back up to sit down on the stone QM steps. He plops down beside me while I expertly twirl the arrow. As Cosmo talks, I think about how kind he's being, about how we're outside instead of at his desk, and about how he brought everything to me so as not to risk having to report this to the Big Gs. I'm sure it's Deya's influence that prompted this undeserved kindness. I feel a tinge of guilt at just how much extra work I've given him of late.

I shake it off quickly, remembering I'm not the one to blame here. I'm the victim, for Gaia's sake. We're all victims of the Fates. Besides, with Deya hanging on Cosmo's every word, at least this mismatch is working in his favor, for a change.

Deya is practically drooling as he reminds me of the reversal process. She lives for the job. She's the best, most competitive Erote I know, and she consistently outperforms even the sixth-years. She's never missed a match, but she's had to wait longer than she's wanted to for the perfect shot. Anything that makes her better understand her "calling" is right up her alley.

I love her, but it's kind of annoying.

When they're done, Deya fills her quiver and Cosmo turns to me. "Do you want to see any of my new arrows while you're here? I just put the finishing touches on a self-guided arrow that your dad is already flipping over."

"No thanks," I tell him. "You know I'm a purist."

"That's why you're Artemis' favorite pupil," Cosmo says.

Deya looks pointedly at Hector, who's still talking with his aunt. "There may be other reasons at play there."

"Shush," I say. "Can I go reverse this already? I really want to get to Flagstaff before lunch."

Deya's mouth falls open. Gaia, is she ever dramatic. "Are you serious? *You*—the goddess of job hating—want to get back to work? Are you planning to match a band geek with the first bully you see? Or a vegan with, I don't know, lunchmeat? I can't believe they haven't yanked your training wings yet."

"The day is still young."

She eyes me suspiciously. "I'm coming with you. Don't even try to argue, or I'll tell your dad."

I glare, but I don't fight her. I may not care about this job, but I do care about not getting Dad involved in this particular screwup . . . or my current ungrounded status. We say goodbye to Cosmo and wave to Hector and Artemis, then head away from the archery grounds and step onto a perfectly smooth stone pathway, surrounded by forests and gardens that would put Eden to shame. We pass amphitheaters created for the Games, theaters cut into hills, and tracks for races, all in ideal condition thanks to the Domestic Comfort department. Hestia, the ancient Goddess who heads the department, takes her job very seriously.

After all, around here, upsetting the boss can make your life Hades.

We wind around the path to the Port. Although we could technically disappear and reappear at will, Hermes and Zeus decided ages ago to track all transportation on and off the mountain. They bent the magic on Olympus to make the Port the only place an immortal can "jump" from, except the Ancients. The Big Gs.

Deya grabs my arm to slow me down.

"Seriously, Kal, you haven't been in a rush to get back to a job since your *Thunderclap.*" I hate the way she emphasizes the word. "What's going on?"

"Nothing's going on. You say we need to reverse Beach Rat's match, so we're reversing it. That's fine. I just want to get to Flagstaff and match Ben—"

Deya's head cocks to the side. "You've named him?"

"Uh, no. I didn't name him, his parents did."

"But you're referring to him *by* name. Don't you think that's a problem? You know what your dad always says about over-familiarity."

"Do you really think my dad should be giving anyone lessons on Erote professional ethics?"

"Okay, okay," Deya says in a placating voice. "So after five weeks of following 'Ben,' why are you suddenly ready to finish? I've had three jobs in the time it's taken you to prepare for this one."

"That's not fair. You're the top in our class, unchallenged."

"And I'm also the most thorough, which only proves my point. Besides, we both know I'm only unchallenged because you stopped challenging me."

"I'm still better at archery," I taunt. She sends me a smiting glare. "What's the point of caring like you do, Deya? The ones that break up, the ones that create problems, the ones that stick? It's all up to the Fates!"

"Then what's the point of any of our jobs at all? What's the point of this specific job? If the Fates have already decided who 'Ben' will fall for and how long they'll be together, then why take *five weeks* on this guy? Why not just stick him already?"

I frown. Why *am* I spending so much time on this assignment? I think of the boy, Ben, and the way he focuses on his notebook when he's writing lyrics, as if the world has ceased to exist. I think of how he checked his phone for hours after he texted his dad last week, waiting for a response that never came, and how he channeled that disappointment into a new song that's *so close* to being just right. I think of how he saw some kids making fun of a freshman girl after choir and how he interrupted them to tell the freshman how much he liked her solo.

He's a good person. He's walled himself off from love, but when love breaks through that wall and allows the real Ben to emerge, he'll become more than he ever thought possible. He needs it.

So why haven't I stuck him, already?

The answer hits me. "The Fates."

"Huh?"

"They made me this way. I'm just their mindless pawn."

"And here I thought the Oracle was the root of all your problems for making you an Erote."

"Don't get me wrong, she sucks, too, but at least she was just doing what the Fates told her."

She takes a large step away from me, hissing, "Are you thanatotic or something?"

Maybe I am thanatotic. I certainly seem to have a death wish, blaspheming like this. But herein lies the problem: my parents may have given me my immortal body, but the Fates wove the thread of my existence. They gave me my personality, the core of who I am. How can they blast me when they made me this way in the first place? Everything I do is ultimately their responsibility. We're all just pawns in their twisted game. It infuriates me. "I'm not thanatotic. But if I am, it's the Fates' cursing fault."

And with that, Deya is sprinting away from me, a blur of chiton trying to outrun the lightning bolt she seems sure is coming my way. I huff, but I can't blame her.

I am tempting the Fates, after all.

I give Deya fifteen minutes before I catch up to her. She's at the Port, talking to our friend Teresa, whose mortie nurse outfit flashes back into her chiton as she returns from a reaping. Of course, because she's a psychopomp—a reaper—her sensible nurse's shoes happen to be steel-toed. She's hardcore like that. She has to be.

When souls separate from their body, the happy ones are happy. The confused ones are confused. And the wicked ones are bundles of boundless, angry energy. They learn fast that no one messes with Teresa. Because she's so tough, it's easy to overlook the fact that she's several inches shorter than me. She's the daughter of Thanatos, the personification of death, and Macaria, who is Hades and Persephone's daughter. So most people give her a very wide berth. All they see when they look at her is death and more death. But I see my no-nonsense, tough-love friend who doesn't take crap from anyone, but who would go to Hades and back for the people she loves.

The chiton looks amazing against the obsidian skin Teresa inherited from her primordial grandparents, Nyx and Erebos. But the look in her eyes tells me she's not planning to talk fashion with me. Not that she ever has.

She nudges Deya, and they both eye me. Deya leans farther back the closer I get.

I hold up my hands. "Truce?"

Deya purses her lips but nods.

Teresa looks unfazed. "So are you done calling down lightning on yourself, or do you need me to knock some sense into you?"

Before I can even frown, Thrax, the god of sexual harassment marches into the clearing. As the son of Ares, the God of war, Thrax comes by his bad boy looks and generally berserk state naturally. He ignores Teresa, like most everyone does, and leers at Deya and me as if we couldn't shoot an arrow through his face. His dad is obsessed with Deya's mom.

"You ladies seeing any trouble down there? Security has asked Demi-Dork to look into some disturbances at the holy sites. Wouldn't surprise me to learn that people are setting up temples to worship your bodies."

Deya balls her fists, not because of what Thrax said about her, but about Cosmo. Calling him a demi isn't just inaccurate, it's wildly offensive. Deya may flirt with Cosmo to get her own way, but she doesn't let anyone talk badly about him.

"Jump in the Styx, Thrax, or I'll drown you in it," she warns. Her threat only seems to excite him. Unruffled, he glances at me.

"What about you, Blondie?" His eyes roam over me, and I want to bleach my soul. "You're not revealing any Olympian secrets, are you?"

"Thrax," I say sweetly and slowly, so he can keep up, "the only secret around here is how your enormous head could hold such a tiny brain."

Teresa and Deya both laugh as Thrax puts both hands to his forehead and storms away.

"Okay, are you ready to fix Beach Rat so we can match Ben already?" Deya asks, still huffing in Thrax's direction.

I'm too high on solidarity to be annoyed that she's acting like my boss again. "Let's go."

We each grab our identical long, bronze necklaces bearing a heart, an arrow, and a single wing. We wave to Teresa, look at each other, and in a blink, we're gone.

Chapter Three

The reversal and match were surprisingly easy. Deya found Beach Rat a match so quickly, I could almost be embarrassed that I didn't see her. If I cared. She owns the coconut stand that Beach Rat makes a point of exercising by. Poor Fifteen was arguing with her parents that she and Beach Rat were made for each other. He was arguing the same thing in rapid Portuguese when Deya made me shoot the reversal arrow. A quick prompting had him looking at the coconut stand owner. I matched them in an instant, and it was like nothing ever happened. They won't remember a thing.

Whoop-de-doo.

So we're just in time for lunch when we transport ourselves from Rio to Ben's high school in Flagstaff.

The smell is the first thing I notice. I step into the gray girl's bathroom at Ponderosa High, wrinkle my nose, and push open an orange stall door that bears the message, "Jake Edwards is a skank." The stall door next to mine opens a moment later, and out walks Deya. She looks more like a runway model than a high school student, but this is as much as she'll water down her beauty.

We both glance in the mirror to do a once over. In my standard mortie uniform of jeans, a concert T-shirt, and Vans, I feel comfortable. For all my famed glory, I love playing mortal. I darken my too-bright blue eyes, turn my honey-blonde waves into shoulder-length curls with a bit of frizz, and add freckles to my naturally tan skin. For fun, I give myself an eyebrow that arches more than the other and a nose slightly too big for my face. I smile at the result. Cute, but forgettable, exactly as I should be. Even Deya is forgettable to mortals. It's part of our anti-glamour, so to speak. We're as pleasant and attractive as we need to be to blend seamlessly into any circle. The moment someone's attention is off of us, though, it's like we never existed.

"You ready to finish your job?" Deya's reflection asks mine. "The bell should ring any moment." She raises a finger and lowers it at the exact moment the bell rings.

"Yes, mother," I mumble.

The gray and orange from the bathroom bleeds into the hallway. Students pour from classrooms, sneakers screech on the vinyl floor. Posters and banners practically scream at us to join this club or sign up for that dance. It's like a full-body cacophony. Add in some wine and a little nudity, and you'd have yourself a good old-fashioned Dionysian revel.

We pass the teacher's lounge, where I see Mr. Gunner, the twenty-something PE and World History teacher who is Ben's favorite. Rumor has it he's quite the archer himself, which naturally piqued my curiosity. But looking at him now, I'm arrested by the sadness that clings to him. Resignation pulls at the corners of his brown eyes in a way that pricks my heart.

What did the Fates do to him?

A nudge in my ribs pulls my attention from Mr. Gunner to Deya. She gestures down the length of the hall to Ben, who's coming this way.

My stomach does a little flip in a show of nerves. I haven't felt these flutters over a match since the Thunderclap.

"So who's his match?" Deya asks.

"Oh, um . . ." I do a quick glance around the hall. "She's not here. I'll just come back later."

She grabs my arm before I can port back to Olympus. "You don't think you should wait for a couple of minutes? She's probably talking to a teacher, or something. You can't tell me you don't know her schedule and habits after five weeks."

I very heroically do not huff, choosing a smile instead. "You're right, Deya. Thank you so much for imparting your endless wisdom to me."

I expect an eye roll—which I kind of deserve—but I get a concerned look instead.

"Kal, I know the last year has been hard on you. Everything with *the Thunderclap* and with Hector."

"Don't," I say, feeling like the ichor in my veins has turned to lava. "Don't bring that up now."

"I'm not trying to bring anything up. I just hope you know I have your back. Matching takes a lot out of a goddess, even without everything you've been through." She puts her hand on my shoulder and squeezes. "I understand why you're mad at the Fates. The Oracle, too. If you'd been called as something else, say as a muse . . ." She stops herself. "Anyway, if I can help, I will. Always."

Emotion tugs my lips tight, so that I'm neither frowning nor smiling when I say, "Thanks, Deya."

She looks back into the hall, and I see her eyes land on Ben, whose eyes are on someone else: Zoe. She's a bold, warm, ambitious, and adorable cheerleader whose only nervous habit is twisting her spectacularly red hair. She and Ben were friends growing up, but her family moved to Sedona a few years ago and just moved back last summer. My research tells me that Ben has had a lot of first dates since Zoe got back into town. A few second and third dates, too, but nothing more. Coincidence? Not even remotely. When Zoe sees Ben between the swell of students, she heads straight toward him. Instead of holding her gaze, Ben looks away, and a flash of doubt and pain wrinkles his brow.

"Oh, wow," Deya whispers. "I know I can't soulgaze like you and your dad, but he's hurting, isn't he?"

She's right. I don't need to use my gift to see the raw need for love that hovers over him like a broken dream. I want to protect him. This beautiful, brooding, remarkably talented bass player with hair that falls in front of his eyes when he's embarrassed and who longs for someone to put him first the way his father never has.

From conversations I've overheard, Zoe first started thinking of Ben romantically several weeks ago, when she ducked into the parking lot in the middle of a cotillion New Year's ball to escape her date. Ben and his band had just finished playing a dance in the neighboring building: a retirement home. As the guys loaded their equipment into the van, Ben was joking around with his little sister, who'd accompanied them to the show. The music from Zoe's dance was loud enough for them to hear, and Ben was spinning his sister around the pavement while she laughed. Zoe ran across the parking lot and said, "May I cut in?" His sister agreed.

Eleven minutes and three songs later, Zoe's stiff-upper-lipped parents found her doing the Cupid Shuffle (cursing Romans!) with Ben and his sister while Ben's bandmates heckled them. Zoe told her best friend later that dancing with Ben was totally worth getting grounded.

Sweet, right?

Thanks to my nudging, Ben hasn't gone out with anyone new in weeks. His heart is locked up as tightly as a Quartermaster vault, but I don't have to be Hephaestus' progeny to solve this problem. Ben needs to let his guard down. He needs love. I could have matched Ben and Zoe instantly, but Deya and I did a research project a couple of years ago showing that matches have fewer problems when they're primed prior to being matched. That's why I've inspired in Ben a newfound school pride—attending basketball games means watching Zoe cheer. It's why he's started inviting her to his concerts, after months of her dropping hints. Hector told me once that musicians are suckers for people who love their music. Zoe loves Ben's band; how could she not?

As I watch Zoe talk to Ben, he ducks his head down to hide something that isn't quite a smile but definitely isn't a frown. His ash-brown hair falls in front of his face, and Zoe has an urge to brush it aside. At least, I imagine she does.

These two could be great together. So what if her idea of good music is Top 40, or if the future her parents have mapped out for her doesn't include a boyfriend until she has her MBA, let alone one in a garage band? And who cares if Ben doesn't actually like sports, has always thought cheerleading was a bit of a cliché, and that his life goals include touring with Arcade Fire? They're good for each other. They push and stretch and support each other.

They're ready.

"Check out Red," Deya says of Zoe. "How bold she is? Looking to take what she wants? If she's not his match, I'm a three-winged harpy. You may not even need the arrow."

Zoe is twisting her hair and taking a deep breath. I see the way her blood is flowing faster in her body, adding a pink tinge to her skin that no mortal could notice. With a little focus, I hear her pulse speed up until it sounds like it's going to drum a hole in her chest. Holy Hades, is she going to ask him out?

"Of course this case needs an arrow," I say quickly, touching my bronze necklace. "It never would have come to us otherwise." My bow appears in my left hand and the arrow in my right. I feel the soft, yet crisp feathers on my fingertips as I nock the arrow and draw it back in one fluid motion, lining Ben up in my sights. He doesn't know what's about to hit him.

Ben glances at Zoe. It's go time. I blend myself into obscurity so that even the sweaty, jostling bodies can't affect me. No one in this hallway is going to thwart the power that masks my kind when we're working. If their eyes spot me at all, they'll pass right over me.

But if that's the case, then why does it seem like Ben has caught a glint of something in the corner of his eye? And why is he, impossibly, turning his head from Zoe and *looking right at me?*

My hands falter, and I put my bow behind me, like a backpack. I twirl the arrow nervously in my hands. He doesn't see either the bow or arrow, of course. He sees something innocuous: a pen. At least in theory. But in theory, our eyes shouldn't be connected right now. And he definitely shouldn't have a small smile on his lips.

For the first time in my life, I fumble with my arrow, and I'm reaching for it before I've even looked away. Something pricks my finger. With a squeal, I pull my eyes from Ben's to look down.

I gasp. My arrow clatters to the floor.

My dad is going to kill me.

Before I can stop myself, I'm looking back up at Ben, who is watching me bend down to pick up the arrow, or pen, or whatever he sees. Please don't see an arrow. *Please* don't see an arrow. He's walking this way. Zoe is staring at his back, looking gobsmacked. She shakes her head and darts for the bathroom, her cheeks matching her flaming red hair. Still crouched and starting to panic, I glance at Deya, who looks confused. She must not see the shimmery point of ichor on my finger from the arrow, just her improbably fumbling friend, being impossibly approached by her target.

"You dropped your pen," he says. His voice is low and soft and could sing the stars to sleep. He picks up my arrow, and for a moment, I see what he thinks he's holding: a pink, glittery pen covered in hearts. I groan internally. Nice, Cosmo.

"Thanks," I say. Our hands brush as he gives me my arrow. Goosebumps spread all over my body, a sensation I haven't felt in ages. Our eyes connect again, and this time the current is electric.

In my periphery, I spot Deya's eyes flicker down to my newly cut—and healed—finger. I see her eyes widen and her mouth fall open.

I don't really process any of this, though. I only have eyes for this gorgeous, awkward boy with hair falling in front of hazel eyes. All I see is the boy of my dreams. The love of my life.

"Benicio," he says, extending his hand. "But you can call me Ben."

"Kalixta," I say. "You can call me Kali." We shake hands, neither of us letting go.

"Kali," he repeats, as if tasting the word. "Are you new? You seem familiar, but . . ."

"I just transferred last month."

"Wow. How have I never noticed you before?"

My heart drops to my stomach. Not because he hasn't noticed me—of course he hasn't. But for him to notice me now, he must see past my anti-glamour. Even an iota of my glory is as powerful as any arrow.

Yet instead of the sonnets and random bits of worshipful poetry my glory inspires in him, Ben is smiling at my T-shirt. "I mean, how many people in this school have even heard of The Smiths, let alone have a shirt from their 'Meat is Murder' tour? Where did you find that?"

My heart goes *tha-dump, tha-dump, tha-dump.*

I smile, thinking about how one day we'll laugh when he learns that I got the shirt from the actual 1985 tour, a gift from Hector, whose mentor was musing for the lead guitarist. It doesn't matter that I can't tell him now, or that in his years I'm older than his grandparents. Someday, I will. Someday, I'll tell him everything.

I won't have a choice.

I've been lovestruck.

Chapter Four

Somehow, Ben and I are still shaking hands. His fingertips are calloused from playing bass, but I don't mind the roughness. Even against my tan complexion, his skin is darker than mine, courtesy of the petite Latina mother I've seen pick him up from school on occasion. I've never seen his father.

"So what's your last name, Kali?" He says this slowly, relishing the words.

"Olympos," I say, thinking fast.

"Like those Greek gods?" he asks. "Venus and Diana and all them?"

Cursing Romans. "Those are the Roman versions," I can't help but say. "But yes, I'm Greek."

"Where do you live?"

I feel a stab of panic before an answer finds its way to my brain. "Um, nowhere yet. We're just renting."

"Do you need a ride home after school? Or maybe a tour of our fine city?"

"Actually, she can't," Deya says, wrapping a hand tightly around my upper arm. "I'm her cousin, and we have other plans. Come on."

Deya is now pulling my arm so tightly, I'm losing sensation in it. I look back as she starts to tug me away from Ben. *My* Ben. His bandmates are surrounding him now, looking confused.

"Will I see you again, Kali?" he calls to me over students, and

I find myself in love with the way he lingers on my name. "Please say yes. Tonight. Come to my show!"

I shout, "Yes!" over the thrum of students and Deya's hisses. I strain to see Ben as Deya forces my retreat.

Before I know it, I'm being pushed back into the stinky bathroom and shoved into a tiny stall. "How could you let this happen? How could you be so reckless?" she asks, punching the words. Without waiting for an answer, Deya grips the wings on both our necklaces, signaling our imminent arrival to Olympus. We blink out and back into existence in the Port.

"Okay, you can stop squeez—Ouch!"

Deya doesn't say a word. She pulls me out of the clearing and down the same paradisiacal, forested path that we took earlier. But something tells me she won't be content to have Cosmo settle this one.

On the way, I see Hector coming from the opposite direction. He looks concerned. "Is everything okay?"

The pain in my heart is beyond anything I've felt in ages. I want to run to him, tell him everything. And above all, I want badly—very badly—to apologize.

But I can do none of this. Deya answers Hector with a single word: "No."

I look at his face, and I ache, knowing how the truth of what has happened will destroy him. But Deya doesn't care. She practically drags me up the steps of our headquarters, heedless of my protests and not caring that she just bumped me into a Doric column. When I tell her to stop, to let me go, that she's not the boss of me, she just curses at me in Ancient Greek and grips me harder.

We cross the marble floor, passing packed classrooms the size of that pathetic little colosseum in Rome. Then we're walking out the other side, into the immaculate, ethereal grounds. After several hundred yards of frosty silence, we reach the open-air theater where my dad and his brothers are teaching a seminar on advanced matching to tens of thousands of sixth-years.

My dad. Eros. The original god of love, wings and all.

His wings perk up when he sees the two of us at the top of the stairs. Then they sag. I'm not sure if he sees something in Deya's face or mine, but I know he doesn't like it. Dad gestures to his brother, Anteros, who is seated on the stage nearby. The god of friendship continues Dad's lecture without missing a beat, looking if anything even happier at the chance to help. It's so sweet, I could almost smile.

In moments, Dad's wings have landed him by my side. He looks at me, then at Deya.

"Let's go someplace more private."

"Someplace more private" turns out to be my house. The expansive marble palace is the pinnacle of beauty and taste and comfort, and unlike most of Olympus, my parents' room even has a roof. The luxury! With natural springs, fountains, and even small glades right in the middle of various rooms, our palace is magnificently awe-inspiring.

It is the last place in the heavens I want to be. At least Deya didn't stay to heap on the shame. It was bad enough that my dad loaded praise on her for her "watchful eye."

"Why don't you tell us what happened," my mom says, sitting on a divan with her arm around me. My dad sits on my other side, his arm also around me.

I tell them everything, and in spite of myself I cry, which—for the record—is a very understated reaction for a goddess. The Big Gs would be flaying people and leveling cities with a glance. A little hysterical crying is positively boring.

My parents hold me tightly, whispering that everything will be okay.

"But what am I going to do?" I ask, drawing a deep, hiccupping breath. "He's all I can think about to the point that I feel like I'm losing my mind! It's physically painful to not be by his side. But how am I supposed to feel happy when I know it's forced on me? How could I have made such a stupid mistake?"

My mom stiffens, which makes me feel worse. My parents have one of the most famous love stories in the world. Morties know it as *Beauty and the Beast.* My mother, Psyche, was the most beautiful woman on Earth, but mortal men were too intimidated by her beauty to court her. When Aphrodite heard that mortals had begun worshiping Psyche, she asked her son—my dad—to go make the woman fall in love with a monster. But when my dad saw my mom's beauty, he accidentally pricked himself with his arrow and fell deeply in love with her.

Meanwhile, her parents consulted an oracle to learn her fate. The oracle told them that she was destined to marry a monster and instructed them to leave her for her groom.

They followed the instructions, and the wind whisked her away to a mountain palace populated by invisible servants and my father: the "monster." (Technically, the term is accurate. I mean, he does have wings.) My dad, not wanting her to love him just because of his beauty, only visited her in the dark of night and insisted that she never try to see him in the light.

Although my mom had grown to care for my dad, she was homesick and asked him to send for her sisters to visit. My dad complied. My mom's sisters grew jealous when they saw how happy my mom was and how beautiful her home was. So they convinced her that my dad was a terrible, hideous monster who was planning to eat her. They armed her with a lamp and a knife to use when he visited her that night. When he was sleeping, she pulled out the lamp and looked at him.

Instead of seeing a horrifying monster, she saw the most beautiful man imaginable. She was so surprised that she stumbled and pricked herself with one of the arrows in the quiver next to the bed. In her enflamed passion, she spilled hot oil from the lamp onto him, waking him from his slumber.

Anyway, long story short, my dad disappeared, my mom repented of her momentary stupidity, and she searched high and low, all the way to the underworld and back, to find my dad, enduring every considerable trial my grandmother could throw at her. With the help of nature and some minor deities, she finally found her way back to him, proving her love.

Zeus was so taken by the story, he gave my mom ambrosia— the drink of immortality—transforming her into the goddess of the soul. And in a twist of the Fates, they have lived happily ever after, as ridiculously in love as a pair of freshly matched morties.

It's so beautiful, you could almost forget how disgustingly fatalistic it all is.

Before the Thunderclap, I never considered what a sham my parents' marriage is or how cruel it is for my parents to be stuck together for eternity, whether their authentic selves would have wanted it or not. It's like being forced into eternal servitude and being given a drug that makes you ecstatic about it.

It's awful, and now I know exactly how it feels.

"Sweetie," my mom says gently. "Whatever you think you know right now, I can promise you that it's not the truth."

I laugh darkly. "What, so you and Dad aren't forced to love each other forever?"

"You don't have to suffer—" My mom says, but my dad jostles her and she looks at him. They're talking with their minds, arguing about what to do with me, no doubt. Annoyance appears and disappears on my mom's face in a blink.

"You don't have to suffer forever, I mean," she says. "You know Zeus has forbidden giving ambrosia to any more mortals, even his own half-mortal children."

I let out an understated sob.

"But when this young man dies," my dad says over my cries, "your love will naturally fade, just as has happened for other immortals who've been lovestruck."

"So, what, the next seventy or eighty years are all I have to suffer?"

"Mortie years, yes." My dad nods. "You'll only have had your wings for a few of our years, though." He says this like the conversion of a mortie decade to an immortal year (give or take) is supposed to make me feel better. "You have an eternity ahead of you."

I double over in heartsick pain. "It feels like it's been an eternity already. How am I going to live like this?"

My mom hugs me tightly, kissing my forehead. "We know, *kopela mou*. We know."

My dad says, "Kali, I wish we could reverse this, but you know as well as I do that a match with an immortal is irreversible." He's right, of course. If it weren't, Aphrodite would have forced my parents to reverse their match eons ago. He wipes a tear from my cheek. "I know what you're going through. You can't understand how it's possible to feel so much love without breaking apart, and yet you know that you're going to do everything you can to feel more and more of that love, no matter how ill-fated it is." He grabs my hand. "Is that about right?"

I sniff my agreement.

"How are you feeling, sweetie?" Mom asks me.

"Gee, I don't know, Mom. How did you feel?"

My mom has been immortal for eons, but the vestiges of her humanity show in her very un-Olympian patience. "I think, if I were you, that I would be upset."

"What do you mean, if you were me? The same thing happened to both of us."

"Yes, but I believe your father is the love of my life. You believe this is all some cruel twist of the Fates, don't you? And if I were you, that belief would make me furious. I would hate to feel like I was some piece in their loathsome game." She sounds like she could be giving one of her psychology lectures right now. For once, I'm listening.

"Psyche," my dad says in a warning tone. His own reactions have been tempered over eons of marriage, but deep down, he's still an Ancient. The dangers of speaking ill of the Fates are ingrained in him.

Right now, I'm with Mom.

"No, she's right, Dad. They're messing with me, and I'm mad! They could have told the Oracle to call me to anything else, and then this never would have happened."

My dad gives a colossal eye roll. (Little known fact: Hera invented the eye roll while at Aphrodite's inaugural All Nude All the Time Olympics viewing party millennia ago. Iris captured an image of it, and it's so epic that immortals refer to eye rolling as pulling a Hera.) "This again? The Oracle is never wrong, Kalixta. If you were meant to be a muse, you'd be one. Besides, what could be more important than bringing love into the world?"

"I'd rather inspire a song."

"No mortie could pen a song more beautiful than the sound of two hearts beating as one."

He sits down beside Mom.

"A cure for cancer. The formula for cold fusion. A sustainable resource that can effectively end world hunger. There's more to musing than poetry, Dad."

My dad has settled down, and his self-control incenses me even more. "All mortals die, Kali. Isn't it better that their lives are short and filled with love than slightly less short and filled with longing and despair? Inspiring them to write a song or create some new technology won't make them kinder to each other. Only love can do that."

"But I hate it! Can't you understand? I don't want to be an Erote!"

"Yes, your last few matches have shown me that."

"Throw me in the underworld already, Dad," I say, causing a shudder to wash over my mom. "Give me my punishment."

"Five reversals *used* to mean a day in the underworld," he says. Anyone else I know would faint dead at this punishment. I know I should, too, but I can't bring myself to care, no matter the haunted look Mom gets whenever Hades' realm is mentioned. "Now it means that you repeat a year of training. Your mismatch with this mortal boy is number four."

My limbs go cold, and I'm overwhelmed with gratitude to Deya and Cos for keeping Beach Rat's mismatch quiet. "A year?"

"An *Olympian* year," he says.

Once every mortie decade, or so, Apollo takes Helios' chariot out for a spin around the Earth. For funsies. That little joyride marks the start of a new Olympian year.

"What?" I scream, accidentally singeing all the murals around the room with my shock and rage. "Dad, I can't stand showing up for another day! Why would you do this to me?"

My dad magicks the murals back to normal with another roll of his eyes. "This goes above my head, Kali. This comes straight from Aphrodite. She's seen the reports over the last few months, and the rise in reversals concerns her."

"This isn't personal, *kopela mou*," Mom says. "We all want you to succeed."

"The Oracle made you an Erote for a reason, Kali. Once you take responsibility for your destiny, you'll see that."

With a scream, I turn on my heel and storm away. It's childish, I know, but I'm a sixteen-year-old Greek goddess, for Gaia's sake, and I have the worst job in the heavens and a mortal match. What else could you expect?

I stomp through the house to my bedroom. My emotions are such extremes that I feel like I'm splitting in two. Half of me wants to go Old World and rain fiery destruction down on everything in sight. The other half is keenly aware of how many minutes it's been since I saw Ben and gazed into his hazel eyes. His absence is like a throbbing pain in my chest. How can I long for him and curse the arrow that matched us at the same time?

I stand in the center of my room and my eyes land on a pillar that Hector decorated a couple of years ago. It looks like the mist rising from a waterfall. He could have made the image appear with a few waves of his hand, a skill he'd mastered before we were ever called. Instead, he painted it with a mortie paint set his mom gave him. It took him days to get it exactly right. I've never had the strength to magic it away.

My throat tightens. I look up at the bright blue sky, wanting to curse the Fates into oblivion. What I wouldn't give for my parents' roof right now. Anything to block out the mocking sun. In fact, as I squint heavenward, I swear Helios is actually laughing at me. No doubt the titan of the sun will report all of my drama to his BFF Apollo the sun God later for their mutual amusement.

The Gorgon turds.

I walk to my bathroom and bend over the marble sink. I splash water on my face for a long time, letting my tears mingle with the brisk spring water that runs through all of Olympus. I leave the bathroom and throw myself on my bed face first to mask a scream.

Never in the history of Olympus has anything been so wildly unfair.

After a long bout of muffled screaming, I hear a clap outside of my ever-open window. The familiarity of the gesture tells me that the immortal outside my window knows me well enough to breach the Styx out of the etiquette my ultra-private parents are known for. That can only mean one god.

I push off of my bed and cross to the window, adjusting my chiton and blue-and-gold fifth-year belt before smoothing my long honey waves.

The concern I saw earlier on Hector's face now borders on despair. "Wanna talk about it?"

I nod and hold out my arms to him. I could easily jump, but I know this gesture means a lot to him. He lifts me out of the window as if I'm no heavier than a bird, and then hugs me. My tears start again, and this time, they're for a completely different reason than my star-crossed love for Ben.

They're for Hector's star-crossed love for me.

"I'm so sorry, Hector. I had no idea how this must have felt, how hard this must have been for you all these years."

Hector just nods against my cheek, still holding me tightly. I don't want to let him go, I hurt so much.

But we eventually do let go and start walking to our spot, the waterfall that Poseidon fashioned that comes from the heavens themselves. Since we were children, we've always come to this spot when we're sad or scared or in trouble. It's where I've found Hector in his darker moments, and it's the only place I can imagine finding comfort now.

We brush hands as we walk, and I want to slap myself for not being more careful. To me, Hector is an anchor, keeping me grounded enough to process, to think. To plan what in all of Gaia I'm going to do. But to Hector, I am his torment. I am the one person he loves more than anything. The one person he can never have. The one match I could never, ever allow.

Because it isn't real.

Olympians get nervous around Erote arrows, because no one wants to be tricked into loving someone, not for a few mortal decades and certainly not for all eternity. Since my parents, there have been a handful of immortal stickings, and only two self-stick-ings. One was me.

The other was Hector.

He was twelve years old. His mom, Calliope, had just left Apollo and decided to return to Earth for good. She's the most famous and prolific of the muses, but she was also a loving mother. Hector was devastated. He came over to our house and stole my dad's quiver, intending to stick his mom with an arrow so her connection to Apollo would be too strong to leave. When my dad tried to stop Hector, he holed himself up in my parents' room, refusing to leave for anyone. When I finally stormed into the room, demanding he talk to me, he was holding one of my dad's arrows. He had a shocked look on his face and a pinpoint of ichor on his finger. And he was already looking at me when my eyes found him.

He blurted out three words: "I love you."

I didn't know anything about one-sided matches then. I didn't really comprehend the power of one of my dad's arrows. So I replied like any eleven-year-old. "Ew!"

My parents rushed into the room behind me. My dad grabbed the arrow. My mom grabbed Hector, and he cried in her arms.

He followed me around from that day forward, telling me that he loved me, telling me that he was going to marry me and that we'd be together forever. We would build our palace at the waterfall, and it would be our spot for eternity. As I grew, I thought everything he said was romantic. He toned it down, getting cooler and more accomplished by the year. But his love for me was steadfast. By the time I was fourteen, I told him I loved him, too.

And I did. For nearly two years—two of *our* years—I did.

As we approach the waterfall now, a fine mist fills the air. The sun is low in the sky, and the sunset is indescribable: splashes of red, streaks of purple, blushes of pink. Helios has outdone himself yet again. The water coming off the falls is refreshing, the roar somehow consuming and calming at the same time. Memories wash over me, all here, at our waterfall. Hector and me laughing. Holding hands. Sharing our first kiss.

Me breaking both our hearts.

No. I squeeze my eyes shut, unwilling to face this vision now. I've had too much. The last thing I can handle is the memory of the event that destroyed my heart and desolated my faith.

With every considerable ounce of effort in my body, I shove the Thunderclap back into the recesses of my mind.

"I'm sorry," I tell him again, though I'm not sure precisely what I'm sorry for, just that my sorrow and regret and longing are swirling into a storm to rival anything Poseidon could create. "I didn't know it was this hard. I didn't know that the feelings the arrow causes are so overwhelming." That's not quite right, but it's all I can let out. "How have you handled it all these years?"

The pain on his face could sink a thousand ships. "Let's not talk about that now, okay? How did this happen? I thought the new model of arrows was supposed to be self-stick proof."

"So did I," I cry. "I don't understand what happened."

"But it can't just drop and stick you, right? Isn't that what this new model—the Omicron, or whatever—fixes?"

I shake my head, wanting to grab his hands and hold them to me at the same time that I think of the calluses on Ben's hands and what it would feel like to run my fingers over them.

I'm splitting in two.

"I can't explain it, Hector. I wish I could. I've been over it and over it in my mind. He just noticed me out of nowhere, and I was so shocked, I could hardly think. The next thing I knew . . ." On comes a fresh wave of tears and an already familiar longing for Ben.

Hector reaches a hand up to my face but drops it before touching me. He wrings his hands in his lap. "Why don't you tell me how you're feeling?"

"Like a titan-sized hypocrite for not understanding what you and my parents have gone through. Especially you. I hate that all I can imagine is doing everything in my power to be with this poor mortie, no matter what. It's not fair. I know that. But I can't stop it."

"What else are you feeling?"

"I'm angry at the Fates. The Oracle, too. They screwed me over."

I know my blasphemy bothers him, but to his credit, he doesn't lean away. "I don't think that's how it works."

My eyes leap to his. I don't bother to hide my incredulity. "Really? Then how do you think it works, when the Fates draw our thread at our birth and determine exactly how our lives will go? When the Oracle condemns us to a calling where this sort of crap can happen?"

"But the Oracle can't see everything and the Fates can be appeased and tricked. Their prophecies can even be beaten. Heracles is living proof of that."

"As far as we've been told," I argue. "How do we know that isn't what they want us to believe?"

"To what end?" he asks, his green eyes glinting. "Why would they lie?"

"I don't know, to make us think that if we work hard enough or worship Zeus enough, that maybe we can actually change our fate? It's all a con. Don't you see that?"

He lifts his shoulders. "No, I don't. I can't believe that our lives serve so little purpose, Kal."

I drop my head, too exhausted to argue anymore. I'm tired. I'm sad. I want to see Ben. I want him to sing to me.

I jump up. "I have to go."

He grabs my hand. "Please don't, Kal. Please don't choose him."

I don't know if it's because we've been best friends our whole lives or if it's because the same impulse drives us both, but he knows exactly what I'm thinking. He knows the desperate need that fills me, because it fills him.

"I'm sorry, Hec. I don't have a choice."

I bend down and hug him, and then I run as fast as I can for the Port.

Chapter Five

I appear in an empty bathroom stall in the all-ages club that Ben and his band, Sasquatch and the Little Feet, are playing. The bass coming through the walls echoes in my chest. I push open the dark wood door that's plastered over with fliers and advertisements and walk straight to the mirror. For the first time in my life, I find myself concerned about my appearance. I want to look indie rock, but not weird. I want to look pretty, but average. And maybe it's horrible of me, but I wish I could show him just a tiny glimpse of my real face.

I slap my stupid thought away. No. Not only do I have to limit myself to the mortal appearance I've chosen, my immortal glory would—at best—drive him mad. At worst, well, bye-bye, Benicio.

The thought tempers my enthusiasm. I mentally tame my frizzy curls a little and squint until a hint of makeup appears on my eyes. I make my clothes fit a bit better, too. Not full-out Deya style, and it won't scorch the eyes from his head (literally or figuratively), but the effect is a touch more flattering.

It'll do.

A girl walks into the bathroom, and I see with horror that she has familiar red hair and her eyes look misty. Her friend follows behind her.

"He's been stringing you along," Zoe's super-tall, blonde friend says. "He's scum."

"No, he's not," Zoe says, glancing at me with a smile that says she's sorry for bringing her drama into my space. I try to smile back. "He's going through a hard time with his dad getting remarried. Besides, we've been friends forever. He doesn't know I was going to ask him out. I obviously thought it was more than it was."

"No, you didn't. He probably smacked himself in the head with his big, stupid guitar. A concussion is literally the only explanation for how he could have forgotten you for whatever tramp he's chasing. Once he gets his head checked, he'll come crawling back."

"It's not the girl's fault." She wipes her eyes. "But now I wish I hadn't gotten into a fight with my parents about coming here tonight. They already think I should be interning somewhere to pad my college applications."

"So why'd you come? Why are you punishing yourself?" the blonde Amazon asks.

"I don't know," she says, smacking the palm of her hand into her forehead to the beat of the music blaring from the other room.

I wash my hands to give myself something to do. I'm having a hard time swallowing. Or breathing. I feel like my lungs have stopped working. Has one of the gods cursed me? I look at Zoe's face in the mirror and know otherwise.

This is guilt. Because I'm the source of all her anguish.

"You look familiar," Amazon says to me. "Do you go to Ponderosa?"

And now I know my lungs aren't working. I feel like I'm going to pass out from lack of oxygen. Do I even need oxygen?

A toilet flushes, interrupting Amazon's interrogating gaze. All eyes turn to the stall as Deya strides out like she's owning a catwalk. And she's made herself taller. Taller even than Zoe's friend. I'm so happy to see her, I could cry.

Deya washes her hands. "We both go to Ponderosa, actually. We just transferred." She pulls paper towel from the dispenser, dries her hands, then throws away the used towel. "We're the Olympos cousins. I'm Deya, this is Kali. And you are?"

"I'm Zoe." She points to herself before introducing her friend Alana.

"Well, it's great meeting you," Deya says, her smile dazzling. "We're going to go watch the next set. See you at school sometime!"

I still haven't done more than mumble unintelligibly, but I manage an awkward wave as Deya links her arm in mine and we leave the grungy little bathroom together.

"What are you doing here?" I ask over the music.

"Like I was going to let you see Yeti and the Younglings without me. They're like my favorite band."

"I think you mean Sasquatch and the Little Feet."

"Isn't that what I said?" She smiles and bumps my arm. "I've got your back. Always."

"I love your guts," I tell her as we walk through the club.

As grungy as the bathroom was, the club is worse. The floor and walls are all the same dark wood as the bathroom, but with even less lighting. The floor is sticky from spilled drinks, and the smell is ripe from all the dancing, jumping bodies. Because it's an all-ages club, the bar is cordoned off from the rest of the venue, and people with green wristbands, glossy eyes, and red noses bob out-of-time with the music. But in front of the stage where the teens are, the energy is raw and alive. Ben's band is up, and they're buzzing with excitement. That same excitement permeates the dance floor, where bodies are squishing together and kids are bumping into each other, and no one seems to mind. In fact, they're grinning wildly.

I look up to the stage where Ben's eyes have already found mine. His sweat-soaked black T-shirt clings to him, and he looks elated. When he sings his backup vocals into the mic, it's with a smile and eyes only for me.

"Okay," Deya yells in my ear. She's watching Ben, too. "I'm not saying I think any of this is okay, but that's pretty cute."

For the two hundred and eighth time today, my eyes well with tears. (Little known fact: the record number of times that someone has burst into tears is held by a satyr. It can only be measured using nanoseconds, because it exceeds the number of actual seconds in a day. Athena turned him into a sloth to shut him up.)

The song ends, and I'm the loudest to cheer. Ben notices. Our eyes are all flirtation through the rest of their set. When they reach their last song, he leans into the mic and says, "This song goes out to a special girl I can't wait to get to know better," and my heart does a triple backflip.

This time, Ben sings lead. The song is slower than the others. Ben has sung it to himself in the last five weeks at least daily, but it's different now. So much better. He's rewritten the lyrics and changed the chorus completely. His words pull at me. The haunting melody speaks of an aching that wasn't there before. I feel like he's singing to me alone.

The song's tenor subtly shifts. The longing fades away, replaced by hope. New love has been found, and it's like no pain could ever exist in the face of such happiness. The song reaches its final chords, and Ben lets go of his bass, grabbing the mic and singing a cappella, the lead singer harmonizing.

When you turn from your fate
Give yourself up to luck
That's how it feels
To be lovestruck.

The words speak directly to my soul, and it's everything I can do to keep myself from running to Ben. How could he write something so profound and so tailored to us? Is it the arrow?

As the lights turn on and Ben's band clears the stage to make way for the next band, I stand enraptured.

"He's good," Deya says. She's being more supportive than I deserve. "Really good. You know how to pick them."

"What am I going to do, Dey?"

To my surprise, she scoffs. "Girl, what do I know? My mother is hardly a role model when it comes to relationships. She has more lovers than a hydra has heads. She'd have no qualms about entering into a fake—" She grimaces, and I feel like I've been slapped. "I'm sorry. That's not what I meant."

I can't pretend her words don't sting, but she's here. I'm not about to drive her away. "I know."

"No, really. All I mean is that I have no room to judge. You've been stuck by an arrow, Kal. I can't imagine what that's like. If dating this mortie for a few decades makes you happy, well, you wouldn't be the first Olympian to do it."

Understatement of the eon.

Her words calm me. When Ben runs down from the side of the stage to greet us, he's beaming. My face mirrors his. His enthusiasm is contagious, but even if it wasn't, my wild, intense obsession makes it impossible for me not to be happy when I see him.

He hugs me, and I feel like I could break into song. He's only a few inches taller than I am, and his muscles don't compare to Hector's, but his arms feel perfect as they wrap around me. "You came," he shouts over the house music blaring from the speakers as a new band sets up. "I can't believe you came!"

I laugh. "Of course I came! What else would I do?"

He grabs my hand like he did earlier today. "I didn't know if I'd ever see you again or if I, like, made you up. You seemed to appear out of nowhere today. Like one minute I thought the world was one way," he says into my ear, leaning in close rather than shouting over the music, "and the next minute, it was totally different. Because you were there."

His words take my breath away. I blush and force myself to find my voice. "You guys were amazing," I call out, and I mean it. Hector has made a point of educating me on mortie music over the years. This was good even by a muse's standards.

"You really think so?" he asks, and now he's dropping his head, and his hair is falling in front of his eyes. I reach up to sweep it from his face before I can stop myself. The gesture is so intimate, I almost expect him to recoil. But instead, his smile softens. Deepens. Like he's let me glimpse right into his heart.

When I drop my other hand, he takes that one, too. "Do you want to go outside and talk before the next band is up?"

I hear an "ahem" behind me and see Deya looking, impossibly, like a third wheel. I close my eyes. "Uh, Ben, this is my cousin, Deya. Deya, meet Ben."

Deya's smile is only slightly pinched. With her competition-induced height, she's a few inches taller than him. He doesn't seem to mind.

"Good to meet you, Deya," he says. "Let me introduce you to my bandmates."

He waves behind him, and two guys come over. Paresh, the drummer, and the unkempt lead singer and guitarist who simply goes by Shaggy. Shaggy eyes Deya appreciatively, and I have to keep from curling my lip at him. Paresh, though, reaches a hand to shake both of ours. No lingering touches or glances, just a nice, simple handshake.

"It's nice to meet you both." It's subtle, but Paresh has the barest hint of an Indian accent that tells me his family probably moved to the States when he was a kid. He looks at me and says, "So you're the reason Ben changed up the love song?"

Ben groans, punching Paresh in the shoulder. "Real cool, dude."

Paresh laughs. "What? You added new verses and changed the chorus an hour ago, didn't you? All that stuff about fate? Don't get your junk in a bunch; I think it's awesome. It's awesome every time you change this song. But this was just so out of the blue, I figured a girl had to be responsible."

I've heard two other variations of this song in the short time I've been assigned to Ben. Paresh's words make me realize that those previous variations coincided with a new girl Ben was interested in. Which means I've inspired this version—the *best* version.

"I don't know about any change in lyrics," I say, "but I do know music, and you guys were great."

"Anyway," Ben says before any of our friends can protest further, "Kali and I are going to hop outside for a bit and chat."

Shaggy gives an "ooh," that makes me like him even less. Ben ignores him and pulls on my hand. We snake through the crowd together where we run into Zoe and her friend. Zoe looks like she's been slapped. We have to get out of here now.

"Hi, Ben," she says, her normally strong voice sounding smaller than I've heard it before.

"Hey Zo," he says back. His hand shifts on mine. "Um, have you met Kali? She's new."

Zoe's eyes don't quite meet mine, which is fair. Mine don't quite meet hers, either. "Hi," we mumble to each other.

"Um, anyway, I just wanted to tell you it was a great show. The new lyrics, the chorus . . . everything about the song really worked," she says. "You finally found your muse, huh?"

"Yeah, thanks." His neck turns red and a little splotchy. "Anyway, we're just heading outside. But I'll see you later, okay?"

She whispers, "See you," back to him. My throat itches. Stupid immortal hearing.

We finally make it to the door and out into the chill spring night. Ben guides me over to a rusted old Ford (we had a whole section on cars in mortal studies). He drops the tailgate, then gestures for me to sit down beside him. I shiver at the cold metal on my legs. Ben reaches through a small window into the cab and hands me a navy zip-up sweatshirt.

"Here." He drapes it around my shoulders.

"Thanks." The sensation of being cold is always fascinating to me, but not as fascinating as the charge I feel sitting next to this boy. I know I should fight this, but there's no denying the sparks flying between us or the butterflies swirling in my stomach.

"I want to know everything about you, Kali Olympos," he says, drawing circles on my palm.

"Like what?"

"Everything. Your first pet, your favorite color, when you'll go out with me."

I laugh. "Just the basics, huh?"

His smile dazzles me. "To start."

"No pets, red, and yes."

"Huh?"

"The answers to your questions."

He smirks. "But you said 'yes,' and I asked you 'when' you'd go out with me."

I interlace my fingers in his. "Whenever you ask."

We shift so that we're facing each other, and Ben brings a hand to my face. Oh my Styx. He strokes my hair and brushes a thumb on my cheek and I forget what I'm supposed to be fighting.

"What about you?" I say, barely above a whisper. "Tell me about your family, your hopes and dreams, your biggest fears."

"Just the basics, huh?" he teases. "It may sound, I don't know, idealistic or naive or something, but music is my life. I want kids to be talking about me in fifty years because I changed the face of music. And to do that, I guess I just want to be . . . *inspired.* I know it's gonna sound nuts, but I've been playing with that song—'Love-struck'—for months, and it never worked like it did tonight. I think you're my inspiration, Kali."

No words could be sweeter to my ears. I positively swoon. And the way he looks at me would steal my heart if it wasn't already his. I want more. I want him to keep talking, to answer every question, to tell me about his family—which I can't help but notice he left out. But those thoughts quickly escape my mind as he leans closer. I could stare past his four hundred and eleven eyelashes into those entrancing hazel eyes all day.

"There is something about you," he whispers, his crystallized breath rising around his face.

"Oh, I bet you say that to all the girls." I mean this teasingly, but his face goes totally serious.

"Are you saying that because of what Paresh said? Because it's not like that. *I'm* not like that."

"Like what?"

"Like some . . . womanizer. I don't—I'm not—"

"Of course not. I know you're not like that."

"How?"

Because I've watched you for five weeks. Because I've looked up every detail about your life. Because I could see into your soul if I wanted to, but I don't have to do that to know how bright and pure it is. And it's the one thing I haven't violated, and I'd really like to keep it that way. "It's just something in your eyes, I guess. I trust you, Ben."

The smile he gives me doesn't last. He looks off into the distance. "You want to know my biggest fear? Becoming my dad."

Whoa. That got real fast. "What do you mean?"

He looks at me with a fire in his eyes that would tempt Prometheus. "Do you ever feel like your life is going a certain direction and you have no control over it? Like, even if it's good it's just . . . inevitable?"

I laugh under my breath. "More than you can know."

"I don't want inevitable. I want a little control over my life."

This must be what it feels like to be pushed out of a plane. My heart is plummeting to the ground, and it doesn't feel remotely immortal right now. "You sound like you're talking from experience."

The flame in his eyes subsides into a sad flicker. "My dad left my mom for some woman he knew for a week. I don't want to be anything like him," he says, and a little parachute pops out, saving my falling heart. "It's such a pathetic excuse, letting yourself be 'magnetically drawn' to someone. Like he didn't have any say in the matter. Like that's any reason to ruin a life. A family." He rubs his eyes, which are now extinguished. "Sorry, I didn't mean to go off like that. My dad's just kind of the worst."

The parachute has punctured and my heart has just hit the ground and exploded into pieces. Ben may as well be talking about us. He would hate me if he found out the truth of his attraction to me, even as the magic of the arrow forced him to love me in spite of the truth. How can I sit next to this sweet, aching boy and just let him love me? Isn't this exactly what I've been fighting against since the Thunderclap? My love is already ruining him.

I don't know what to say. I take off his jacket and drop it on the back of his truck before jumping to the ground. "I'm so sorry, Ben. I shouldn't . . . I have to go." My words sputter out, and I feel like I'm spinning out of control.

Ben gets down from the tail. "Kali, what's wrong? Did I say something—"

I shake my head, already running back into the club. "No, it's me. I can't . . . I just have to go."

"Kali, wait!"

But I'm already inside the dank club, my eyes searching everywhere for Deya. I see her sitting on a stool, surrounded by boys. I break through her worshippers and grab her arm. "I need to go. Now."

Deya doesn't question me. She stands, dismissing her fans, and strides with me to the bathroom. She doesn't ask any questions, just rubs my shoulders while I shake with guilt and anger.

When we get back to Olympus, the Port is busy. Among those coming and going from assignments, a lot of immortals are popping down to Earth for a bit of fun.

We move away from the gabbing immortals. I stare at my feet, clad in sandals again instead of Vans, and let Deya steer me away. Before we've left the Port, someone bumps into my shoulder. I look up to see the goddess of aggravating the styx out of me: Ianira.

Oh, this is just perfect. She's in her chiton, like the rest of us, but—and this is the third biggest reason why I can't stand her—she's also wearing glasses. Not because she needs them, of course; she has way-better-than-hawk-vision, like the rest of us. No, she wears glasses with her sleek black hair in a sophisticated ponytail because she wants us all to remember that she's a genius muse. She's mused for several renowned scientists and a Nobel laureate. Those glasses are meant to remind us that she's smarter than we are.

It totally works.

Gaia, she bugs me.

"Whoops, sorry, Kali," she says in a falsely sweet voice, looking over her lensless—lensless!—glasses at me. "My, you look *awful.* Have you just returned from *another* mismatch? I swear, Kalixta, it's almost like you're *excited* to get sent to the underworld." She tsks. Second biggest reason I hate her: overemphasizing words for dramatic effect. "But then, I've never understood your taste, letting *Hector* go like that."

Reason number one? Her titan-sized crush on Hector.

"Ianira, hon," Deya says, "you have a spot of something, right here." She gestures vaguely to Ianira's cheek, making a grossed out face. "It looks like . . . well, you should probably just go wash up. Now."

Ianira tries not to cover her face with both hands, but I can see her fingers twitching. "How immature," Ianira snaps.

"How attractive," Deya says, still fixating on the same nonexistent spot on the girl's cheek. Ianira turns from us and marches away. Deya and I share a dark laugh and wander over to our training fields. A handful of overeager (or overly bad) students are practicing with bioluminescent arrows and targets, though the constellations are so bright, no extra light is needed.

"Are you going to tell me what's going on, Kal?" Deya asks. "Did something happen?"

"No. It's just . . . what am I doing? To either of us? How could I just let myself be with him when this is all forced?"

"He doesn't know that."

"But *I* do!" My voice is loud enough that one of the students glares back at me. "My cells are vibrating differently since the arrow, Deya. The distance from him is physically painful for me, which means it's painful for him. I can't do this to him. I can't do this to *me*, no matter how badly the arrow makes me want to." And boy, how I want to.

She's quiet for a long time. "So, what are you going to do about it?"

I sigh and lean my head on her shoulder. "I don't know."

Chapter Six

At headquarters during school the next day, I'm a mess. Memories of Ben's eyes and touch haunt me as I go through the motions. Since the Thunderclap, I've made it my life's mission to prove to the Erote department that the Oracle made a mistake. I've purposefully botched exams, conveniently forgotten to hand in homework, and have made a few colossally bad matches. Not even a day in the underworld was enough to control me. But now that my dad has announced I'll have to do an entire year over if I hit five mismatches, I'm stuck. My dad's parting wisdom from yesterday—that I'll feel better once I take responsibility for my fate—mocks me. He's asking me to do the impossible.

Near the end of the day, I'm not surprised when all eyes are on me. Everyone just received the same message about a special assembly that will take the place of our last class. Sixth-years stare down their noses at me, first-years look at me in horror, and my classmates—the other fifth-years—just pull a Hera and roll their eyes. We've had a handful of special assemblies since the Thunderclap, and there's no denying that most of them were because of me. The lecture "The Pygmalion Problem: Why We Don't Match Humans with Inanimate Objects," was of particular note.

A sixth-year claps me on the back. "Thanks for getting me out of my advanced research dissertation, Kali."

A pair of glistening green eyes in the crowd catches my

attention before I can even pretend to deny it. I snake around the sixth-year and grab Hector's arm. "What are you doing here?"

Hector's grin is unabashed. The turd. "I heard there was a new special assembly on your account. What kind of friend would I be if I missed it?"

"The best kind," I mutter, picking up the pace.

He follows me through the building and outdoors to the amphitheater. "No, no. Best friends support each other when they get lectured in front of their entire department. Besides, if this is anything like 'Just Because Zeus Turned Himself Into a Bull, Doesn't Mean You Can Match a Matador with One,' I wouldn't miss it for all the stars in the sky."

I hate that he's enjoying this so much. Shouldn't this particular assembly hit home a little harder for him? He's always doing this: acting like his ever-breaking heart isn't killing him. I swear, he does it just to drive me wild.

Okay, I know how selfish that sounds. If this is how he copes with his one-sided match, who am I to blame him? I just wish he didn't have to cope at my expense.

I spot Deya at the top of the amphitheater and she waves us over to a few spots that she's saved . . . beside Cosmo and Teresa, neither of whom needs to be here.

"Wow," I say dryly. "Thanks for the support, gang."

"We wouldn't dream of letting you face public humiliation alone," Teresa says with a sharply arched brow. She leans back and bumps into a sixth-year.

The older girl looks at Teresa, eyebrows raised. "Excuse you."

Teresa grins at her. Then snaps her teeth down. The girl blanches and scoots down the row. Far down. She grumbles to the student she bumps into, and they both stare down the row at Teresa. The other student asks, "Is that Iron Heart?"

"Sure is, buddy," Teresa says pleasantly, waving.

In spite of myself, I snort. I'm about to slide in when Deya steps out of the row, ushers Hector in to sit beside Cosmo, and then sits back down. I drop beside her. I'm relieved to have a little distance between Hector and me. I know he's acting like this assembly won't dredge up some painful memories, that it's just the same old "Come watch the consequence of Kali's latest antics." But I also know that he likes to power through the pain.

A pain I already know too well.

I keep remembering Ben's face last night when he said that he doesn't want something inevitable, that he doesn't want to be forced. It's the same way I've always felt. I yearn to be with him. I ache to feel his arms enfold me. But the hypocrisy is suffocating.

I can't be with him.

I *must* be with him.

My dad and Uncle Anteros get to their feet on the stage at the bottom of the semi-circular theater. Their voices project in such a way that the thousands upon thousands of students can hear them as if they were in the first row. But at least here near the back, my dad's eyes aren't burrowing into me.

"Today we need to discuss the importance of arrow safety," my dad says over a collective, muffled groan. My dad's eyes narrow just a fraction, and, what with our better-than-perfect vision, the enormous crowd goes deadly silent.

"As a reminder, being immortal does not mean that you are invulnerable, only that you cannot die. But our bodies are still susceptible to things like being stabbed or shot or being hit by a car, even if the results won't be fatal. If we are cut, we *will* bleed ichor. Our bodies work perfectly, so we heal rapidly and won't scar, but we can be injured. By now, you all know that we're as easy to injure as mortals, if impossible to kill."

Teresa mutters, "Is that a challenge?" making Hector and Cosmo laugh under their breath.

"Because our immortal skin is not impenetrable, you must remember that our own arrows can pierce us." A shudder takes over the entire theater in a wave. I feel like everyone's eyes are burning into me. Yet when I glance up, I see the students are too busy worrying about themselves to judge me. We've all seen too many bad matches to want one for ourselves.

A hand goes up somewhere in the middle of the theater, and Uncle Anteros calls on the boy, a second-year, judging by the yellow threads in his gold belt.

"B-but I thought that shooting an immortal was banned by Zeus?"

"Oh, it is," my dad says. "The minimum sentence is five years in the underworld."

Hundreds of immortals hiss. This is hardly news to an Erote; it's just that strong a deterrent. Even Teresa's eyes widen, and Hades is her grandfather. Another hand goes up. "And our arrows . . . aren't they immortal-proof? Because immortal matches can't be reversed, I'd heard that the Omicron was specifically designed not to work on immortals."

"It is," Anteros says, a little too brightly. He can't help himself. "*Theós* Eros and I have checked every arrow personally, and I hate to have to admit this, but we found two faulty arrows. Both have been destroyed. Moving forward, every Omicron from now on will be personally inspected by an Ancient to ensure that they are immortal-proof and that no immortals will be susceptible to an irreversible match." No *more* immortals, he means. Because of course, my arrow had to be one of the faulty ones.

No one else knows this, though. A huge sigh of relief releases into the sky.

"But you must all still be vigilant," my dad says. "An Ancient's power may seem limitless, but combating our own power is one of those limits. Who remembers some of the famous immortal stickings in our history?"

Hundreds of hands shoot up, including Deya's. My dad calls on her.

"*Theós* Dionysus and Aura," Deya says, using the formal address but going straight for the kill. I shift in my seat, as do many, many others.

The God Dionysus and the nymph Aura are a textbook example of a mismatch. They were incompatible in every way, but they were matched with a stolen arrow because Aura had the nerve to compare herself to a goddess. (Aura is also a textbook example of why no one should ever, ever challenge a Big G, whether it's in a beauty contest, an archery contest, a musical contest . . . Styx, even an eating contest. Don't do it. Ever.) Aura was forced to love the God, but it was an obsessive, hysteric love that went very bad very fast. She went insane. She started killing sheep and desecrating shrines and even tried to kill her own children. One of the gods changed her into a spring to stop her. Not exactly a bedtime story on Mount Olympus.

"*Theós* Apollo and Daphne," another student says.

Hector and I glance at each other, smirking. This one's all my dad's fault. When they were both young Gods, Apollo tried to tell my dad that he was the better archer, so my dad showed Apollo just how good an archer he was. He shot Apollo and made him fall in love with a nymph who hated him. A classic one-sided match. Apollo chased the nymph long and hard until she asked her father, a river god, to change her into a laurel tree. Apollo, to his credit, developed a sense of humor about the whole thing. He and my dad are friends, and he made the laurel tree sacred.

"*Theá* Aphrodite and Adonis," another student says, and now it's Deya's turn to sigh. As if her mom needed more excuses to make bad choices with men, she grazed herself on one of my dad's arrows and fell in love with Adonis, the most beautiful mortal man in history. She even convinced Zeus to make him immortal, though she shares him with Persephone, in the underworld. It's a mess. Like Aphrodite's love life.

A tiny first-year shoots up his hand near the front. "Maybe this isn't a real one, but I heard that *Theá* Artemis and Orion—"

Gasps envelop the first-year's voice. A student next to him elbows the kid in the ribs and points up at Helios overhead. The titan drives a chariot carrying the sun across the sky every single day. He has nothing better to do than listen to gossip.

The first-year seems to realize what he just said, because he blanches and hunches far down in his seat. Because the truth of Artemis and Orion is far worse than a simple arrow, and the consequence for even mentioning that Artemis fell in love is so bad, not even my dad would risk it.

Apollo can be one of the coolest Gods out there, but he can also be straight-up Old-World vengeful, especially when it comes to his sister. He doesn't let anyone talk about her. And everyone knows Helios reports everything concerning her back to Apollo. The snitch.

My dad silences the theater with a single look, then turns to the first-year. "No. You are mistaken."

The lecture continues, and I'm left thinking about how there are even worse messes than my own out there. And my mind, naturally, goes to the cause of all my woes:

The Fates.

I sink deeper into darker and darker thoughts, missing much of the lecture, until we reach the Q&A portion and a question pulls me from my head.

A third-year has her hand up. "When a mortie match happens, how do you decide if it should be reversed or not? Is it chosen by the Fates or by you?"

"What an excellent question!" Anteros says, as if this student is the first to ask it in all of history instead of the first to ask it since, oh, lunch. "What do you all think?"

Dozens of hands pop up, and Anteros picks a few.

"The Fates decide and you get a report from them daily of the ones that need to be fixed."

"No way. The Fates don't care. It's up to the people involved to make a good match."

"I think everyone has a handful of possible matches based on their personalities, history, interests, everything like that. I assume *Theós* Eros soulgazes every match to determine if they're right or not."

I hate this debate. I've heard it so many times, I want to jab arrows in my ears to blot it out. My dad and his siblings love it. So even though they never tell people the actual answer—not even their own children—they encourage the discussion. My dad says it's good for his students to think through problems like these and find out the truth for themselves. Which no one ever does. Because no one is willing to admit the truth, bleak as it is:

The Fates decide everything.

I peek down the row and see Hector and Cosmo glancing around, unfazed by a conversation that engrosses any Erote. Cosmo may be assigned to the Erote department, but he's still a QM, a scientist. And Hector, despite getting stuck by an arrow, works in a department that doesn't much care if Fate is involved at all.

It must be nice.

Children on Olympus have until the age of twelve to dream that we can be whatever we want to be before our hopes are either granted or cruelly smashed into oblivion. On our twelfth birthday, we're taken to Delphi to the Oracle to learn our "calling," by which I mean our fate.

Truth bomb: the Oracle invented the dead-end job.

Olympus departments run the gamut from weather to war to wine. Most everything in the Western World is in our domain—the monumental, the superfluous, and everything in between. One of the Twelve runs each department, and all positions involve years of studying and on-the-job training. Erote training consists of six years of school, including shadowing and monitored probation by quartermasters like Cosmo. After those six years, there are two more years of unmonitored training with reversal arrows. Post-graduate work, so to speak. If we do well, we get our wings. If we don't, they strip us of our glory and send us down the mountain to live out our immortal life on one of Olympus' lesser tiers. Very little responsibility, very little reward, a lot of boredom.

This is my fifth year in school and my second year as a pro-bie, and it has been the longest immortal year of my eternal life, thanks to the Thunderclap. Before that, Deya and I were constantly fighting for top in our year, both in subjects like archery or the psychology of love and in our matching accuracy and compati-bility. Existential questions about fate never bothered me; I was convinced that my actions were mine and that they mattered in the greater scheme of the universe. But in the months since the Thunderclap, I've grown jaded.

I loved this calling once. I put my soul and my considerable skill into every match, and I destroyed a mortie's life—

Stop thinking about it, Kali.

Anyway, I stopped trying. And since I've stopped trying, I may have had a few reversals, but at least no one was hurt. And in the end, the Fates have won out, anyway.

So why try?

Mercifully, the seminar comes to an end, and my dad leaves everyone with a warning, a handful of answers, and a million more questions. But hey! At least we all know not to be stupid like Kali and her faulty, cursing arrow!

"So, how is everyone feeling?" Deya asks. "Can we all agree not to stab ourselves with arrows in the future?"

Hector and I lock eyes and groan. Deya's smile sparkles. "Good."

"And can we all agree that if the Fates created us, then they're ultimately to blame for everything we do?" I retort.

Deya and Teresa shake their heads.

Hector nods to Cosmo and the girls, then puts a hand on my elbow. The tingles his touch causes don't overwhelm me, a pleasant side effect of my mismatch with Ben. "I need to run," he says. "I have a meeting to get to."

"Meeting?" I ask. "Whatever. I bet you're getting an award."

"Better than a lecture."

I bite back a smile. "You loved it. Nerd."

"Rebel."

"Suck-up."

"Poser."

Deya makes a gagging sound. "Enough with the flirting, you two. Get back to work."

"I'll walk out with you," Cosmo tells Hector. "I'm helping out Security for the next few nights, watching the holy sites, so I need to get back. See you all later." Cosmo leaves with a backward glance at Deya, who smiles. Hector doesn't look back.

Most of the Erotes have cleared out of the amphitheater. Teresa, Deya, and I follow suit, leaving the expansive Erote grounds and heading for a glade of evening stock nymphs. Because the nocturnal creatures sleep in plant form during the day, their shade covers Helios' mocking eye. It's a safe place to gossip and, for me, blaspheme. Which is all I want to do right now.

Teresa preempts me. "Don't, Kali."

I frown. "Don't what?"

"Don't complain about how the Oracle and the Fates and the universe are out to get you."

"What am I supposed to do? I'm going out of my mind with a need to be with Ben, but I don't know how I can after . . . after . . ."

"Screwing Hector over?"

This hits me like a lightning bolt from an enraged god. I glare. "How did I screw him over? It's a one-sided match, remember? He was looking at me when he pricked himself with the arrow, but I wasn't looking at him. The arrow *forces* him to love me; it didn't force me to love him back. I chose that! Do you think I wanted to hurt him? Do you have any idea how badly it hurt *me*? At least Ben and I are stuck in this together." My eyes sting with an eternity's worth of unshed tears. "Gaia, the Fates are probably laughing their shriveled butts off at me right now."

"So laugh back," Teresa says.

"Don't encourage her," Deya says, but it's too late. Teresa's words ring in my ears, calling to mind what my dad said yesterday: I need to take responsibility for my destiny.

I think about what Hector said about Heracles beating the prophecies that foretold his doom. My brain kicks into motion, and I swim in my thoughts until I realize both of my friends are staring at me.

"What?" Deya presses. "Kal, what are you thinking about?"

"Laughing back."

Chapter Seven

Deya is the opposite of moved to action. "Hold up, Kal, I know that look. That's the look that had us running out of Athena's library in nothing but our underwear when we were twelve. What are you planning?"

"Deya, come on. Do you trust me?" I look at Teresa, too.

"Underwear. Athena's library. Remember?" Deya says.

"Dey."

She sighs and runs a hand through her caramel locks. "Of course I trust you."

"Then I need your help."

"Is this about Ben?"

"No," I say honestly. "This is about me. I need to see the Oracle."

She spits three times into the grass, as if it will protect her from whatever evil she thinks I'm inviting. "Don't ask this. Please."

"I would never ask you to come with me. I just need some distraction."

She sighs and looks at Teresa, who nods. "Okay, but don't thank us yet."

"What's the plan?" Teresa asks.

The plan is coming too fast for me to process, but I tell them my thoughts as they come, and soon they're filling in the blanks.

"Leave transportation to me," Teresa interrupts at one point before addressing Deya, "and you can cover detection."

"Fine," Deya says. "But the Oracle is all Kali, right?"

Gaia help me.

By the time Helios sets the sun, we're ready. Our first stop is the vault right off the archery field, where Cosmo is working late. Deya knocks on the heavy masonry door with torches burning on either side of it. A small metal cover at eye-level opens to reveal Cosmo's dark eyes.

"Hey, Cos," she says in a throaty voice. "What are you doing?"

"Running those detections for Heracles." He sounds reluctant. "I really have to—"

"I forgot to tell you how amazing I think it is that you're being loaned out to Security. Heracles doesn't let just anyone help his department. That's huge, Cos," she coos. "So what are you doing for them?"

"They've been having some weird intrusions at a temple site, so I'm supposed to look out for anomalies." He keeps turning his head around. "I actually have to—"

"Can I watch?"

He glues his eyes to hers. "Wh-what?"

"Sorry, I'm being stupid. I understand if you'd rather not have company—"

"No! I mean, yes! Please, please come in!" He slides the metal cover back into place, and a moment later, the door glides open.

With a backward glance and a wink, Deya follows Cosmo into the vault.

"One down," Teresa mutters. "One to go."

"Two to go," I correct her.

"Not for me."

Can't argue with that.

Thanks to the genius of the Twelve, the path to the Port

never takes longer than ten minutes from anywhere on Olympus. Something about temporal folds. All I know is that even though Olympus itself exists outside of space, occupying the heavens in a way that even few immortal minds can fathom, if you stay on the far left path at every fork, you find yourself at the Port ten minutes later. Which is where we're descending now.

"You okay?" Teresa asks.

"I'm fine," I say, rubbing my arms against a cold that exists only in my mind. "Thank you, again and again and again, 'Resa."

"It's not like it's going to ruin my reputation."

"Don't talk like that, and don't you dare buy into their 'Iron Heart' crap," I snap. "Teresa, you are a brilliant and kind reaper as often as you are a terrifying one. People's fear of you because of your dad is based in fiction, not fact. I know your dad. Every time I'm at your house, he gives me baklava that he made himself. He's a dear, and you're a dear, and anyone who thinks otherwise can drown in the Styx. Okay?"

She arches her brows. "Kal, we both know I'm not a dear. And I don't need a pep talk. I know who I am, and I like it."

"Yeah, well, we should all be so lucky."

It's Teresa's turn to snap at me. "Okay, are you going to whine about your fate all day or take control of it?"

An image of Ben's hair falling in front of his eyes hits me, filling me with a need I haven't felt since Hector. "I'm gonna take control."

"Good. Because I want the old Kali back."

"Old Kali?"

"Yes, the old Kali. I'm supposed to be the hardened, jaded one of the group. You're seriously encroaching on my turf. So go fix that," she says.

"Yeah, yeah, love you, too," I tell her. She smiles.

At the Port, Teresa spots an agent who looks like he'll wilt at the slightest breeze. She marches up to his desk between two columns. The guy's rust-colored hair seems to stand higher and higher on his head. "I need to access my transportation log," she demands.

"I-I can't just let you—"

"You'd better believe you can," she says. "My log and your log don't match up, and now I'm being told I'm not meeting my assignment requirements. I need to prove that you messed up so I can show my mentor."

The agent's voice takes on a higher pitch, but still, he argues. "That can't be. All due respect, of course! But, no. My logs are never wrong."

Teresa's voice gets scary low. "Never? So are you saying *I'm* wrong?"

He leans back. "No! Of course not. But c-could your mentor be?"

Teresa gets in his face. "Obviously my mentor has the wrong hours. And obviously they came from somewhere. Now, do you think that's from me or from you?"

The agent looks like he wants to seep into the Earth. But he doesn't. "Well, it's just, it can't be from me."

Curse his stupid gumption. Just give in already!

"Do you realize who you're talking to right now? Do you realize what I could do to you?"

His head looks like it's ready to jump off of his body. "Yes! But that wouldn't change the fact that my logs are right."

Okay, I did not see this coming. They're actually getting into a legit argument, and this stupid, thanatotic agent isn't backing down. As Teresa's voice gets lower and the agent's gets higher,

I get more and more nervous. I have a small window of time to port, and if Teresa can't distract him from watching his station, I won't be able to port at all. The agent stands up and gestures at the aqua screen that separates the agents from the Port itself. No. He needs to look away from the Port. *Away from the Port!* Ugh, why can't I communicate telepathically, already? Teresa's eyes flash up to mine, as if to say, "What do I do?"

I move my fingers in a rolling motion, mouthing, "Turn him!" She gives a tiny nod.

"So you think I'm just supposed to trust that your screen," she says distastefully, adjusting her body so that he has to turn away from the glass to look at her, "hasn't been tampered with in some way?"

"Tampered?" he repeats. "You think Iris would let someone tamper with her screens?"

"I don't know. Maybe it's you." She puts a hand on her hip. "For all I know, someone's bribing you."

"Bribing me?" he scoffs, his back finally turned to me. "Are you serious? Who would want to—"

Low enough that the agent can't see, Teresa makes a "run along" gesture to me. I dart into the Port, relieved but freaking out inside. This has to be the worst idea I've ever had. What if the Oracle won't help? What if Apollo finds out? Or worse, Zeus?

But if I don't go, I'll regret it for eternity.

I take a deep breath and close my eyes. I don't grab my necklace, because I don't want this jump registering at school. I just vanish.

I reappear at Delphi, where a four-day-old Apollo once slew the Earth-dragon Python when it tried to attack his mother. It's one of the holiest sites on Earth.

The home of the Oracle.

It's no coincidence in my mind that a harsh wind blows and a pack of wild animals cries and moans in the distance. I look up at beautiful Mount Parnassus, which stands high above the countryside. The ancient sanctuary of Delphi is on the southern slope, a famous, abandoned archaeological site. All around me are the crumbling stone ruins of temples and treasuries, altars and votive statues. The enormous ancient theater packs in the mortie tourists year round. When they visit this place—one of the holiest in the world—all they see are the ruins, impressive as they are. But I see more.

With torches lining its columns, the Temple of Apollo stands as proudly as it did thousands of years ago. The moonlight casts a glow on the ruins that is positively otherworldly. The forlorn howls add to its mystique.

Only our kind can see the temple, let alone enter. It's the last of the ancient structures at Delphi that still exists in the immortal plane. I've ported behind one of the nearby treasuries in the sanctuary to hide myself from the lone priest who guards the entrance. Getting around him won't be easy.

My feet crunch softly on the rocky terrain. I silence my steps the way Artemis has taught me. I'm only a few dozen yards from the temple and could sprint there in seconds, but I can't risk the robed priest glancing my way. I would be in an underworld of hurt. I wait with a pounding heart, crouching behind cool stone, until I hear his quiet footfalls getting farther away. With his back to me, I make a break for a votive, pause behind it, and dart for an altar.

The wind whips my hair into my face. I hide and try to listen for the guard over the pained howls of the animals. Their cries make the hair on my arms stands up. Then I hear a scuff of rock only a couple of yards away. I whirl around, but nothing is there.

In the opposite direction, I hear another scuff. I whip around, this time clutching the arrow on my necklace. Again, nothing. In a heartbeat, my bow and arrow are in my hands. It doesn't matter that these arrows aren't lethal. I'm happy to make a feral animal devote itself to me forever if it keeps me from being eaten alive, or, worse still, caught by the Oracle's priest.

More movement sounds behind me now, and a long, mournful moan reverberates through my chest. With heart racing, I spin around, armed and ready to shoot. Then my eyes pop. My mouth falls open. And for the second time in as many days, my arrow clatters to the ground.

Three old crones stare at me.

They are hideous, their bodies bent and knotted. All robed in black, they move in unison. One holds out a spindle, her beady, piercing eyes staring longingly at the glistening threads. One clutches a staff with her worn and wizened fingers. The last grips a pair of wicked scissors that she snaps hungrily at me. I shudder.

The Moirai.

The Fates.

"Hello, Kalixta, daughter of Eros," they say in a creaking voice that sounds older than the Earth.

I wince at a high-pitched squeal before realizing it's coming from me.

"Why are you here?" they ask, taking a step toward me. I try to back up but trip on the uneven ground, crashing to my back. They step toward me again, hunching lower so their eyes are almost at mine. Their eyes . . . nothing should move inside eyes like that. "Why are you here?" they repeat.

The words are out of me before my courage can fail. "To take back my fate."

They straighten with a collective hiss. "You do not care for us," the one holding the scissors says. Her voice is so sharp, I think she could cut the thread of my life with a single word. "Do you?"

They already know, so lying does nothing for me. Rocks bite into my palms. "No," I whisper.

They cackle now, the three voices discordant and screeching. I am terrified. I glance around me, praying for a wild animal or the priest to devour me. Surely, that would be a better end than whatever the Moirai have in store for me.

The one holding the staff points it at me, grinning to show no teeth in her black hole of a mouth. "I like you," she says in a hollow, rasping voice.

I blink.

The Fate holding the spindle of thread gestures to me to stand. I do, wiping my dirty, sweaty hands on the back of my chiton. She pulls a long thread slowly from her spool and shows it to me. As thick as my finger, the iridescent thread radiates a life of its own. When she speaks, it is the sound of ancient bones crumbling in the Earth. "What do you see?"

I stare at it for a long moment. I squint. I cock my head to the side. It's almost as if I can catch visions of the strange life pulsing from the thread. Almost.

But not quite.

I deflate, wishing I had a different answer. "A piece of thread. I'm sorry, that's all I see."

"A piece of thread," Spindle says, "that we control. Yes?"

My breath hitches in my throat, but I force out the word. "Yes."

She doesn't respond. Her beady eyes narrow, and for a second, I swear she's closing in on me. They're all closing in on me. Studying me. About to suck out my soul.

Then they cackle again. The sound turns my bones to ash and my hair to serpents.

"Oh, I like her, too," Spindle breathes, holding out the thread to her sister.

The crone with the scissors snips it.

I gasp, watching the thread fall free of the rest of the spool.

What have I done?

I drop to my knees. Have they just ended someone's life? Because of me?

Or is that life mine?

My breath grows shallow. My heart seems to constrict. My throat, too.

Sparks of light fill my vision, tiny spots that I want to bat at. Everything else is going black.

I feel myself slowly falling to the ground.

I am dying.

"Oh, quit being so dramatic," Scissors says, snapping her fingers. Her razor-sharp voice cuts through my fog. "We have done nothing to you. Get up."

What? I lift myself up from the ground. I try breathing, indescribably relieved when air fills my lungs and the spots in my vision disappear. I tentatively stand, feeling like at any moment, I'll be right back on the rocky ground again.

"Here," they say together, handing me the thread. I recoil.

"I-I can't. I don't even know who that is."

Their laughter punches the air like squawks from geese.

"It is no one," they say together. "It is just a piece of thread."

Scissors extends her wrinkled, arthritic hands with the thread in her palms.

"Take it," they order.

I take it.

They smile their wicked, toothless smiles and turn around.

For old crones, they sure move fast. I stare at the back of their black robes. "What am I supposed to do now?" I call out.

"Whatever you do, it will be what we want," they say with a final, awful cackle.

What are they saying? That I really am a prisoner of fate? Or that they want me to do what I want? Is that the same thing? Oh, leave it to them to speak in riddles.

Their forms are gone before their echoes of laughter have faded. I look around, uncertain, vulnerable. What just happened? How did I face the Moirai, *insult them*, and live to tell about it? Not that I'm telling anyone. This little sliver of madness is all mine.

I shake my head, trying to break through the cloud of terror fogging my mind. I turn to the temple, where the priest is nowhere to be seen.

Right. The temple. At least I remember what to do next. Emboldened by my encounter, I bolt past the final altar, up the steps, and dash through the door before the priest can return.

Time to see the Oracle.

Chapter Eight

Inside, dull light guides my path. As high as it is, the heavy, gilded roof above makes me feel claustrophobic. Because the temple is Apollo's, much of the interior is golden, and the notes of an enchanted lyre fill the temple. Friezes of Apollo's hunting conquests and of him playing instruments and riding a golden chariot line the top of the walls. I have to walk through the *pronaos*, the foretemple, where I tiptoe around marble statues of Zeus and Poseidon and the Fates. The statues are hardly faithful representations. In reality, the Gods are far more stunning and the Fates far more ghastly. I give the marble crones a wide berth, hugging the colonnade surrounding the interior wall. Then I follow a small row of columns that runs perpendicular to the colonnade, leading to the entrance of the *cella*. The inner shrine.

I take several shaky steps down to the shrine, my eyes darting from left to right. The emptiness is unnerving. At the far end of the *cella* is the walled off *adyton*, the holiest part of the temple. Through the door of the *adyton*, a statue of Apollo gazes down on me. I step silently, hoping not to call the God's notice. My hand tightens as vapors begin rising in the holy room, and I realize I'm still holding the thread from the Moirai. I stuff it in my pocket.

My throat is dry when I approach the holy room. The vapors grow thicker and thicker, and the smell of laurel is cloying. I cough, putting my arm in front of my face. I don't know whether to call out to her, walk in, or leave while I still can.

But the decision is not mine to make.

"What desirest thou?" a powerful voice asks.

I know it's immature, but I can't help but pull a Hera and roll my eyes. If the Fates, who are older than dirt, can tell me to stop being such a drama queen, then the Pythia—the Oracle chosen anew each generation—can just ask me what I want.

I spot her through the laurel vapors, and my snarkiness vanishes. The Pythia's eyes are pure black, and yet I swear she's looking right into my soul. It's creepy. She sits on a three-legged stool wrapped in red robes, surrounded by the swirling, prophecy-inducing vapors that rise up from the final resting place of the Python.

"I've come to reclaim my destiny."

Her smile is even creepier than her eyes. Her skin sags around her grin. I'm shocked by how much she's aged since she handed me my fate as an Erote when I was twelve. But then, she's mortal, and that time has passed far, far more quickly for her than it has for me. She'll be in the constellations before I've even graduated.

The thought makes me sad.

"Thy destiny?" she asks. "Countless are the stars that make up thy heavens, Kalixta. Tell me: what precisely dost thou desire to reclaim?"

I think of Ben singing "Lovestruck" and the intense look on his face as we locked eyes. I felt like a fire was alive inside me. That fire warms me right now, crackling pleasantly inside of me, roaring a little harder and hotter just by me thinking about him. But I know that fire could spread beyond my control, consume my insides, and leave an empty husk.

I've seen it happen.

I won't let it happen to me.

"My heart," I say. "And my calling."

Another smile. "Better." She grabs a laurel leaf from the small pot on the stand beside her and pops it into her mouth. "But thou must choose. Which dost thou value more?"

This isn't how it's supposed to go. I shouldn't have to choose. My calling or my heart? A calling where I'm the Fates' pawn, matching poor fools who don't realize they're merely playthings, or one where I never have to fear ruining a life again? But is that more important than my heart? Than having a future of my own making, a love that I choose and that freely chooses me? Or do I risk having a fate like my parents? I can almost see the Moirai laughing at me. Those wretched old hags must have planned this the whole time.

"Which dost thou value more?" she repeats.

Thoughts of Ben and the Thunderclap and Hector swirl and crash inside my mind, creating a tsunami that leaves confusion and devastation in its wake. But each of these thoughts has the same central theme: love.

"My heart. I don't want to be forced into love." No matter how good it felt when I believed Hector loved me for me. No matter how good it feels to think of Ben. Love has the power to heal, enrich, and beautify, but when it goes wrong, it has the power to destroy. I can't do that to any of us.

"A wise choice. What art thou offering?"

"Um . . ." I forgot this part.

She closes her eyes and sighs. "Why dost thy kind always ignore the offering?" She gives an exasperated shake of her head and eats another laurel leaf.

"No! No, it's okay. Hang on." I pat my chiton, as if something good will magically appear. Nada. Time to try another tactic. "Um, is there anything you want?"

With a curl in her lip, she leans toward me. "Didst Veronica and Logan end up together?"

"What? How do you know about *Veronica Mars?*"

"Thou art not the first rogue goddess to darken my doorstep. The last one who came offered me a tablet loaded with all three seasons."

I close my eyes and concentrate, searching my memories. After a few heartbeats, I find it: an assignment from a few years ago. I was in a park observing my target while two girls running around the lake discussed the movie and subsequent books for four straight laps. I didn't pay attention at the time, but my perfect recall pulls it up now. I tell her everything.

When I finish, she sighs, a hand over her heart. "I couldst swoon forever."

Before I can even laugh, her entire body goes rigid. She sits stark upright. Her head snaps back, and the vapors stream through her, pouring from her mouth, her nose, her eyes. Her head drops down and she looks at me with eyes of pure white. I actually miss the black.

She speaks, and her voice sounds like it has split in two. "To reclaim thy heart eternally, thou must complete these tasks three: heal the heart of a desperate maiden, restore to greatness a fallen champion, and save a soul from an unjust union. Should success be thine, thy destiny wilt thou find." My mind jumps and races at her words. I file away the exact phrasing for safekeeping. But her face grows redder, and her body writhes as if she's fighting some invisible foe. When she speaks again, her voice is frantic, and she almost screams. "But beware the eye of the jealous son," she cries, her face pure agony as she fights to get out her final words, "lest thy quest for heart end in none!"

Her head slumps down, and the vapors dissipate, leaving a stale room and an unconscious Oracle. Her final words chill me to the core.

I don't dare move, but I have to make sure she's okay. She's so old. I creep over to her. When I reach her, I grab her hand, which doesn't so much as twitch. It's somehow hot and cold at the same time.

"Pythia?" I ask, tilting her head up. After a moment, her eyelids flutter, and I release a long, slow breath.

"I'm fine, dear," she says, sounding like any mortie's grand-mother. She blinks, and the creepy eyes are gone, leaving normal, pale-blue irises. Her laurel-laced breath comes out in huffs. "Go."

I look at her uncertainly, and she glances behind her at the statue of Apollo.

"Go," she whispers. "Run now, before you're seen."

"Thank you."

I run out of the temple, down the dark slope, and dematerialize before the howling animals or priest or Apollo's gaze can catch me.

Back on Olympus, the stars are so much brighter, I feel like I can see everything. I spot my friends at the archery field before they see me. They jump when I approach.

"It's just me," I pant.

Teresa exhales, the only indication of her nervousness. "Kal, you made it."

"You scared us, you turd!" Deya says, throwing her arms around me. "What took you so long?"

I hug her tightly, wondering what I should and shouldn't say. The run-in with the Moirai ... I shudder. I'm both protective and superstitious of our exchange. And I'm still too confused to know what to make of it. Shivering, I jam my hands in the pockets of my chiton and wrap my finger around the iridescent thread.

"I had to wait till the priest made his rounds. I think the disturbances Thrax and Cosmo mentioned are just wild animals, at least at Delphi."

Deya nods her head. "Cos couldn't find anything but animals as he went over the archives, too. It was everything I could do to keep him from looking too closely at Delphi tonight," she says, a flush on her cheeks. Drown me in the Styx, Deya is blushing.

"Wanna talk about it?" I ask, sharing a grin with Teresa.

Deya fights a smile. "Nope."

"Well, I ended up forcing the Port guy to get in his system and show me every port in and out I've made in the last month, which took some time. Then I made him check on someone else's aqua screen because I told him I didn't trust him. He was *not* happy. At all," Teresa says with a smile. "I checked only a few minutes ago, and his supervisor was yelling at him for the distraction."

"He was still getting yelled at about being distracted when I ported back up. They didn't even see me coming," I say, still grinning. "Irony is my favorite."

Teresa chuckles.

Deya's relief is palpable. "So it worked? I can't believe it. I know we prepared, but this was almost too easy."

I think of my conversation with the Fates, of the scissors slicing through that thread with awful finality. Maybe not so easy.

Deya gets between Teresa and me and loops her arms through

ours, not letting Teresa shake her off. "So, what happened?" Deya asks.

We walk over to the far end of the archery field, passing arrows so far off target, they could only have come from first-years. The archery field ends abruptly, dropping down a cliff to overlook the lower peaks of Olympus where minor deities live. The top three peaks are for Zeus and Hera, the Twelve, and the Ancients, respectively, while the departments come next. The remaining tiers are for immortals and minor deities of lineage too far removed from Zeus for the Big Gs to care about. There is a definite hierarchy to Mount Olympus.

We sit down and swing our legs over the edge of the cliff, looking over the numberless tiers of our mountain home. Several peaks down, I see naiads have invited some river gods over for a serious pool party. I avert my eyes. Looks like clothing is optional. Thanks for nothing, hawk vision.

"Kal," Teresa prods, "what happened?"

I don't mention the Fates, but I tell them everything that happened with the Oracle.

"Repeat the prophecy," Teresa says. I do. "Typical. There are probably a thousand different interpretations. Do you have any idea who the three are you need to help? The desperate maiden, the champion, the unjustly unioned? Or, more importantly, the 'jealous son' you're supposed to watch out for?"

"No, no, no, and no," I say.

Deya picks a petal off of a white hydrangea and throws it over the edge, watching it turn into a butterfly and flap away. "The jealous son could be Thrax, that dirty son of a Gorgon. He actually came to check up on Cosmo tonight and when he saw me there, he went berserk. More than normal, I mean."

"I don't know. He's more into you than he is me," I say.

She shrugs, tossing another petal-turned-butterfly. "Only because I'm Aphrodite's daughter. The jerk is just like his dad; you know he thinks he's destined to be with one of Aphrodite's descendants. He can't stand seeing any of us with someone else, just like his dad can't handle seeing my mom with anyone else. If it were up to Thrax, I think he'd marry us all. And, with him being in Olympus Security, he could meddle with your plan pretty easily."

I can sort of see what she's saying, but I didn't get a douche vibe when the Oracle mentioned the son. It felt more menacing. I tell my friends as much. "But we should probably keep an eye on Thrax, just in case." My friends nod. "Now what about the others? We need to figure out—"

"How long you're going to be grounded for?" a voice says behind us. We all turn to see Artemis standing over us. She looks no older than we do, but power rolls off of her in tumultuous waves. "You're in a world of trouble," she says. "Come with me."

Artemis sends Deya and Teresa away without argument. They cast me worried looks, which are warranted, because I may be immortal, but I'm dead. We set off to my house on the temporally folding paths, but now that we're moving, I get the sense that she isn't in a rush to get me home, particularly as she could just teleport us in an instant. Her eternally youthful face looks so sad, her green eyes so haunted. I hope she's not too disappointed in me.

"*Theá* Artemis, please," I beg. "I can explain everything."

She waves her hand. "Don't be so formal."

We pass a handful of little Gs scampering around couch-sized mushrooms—lesser nature deities and immortals a hundred generations removed from one of the Twelve. They nod respect-fully when they see Artemis. Once we're past them, she shakes her auburn curls, which are pinned up, as always. "I'm just the messenger, kid. Your parents have been worried, and I volunteered to find you."

Of course, the Goddess of the hunt would find me. I wonder how long she took.

"It took all of two minutes to figure out what you were up to."

Right. My ego is officially gone.

"Artemis, please, just understand that I'm not trying to defy anything. I'm stuck loving this boy, and I can't live knowing that the way we feel is a lie! I had to know if I could fix things so I can be in control of myself again. I just had to."

She looks down at me with pity. "And what about Hector, Kali? Why is there a different standard for you than for him? You know how he feels about you."

"But that's just it! Reversal arrows don't work on immortals, but if I can reclaim my heart, it won't matter that I ever stuck my-self, because I'll be in control. No double standards. It'll be proof that the Fates really can be beaten." Why does no one understand how much this matters?

"I get it. You're desperate. Love makes you do stupid things. But going to the Oracle? Do you know how foolish that was?"

"Does your brother know?" Please, don't let Apollo know.

"Fortunately for you, no. The priest didn't know you were there, so the Pythia was able to go rogue prophesying for you."

I exhale in relief. "So how did you—"

"Goddess of the hunt, remember? Everyone leaves a distinct trail to me. And because I know you as well as I do, it made you even easier to find."

The temporally folding path has us only yards from the house. I turn to her. "Please, Artemis. You have to help me. The Oracle gave me a way that I can make everything right. I know I'm raving right now. It's the arrow. Just being away from him for a day makes me feel like my heart is clawing to get out. The longer we're apart, the more I feel like I won't be able to exist without him." Memories of Ben's voice, of his fingers laced in mine and his hand stroking my cheek fill my mind, and it's everything I can do not to cry. It's a testament to Artemis' coolness and my desperation that she's letting me talk to her like this. "I don't want to feel like this, Artemis. Please help me."

She sighs. "What could I even do, Kali? I'd love to help, but I won't defy your parents."

"Just convince them to let me see this through. I can still do all my jobs and my class work. But when a match is separated, they can go insane with the need to be together. If I can just be near him while I sort this out . . ."

She clutches the necklace she usually keeps hidden beneath her chiton and stares up at the stars. For someone who chose to stop aging before the peak of maturity, she really is stunning. She's beautiful in the way that a gazelle is beautiful, or an eagle: majestic, fierce, and unstoppable. Yet I see the vulnerability she hides; it surpasses even her fierceness. She's still looking heavenward, and her eyes reflect a single constellation: Orion.

I reach a hand to her bare shoulder. "Artemis, are you okay?"

She drops her glorious head and tucks the necklace back into her chiton. "I'm fine." She sets her green eyes on me, eyes so much like her nephew's, but infinitely sadder. "If I could help you, kid, I would."

I hate that we're not allowed to talk about Orion to her. I hate that she's not even allowed to admit that she was once in love when it's obvious how much her heart still aches for him. I wish I could distract her, or at least give her a break from her brother's prying eyes.

"Wait, Artemis," I say, the words tumbling from my mouth. "I think I know how you can help me."

She studies me like I'm her prey. "Does it involve disobeying Zeus?"

"No."

"Will it betray your parents? I like your parents. If I don't get invited to one of their game nights because of whatever stunt you have planned—"

I brave a hopeful half-smile. "I promise, you'll still get invited to game night."

"Will it hurt Hector?"

My brow furrows. "No. Nothing you do will hurt Hector." What I do, on the other hand, seems to hurt him no matter what.

When her eyes meet mine, they're sad, but understanding. "Okay. I'm listening."

Chapter Nine

Artemis has been talking to my parents in their room for a long time. Because Aphrodite's almost never home, Deya's sleeping over, like usual. We're lying on the bed in one of my siblings' old rooms. I have hundreds of siblings, and this one is one I don't know too well. She's one of Demeter's Earth mothers, and she's way older than I am. By order of Zeus, all immortals are limited to one child every two mortie centuries for immortal population control. However, that decree doesn't keep them from having children with morties, which countless of them do. Hence Zeus' decision that no demis can find out about their heritage or be made immortal. If they were all made immortal, Olympus would fill the galaxy. Raunchy, horny immortals.

As much as I mentally look down on my parents' marriage, it's secretly one of the things I appreciate most about their relationship: no affairs. Not a one.

"So, do you really think they're going to go for this?" Deya asks as we lie on her bed and look up at the stars.

"If Artemis can't convince them, no one can."

"I still don't understand how you managed to convince Artemis."

I roll over onto my elbow to look at her. "I think she feels just as lost as I do. You should have seen her tonight, just staring up at the stars like they could guide her home. It broke my heart."

"It probably broke hers, too."

"I know. It's so stupid."

"Stupid or not, she shouldn't have risked that relationship."

"Like she knew a giant scorpion would kill Orion!"

Deya rolls over, too. "You're kidding, right?"

"What do you mean? You think Orion deserved it?"

"No! Kali, do you really mean to tell me you don't—" She claps a hand over her mouth. Then she grabs a blanket to throw over top of our heads. "You really don't know what happened to Orion?" she whispers.

"Yeah, the scorpion—"

"No." Her voice drops even lower. "A few years ago, I heard my mom gossiping about it with some sirens over a bottle of Dionysian wine. It sounds like no one knows for sure, but the story she heard at the time was that Apollo was so overprotective and upset by Artemis' love for Orion that he challenged Orion to see how far he could swim. When Orion was miles and miles out and only his head was visible, Apollo bet Artemis that she couldn't hit the animal, way, way out in the water. And because she's Artemis . . ."

"She hit him," I whisper. It's the most awful thing I can imagine. I hope for her sake that it isn't true.

"Exactly."

"This is so much worse than the scorpion."

Deya nods. "Yes, but what else can she expect when she took a maiden-oath to Zeus?"

"She was a child when she took that oath. No one should be held to a promise they made when they were three."

"But she's a Twelve, Kali. At three years old, she had a greater mental capacity than you or I will ever—"

"Deya, she asked to stay a virgin for eternity, for nymphs to watch over her bow when she's not hunting, for a choir of nine-year-olds to sing to her all the time. These are hardly the wishes of a mature mind. Zeus should—"

Deya hisses. "Are you out of your cursing mind? Why are you trying to get us killed?"

I can barely make Deya out, even with my hawk vision. "The sun set hours ago, Dey. Helios can't eavesdrop, and everyone knows Selene hates Apollo. The titan of the moon won't tell him a thing," I say, pointing upward.

"The moon is hardly the only one I'm worried about. Zeus doesn't need Helios or Selene to know when you're blaspheming, you fool!"

I huff, but she's right. Although I doubt Zeus cares what a probie says, he doesn't deserve my disrespect. Besides, I'm sure he found Artemis' oath as silly as I do.

"I'm sorry, Dey." Underneath the blanket, it's getting uncomfortably stuffy. "I just wish Artemis didn't hurt so much."

"Me too."

We both fall silent. I pull the blanket off of us and stare back up at the sky. Of course, I only have eyes for Orion after the story. I want to help Artemis more than ever. As much as I want to help myself.

Eventually, Deya falls asleep, and I keep staring. Staring and hoping. Thoughts of Ben and Artemis swirl around in my mind until a knock on the door sounds.

"Good luck," Deya murmurs, turning over. "Tell me all about it. Tomorrow." Her breathing regulates, and she's back asleep before I've left the room.

I step into the expansive marble hallway, rubbing my eyes to blot out the bewitched torchlight that illuminates the house. My parents direct me down a hallway lined with pottery, plants, and bronze statues. They guide me into a room where Artemis stands with her back to me, looking into the hearth. Oh no.

My dad stares me down. "Artemis told us that she found you sneaking off to see this mortal." This lie was Artemis' idea, seeing as my sneaking off to the Oracle is definitely the kind of offense that would get me grounded for a century. Unfortunately, the look on my dad's face tells me that even coming from a Goddess, he isn't as moved as I'd hoped he'd be. "Your mother and I want to impress upon you the enormous risk it would pose to let you be with this mortal boy." Despair claws its way up to my throat. "It would involve multiple departments and require approval from the head of your department, as well as from your own parents."

"But Dad, *you're* the head of the Erotes!"

"In practice, yes, but technically, your grandmother is, as all departments report up through one of the Twelve." He says this as if it's bad news, but Aphrodite is a sucker for love. I'm in! "But because this request involves a probationary goddess and impacts another department, it has to be approved by another God, as well."

"Who?"

"Hephaestus."

My legs go weak and I drop to a divan. Hephaestus: Aphrodite's spurned ex-husband. My dad is the product of an affair Aphrodite had with Ares while she was married to Hephaestus. He may be the last God willing to sign off on an ill-fated quest by one of her descendants. I'm doomed. The thought of the arrow controlling me, of going mad with a need to be with Ben, is more than I can take. "Why would Hephaestus care?" I ask weakly in what is surely my last and most futile effort to take control of my life.

"Because your QM isn't authorized to create whole lives out of thin air the way he would have to do for you. You'd need lodging, transportation, identification . . ." He looks at my mom, as if she'd know all the modern earthly amenities and alibis necessary to pull this off. She holds her hands up in a "How would I know?" gesture.

"Stuff, Kali," my dad says. "You would need a great deal of stuff. Hephaestus would be inviting unnecessary risk into his department."

"So that's it, then," I say, fanning my face, because it's suddenly sweltering in here. "I'm done. I'm going to waste away here on Olympus forever, and in another seventy mortie years, I'll be so far gone, it won't matter that—"

"She gets the dramatics from you, Monster," Mom says.

My eyes narrow at my mom. "I don't think making fun of me is really helping right now, Mom."

"I'm not making fun," she says with a long-suffering smile that she probably mastered eons ago, when my oldest sibling, Hedone, was young. "But if you'll stop feeling sorry for yourself and listen up, you'll get better results."

"Results? What are you talking about?"

My parents look at each other. (They carry on so many tele-pathic conversations, it's rude.) My mom's nostrils flare slightly as my dad talks. "Your mother is trying to say that Artemis reminded us that the risk of keeping you and this boy separate is insanity." Hope stirs in my gut. "We've had enough rampaging immortals over the years, and no one is interested in the fallout and cleanup from another such incident. So it is with the gravest of misgivings that I tell you we've decided to let you be with this mortal boy."

I hop up and grab my dad's arms. "Are you serious?" I jump up and down, squealing, but he silences me with a finger in the air.

"You are allowed to spend time with him on the following

conditions," my dad continues over my squealing and hopping. "You will still be expected to stay current on your Erote classwork, and do a *far* better job than you've been doing."

This is no more than I had proposed to Artemis, yet somehow, I'd hoped they'd let me quit. After all, the Oracle said I can change my destiny if I meet the other terms of the prophecy, which I will absolutely do. And what is my destiny if it doesn't include my calling? I'm almost tempted to tell him about the prophecy. But remembering that I don't want my parents to smite me, I keep my mouth shut.

"Your probation matching will be temporarily suspended. You already have four mismatches, Kali. You need to rediscover yourself while you spend the next few mortal decades with this boy before you end up drowning in a pile of homework in the underworld," he says, being disturbingly literal. "You will spend your weekends here, not on Earth with the mortal boy. Artemis has agreed to chaperone your mortal stay for the time being."

At this, Artemis winks at me. It's exactly what we planned, and it worked! No matter how hard she tries to be cool, I see the little smile she's trying to hide. She needs this change of pace.

"Additionally, I'm going to assign Deya to come with you." His eyes flash a warning not to complain, which is both justified and insulting. And maybe a little hurtful, honestly. If she were coming as my best-friend-slash-de-facto-sister, I'd be all for it. But that's not what this is. She's going to be there to supervise me and make sure I don't do anything stupid, day in and day out.

My stomach twists. She's going to be there because my parents trust her more than me.

"We will reevaluate your stay, oh, whenever we want," my dad adds. His wings stand tall behind him, so I know he means business.

"Monster." My mom chides him gently. From her seat across from me, she smiles. "You are our daughter, Kali. We want you to be happy and we know that you feel that your happiness depends on this boy. Remember that your happiness is also made up of the relationships you have with your family and friends. Don't let a quest for freedom overshadow the happiness you've already achieved."

Her words are sweet, but too Mom-ish to take seriously, especially because one fact distracts me: it worked. My plan actually worked. I'll get to be with Ben, thus staving off insanity and also satisfying this insatiable need I have to listen to him sing and run my hands through his hair. More importantly, I'll get to work on the prophecy and take my heart and fate back from the Moirai.

"I'll do whatever you want," I promise, excitement filling me in a way I haven't felt in months. "Thank you, thank you, thank you!" I jump up and down again, rushing between them to kiss their cheeks and hug them tightly. I go between them so many times that they both start laughing.

"Okay, okay," my dad says. "You're starting to ruffle my feathers."

I laugh and just squeeze him again. He hugs me back, a tight, loving hug that I never tire of. Artemis wears a wistful smile as she watches our exchange. I catch her eye and mouth *Thank you.*

She returns my smile and mouths back *See you tomorrow* before she disappears completely.

I won't sleep a wink tonight.

How could I?

Tomorrow, my new life begins.

Chapter Ten

I try to fight the feeling all morning, because this is the most fatalistic thing I've ever willingly done. But the truth is, I'm all aflutter. I'm going to see Ben in a matter of minutes. Even knowing I wouldn't wear my chiton on Earth, I changed it twice. Deya rolls her eyes at me while Artemis chuckles. I don't care. I'm going to Earth indefinitely with my parents' blessing.

Maybe the Fates really do like me.

It's been ages since I've felt so happy. The day seems even more perfect because I know what's in store. Somehow, the sun is brighter, the birds are chirpier, and the forests and flowers and springs we pass are more breathtaking than ever. As we meet up with the temporally folding path, nothing can dampen my mood.

Until the path Hector is taking intersects with ours. And of course Ianira is with him.

Ugh.

They're only a couple of steps in front of us, deep in conversation, when Artemis says, "Nephew!" Hector turns around in surprise and gives his aunt a big hug. His green eyes light up before catching mine. His smile falters, yet when he and Artemis separate, he's the picture of cheer.

"What are you doing using the folds? I thought all you Twelve liked showing off your port-free mobility by disappearing and reappearing at will," he says.

"We're not all show-offs like your dad. Speaking of whom, how is my brother?"

"He's good. He misses you. It's been too long, Aunt Artemis."

She doesn't respond to this, instead asking, "So what are you two doing this morning?"

Ianira adjusts her glasses. "Hector and I are going to be working together. You know, I'm *normally* dedicated to the sciences, of course," she says, because we all care so much that *of course* we track her every musing. "But the subject *I'm* musing for has just been asked to consult with *Hector's* subject, if you can believe it." She starts explaining why while Artemis nods and carries on the conversation.

Meanwhile, behind their backs, Deya flashes a "gag me" look. She's just slowing down to hang back with Hector and me when Artemis grabs her arm. The Goddess speeds up, with Deya on one side of her and Ianira on the other. Ianira is ambitious and smart enough to know that when you have a Big G talking to you, you listen, no matter how badly you want to flirt with the sexy immortal who's now talking to his best friend.

Ha!

Wait, Artemis has left Hector and me alone together. To talk. Ah, Styx.

"So you're really going through with this?" Hector asks, kicking at an imaginary pebble with his gladiator sandal.

I nod and kick the same imaginary pebble. I could tell him about the Oracle, but that doesn't change the fact that I'm going to be with Ben in the interim, however long it takes. I can't *not.* "I'm sorry, Hec." What else can I say?

"If I—" he stops himself with a shake of his head. "How long is this for? What's your plan?"

I tell him about my parents' rule that I spend weekends home and keep up with my schoolwork. "I'll be back every weekend. So we'll still see each other all the time."

"Well, maybe not all the time," he says. "The filming schedule for *Most Dangerous Game* is around the clock lately, and Ianira isn't familiar with the arts, so she's going to need extra help. I'll be gone a lot."

I click my tongue in annoyance. "Right, because Ianira needs so much help with her assignments."

We're almost to the Port, but he slows down. "What do you mean?" There's a look of steel beneath the question in his eyes.

No, I think with a pang. I'm not allowed to do this to him. It isn't fair for me to keep him from seeing anyone else when I have no intention of ever giving him the relationship the arrow has convinced him he wants. Besides, he's too smart to be taken in by Ianira. He'll see right through her lensless glasses. "Nothing," I tell him, stepping over to the Port where Artemis and Deya are waiting. "I just hope we'll still get to see each other sometimes."

"You can't hope too much, considering you're the only one keeping us apart," he mutters before grimacing. Ouch. His perfect jaw tenses, and he shakes his head. "Good luck in Flagstaff, Kali," he tells me, stepping into the Port beside Ianira. She and I don't make eye contact.

My throat feels hot, but I pretend I didn't hear Hector. As if. "Thanks, Hec. Good luck in—where are you going, anyway?"

"Phoenix." He smiles, already returning to the cavalier happiness that always bothers me. "Phoenix, Arizona."

I clutch my necklace and try to process whether I'm happy or not that we'll be so close, but I push the thought from my mind. He'll be working. I'll be with Ben.

And even though I should stop myself from feeling this way, I cannot cursing wait.

A moment later, we appear inside a cabin in Flagstaff, Arizona, wearing mortie clothes. Artemis is wearing jeans and a fitted white T-shirt with a target on the back that looks amazing on her, especially with her auburn curls piled effortlessly (and sexily) on top of her head. Her mortal form looks like a fitness model: tan and toned and like she was made to dominate at beach volleyball. She's aged herself to maybe her late-twenties, which suits her far better than her usual preternaturally wise fifteen-year-old look.

"Sorry it's so small," Artemis says, gesturing to the cabin, "but it was the biggest house the mortal liaisons could get on such short notice." She looks up at the twelve-foot ceilings. "I already feel claustrophobic."

My time among mortals has been limited to my assignments, which are always in public places. Yet I know that this three-story house is luxurious by mortal standards . . . and totally confining by immortal ones. The floor-to-ceiling windows all have glass on them instead of giving open access to the outdoors, and while we all have our own bedrooms and bathrooms, they're cramped. The floor of my bathroom on Olympus is a bed of moss softer than goose down, and it leads to a natural hot spring that could comfortably hold a dozen people. I can barely lie down in this "Jacuzzi tub."

Even goddesses have to make sacrifices.

When we've finished the tour, we step onto a balcony off of the kitchen and lean over the railing at towering ponderosa pines, oaks, and quaking aspens.

"How much of it is ours?" Deya asks.

"Only four acres," Artemis says, making a face. "But the liaison assured me that this is a lot to modern mortals. I haven't left Olympus in a long while, so I may be a little out of touch."

"It'll be fine," I say brightly. School starts in fifteen minutes, and I don't intend to let anything bring me down today. "I should probably head to school now while you go find your assignment, Dey. I'll see you two—"

"Nice try," Deya says. "I'm following you and you're shadowing me, remember? Your dad just told us this morning. We're both going to school so your dad can exempt us from mortal studies for the rest of fifth year." She keeps talking, reminding me about the classes we'll be attending and the ones we won't, but now that I'm on Earth, I can feel my proximity to Ben, and it's taking over my thoughts. My stomach is in knots that my rational mind can't untie.

Deya snaps in front of my face. "Kal. Get out of la-la land and get your mind back in the game."

"Right, totally. We'll take classes with Ben, I'll follow you on your assignment. Done." I grab Deya's arm before she can get upset. "Now let's go."

I reach for my necklace to port over to school when Artemis stops me with a glance. "No way," she says. "You two are visible now, which means you can't use Olympian powers for everything. The risk of exposure is far too great." We both start to protest, but Artemis raises her eyebrows. "Welcome to Earth, probies."

Deya looks horrified. "Artemis, what are you saying?"

Her smile is nowhere near apologetic. "Unless you're here at the house, you change, do your hair, communicate, and travel just like morties do."

Deya turns on me. "Look what you've done!"

I flinch. "It's okay! It's all going to be okay. We just have to get to school, and I promise you—"

"And how are we supposed to get to school?" she snaps. "Are we anywhere near it?"

Artemis laughs and a set of keys appears in her hands. "Come on, probies. I'll drive you." She grabs a bow and quiver of arrows out of thin air and jumps over the balcony, landing silently on the forest floor two dozen feet below. Deya and I follow her. Several cars are parked in the driveway. Artemis is already jumping up into a vehicle that looks like a box without a top.

"It's a Jeep!" Deya yells excitedly, shoving me in the back seat so she can sit in the front. I tune out her prattling about how Cosmo knew she always wanted to drive one, thinking of a pair of hazel eyes I'll see any minute now.

The tires squeal, spitting up rocks and dirt. "Hold on tight!" Artemis yells.

I do. I hold on as tightly as I've ever held on to anything in my life. Deya screams and whoops as Artemis steps on different pedals and jerks the steering wheel and narrowly dodges trees and signs and other cars. My heart has stopped and restarted a dozen times. Twice, it has tried to force itself out of my body through my throat, along with the contents of my stomach that are now scattered over the highway. Admittedly, I know nothing about driving. But I know beyond all doubt that Artemis is the worst driver in the history of Olympus.

She's so bad that when we fly through an intersection, a voice sounds next to our ears. "I'm switching this car to 'Cos Control' before you get yourselves killed," Cosmo tells us with a laugh. As the speed and steadiness regulate, I breathe out a thank you to him.

Artemis, meanwhile, is cursing. "Listen, little quartermaster, I was doing just fine."

"Of course you were! You were just, um, attracting the notice of f-four mortal police," he stutters. "I had to intervene before you were detained and possibly arrested. I'm really sorry, *Theá* Artemis. Please don't smite me."

As Cosmo pulls us gently into the school parking lot, I say, "Cosmo, don't you dare apologize for not letting her kill us. I'd rather take a ferry ride with Charon."

"Oh, quit your whining," Artemis says. "Or I'll make that ferry ride happen."

Cosmo parks the car and we hear him clear his throat. "Um, *Theá* Artemis, the school needs to have you sign some papers for the girls to transfer here. I would have made the problem go away, but I was explicitly asked not to because the girls are visible."

"It's not a problem, kid," Artemis says.

The relief in his voice is tangible. "Deya and Kali, you have bags in the backseat with phones, identification, class schedules, and everything you'll need to get by today. I've made you familiar to your classmates, but you may still be overlooked a little."

Deya chuckles. "Not likely."

Cosmo sounds choked. "Right. Well, if you encounter any problems, press your charms and I'll take care of it."

'Thanks, Cos,' we say before we all hop out of the car. I smile at students and beam at teachers. When Mr. Gunner, the World History teacher, walks by, I wave.

"Hi, Mr. Gunner!"

He gives me a look like he should be able to place me, but can't quite. Then Artemis' bow in the back of the Jeep catches his eye.

"That's a beautiful bow," he says. "Does this belong to one of you?"

"It's mine," Artemis says. "Do you shoot?"

He hasn't looked at Artemis yet; he's too busy admiring the

bow. "Um, yeah, I mean, no. Not anymore. May I?" She nods and he picks up the bow, admiring the expert craftsmanship. "This is stunning. Who made this?"

"I did," she says.

His eyes move to Artemis and widen. After a pause in which he seems to be studying her, he says, "Impressive. Madagascar rosewood?"

"Close enough," she says. It's Olympian Rosewood.

"Wow," he says, putting the bow back down carefully in the Jeep. "Are you going into the school? Can I show you around?" They start toward the school. Finally. I'm bouncing as I look over heads and through arms for a sight of Ben. "So are you any good?" Mr. Gunner asks.

Artemis smirks. "You could say that. You?"

The sadness I've associated with Mr. Gunner in the past few weeks seems to lift. "You could say that."

I glance back to give Artemis a wave, but she and Mr. Gunner are still talking. Her eyebrows are raised, and a slight smile graces her lips. I'm relieved to see that she already looks happier than she has for ages.

I run ahead, looking for our first class, which Cosmo's schedule tells me is World History with Mr. Gunner. The warning bell rings as I sneak in. And I see him: Ben Vega, with his ash-brown hair covering his face and an empty seat beside him. My heart does a million jumping jacks while my head tries (and fails) to keep it in control. I feel like I'm going to fly apart. I flash Deya a tight smile and walk over to the open desk.

When I slide into the seat, his eyes pop. "It's you. You're here."

I squeeze my hands into fists. It takes all of my self-restraint not to throw my arms around him and declare my eternal love.

"I'm here. Is that . . . okay?" I ask, all too aware of the arrow on my necklace.

"Of course! It's just, after the other night, I didn't know if I'd see you again. I thought I may have made you up: the beautiful girl with the Smiths T-shirt."

My cheeks flush. "I had to take care of something . . . a family problem. But it's all better now."

"Does that mean you're not going to disappear on me again, then?" he asks. My stomach flips at the earnestness in his eyes. Calm down, Kali.

I don't calm down. I flirt. "Give me a reason not to," I say. He grins. In spite of myself, I grin back.

Mr. Gunner gets into the room just as the bell rings. He instantly starts his lecture, so Ben and I can't really continue. But Ben opens up a notebook and writes on a piece of paper, which he then slips in front of me. All it says is "Reason=Me."

I pop the lid off of my pen and write, "Yeah?"

"Yeah," he writes. Then he draws a quick sketch of himself from the ground up, starting with his beat-up, blue-and-gold Adidas shoes. I'm surprised by his talent, how he captures the frays in the jeans that sit just a bit too big on his wiry body and the way his lean arms jut out from his plain navy T-shirt. When he gets to his face, he doesn't draw any features—no eyes or nose—just a huge, sloppy grin with hair.

I have to keep myself from succumbing wholly to the arrow's power. I want to draw a picture of me with my heart full to bursting. I manage to simply write "Cute" on the paper, instead.

He writes, "Little ol' me?"

I write, "I loved your song."

He draws a picture of a perfectly fat, cherubic baby cupid with wings and an ill-proportioned and completely inaccurate bow. The sight turns my stomach, not just because of the cursing Romans, but because it's a reminder of how wrong this all is. From the cupid's bow, Ben draws a zooming trajectory of an arrow that spells out "Lovestruck" in cool punk rock lettering.

"Ben," Mr. Gunner says. "You and your friend have been taking notes rather furiously. Would either of you like to share with the class what you've just learned about the historical inaccuracies of the movie *300* compared with the actual events of the Battle of Thermopylae?"

My in-depth knowledge of Ancient Greek history aside, this is a trick no teacher on Olympus would ever pull. While being immortal doesn't make you an instant master in every subject, it does mean that your brain works vastly more efficiently than a mortal's brain and that most of us have near-perfect recall. So simple multi-tasking like flirting and paying attention to a lecture? Come on.

Also, I've seen the movie, and it's hysterical.

I sit up straight. "The number is off, for starters. Sure, there were three hundred Spartans fighting that particular last stand, but there were also over eleven hundred other Greeks from other cities. And the Spartans forced their slaves to fight, too, which is just wrong on every level and ups the count of soldiers. The Spartans had some of the most advanced armor of their day and would never have fought in just their underwear—"

"And abs," Ben says. "They also had their abs."

"Good point," I say with a smile. "And while Leonidas' queen was very active in running Sparta, she didn't kill anyone. Though you better believe she'd have killed any fool who thought he could lay hands on her." I smile at Mr. Gunner. "Is that enough, or should I move on to the absurd hypocrisy of King Leonidas calling Athenians 'boy-lovers'?"

Students call out "snap," "check," and "burn," earning a chuckle and nod from Mr. Gunner. He raises a hand, quieting the room. "That'll do. Thank you, Ms. Olympos."

I smile back and settle into my first day of school.

Chapter Eleven

At lunch, Deya and I sit with Ben and his bandmates, Paresh and Shaggy. The cafeteria is the same color scheme as the rest of the school: gray walls with orange stripes at the top and bottom; gray vinyl flooring; gray, round tables with orange chairs. The school mascot, a cartoon jackrabbit, snarls at us from the wall.

This place is hideous.

I stare at the contents of Ben's tray, not believing that mortals actually eat this . . . stuff. Part of me thinks Cosmo is playing a prank on us. Bet when I see Ben and Shaggy pick up their—what were they called? Sloppy Joes?—and take big bites, I realize that this is really happening.

"What is that made of?" Deya asks, grimacing.

"Sloppy Joes?" Shaggy asks. "In theory, that's bread and ground beef and some kind of tomato sauce. In reality, though?" He looks at Ben. "What do you think, goat?"

Ben nods, swallowing his bite. "Yeah, probably goat."

Deya and I share a look.

Ben and Shaggy both start laughing. "We're just messing with you. It's totally safe. Just good ol' cow." Shaggy says. He says something else to Ben, during which time Deya and I lean toward each other, still looking at the guys.

"I don't get it," she whispers to me. "Is it somehow better that it's cow and not goat?"

"You got me," I whisper back. I notice that Paresh doesn't have any of the weird cooked meat on his plate. His tray is covered with vegetables and rice, just like ours.

"So where did you guys go to school before this?" Ben asks me.

Cosmo prepared us for this, and Deya loves attention, so she answers. "We went to a private school in Phoenix, and then we were homeschooled for a bit. In fact, we're still taking a couple of homeschool classes, so we won't be around all day."

"What," Shaggy says, "your family sent you to real school so you could finally get a life?"

Deya smiles so seductively at him, I don't know how he isn't melting. "Shaggy. Look at me." He does. "I've turned down more dates today than you'll have in your miserable, rejection-filled life, you sorry turd."

Ben and Paresh snort, and soda comes out of Paresh's nose. Through sniffs and coughs, Paresh yells, "Burn!" to Shaggy, earning him several attempted punches to what I'm pretty sure is his crotch.

While the other two continue their slap fight, Ben turns his attention back to me. "So you were at a private school? What was that like?"

On the surface, Erote schooling isn't drastically different from mortie schooling. For a fifth-year, three days a week are devoted to classes and two to probationary training. In sixth year, it'll flip. We have classrooms with aqua screens, not so unlike mortie classrooms with their tablets. We take classes like history, human psychology, physics, and mortal studies. And, sure, our classrooms make the Sistine Chapel look like a mortie toddler's art project, and our infinitely superior screens respond to thought, and our teachers didn't just "write the book" on a subject, they literally created the subject from the primordial ooze. But, hey! Morties have way better student-to-teacher ratios.

To say nothing of detention.

Ben looks at me earnestly, so I tell him about as much of the truth as he can handle: "It was intense."

"I bet," he says with a nod. "So you said the other night that you're renting a place? Where's that?"

"We're staying with our aunt in a cabin just outside of town," I answer. I remember a sign over the gate that Artemis almost knocked over. "Observation Ranch."

The guys stop their junk-punching. "You guys are renting the O-Ranch?" Ben says after a long pause. "For how long?"

Deya and I look at each other and shrug. "For the time being, I guess, until we find something that suits us better."

Ben's face has gone from tan to deep red and he's avoiding my eye. "What, like Buckingham Palace?" Shaggy asks.

I sense that Deya is about to make another snide remark, but I need to fix this sudden awkwardness with Ben.

"I just mean that it's a bit much for the three of us," I lie, but it's the right lie. Ben is still flushed, but he's nodding, at least. I squeeze Deya's hand under the table, willing her to go along with what I'm saying. "Our parents both travel for work internationally, so they aren't really in touch with reality."

"Right," Deya says. "Good thing we have our aunt to keep us, you know, down to Earth. Right Kal?"

I nod, relieved when Ben returns his eyes to mine. "Your parents aren't around much, huh?"

I hesitate. Fatalistic love aside, my parents are actually the best. All of my friends like spending time with them because they love each other and they love us. Sometimes it bugs me how much my friends will talk to my parents instead of me. But I get it, too. Compared to the vast majority of Olympian offspring, my home life is a fairytale. I can't tell Ben this, though. The vulnerability on his face is too heartbreaking. "We have a complicated relationship." That's true, at least.

"I know the feeling." He rubs his nose. "So, what are you doing after school?"

"Deya and I have homeschool classes with our aunt." The warning bell has rung, and everywhere, kids are picking up their trays and throwing out their trash. We do the same.

"That's no problem," Ben says. "Meet me at band practice, then. Or after. Or for a super-sexy, moonlit walk." I laugh. "I don't care what we do. Just tell me I can see you later."

My chest grows warm. "Yeah, okay."

"Give me your phone," he says.

"My phone? Why?"

"So we can trade numbers." I hand him my phone and he enters his number into my phone, then texts himself my number. When he gives me back my phone our hands brush, and a lightning bolt seems to shoot up my arm and through my body. I want to revel in the feeling—Hades, I want to live in the feeling—but I give myself a mental shake and look for Ben's number in the phone. Cosmo's cover is impressive. I have hundreds of numbers stored. I recognize the name of every immortal I know with a visible mortie assignment, including Hector and, yuck, Ianira. I keep scrolling "Wait, I don't see you."

He grins. "It's under 'Handsome Devil.'"

"From the Smiths song," I say. His grin is only grinnier.

"Yep, and you're 'Pretty Girl' in my phone." He shows me the entry.

"Also from the Smiths."

Ben's friends are calling him away, but he stops just long enough to tell me, "Exactly right, Pretty Girl. I knew I liked you." He walks backwards with his friends, almost getting lost in the crowd of kids leaving the cafeteria for class. Right when he's about to disappear from my view, he runs back towards me and whispers in my ear. "I'll text you, okay?"

"Okay," I say, but it comes out airy. His nearness takes my breath away.

That arrow magic is no joke.

I let Deya pull me through the halls and out into the parking lot, barely noticing where I am. Ben is already texting me.

We still on for tonight? Say yes

My fingers are clumsy on the screen, but I type.

Of course! It's only been 10 seconds, silly.

Everything can change in 10 seconds, that's all it took for us to meet. Or for Shaggy to choke on his sloppy joe.

I laugh. The texts keep coming, and several times, I have to buzz in Cosmo to translate for me.

"Okay," his voice says between Deya and me as we drive to downtown Flagstaff to find Deya's assignment. Artemis was kind enough to leave the Jeep for us. "That image is meant to convey his current mood. So when he says he wants to see you along with this picture of that depressed-looking lizard lying belly-up, it's meant to represent how he's feeling without you." He clears his voice. "Are you sure you want me reading these messages?"

"I don't have another option, Cosmo! The 'Mortal Communication Devices and How to Use Them' seminar didn't exactly cover ever-changing text etiquette. What should I say back?"

"IDK," he says.

"IDK?" Then I get it. "Cos, please."

Next to me, Deya is driving like a pack of cyclopes are on her tail. Our tires are screeching, pedestrians are shouting unkind things, and other drivers are honking their horns. Crappy driving obviously runs in the Olympos family.

"Gaia's tears, Kali," Deya says, zooming past a sign instructing her to STOP. "Just tell him you can't wait to see him. Who cares if you use that stupid language or not? He understands English."

Oh. That's actually quite smart.

When we pull into a parking spot—no, two parking spots—and step down from the Jeep, I stow my phone in my pocket. "Dey, is it just the arrow, or is he like ridiculously cute?"

"He's pretty cute," she says begrudgingly.

We walk through the quaint, historic downtown, where the brick buildings have an "Old West" feel. Cute shops and restaurants line the streets, and the people walking around all wear jackets and scarves to ward off the chilly air. We cut through a courtyard and walk into a rustic pizzeria all decorated in red, green, and white. The smell of sauce, seasoning, and garlic makes my mouth water after the pitiful non-lunch at school.

Deya asks the hostess for a table for two. The hostess seats us near the hot, noisy kitchen, at Deya's prompting, I assume. Only a half wall separates the kitchen from the dining area, so we can easily see and hear everything that's happening within.

"So who's your target?" I ask her once the waiter goes to get our drinks. Crappy cafeteria food aside, I actually quite like mortal food. I bite into a hot, buttery breadstick.

"I'm supposed to match the owner," Deya says, glancing into the kitchen.

We see a black woman in her forties, her hair pulled back from her tired, round face. A server drops a dish, but rather than yell at the girl, the restaurant owner bends down to help her clean it up.

I look around at the patrons and staff. "Who are you thinking?"

"Maybe the dish boy, for a little fun. He obviously has a crush on her."

I frown, looking in the direction Deya's pointing. The "dish boy" is as much a boy as the name promises. He can't be older than twenty. Fine for Deya, maybe, but not for a woman twice his age. "Right. Like you would ever set those two up."

"Right," she mimics, "and like you would care. Aren't you the one always saying that it doesn't matter who we match because the Fates will do whatever they want, anyway?"

I return to my breadstick. "You're exactly right. Match her with the dish boy."

Deya growls. "I'm not going to match her with the dish boy. I just wanted to see if you'd care enough to stop me."

"Well, I don't. Are you satisfied?"

"You're lying, Kal. I saw the fire in your eyes when I pointed the guy out to you. You *hated* that I was going to match them. Admit it."

I'm not going to admit anything of the kind. Besides, if I did have a moment's hesitation, it's because of my training, not because of some misplaced conviction. "No."

"Fine." She says, but goes back to surveying the restaurant. By the time we've ordered and our food has come, she's fiddling with an earring. "Okay, who would you match her with?"

My eyebrows jump. "Are you serious? Anyone. That old guy there with the *Bachelor Nation* T-shirt. You're asking the wrong girl."

"Kal, just pretend that our actions and calling have meaning for a second." I scoff, but she jabs a finger toward my face. "Hey, I'm sacrificing a lot to be here with you when we both know I don't have to be. But because we're basically sisters and I love you, I'm supporting you. So the least you can do is knock off the fatalist crap for two seconds and support me."

"Okay, okay. I'm sorry. I didn't realize this was so important to you."

"It should be just as important to you. If you don't take this seriously, your dad is going to change his mind and take you out of here, whether the distance from Ben drives you insane or not. Your dad specifically instructed me to give him honest feedback on your performance, and I'm not lying to him. Not even for you."

Her loyalty to my dad—and his to her—is either endearing or irritating, depending on the day. Today it's both. "I would never ask that, Deya."

She ignores me. "The assignment notes indicate that I shouldn't need to leave the restaurant to find her match, which makes me think it's a regular customer or someone on staff. But your dad said I needed to be careful because a lot was riding on this one," she says. I hold back the snark and listen, like a friend should. "What do you think he meant by that?"

I look around the restaurant. It's still busy past the end of the lunch rush, so I doubt the restaurant is going under. Her employees are all hustling, but no one looks disgruntled. I glance into the kitchen. The equipment seems high end, the workspace clean, even the posters and artwork on the staff bulletin boards look—oh.

"She has kids."

"What? How do you know?" she asks.

I gesture back towards the kitchen. "Look at the drawings on that far wall, the one with all the safety posters on it? They were obviously done by kids, two different ones, if I had to guess. Who else but the owner would display it?"

Deya purses her lips. "That makes sense. Your dad wants me to make the right match for her kids, too." She stares at the owner. "Look at her, Kal. She's exhausted. She needs someone to help out around the house and tuck the kids into bed when she's working late. Someone to rub her feet when she gets home after a long day." She gives me the biggest puppy-dog eyes you can imagine. "Please. I just want to find him."

I laugh: a low, defeated sound. Deya's laying it on thick, but after seeing the pictures drawn by her kids, my heart's been softened. A little. "You suck, you know that?"

"Yeah, and you love me, you know that?"

We study the patrons through the meal and dessert. So far, no one has caught my attention. "What do you think about that guy?" she says. She's looking across the room to a middle-aged man in a suit who just sat down. He pulls out a briefcase and starts poring over files before the server has even brought him water.

"Uh-uh. He's working over lunch, which means he probably takes work home with him all the time. If you want someone who can balance her out, help her live a little, that's not the guy."

She nods. "Okay, what about him?" She points to a kind-looking man in khakis and a polo shirt sitting with a college-aged girl. He's not wearing a wedding ring, and his left hand doesn't have a white ring line like his right does, where I'm betting he typically wears his college ring. Yet something about their body language tells me that this girl is family. They're laughing, and she's showing him a video on her phone. When he teases her about something, she pushes the hand holding his fork into his meal and he flicks water on her face. The exchange is sweet and good-natured. I glance back at Deya, whose eyebrows are creasing in hope and concern. I look back at the man and examine him closer, but not too close. I think of what my mom has taught us in class about compatibility and the psychology of love.

This man has very little trouble in his life. He has fewer wrinkles than you'd expect from a man with that much gray in his hair. No frown lines at all. He wears a gold watch, a tan he probably got in Hawaii, and has a blade of grass on the hem of his pants. The girl's white sneakers have a grass stain on them. They've been golfing. He asks about her mom, but with no reluctance or awkwardness, and her response is equally comfortable. Not his daughter, then. A niece or goddaughter, probably.

"What are you thinking?" Deya asks.

"That this man lives a life of leisure."

"So?"

I glance back at the overworked restaurant owner and the artwork catches my eye. One of the kids has drawn a picture of her stick figure hugging her mom's stick figure, and the words, "I miss you Mommy" above it. I hesitate. I don't want to get invested in this woman's happiness, kids or no kids. But I'm one of only two immortals with the power to soulgaze, a skill I've neglected for months. This muscle is begging to be flexed.

So when I look deeper into her, I do it for me. For Deya, even. Not for her.

I focus and there's a moment where my vision doubles, and I'm looking at her, body and soul. Deya was right: she is tired. She's been tired for a long time, but that doesn't stop her. She's like a forest weathering a thunderstorm, and it's been raining a long, long time. But her roots have sunk so deep into the ground, she can withstand just about anything, and her limbs have come to stretch so high, that when the sun finally comes out, she's going to be stronger than ever. The joy and pride she feels in her children . . . it's intense. Overwhelming. I pull myself out of the moment before I get lost in the feeling.

"I don't know," I tell Deya. My head is swimming with so much emotion, it's spilling into my eyes. "They don't feel wrong for each other . . ."

She stares. "Did you just soulgaze? For me?"

I look away from her. "Yes, but don't get used to it."

"I knew you loved me," she says, her voice catching. "Now tell me everything."

I tell her what I observed in the golfer and what I gazed in the restaurateur, and Deya takes it under advisement. "But it could be him," she says. "He could be her forever."

The old me never would have matched them, but Deya is the best in our year and basically my supervisor, so I'm not going to tell her no. "Sure, he could be. What do I know?"

My phone chimes, and I lunge for it, the arrow making me eager to see Ben's next message. Instead, I see the name Hector appear above the message alert.

I open the message, and it says:

You have a cell phone. You have officially entered the mortie world.

I respond:

Who is this? How did you get this number?

His reply:

Sorry, I must have the wrong number.

Okay. But what's a mortie? And you implied that I had entered a different world?

I snicker, waiting for his response. Nothing for two straight minutes, then:

I just double-checked with Cos. You suck.

I shoot back my reply.

Says the guy who just about revealed the existence of Olympus to the entire world.

His reply is almost instantaneous.

That's a bit of a stretch, but you're not exactly the goddess of proportional responses.

WHAT? HOW DARE YOU? I WILL SMITE YOU FROM THE FACE OF THE EARTH I write, biting back a smile.

"Another text from Ben?" Deya interrupts.

I wait for Hector's next message. "No, Hec."

"Oh. Of course."

"Huh?" I ask, glancing up.

"I should have known, that's all." She turns back to the kitchen.

I stuff the phone in my pocket, annoyed, even if I'm not sure why. "So, any other options for . . . what are you calling her?"

We never refer to targets by name, only by code name. "Ro."

"Row? Like a boat?"

"R-O, for Restaurant Owner."

"Works for me. Who else are you seeing?"

She nods to the back of the kitchen. I strain my head to follow her finger. Wide double doors are open to the outside where a burly deliveryman is unloading boxes. He's bald with a black-and-gray streaked beard, but he can't be much older than Ro. He has tattoos up and down his brown arms, rows of tiki eyes and shark teeth and other geometric symbols that tell me he's probably Samoan. Some younger men continue to unload boxes while the bearded delivery guy pulls out a clipboard with a form for the owner to sign. She grabs the pen, and despite the flour on her arms and her hastily pulled back hair, he's studying her rather than the clipboard.

His soul pulls at me. Without meaning to, I get drawn in, and a vision of his true self snaps into place over his physical self. It's like looking through two different lenses at the same time. His soul is weathered. He's seen his share of storms and been waylaid by more than one. But through it all, he's learned to love the rain. He doesn't notice the stressed woman who resents her ex, drinks too much coffee, and feels guilty for leaving her kids with friends and her mom so often. He notices the smile that eclipses her face when she talks about something that excites her. He sees the way her light brown eyes sparkle when she talks about the new recipe she'll try with the equipment that he's brought her. But she doesn't see him at all. And he wishes so very badly that she would.

"Are you getting something?" she asks me.

My heart seems to double in size. "He'd be good for her, Dey. Great, even. Do it."

Her head tilts. "I haven't vetted him out yet. She's never even noticed him. I don't want to uproot her entire life because the delivery guy has a crush on her."

"Suit yourself," I say, ignoring the ache in my chest I feel looking at these two. Excepting Ben, this is already more work than I've put into a match in months. I can't let myself get sucked into caring about all of this again.

As if reading my thoughts, Deya's eyes narrow. "Suit myself? No, how about I suit the kids who drew those pictures? Or the woman working her butt off to provide for them? Sure, these two have a charming odd couple thing going, but what if he doesn't want forever? What if I match them, but when he realizes she has kids, no amount of forced love in the world will make him a kind father? Don't they deserve someone who's going to love them unconditionally?"

I've struck a big fat nerve. I love Aphrodite. She's fun, and it's always a party visiting with her. She talks about boys non-stop. Who do we like, what did he say, how are we going to do our hair when we see him next, and so much more. She's like a really, really, *really* experienced older friend. But she's not maternal at all. Even though Ares is technically my dad's father, Hephaestus pretty much raised him, despite divorcing Aphrodite (probably why Hephaestus approved my little expedition to Earth, come to think of it). My dad has made a point of paying that favor forward to Aphrodite's other children—his siblings—including Deya.

Meanwhile, Deya tries desperately to get her mom's attention by having more successful matches than any probie in the history of Olympus. She hates her mom in some ways, but that doesn't stop her from craving her attention and love.

After the server clears our table, I apologize. "You're right, Dey. I'm sorry for not being more supportive. We'll do a little more research on these two. Okay?"

Her misty eyes are still fixed on the kids' artwork. "Thanks, Kal."

Chapter Twelve

At the door to the restaurant, Deya tells me she's going to scout out Delivery Guy a little more and she'll pick me up when she's done. I'm waiting by the "To Go" entrance, rubbing my arms for warmth, when Mr. Gunner runs into me. In his khaki shorts, an orange polo beneath his jacket, and running shoes, he looks like he's popping here between PE classes. A "Ponderosa High Jackrabbits" hat covers his short, sandy-blond hair. His brown eyes narrow.

"Olympos, right? Kali?"

I nod. "Yep, the one who talked about Sparta's penchant for institutionalized ped—"

"I got it," he assures me. "Shouldn't you be at school?"

I explain about our afternoon homeschooling. "But, shouldn't *you* be at school?" I ask him.

He holds out a slip of paper with orders on it. "I don't teach a class this hour, so I've been sent to get some of the other teachers lunch. Nothing like being the noob." There's an awkward silence, then he says, "Hey, so your aunt, Cynthia"—I mentally remind myself to call Artemis by her nickname—"She really knows archery, huh?"

I stifle a laugh. "Oh, yeah. She's the best you'll ever meet."

He grins, like for some reason, this is good news. "And . . . uh, your uncle? . . . Is he any good?"

"Her brother is, yeah," I say. I suspect where he's going with this, but I want to make him work for it.

"And, uh, your *other* uncle?"

"Hmm?"

He gives a vexed huff just as Deya is pulling up. "Is Cynthia married, or not?"

With a huge grin, I climb into the Jeep. "Not. See you tomorrow."

"Was that Mr. Gunner?" Deya asks when we start driving.

"Yep." I pull out my phone on the off chance that I've missed a message. Nothing, not from Hector or from Ben. "What am I doing here, Dey? Waiting around for Ben to get off school? This is brutal." I sink farther down into the passenger seat.

"Are you starting to regret that your dad didn't give you an assignment? I can't blame him. With your judgment lately . . ."

"Yeah, yeah, I'm a danger to us all. Just like you are! Watch out for that—" Deya slams on the brakes and we fling forward against the taut seatbelts. The smell of burned rubber fills my nostrils. At least we didn't hit the cat.

"So, what should we do with the rest of our day? I don't suppose you want to quiz me on chapter 1117 of Advanced Match Theory?"

"That's a no," I pant. I'm still rattled from our near felinicide. "But don't you find it dark that you want to review pet matches after almost killing that cat?" Deya smirks at the question. "What's that for?"

"We haven't studied chapter 1117 yet, but somehow you know that it's about pet matching. Interesting choice for someone who hates her calling."

"Nice try. I looked at the index last year. Perfect recall, remember?"

She sticks out her tongue. "Fine. So what's next?" I'm about to mention Ben, but Deya answers her own question before I can. "Should we try to decipher the Oracle's prophecy?"

"Definitely," I say. Because of course that's what I should be doing. I haven't even been here a day, and already thoughts of Ben are clouding my judgment. I can't reverse this match fast enough.

For the next few hours, Deya and I walk around the woods back at the cabin and discuss the different parts of the prophecy. We start at the top.

"So, you have to heal the heart of a desperate maiden. Why that wording, specifically?" Deya asks.

"I wondered that, too," I say, kicking the ground. "It always makes me think of the maiden goddesses."

Our heads snap up at the same time. "Holy Hades, what if it's—" I look up at the sun and catch myself just in time. Am I thanatotic? My heart hammers wildly. I grab Deya's hand and pull her under a canopy of branches so thick, the sun can't penetrate it. "Deya, could it possibly be—"

"Don't," she says in a sharp whisper. "Don't say it, Kal. Don't even think it."

But I can't stop. The Oracle was so obviously talking about Artemis. "It has to be her. I have to help her."

"Kalixta," she says harshly. She puts her hands over her mouth, an extra layer of protection from Helios' prying eyes. "Please don't tell me that you're actually considering this. This wouldn't simply be about helping Artemis. This would entail defying the God who is so over-protective of her maidenhood that he's killed over it! Do you think Apollo would just let this slide? Not to mention *her father?* Zeus won't just kill you, he'll eradicate your existence. No afterlife, no Elysium. You'll just be gone. Tell me you aren't that stupid!"

Every part of me shudders, but I can't ignore this. "She was a little kid when she made those promises, Deya," I protest. "Just because she's a Goddess doesn't mean that she's omniscient. She didn't know what would be best for her eons later in life."

Deya just holds up her hands. "I'm sorry, but you're on your own with this one. I'm not playing with lightning."

I grab a leaf off of a tree and tear it into pieces. Then I grind the pieces into the soft forest floor beneath my feet. My chest burns with anger, but it's not fair to take it out on Deya. She's only trying to keep me alive. "Fine, let's just move on to the next point: saving a soul from an unjust union. That could be anyone, couldn't it? With so many Erotes on assignment every day, you know there are plenty of crappy matches."

"A lot fewer with you out of commission," Deya says.

"Ha ha."

We go through a mental list of the Erotes we know who've made terrible matches, but no one seems to jump out at us.

"Styx, I don't know," Deya says eventually. "Maybe it's the restaurant owner. Maybe you saved her from a bad match today, and it's already done."

I chortle. "Yeah, I'm pretty sure I would have matched her with the tablecloth. If anyone saved her, it was you. Besides, I think the Oracle was talking a little more fatefully than that. And the word soul . . . 'save a soul from an unjust union.' It doesn't strike me as just any match."

"Okay, then who do you think it is?"

I look around the forest, mentally running through faces and relationships, but I draw a blank. "I don't know."

"Next point?" she asks. I nod. "Okay, 'Inspire most truly a fallen champion.'"

I've tried not to make this a big deal, but I love this part of the prophecy. It's like she's telling me that to get my life back, I have to become a muse. I've gone over and over all the heroes I know: Heracles, Achilles, Perseus, Jason, Odysseus, Atalanta, and others. They've all either been *apotheosized* and are full gods on Olympus now, or they're in Elysium with the other just souls. So clearly she can't mean any of them. But somewhere, there's a fallen champion I'm meant to muse for. I'm desperate to start.

Deya holds her necklace and calls out, "Cos?"

His voice is there in an instant. "Yes?"

"What does it take for morties to consider someone a champion?"

"Checking . . . Um, okay. It's pretty simple nowadays. If a person or team bests all of their competition in a particular field, usually a sport, then they're considered a champion."

"So how many different champions are there?" I ask him. His voice hovers around my ear.

"More than I can easily count. There are champions for every different sport at every different level and age group, professional and amateur. And even within those sports, there are categories depending on things like weight or number of students at the school or country."

I rub my head. "So we're talking thousands. Tens of thousands."

"More," he says.

I groan. "This is going to be impossible."

"Sorry?" Cosmo asks. "Am I missing something?"

I bite my tongue at the same time that Deya gestures for me to shut up. Cosmo doesn't know what we're talking about.

"Nope, you're not missing a thing," she tells him, smiling. "The topic came up today, and we were just trying to get a better understanding. We'll talk to you later, okay?"

"Sure thing. I'll see you both this weekend."

I pace around the forest, touching the rough, cinnamon bark of the pines as I pass them. Their tufts of cool needles tickle my hands, and I find myself rubbing my arms for warmth. What am I going to do? The Oracle was pretty clear about the stakes involved in my little quest: it's not just my heart that's in jeopardy here, it's Ben's, too.

Ben.

The pull is immediate and undeniable. I pull out my phone and text him.

Can I meet you after school?

A few moments go by, during which time, my gut twists into a thousand knots.

YESSS/:

Huh?

Sorry teacher watching didn't know what I was hitting. Parking lot OK? Right after school?

Perfect.

See you in 10

I feel more settled now that we have a plan to meet, although my stomach won't stop knotting. What's that about? I look up. "Deya, I need the keys."

"No way. You drive your own car. I stole that Jeep from Artemis fair and square. Besides, Cos ordered it for me special." Her smile is real. Deep. "He knows that was my favorite vehicle we studied."

"Fine. Keep your pilfered goods. I'm heading out to meet Ben."

I'm already running through the forested yard when Deya yells, "I won't wait up!"

I grin. In front of the house, more cars are parked. I open the door to another boxy vehicle. The keys are in the ignition and I'm off.

Driving, it turns out, is harder than it looks. After the first time I fishtail, I patch Cosmo in to drive for me.

"You know you two aren't my only assignments, right?" he asks me as he takes control of the car.

"I know, and I'm sorry, Cosmo. I wouldn't ask this if it weren't important."

"Just make sure you two stay safe, okay?"

He's the perfect quartermaster for people like Deya and me. Mostly Deya. She likes being catered to, and no one could pay her more attention than he does. But I normally pride myself on being the opposite. I don't like to play the 'Aphrodite' card that all of her kin are only too capable of playing. But here I am, taking advantage of Cosmo because he's in love with my friend.

"Thanks, Cosmo. Honestly. I'm sorry for taking so much of your time today."

He doesn't answer at first. "Thanks, Kali."

Once I'm a few blocks from school, I ask Cosmo to let me drive. After all, I need the practice. If I drive anywhere with Ben, I can't exactly have my quartermaster take over in front of him.

I arrive at school as the bell is ringing. My stomach is writhing with serpents, I'm so anxious to see him. After only a minute, I see him come out of the school with Paresh and Shaggy. He's searching around for me when I realize that he doesn't know what car I'm in. After trying all of the wrong buttons, I finally manage to roll down my window (and every other window) and wave him down.

His face lights up when he sees me. He elbows his friends in the ribs and they walk up to the vehicle with wide eyes. "Dude, this is one sick whip," Shaggy says.

I don't have a clue how to respond.

Shaggy keeps talking about the car—a Range Rover, I hear him say in a reverent tone—and he opens the back door. Before he can jump in, Ben pulls him out and closes the door behind him. Through my open windows, I hear Ben say, "Dude, you're killing me. I like this girl. Just give me a little time with her, okay?"

"Yeah, fine," Shaggy grumbles. "Just don't be late for band practice, okay? Six o'clock at Paresh's."

"Of course. I've never been late yet, have I?"

The three guys bump fists, and then Ben is getting into the passenger seat. "You wouldn't want to drive, would you?" I ask.

He practically salivates. "Are you sure?"

"You'd be doing me a favor. I'm used to a, uh, smaller ride." Considering I'm used to traveling through space at the blink of an eye, I'd say that's an understatement.

He agrees, and we switch places in the SUV. I'm already more comfortable.

"So, uh, where to?" he asks me, pulling into the line of cars waiting to leave the parking lot.

"Oh, I don't know," I tell him. "Maybe you could take me on a tour of the town? Or I'd love to see your house—"

"A tour sounds perfect," he says. "Let's do that."

Ben grew up in "Flag," he tells me. We drive through the residential side of town, or East Flag, as the locals call it, and then the college side, West Flag. He points out all sorts of cool local spots, great burger places, the tiny all-ages club where his band played their first gig.

"Right over there," he says, pointing to a hill, "is where, at the tender age of seven, I realized I would never be a BMX racer."

I don't know what this means, but he has a playful smile that would be cute even without the arrow. "What happened?"

"I was racing Jason Chrysler down the hill and a rabbit darted across the street in front of us. I slowed down, but Jason sped up and jumped the thing. Literally soared over it on his bike. It was awesome. At least, I think it was. I wiped out right there at the bottom of the hill and got a mild concussion and my first stitches." He lifts his elbow up to show me a shimmery purple scar about an inch long.

"And your BMX dreams went down with you." I tut. "Probably for the best. Music is definitely the right move for you."

He looks like he's trying not to smile. "Are you implying that I don't have the skills to make it in the competitive racing circuit?" We stop at a light and he pokes my side. "That's cold, Kali Olympos. Ice cold." I squeal when he pokes me again and grab his hand to stop him. He threads his fingers through mine, but he lets go when the light turns green.

I kind of hate that he let go of my hand.

He keeps giving me the tour, pointing out the place where he lost his first tooth in a pastrami sandwich and how he cried, not because of the tooth, but because his grandpa had always told him that pastrami was the sandwich of men, and now there was "blood on his man-sandwich." He takes me past the drive-thru where he got rejected by Amanda Meyers when he asked her to the Sadie Hawkins dance in seventh grade, not realizing that it was girl-asks-guy. His stories are hilarious and heartfelt. He's so adorably animated, I find myself staring at him even when I try not to.

When we get to the university, we drive up around a large dome.

"That's the Lowell Observatory," he says, parking in front of one of the buildings. "It houses the telescope that was used to discover Pluto. Paresh's dad is one of the head astronomers in the country, and he works here. He actually got me a job here." He keeps his eyes on the building, and his face flushes. Is he embarrassed? "I take tickets on Sundays, which is kinda cool. I'm a night janitor the rest of the week, though. Eleven p.m. to one a.m., Wednesday through Friday. I just got moved to this shift, but I've been working since I was fourteen." When he says this, it's almost with a hint of challenge in his voice.

"Me too," I say. I'm not sure what response he's looking for, but this one is the truth. Erote students start shadowing when we're fourteen. We shadow for one full year before we become probies and start going on monitored assignments, like all of mine are now.

"You have? Why?"

"What do you mean? What else would I do?"

"I don't know, whatever people with money normally do?"

Ah ha. I realize this probably wasn't a subtle cue, but I'm new to morties, and Ben's periodic embarrassment has been confusing until now. My mortie cover is rich; Ben is not.

"Sorry," he says, running his hand through his hair. "That sounded super douchey. I've had to work to help my family get by. I just assumed that if someone didn't need to work, they wouldn't. Most people in your situation would be content to sit around and look pretty. Guy or girl."

I laugh. "My dad would never be content with me just sitting around looking pretty." Truth. If I tried to pull crap like that, my dad would send me on a summer internship. To Hades. Where it would stay summer for a long time.

Ben seems relieved, and the tension I've felt on and off all day is gone. "I'm glad. I like a girl who knows how to get her hands dirty. So, what do you do?"

Right. "Um, just stuff for my parents."

"What, like secretarial stuff?"

I don't know what "secretarial stuff" is, but I nod.

"That's cool," he says. "My mom is the administrative assistant at my little sister's school."

"Tell me about them."

He finally shifts to face me. I pull my legs up on the seat and turn so our faces are only maybe two feet away. But those two feet agonize me; my head and heart war between getting closer and backing way up.

Ben tells me about his mom, who was born in Mexico and who moved to Phoenix when she was seventeen. He tells me about how she went to night school for years to get her degree and that now she's working on her master's in school administration so she can become a principal one day. Through the course of the conversation, he reveals that they live in his grandpa's house—but it must be his dad's dad, because his mom's family is all still back in Mexico. Part of the reason Ben works, I gather, is because he and his mom are trying to find a way to sponsor her family so they can move to the States. He's proud of this, I can tell by how he straightens when he talks. But he's a little defensive, too. I gather he's had to defend himself to a lot of people, and this makes me want to destroy everyone who's ever made him feel this way.

When he talks about his little sister, Isabella, he relaxes. Isa is, he tells me, a spitfire. She plans to be the next Oprah, so she loves interviewing people. She's twelve years old. "She'll talk your ear off, if you let her. So when you meet her, be careful." He stops himself, as if the assumption that I'll meet his sister could be anything but music to my ears. "Anyway, this is boring," he says. "Tell me more about yourself. Do you actually speak Greek?" I nod. "Will you say something to me?"

"*S'agapó,*" I say instantly. I love you.

Where the Styx did that come from?

I prattle away in rapid Greek so it doesn't stand out.

He bends over the cupholder, which brings his face that much closer to mine. "So, what did you say? Did you tell me how much you like me and how you can't wait to kiss me, already?"

My body is aflame. Actually, all the extra stuff I said was about how driving a car is unexpectedly complicated, but I'm not going to tell him that. I also lean in, pretending to be very interested in the same cupholder. Our hands bump, and he grabs mine. He rubs my hand with his thumb, and my insides dissolve into puddles of need. Need for him to feel for me what I feel for him. Need for my lips to touch his. We're no longer feigning interest in anything except one another's hands. He brings his feet up onto the seat, sitting cross-legged like me. I wish the SUV wasn't so huge, because his lips are still so far away. Less far . . . less . . .

Our faces are only inches apart now. I tilt my head and my eyes close of their own accord. I feel Ben's breath on my mouth. The sensation is enough to drive me wild. His hand brushes the back of my neck and he guides my face into his—

A horn honks, breaking us apart. My eyes fly open, and I am about to start flaying morties when I see Ben's face. He looks equally upset, staring out the window at the random man waving from his car to someone on the sidewalk.

Ben turns back in the driver's seat towards the steering wheel. He gestures to the clock, which reads 5:49 p.m. "I should go meet the guys. Not the best timing, I guess," he says, putting the SUV in reverse. At least he grabs my hand after he shifts back into drive.

"No, it's okay. I've really liked getting to talk."

His eyes are on the road, but he's smiling when he says, "Yeah, me too."

Chapter Thirteen

When I get to the cabin shortly after six, I'm a bundle of emotions. Ben gave me the biggest, longest, tightest hug when I dropped him off at Paresh's. I didn't want to let go. He promised to text me tonight, sometime between practicing with the guys and doing homework.

I drag myself toward the sounds of dishes clinking together. I get to the kitchen and pull up a stool next to Deya. It screeches on the hardwood. Then I drop my head to the countertop with a groan.

"Oh, is someone missing her boyfriend?" Deya teases.

"Yes!" I roll my forehead back and forth on the cool granite. "Why does the arrow have to be so friggin' powerful? Why does Ben have to do other things? Why can't he just stop doing everything else in the world and just be with me forever and never leave and never talk to anyone else?"

Artemis' voice is flat. "That is the worst idea I've ever heard."

I pull my head up. "Okay, maybe that's a bit much. But still! Things were going so perfectly and we almost kissed! With lips!" I drop my head back down. "This is so much harder than I thought it would be."

"Someone isn't guarding her heart the way she thought she would," Deya says, patting my head. Then she and Artemis continue with the conversation I interrupted.

"So what are your hunting companions doing while you're

here?" Deya asks Artemis, who is pulling ingredients from the air to make dinner.

"My little she-bears are with the Hyperboreans. They've been leading the hunts for decades now."

Deya's leg bumps mine, and I listen up. "Why aren't you leading them anymore?" Deya asks.

Artemis pinches some seasoning into the bowl containing our dinner: salads with the most luscious, exotic vegetables and fruits imaginable. Better, actually, because they're from Demeter's garden. Mmm. "Oh, I suppose after several millennia of doing the same thing, it's lost some of its charm."

I put my elbows on the counter. "Didn't you go hunting today?"

"I didn't say it had lost *all* of its charm." She smiles, and plates and utensils appear before us. After thanking Demeter for the bounty, we dig in. "I may have Atalanta running my department, but I'm still Goddess of the wild. It's my duty to oversee the balance of animal life."

Over dinner, we talk about the day and about Deya's current assignment. Artemis approves of Deya's slow approach and of getting to know what her target needs. My dad talked Artemis into returning to teach his students archery several decades ago, and since then, she's spent more and more time on Olympus and less and less time in the mortal world or with her own department. That means she's become pretty familiar with the Erotes. As we talk about the things we did today, though, I get the feeling that she's missed Earth.

"Oh, and I forgot to tell you. We ran into Mr. Gunner after Deya's assignment, and he asked about you." I say this casually between bites, earning a pinch from Deya.

"Oh, yeah?" She spears a spinach leaf and strawberry, then

takes a bite. She takes a long drink of water. Another bite. "What'd he ask?"

I hide my smile. "First, he asked if you were really that good at archery."

"Why is he so interested in that?" she asks.

"Rumor has it he used to be a champion archer."

"That's why he's so familiar," she says. "He's Tony Gunner. He was on pace to become the greatest archer of the modern era. He's never lost a tournament, and he's come the closest to shooting a fourteen hundred with a recurve bow that any mortal ever has. Thirteen ninety-four, if you can believe it."

"That's incredible," Deya says. The recurve bow—an Erote's bow of choice—is a classic. It requires greater strength and steadiness than the compound bow, but the draw and release are more fluid, so we can better see our arrow strike. My dad and Artemis feel that this experience makes for a greater connection with our targets. So although a compound bow is easier, faster, and more powerful, in many ways, it's more impersonal. Almost like cheating.

For Mr. Gunner to be so close to reaching the elusive score of fourteen hundred with a recurve bow is monumental.

"You said he was on pace to become the greatest modern archer. What happened?" I ask.

"I don't know. Four years ago, he was preparing for the Global Archery Tournament, breaking all sorts of records. Then one day, just after the best tournament of his life, he quit. He left the sport behind and no one has seen him compete since." She stabs another spinach leaf with her fork. "It's a shame, too. I've only ever seen one mortal better than him. But with time, who knows what Tony could have accomplished?"

We go back to eating, but I can feel Deya's eyes on me, begging me not to push this.

I push. "You should take him hunting."

Artemis lowers her fork. "Why would I do that?"

My cheeks grow hot. "That's what you used to do, isn't it? Find exceptional mortals and help them become legends?"

"Right, I *used to*. Now I teach brats how to shoot straight. Present company included."

Her fiery tone boils my insides. "Artemis, I wasn't trying to—"

"I know what you're trying to do, kid."

"Y-you do?" *Please don't smite me*, I silently beg.

"Yes. Don't think I haven't noticed you trying to reignite my passion," she says, and I brace myself for the smiting. "But it's not like I've lost my true love here, guys."

Huh?

"It's not?" Deya asks.

She smiles. Why is she smiling? "Not at all. I'll admit, hunting with an audience for eons has gotten a bit old, but my love for the hunt itself is as strong as ever. Don't worry about me getting bored. I've never been to these mountains, so believe me when I tell you I'll have plenty to do."

It's a good thing Deya speaks up, because I'm temporarily speechless. "Of course you will, Artemis. We were silly to be worried. Right, Kali?"

I nod weakly.

The following morning at school, Ben is waiting for me in the parking lot when we step down from Deya's Jeep. My face splits into an enormous grin when I see him. I jog over to him, and he pulls me into a bear hug. Happiness rushes through me before I can brace myself. "Am I crazy, or do you look even hotter this morning than you did yesterday?" he says, grabbing my hand and guiding me into school.

He's not crazy. This morning, I adjusted my mortie look just the tiniest bit—so tiny, he really shouldn't have noticed it. I tamed my hair a little more and made my features *slightly* more symmetrical. That's it! Still, Deya shoots me a look that screams, "Told you." I wrinkle my nose at her and turn back to Ben.

"So, I thought maybe you'd want to come to band practice tonight. Deya, too, of course." He looks at her. "If you want."

She holds out her hand, navigating the halls beside us. "I'm all right, thanks. That's more Kali's thing than mine."

"Okay, so I thought because it's Friday, maybe we could go out afterwards."

"Are you asking me out on a date?" I ask, with as much self-control as I can muster.

Ben's neck goes red. "Yeah, I mean, I was thinking about it, but if that's not—"

"I'd love to," I blurt. *Freaking arrow.*

I don't mind my lack of self-control when I see Ben beam, though. The morning classes are a blur of flirting, bumping legs, and kicking each other's feet. In every class, we pass notes and brush hands. By the time we separate for PE, the charge between us is electric. I hardly even talk to Deya as we change into our gym clothes. I move as quickly as I can, willing her to do the same.

"Come on," I beg. "We need to get out there."

She flushes the toilet and waltzes out to the sinks, washing her hands leisurely. I grab and thrust paper towels at her, forcing her to pick up the pace. I push her through the changing room toward the door leading into the gymnasium, when she says, "I thought you were trying to fight this, Kal."

"I am. Believe me, this is me fighting this."

"Well, you're only going to look desperate. No one likes desperate."

I curse in Greek but slow down all the same, because she's right. I let a couple of other girls move past us into the gym. One of them is . . . ah, Gorgon crap. It's Zoe. She gives me a smile that doesn't look totally forced as she passes. When enough girls have passed us, Deya nods, and we walk into the gym.

A row of archery equipment lies on the ground outside Mr. Gunner's office. Deya and I look at each other with matching grins. Callings aside, we love archery and are fiercely competitive. I'm a little better than she is, which bugs her to no end. As students congregate to talk, Deya and I head over to Mr. Gunner, where he's stringing bows.

"Did you need help with the rest of these?" Deya asks.

"No, I'll string them while Josh shows the rest of the class how to shoot," he says, gesturing to one of our classmates: a tall, muscular kid who usually wears nothing but camo. "He's been hunting with them for years."

"Are you sure you don't want help?"

He looks from Deya to me. "You both know how to shoot, too? It's not just your aunt?" We nod. He seems skeptical, but he hands us bows and string. "I'll inspect them when you're done."

"Fine by me," Deya says casually, as if she didn't take it as a challenge. The offspring of gods and goddesses aren't generally accustomed to people doubting we can do something. Especially something as simple as stringing a cursing bow.

Ben and Shaggy walk into the gym, their sneakers squeaking

on the floor, and cross over to us. Ben and Zoe share an awkward smile on his way over. "What are you two doing?" Ben asks.

"Stringing these bows," I say, gesturing to the pile of bows we've already strung.

"Are you sure you're doing that the right way?" Shaggy asks.

"Watch and learn," I tell him.

Shaggy's question is understandable, even if his tone is unforgivable. Recurve bows have a sculpted handle and flat limbs, but the tips point away from the archer. I've always thought an extreme recurve looks a little like a lyre, but the unstrung shape always confuses people; they think the curves should face the archer instead of away. Because they don't know what they're talking about.

When the bell rings, Mr. Gunner takes a look at our bows and nods appreciatively. Then he turns to the class.

"Against my better judgment, the school district has decided that we will study archery this semester in PE. Today, I'll give you a brief introduction to the sport and, if we have time, we'll practice shooting outside. But first, everyone, please put on your protective gear. Arm guards and finger tabs go on like this," he says, putting both on. Deya and I look at the gear distastefully.

"Mr. Gunner?" Deya asks. "What if we prefer to shoot without the gear?"

Josh, the tall hunter, smirks at us. "Don't worry, princess, it won't hide your manicure."

I grab Deya's hand before she can break his face.

Mr. Gunner just says, "Put it on, Ms. Olympos. Both of you."

We grumble but do as we're told.

"Now," he continues, "break into groups of five, and we'll have one bow per group." Ben runs to grab us a bow before Deya or I can. He comes back to our group with a bow in good condition. As groups form, Zoe looks around the class. Ben and I make eye contact, and I hazard a smile. Ben smiles back before waving Zoe over. She holds her head up and walks to us, looking a little like a warrior goddess. It weirdly makes me like her more.

"Nice gesture," Deya murmurs to me. "But she could have gone with any group. You know that, right?"

Before I can tell her I'm not threatened, Mr. Gunner silences us with a look and goes back to his explanation.

Deya whispers so quietly, only immortal ears could hear her. "Talking in class would be a lot easier if you would just learn to flash your thoughts to me, already."

She has a point.

Mr. Gunner is explaining how to check the upper and lower limbs, the nock, the arrow shelf, the grip, and the bowstring. Ben holds the bow, but we all inspect it as Mr. Gunner talks. Then he instructs us on the arrows.

Twenty minutes later, the class has practiced form and reviewed the rings on the target. We are chomping at the bit to shoot. When Mr. Gunner reviews safety rules for the tenth time, the class barely pays attention.

"Okay, class, outside to the range."

Finally.

Outside, the air is cool, but still. We walk over to a range set up on the football field. Mr. Gunner explains archery terms using Josh as his model. "Take your mark." Josh moves away from the group to stand about two feet behind the shooting line, facing the target some twenty yards away. "Ready on line," Mr. Gunner says. Josh steps forward to straddle the line, with one foot in the range and one foot out. "Nock." Josh pulls an arrow out of his quiver and puts the tip down on the ground outside of the range. Then he raises the arrow and lines it up with the arrow rest, locking the nock on the serving of the bowstring. "Draw." Josh places his fingers around the nock and pulls back the bowstring until his hand is near his ear and his elbow is high. "Aim." He aims. "Fire." He releases the bowstring, and the arrow flies at the target, sinking into a red ring. A good hit. The only ring better is gold.

Mr. Gunner barks out some more orders, but our group is already talking. "So who wants to go first?" Shaggy asks.

"Me," Deya and I say at the same time. We smile at each other. "After you," we say, speaking together again. The rest of our group laughs, including Zoe.

"You two aren't competitive at all, are you?" she teases.

"Show us how it's done, Dey," I tell her. With arched eyebrows, she grabs a quiver with ten arrows. She straddles the line, nocks an arrow, and draws in a motion so graceful, it's like dancing.

"Nice form," Mr. Gunner calls out to her. "When you aim, be sure—" She's already fired. The arrow hits a perfect bullseye before he's finished speaking. "Oh."

He comes over to our group. Deya sinks the rest of her quiver, one arrow after another, before another person on the field has gone a second time. She turns around with a fierce grin. Mr. Gunner studies her. "You weren't kidding when you said you know how to shoot."

She tosses the quiver to me, which I catch deftly. "We weren't."

Two students in other groups are still trying to draw, but the rest of the class has turned to our group. Ben leans over to me, our shoulders touching. He puts his mouth so close to my ear, his nose tickles my cheek. A tingle runs over my body. "Please tell me you're better than she is," he whispers.

"Oh, I am," I say with a wolfish grin. I fill my quiver while Deya retrieves her arrows. "Mr. Gunner, can we move our bale back?" I ask.

Josh scoffs, but Mr. Gunner nods. "How far, Ms. Olympos?"

I look at Deya, who's returning from the bale. "How interesting should we make this?"

"How badly do you want to get exposed?" she asks pointedly. What sounds like a taunt to the others is really a reminder that we can't make this so interesting that we expose our immortal abilities. When she gets right next to me, I whisper a quick plan. She smiles. To Mr. Gunner, I say, "How about Olympic standard?"

His face tightens, but he asks Josh, "Put the bale around the seventy-five yard line, would you?"

Josh shakes his head, mumbling jealously, and I smile to myself.

Soon, Deya and I are at the line. In mortal archery, shooters both take polite turns, give each other ample time to aim and fire, and would never, ever heckle each other.

Immortals don't follow the same rules. We also don't just aim for the bullseye.

But I keep it civil, starting with the bullseye just to show the class that I can. Unlike Deya's, my movements are more song than dance. When I step to the line and nock, my motion is like a symphony at *pianissimo,* delicate and so soft you strain to hear it. When I draw, the music reaches a crescendo, continuing to swell more and more forcefully until it begs me to fire. The tension is so high that your ears almost ache. I release with such force that the symphony reaches *forte fortissimo.* The thrum of my bow is resounding; you feel it deep in your chest, but you can't turn away from it, you can't imagine tuning it out. Then, when my arrow strikes its target, the music comes to a halt so final and shocking that you feel like your heart has stopped with it.

Or that's what Hector told me once, anyway.

When I sink arrow after arrow into a perfect heart shape starting and ending with that first bullseye, I know the class agrees.

I turn around, and Ben is looking at me like he's never seen me before. I shiver. *Styx.* I've crossed the line. Shaggy pushes Ben, and he almost tips over.

The look on Deya's face is distasteful. "A heart? You don't think that's a little on the nose?" I frown, still trying to gauge Ben's reaction.

Deya walks forward to straddle the line. She rapidly draws, aims, and fires in her taunting dance. I'm distracted as her arrows land exactly in between mine, adding precisely spaced dots to the outline of my heart. Deya gestures to me to go again, but I shake my head.

"Come on!" someone in the class yells. "You've gotta do something else for her to match!"

"All right," Mr. Gunner says, studying Deya and me. "Obviously the Olympos cousins don't need the practice, but the rest of you do. Return to your groups and take your marks."

"But Mr. Gunner, aren't you going to show these two up?" someone else calls.

Mr. Gunner's face clouds. "No, you've had enough showmanship for one day."

"But Mr. Gunner, you have to!" another classmate calls.

"Yeah, please!"

"Come on, Mr. Gunner!"

The pleas are coming from every member of the class, including Zoe. "Show us what you got," she says.

But instead, he meets my eye, as if I'm the cause of all of this trouble. After a moment, he walks away.

"Aww, come on, Mr. G!"

"You can't just walk off!"

Ten yards away, he bends down and picks up a bow. Then he stalks back towards us, a no-nonsense gleam to his eye. He scoops up a quiver and puts it across his back. He straddles the line, rocking back and forth from foot to foot. I see him mouth something that I can't quite make out. Then he nocks an arrow, draws, and aims in a motion so slick, any immortal would approve. His draw is powerful. He's a well-built man, but that draw is the draw of a god. The bowstring touches a point at the bottom of his mouth, and he moves his lips again. This time I read them: "Forgive me."

He releases, and the arrow goes *thunk* in the tiny space right between Deya's arrow and mine at the base of the heart. He repeats this nine more times, saying "Forgive me" before each shot. And each arrow lands between ours. I'm holding my breath as his last arrow lands just as perfectly as the first. The heart is flawless.

When he finishes, the class is quiet. Then Zoe lets out a loud, "Whoop!" and everyone follows.

Mr. Gunner holds out a hand, trying to still the cheering students. "All right, all right. Back to your groups and take your marks."

Chapter Fourteen

"It's Mr. Gunner. It has to be," I tell Deya in the changing room after class. "That man is a champion, right there."

"Totally," she agrees, tossing her gym shirt onto the bench and rifling through the locker for her clothes. "And did you see his face when he was shooting? It was like nothing I've seen before. So intense, so . . . so . . ."

"Homesick?"

"*So* homesick," she agrees.

Other girls start to change around us, but they quickly turn their backs. With all of our toning down our beauty, we probably didn't pay as much attention to our bodies as we should have. I hate thinking that we've made anyone self-conscious. I promise myself that we'll use the changing rooms next time.

When we're fully dressed and about to leave, a few of the other faces relax. But one girl, at least, doesn't mind meeting our eye. "That was one of the coolest things I've ever seen," Zoe tells us, stuffing clothes into her bag. "You two are fierce. Josh can be such a ginormous douche about his 'bow hunting skills.' I bet he's gonna give that a rest for a while," Zoe says with a laugh. "See you around."

We thank her as she passes us out of the changing room. Deya looks at me as she leaves. "So, she's super cool."

"Yeah. Super cool." Which only makes me feel horrible that I've stolen her almost boyfriend.

No. I haven't stolen him. The arrow did. And just because I can't fight it as well as I'd planned, doesn't mean I've done this to her.

Outside the changing room, Shaggy and Ben are talking against the wall opposite us. Ben's hair is all the way in front of his face. I stride over to him, forcing other students to step out of my way, and stand right in between him and his friend. "Hey," I say. I reach up a hand and smooth his hair out of his eyes. He catches my hand and drops our clasped hands in front of us.

"Hey," he says back. He's been so happy so far that I forgot that he's a brooder. I forgot the feeling that came over me when I first got my assignment and saw Ben. He'd been working on a song, singing lyrics softly to himself. He kept stopping and looking at a picture of his family on his phone, his shoulders hunched almost up to his ears. When he finished the song, he deleted the picture. I felt a pang in my heart that I'd stopped feeling for other assignments. I felt a desire to make him happy.

I worry I'm failing there.

"So. I'm really good at archery. Are you okay with that?"

He lets go of my hand, and for a moment, my heart withers inside of me. Then his hand reaches for my necklace. He fiddles with my arrow, my wing, and my heart. "Yeah, I'm okay with that." He screws up his face and pulls his eyes up to me. "It just took me by surprise. You're good at basically everything, and I'm—"

"Terrible at BMX racing?"

His lips tug into a smile. "Nailed it." But his smile doesn't last. "I'm a poor kid from Flag whose parents could barely afford to give me piano lessons and you're an expert at history and archery and

Lovestruck

foreign languages, and I bet you're secretly the youngest spy the CIA has ever had and have like six gold medals from the X Games."

"Seven, actually," I tease. "So?"

"So I'm not sure how I fit in your world. I'm not sure how to compete with all of that."

"Why would you want to compete with any of that?" I ask, equal parts annoyed and sympathetic. Of course he can't compete with me. I'm a goddess. "I'm not going to pretend that I'm not good at things so you don't feel threatened, and I know you don't actually want that."

"I don't," he says, though I'm not sure he realizes how little conviction he has. I'm about to continue my tirade, but a wave of affection overtakes me. How would he not feel threatened? I'm incredible. Astonishing. He will never know someone more amazing than me at virtually anything in the world. At least, not a mortal someone.

I change tactics. "But who cares if I'm rich and absurdly good at archery? I'm literally the worst driver you will ever see, unless you get in a car with someone else in my family. I suck at biology and I don't understand how the most basic things work, like pipes or batteries. I'm not sure I even believe in electricity. It's too much like magic." He laughs, and my stomach flips. "I like you, Ben. I know you say you don't know how you fit in my world, but that's the last thing I want. I'm sick of my world." His eyes are jumping back and forth between my eyes, and the crease between his eyebrows has smoothed. "Since we met, you've been on my mind way more than you should be." And I'm not sure I can fight it much longer. "Okay?"

He drops my hands and puts both of his hands on the sides of my face. We peer into each other's eyes. "Okay," he says.

He brings my face closer to his, and this time, there's no hesitation. His lips meet mine before my eyes can even close. But then they close, all right. Because he is kissing the Hades out of me. We are all lips and breath and hands on each other's faces. He moves a hand to the back of my head, and our kisses deepen. I'm not aware of anything except for him. The taste of his breath. The feel of his heart beating against my chest. The sound of—

"No kissing in the halls!"

We break apart like a bolt of lightning has hit us. I'm so dazed, I can barely think straight. I look around, trying to find the source of the interruption to curse it into oblivion, when I see a teacher staring us down over her glasses and wagging a finger at us. Ben waves an apology, grabs my hand, and pulls me through the hallway. We bump into kids who are catcalling and whistling at our retreat. When we get outside, we look at each other and laugh. Ben pulls me to a grove of aspens past the parking lot. We drop to the ground underneath the tree and immediately start kissing again. And kissing. And kissing.

We kiss until the bell rings and lunch is ending.

But as Ben runs backwards into school, giving me a look of such intensity and joy that I can't stand straight, I know this is just beginning.

I find Deya at the pizza restaurant, sitting at the table next to the kitchen. She's studying the owner like she did yesterday. She startles when I sit down across from her.

"I didn't even hear you—whoa," she says, laughing. "Your face is raw."

"What do you mean?"

"I mean," she says, leaning in and dropping her voice, "that you need to magick your face back to normal before someone thinks your lips were burned off."

I run a hand over my face and concentrate for a moment. Then I drop my hand. "Better?"

"Better." She returns her attention to the owner. "So? You and Ben are good, huh?"

My smile is so big, my cheeks hurt. I shouldn't be this happy, given that we've been forced into this. But I am. "I can't help it, Dey. Like I literally cannot help it."

"Tell me everything."

I tell her about our conversation in the hallway, which she ditched out on immediately, she says. When I get to the kissing, I'm about to gloss over it when she says, "No way. Don't skip over the good stuff. Is he a good kisser?"

I gush and blush and glow, and all the while, Deya smiles and *ooh*s and watches the kitchen.

Like I said, immortals are good multi-taskers.

"Okay, okay," she says, interrupting me. "Look."

I peek into the kitchen and see a woman who looks like an older version of the restaurant owner come in with a little boy of about four and a little girl of maybe six. They run up to their mom and hug her tightly. Instantly, the worry lines on her face disappear and she gives them huge, smiling hugs. The older woman apologizes for something before running out the back door. With immortally keen ears, we catch the owner explaining that grandma has to run a quick errand, so the kids will have to help her for a couple of hours. The kids are elated at the news.

"I did that," Deya says. "Grandma just got a 'reminder' from her doctor about an appointment."

"Nice."

We spend the next hour slowly eating and ordering more and more to justify still being at the restaurant. The server actually gets switched partway through the wait, making us feel more comfortable. Before we became visible to mortals, we could stay at a table like this for hours, knowing that the servers would forget us the moment they moved on from our table. But now, we have to think about things like servers and their suspicious glances. Thank Gaia for the server change.

Finally, just when we worry that today is a bust, Delivery Guy, with his big beard and kind eyes, shows up. He only has a single package today, and he watches the owner just as intently as he did the day before. Until he notices her children.

I hold my breath.

Delivery Guy looks floored. He blinks at them, then his gaze jumps back to the owner. He rubs his forearm with a meaty hand, covering and uncovering his tattoos with the movement.

She holds out the pen and clipboard to him, but he doesn't see. He's still looking at the kids, who are hiding behind their mom's legs. The scene is heartbreakingly awkward.

"I'm sorry, Dey," I tell her, and I'm surprised to mean it. I feel sad for these two. These four. They deserve happiness.

"Wait," Deya says. I turn my eyes back to them. Delivery Guy is moving his head from one side of the owner's legs to the other side. And the kids are following suit. Deya and I look at each other, then right back. They're playing! The kids are playing with him, and as he reaches down to pinch one of their noses, we see the owner smile.

It's a beautiful thing.

"So?" I ask. "Will you just do it now?"

She frowns. "Just because he didn't run the second he saw her kids, doesn't mean he's ready to become a dad. I should follow him a bit, have Cosmo run a background check—"

"A background check! Deya, are you kidding me?"

"What if he's an ex-con? What if he goes home and it turns out he lives in his mom's basement, and he does nothing but play video games till it's time for bed? Or what if he doesn't *mind* kids, but he's not interested in being a dad? There was a time when you'd have done research on all this, too, you know." Deya stands up and plops her napkin over her plate, along with a handful of bills to cover the check and tip. "Now I'm going back to the ranch to do psych homework. Are you coming, or are you planning to drop out before your mom's exam next month?"

"I'm coming, of course." I run to catch up with her, but she's already gone.

Fortunately, by the time we're back at the ranch, Deya's frustration has settled, and she's playing nice again. We do Erote homework until school ends, when I get a text from Ben asking me to meet him at Paresh's. I run downstairs from my room, shouting goodbyes to Deya and Artemis. I drive with either more confidence or less inhibition due to my excitement. Either way, when I arrive at Paresh's, I practically float from my car to the open garage.

Paresh's family appears to be well off, by mortal standards. The guys are set up in the third car garage, and it looks like it's exclusively their space. I know something of garage bands. Hector has mused for a dozen bands that got their start in exactly this way, and he always invites me along to the bands that he thinks I'll like. I pull out my phone, thinking how much he'd like Ben's band, thinking of the way his green eyes tense when he's focusing on the music, thinking of how something inside of him seems to sway to a beat, even when he's holding himself perfectly still.

I stop myself with a mental slap to the face.

What am I doing? What the Styx am I doing?

I tell myself not to overreact. It's habit to share things I love with Hector, especially music, and it's natural that I would think about him when music moves me. We've been best friends since we were babies. That's all this is.

As the guys rock out, I sit cross-legged on the rough pavement. I shake off all thoughts of Hector and get lost in the band's talent and in Ben's raw energy. Several songs pass before I notice the two kids beside me: a girl of maybe twelve with Ben's eyes, and another girl a year or two younger who's making faces at Paresh. Their little sisters.

When the guys take a break, Ben's younger sister, Isabella, turns to me. She's holding a clenched hand up to her mouth as if she's holding a microphone. A half-dozen multi-colored bracelets adorn her thin wrist. "So, Kali . . . can I call you Kali?" she asks, in full interview mode. I nod. "Where have you been hiding? I mean, look at you. You're adorable!" She holds her hand to my mouth, indicating that it's my turn to answer.

"Well, we lived in Phoenix before—"

She pulls the phantom microphone back to her face. "Who's 'we'? Your secret lover?"

I snort out a laugh. "No, my cousin and my aunt."

"And what brought you to Flagstaff, Arizona? Not exactly the metropolis you're used to, am I right?" She winks.

Shoot. Why hadn't I thought about this before? "Um, well,

my parents travel a lot, and my aunt is really outdoorsy, so we thought this would be a nice change of pace."

"Hmm," she says, as if she's not buying it. "And why don't you live with your parents? Travel the world with them?"

I pause. "My parents want me to take over the family business some day. I want to be the master of my own fate. I guess I need a break from them."

"What teenager doesn't want a break from her parents, am I right?" she asks and I chuckle. She drops her hand, and her demeanor shifts. "I'm taking a break from my dad."

"Wanna tell me about it?"

She chews the inside of her cheek. "More like he's taking a break from us, actually. He was promoted to bank manager last year and fell in love with one of his tellers. When he told my mom, he said they were 'magnetically drawn to each other' and he 'couldn't explain it,'" she says, using air quotes just like Ben did. "My mom cried all night. My dad moved to Tucson to take over a branch there. Since then, we see him two weekends a month. His stupid girlfriend, too. I mean, fiancée." She almost spits the words.

"How long ago was this?"

She rubs an eye. "Fourteen months and eleven days ago."

The accuracy of her count hits like a blow. "How's your mom doing?"

"My mom is the best," Isa says. "She's not going to let a man define her worth."

I smile, knowing this must be an exact quote. I look at Ben. He's still playing, but he's also intently studying us. "How's Ben?"

"It's hard for him. Our parents used to be really happy, but when they split up, he couldn't understand it. Since then, he dates a lot, but he'll never get serious. I think he's afraid of being hurt by someone, too." She glances at her shoes—black Vans with pink flamingos on them.

He's afraid of becoming his dad. He admitted as much that night after his concert, but that's not my place to share. I lean a little closer to the younger girl and bump her gently with my shoulder. "So how's Isa?"

She doesn't answer through the rest of the song. I finally dare a glance down at her. Tears are spilling down her cheeks. I catch Ben's glance—protective and nervous—and I turn back to his sister. I put my arm around Isa's shoulders and lean my head against hers. "I know it doesn't feel like it now, but it's going to be okay. I promise."

After a few minutes, I look up at Ben. He's smiling gratefully, and his eyes are full. "Thank you," he mouths to me.

I smile at him. Then to Isa, I say, "Now, Miss Vega, I believe you promised to interview me. And I have a lot more to say, thank you very much."

Isa wipes her cheeks, but her eyes are bright. She sits up and puts her phantom microphone to her face.

"So, Kali, darling, how does it feel to be dating a future rockstar?"

Chapter Fifteen

In spite of the voice inside my head telling me to slow down while I figure out the prophecy, Ben and I are on a date. A real date. With dinner and a movie. In fact, we're at the movie now, and we'll go to the observatory where Ben works afterwards. We're holding hands and I'm trying to pretend that I'm interested in this movie about an Egyptian god let loose on the mortie world, but it's too ridiculous. I know some Egyptian gods. They're weird and some of them have animal faces and they're obsessed with suns and moons—and, frankly, phalluses, which is just gross. But they're practically family, and they're nothing like this scarab-spitting wacko trying to sear New York City with the power of the sun he holds in his staff.

After Ben's rehearsal ended, Isa and I gave each other a big hug, and she asked me to come over to her house tomorrow to see her room. By that time, Ben was standing beside us, and I explained that I had to go home for the weekend. The look on his face told me he was disappointed that we'd have to be apart for even two days. He grabbed my hand then and held me close. He hasn't let go of me since.

With our hands entwined and our legs practically glued together, neither of us is paying much attention to the movie. Halfway through, and we're tracing shapes on each other's palms and tickling each other's knees. Honestly, I want to kiss him so badly, I think *I* might unleash the power of the sun. So when he leans over to me, his lips on my earlobe, and suggests that we leave now, I don't even answer. I just jump out of my seat and over the people in our row, leaving Ben to catch up.

Once outside of the theater, we race to my SUV. By mutual agreement, Ben is the usual driver, but he follows me to the passenger door. I'm sure he's going to open the door for me, but I'm not in the mood for chivalry. I grab the collar of his jacket and pull him toward me for a kiss. I hear an *oomph* of surprise from him, followed by nothing but the delicious sound of kissing.

I love kissing. I love it so much. I want to do nothing but kiss Ben for the rest of my immortal life. Well, until I fulfill the prophecy and get my heart and frigging brain back. Seriously, I'm getting so lost in this arrow spell that I can't see straight anymore. And if we fight a little for who gets bottom lip, so what? I love kissing him, and his bottom lip is delectable.

Several minutes later, we climb into my car. "So, uh, how did you like the movie?" he asks me, pulling out of the parking spot.

I giggle. "Apart from the historical and mythological inaccuracies? I loved it."

He laughs. "Yeah? What was your favorite part?"

I put my hand on his arm, tickling my name over it. "Oh, I thought this part was pretty good."

"Funny," he says, turning onto the main road. "I liked that part, too."

The two-mile drive to the observatory is quick. Soon, we're opening the sunroof and leaning our seats back to stare at the stars. Our hands are clasped over the cup holders, and occasionally, we lean over to steal a kiss.

"It looked like you and Isa were getting along earlier," he says.

"She's a really cool kid."

His brow darkens, hiding his eyes. "Wh-what did you guys talk about?"

I know that look and that stammer. I watched him do this when I was observing him for all those weeks. It means he both does and doesn't want to know. It means he's about to brood.

"Oh, just family stuff," I say, watching his face cloud further. I need to fix this. "And maybe a bit about you. And all your girl-friends," I tease.

Wrong move. Ben's whole face has darkened now. And worse, he looks offended. He shifts away from me, folding his arms over his body. He's closing himself off. Next stop, total shut down.

Think, Kali. "But what I thought was especially interesting were all your secrets." He narrows his eyes. This can only go one of two ways. "I mean, 'Kitten of the Month' calendars? Sleeping in Katy Perry boxers? Knowing all the words to Celine Dion's entire musical catalogue and singing the songs in the shower? Bold choices, Ben. Bold choices. I'm only the tiniest bit afraid of you after learning all of this."

His face clears. "And the tiniest bit aroused, am I right?"

I give him a playful shove, glad the moment has passed. With our clasped hands, Ben points to the sky.

"So, do you see Orion?" he asks, and he points to the red super giant that makes up Orion's left shoulder. "That star is Betelgeuse. Dr. Kapur, Paresh's dad, has discovered . . ." He tells me about a recent discovery related to mass loss that Paresh's dad has made. I love astronomy, and I could tell Paresh's dad a thing or two about that mass loss, but now isn't the time for showing off. Ben points to another star at Orion's left foot, Rigel, and explains something else that Dr. Kapur taught him. He doesn't speak with any particular passion about astronomy, but I think he's proud that he can tell me something that (he thinks) I don't know. And I can tell he respects Dr. Kapur by the way he says his name.

When he finishes, I want to reciprocate, to tell him something about someone that's important to me, regardless of the fact that he won't believe it. Fortunately the sun has set. "You know, Orion is named after the ancient Greek hunter. He was considered the greatest hunter of all time."

"I thought he was Roman."

"Hmm?"

"You said Orion was Greek, but isn't he Roman? I thought all the constellations and planets were."

He can't know how much this bugs me. He can't. "No, but that's an easy mistake to make." Cursing Romans. I don't know everything about mortie history, but when it comes to us versus those hacks, I could write the cursing book. "The Latin poet Ovid wrote about him around eight A.D., but the Greeks were telling stories about him ten centuries earlier." Ben shrugs, as if this information isn't of Earth-molding importance. Ugh.

"Anyway, he fell in love with the Goddess Artemis, and, even though she was a sworn maiden, she fell in love with him. They hunted together, and his skill rivaled even hers, the Goddess of the hunt. She loved him so much, she was willing to turn her back on the promise she made her brother and her father, Zeus, to remain a maiden for eternity." A lump forms in my throat. "His death is a mystery. Some say the Earth Goddess, Gaia, feared that he would eventually hunt every living animal, so she created the scorpion to kill him. Others say that Artemis' brother tricked her into killing her one true love. But either way, he was killed, and Artemis' sorrow was so profound and her love for him so great that she begged Zeus to put him in the stars so she could always see him."

"Wow," he whispers. We both stare up at the sky, and my thoughts turn to my favorite teacher, who is back at the cabin, probably looking at the same night sky. "I want a love like that."

I turn my head to him and time seems to slow. I take in the way he's chewing his cheek, how he's fidgeting with his cuticles, the hint of a question in his eyes. "Me too."

I put my hand on his cheek and he puts his hand on mine and we just look at each other for a long time.

Then he's shaking my shoulder and my eyes are fluttering open. "Kali," he whispers. "You fell asleep." I sit up. It's almost eleven. "I have to get to work."

"Oh, right," I say, rubbing my eyes. "I'm sorry. Did you fall asleep, too?"

He shakes his head and I notice that his seat is already upright. "No, I was just watching the night sky. You actually gave me an idea for a new song."

A volcano erupts in my chest, but it isn't joy, it's pride. Maybe I really am cut out to be a muse. "Really? What's it about?"

He leans over and kisses me for long enough that I'm not even remotely sleepy when we break apart. "A love that's written across the stars. Text me tomorrow when you're safe at home?"

I nod then watch him get out of the car and head toward the observatory. He stops and waves at me before unlocking a door and disappearing inside.

All I can think about when we port home is what Ben said about wanting a love that's written across the stars. It's not just the arrow, though. It's the fact that I was his inspiration. Every time I think about his words, I remember the spark in his eyes as he said it. Deya and Artemis have already told me to shut up about it at least a dozen times this morning.

Teresa is waiting for us when we arrive. She strides into the Port, nodding respectfully at Artemis.

"Now that you're safely back, I'm going back to Earth to hunt. See you kids Monday morning," Artemis says before disappearing.

Deya and I give Teresa a big hug, something she normally doesn't allow. But she's missed us. "So?" Teresa says directly to me. "How's it going?"

My mortie clothes fade away, replaced by my chiton. I know it's only been a couple of days, but the Olympian clothes I've worn my whole life suddenly feel like a uniform. I thrust my hands in my pockets, clutching the phone I get to keep on me now that I'm visible.

The three of us start walking down a lazy path that winds through forests and rose patches and gardens where butterflies sculpt themselves into living, flittering statues of the Twelve. It's as beautiful as can be. In fact, it feels too beautiful. Too green, too bright, too cloudless. I find myself wishing for a cold breeze and brown leaves. "It's actually awesome. Ben is so much more than I thought he was. He's cute and talented, but he's deep, too."

"You know I was talking about the prophecy, don't you?" Teresa asks. Then she looks at Deya. "Has she been like this the whole time?"

"No," Deya says. "She put up her guard at first. But it's slipping."

"It's obnoxious."

"Hello, right here, guys."

"Yeah, I know," Deya says. "Imagine what I'd tell her if you *weren't* here." I glare. To Teresa, Deya says, "She's trying to stave off madness; I'm trying to give her a pass."

We reach a pond and step on enormous lily pads to cross, our sandaled feet getting wet in a way I would normally find refreshing. But I'm still annoyed when we reach the path on the other side of the pond.

"I'm just chuffed that you and your mortal are having such a nice time together," Teresa says with false brightness. Then she drops her voice, "But have you made any progress?"

"Yes, actually," Deya says, as if it's some kind of surprise. Which it completely isn't. "We know the *maiden*." Deya says, raising her eyebrows.

Teresa's eyes widen. "We're sure it's . . . her, then?"

"You should have heard her, 'Resa. She's hurting bad," Deya says.

"How about the unjust union?"

I turn to Deya. "I actually have a theory: I think it could be Ben's dad."

I may as well have told her the Earth is flat. "Seriously, Kal? I thought you said he met a hot younger girl and left his wife. It's the oldest story in history. Zeus literally invented that story. Thousands of times over."

This isn't lightning-worthy. Zeus may have mellowed in the last several centuries, but he's absurdly proud of his sexual prowess. It's creepy.

"No, I really think this could be it." I tell them both about Ben's dad just suddenly leaving his wife and kids, claiming that he was drawn to her in a way he couldn't explain or deny. They look skeptical, but not altogether disbelieving.

We stop in a glade where the flowers float like soap bubbles.

We sit down cross-legged in a circle, poking at tulip bulbs and flicking daisies so they spin like tops in the air. "So how can we confirm if he was matched?" Teresa asks. "Just ask your dad? If this were a sanctioned match, he'd know, right?"

"Right, but my dad would never allow a match that broke up a marriage. That's one of the rules he implemented when he took over the department for Aphrodite. Mortals have to end a relationship on their own terms before we'll intervene."

"Sure, but who says it was a sanctioned match?" Deya asks.

We stare at each other. "Security is in charge of tracking down unsanctioned actions across departments, right?" Teresa asks. "So we go talk to Security."

Deya and I look at each other, groaning.

Teresa looks back and forth at us. "What am I missing?"

"Only the fact that the god of sucking at life covers Erote security."

"No." Teresa starts.

"Yes," Deya says, spitting a curse. "Thrax."

The Security headquarters are on the fourth peak, an easy jaunt from the Port, which exists on all peaks simultaneously. It's all gorgeous marble and columns, but without any of the friezes or fluting that make the buildings beautiful. Thrax's place of work is the only building I've been to on Olympus that feels like a compound, though, in fairness, I've never been to Ares' headquarters. I'm sure the God of war's headquarters make this look like a fairy palace.

Heracles is over Security. His is the only department that isn't controlled by one of the Twelve. Although it isn't beautifully decorated like Erote headquarters, the Security department does have some art. In fact, it's filled with statues of Heracles accomplishing the Twelve Labors. Him slaying a lion, him slaying a hydra. Well, they're mostly just him slaying things.

A Security goddess stops us. Over her chiton, she wears armor, a helmet, a belted sword, and she carries a shield. Armed goddesses and gods, no matter how lower-case the "g," are the height of overkill in my eyes. But after some vicious prank wars with the Norse deities a few centuries ago, Heracles feels it's necessary, and you don't argue with Zeus' favorite son. (Unless you're Thor. Thor argues a lot with Zeus' favorite son.)

"Why are you here?" the immortal asks. Her helmet sits low on her face, but her brilliant green eyes are visible.

"We're here to see Thrax. Ares' son," Deya says.

The Security goddess instantly escorts us. Thrax is only nineteen, which means he would normally be a peon in an operation this big. But because he's the direct son of Ares—who doesn't exactly have a reputation for being hinged—he gets a lot of latitude. No one wants to mess with Ares. Dude is not right.

The guard marches us through the stoic building where everyone is on high alert. After passing countless closed doors, we finally stop. The guard approaches a closed stone door and communicates with someone on the other side. Then the door opens to a dark, ceilinged room. Torches line the walls, but the lack of any direct sunlight is uncomfortable. The room is full of immortals, including some gods and centaurs. They're all staring into pools of water with smaller aqua screens at their sides. Information appears on the screens faster than the blink of an eye. The immortals in the room think back their responses or commands, which transmit seamlessly on the screens. With swipes of hands, the images in the pools change, move, focus, and zoom.

The guard who escorted us here finds Thrax talking with a small group. She says something to Thrax, whose head flies up to find us. He walks around pools and immortals to get to us.

"To what do I owe the honor?" he says to Deya and me. Like always, he ignores Teresa completely.

"Hi Thrax," Teresa says, leaning in closer to him. I swear, he actually flinches.

"We were hoping to ask you a favor," I say before Teresa can dissuade him from helping us.

His smile is predatory. I fight a cringe. "Favors come with a price, Kalixta."

"Name it."

"Go out with me."

Ew.

"Thrax, you know Kali's heart belongs to someone else," Deya says in a purring voice that would normally have him lapping at her feet. But not this time.

"Don't tell me that rumor is true. You stuck yourself? You fell in love with a mortal?" The outrage in his voice takes us all off guard. I glance around the compound, and a handful of immortals have stopped to look at us. I give them a little "move along" wave, praying to Gaia that they don't know who I am. Thrax hearing a rumor like this isn't too surprising, considering his job and what close tabs he keeps on the female descendants of Aphrodite. But I don't need every immortal knowing what a lovestruck fool I am.

"Thrax, please, just help us," I beg. "It's a tiny favor and would take you less than a minute."

"No," he shakes his head. "Not until I find out that you've broken it off with the mortal."

Teresa pushes between Deya and me and gets in Thrax's face. "You don't want me for an enemy, Thrax. I will take you so far into the depths of the underworld, even Hades himself won't be able to find you."

Thrax's olive skin blanches, and for a moment, I think Teresa has saved the day. But then his eyes fall on a statue of Heracles, and he looks at the guard who brought us here, as well as the two other guards in the room. Emboldened, he bends down to growl at Teresa. I'm reminded just how much shorter she is than Thrax. It's easy to forget with a presence like hers. "Save it, Iron Heart. You may put the psycho in psychopomp, but I'm not scared of you."

Teresa stands up on her tiptoes and stares him down. "Yes, you are. And you're about to learn why."

"Okay, okay," I say, stepping between them before Teresa does something she definitely wouldn't regret but would cause a lot of paperwork. "Thrax, obviously you don't take Olympian security as seriously as I'd thought. We'll get out of your way."

I pull my friends' arms towards the compound doors, waiting for Thrax to take the bait. And still waiting. We're actually at the doors and he still hasn't stopped us. What gives?

I glance behind me, and his arms are folded. He gives me a nod that tells me, clear as an Olympian sky, to keep walking.

We do.

Chapter Sixteen

My parents act like it's been a year since they saw me instead of five days. When we show up after our encounter with Thrax, they rush to the door to hug me. My dad's wings actually pick him up off the ground a couple of inches.

"Oh, how I've missed you," my mom says, squeezing me. Then my dad swoops in for a hug.

"How are you?" he asks.

"I'm fine, guys, things are going really well." I wish I could tell them about the prophecy, but they still don't even know I went to the Oracle. Explaining the lengths I'm going to in order to prevent a fate like theirs may not be the kindest truth I could tell them.

"Oh, my darling girl, you have to tell me everything!" another voice says, and I look around my parents to see my grandmother. Aphrodite.

I've mentioned that I'm basically the paragon of beauty, right? Well, Aphrodite *is* beauty. Beauty and desire, lust and love. When she comes into a room, it feels like the heavens have parted and perfection is all around you. You can't even remember ugliness, let alone imagine that it could exist in a universe that could create her. And when she leaves, the emptiness is so heavy and the void so vast that you actually mourn her absence. And that's just to immortals. To mortals, she becomes everything they could ever desire to an infinite degree. Morties would literally combust if they saw her in her glory.

So it's tough to get a big head about being beautiful around here.

Aphrodite sweeps the three of us up in her arms and gives us a huge, loving hug. "Oh, my girls! Do, tell me everything."

Her blonde hair glistens in Helios' rays, and the reflection sends beams of light around the room like sunbursts. Her chiton clings to her in a way that I'm pretty sure I shouldn't see on my own grandmother. But considering she used to parade around Olympus naked most of the time, I'm more relieved than anything else. Her smile reveals dimples and cheekbones that make it anyone's guess what age she chose to spend eternity at. She could be my older, infinitely more perfect sister.

She pulls us over to a divan to sit. Sitting on one side of Aphrodite, Teresa is patently uncomfortable. She's the least superfluous immortal I know, and Aphrodite is the most, so they never have much to talk about. But Deya, who sits on Aphrodite's other side, stares at her mom with undisguised worship. I sit on the floor across from my friends and my parents sit on the divan behind me. My mom plays with my hair, and I lean back against her legs.

"Details, girls," Aphrodite demands. "I need details now."

I let Deya do the talking, and she plays up the details of my relationship with Ben, explaining everything and even embellishing a little, despite my parents being in the room. My mom's hands hesitate when Deya tells Aphrodite that Ben and I kissed.

Aphrodite squeals and claps her hand, turning the full force of her charm on me. "Oh, Kalixta, my beautiful girl! Nothing beats a first kiss with a new love. Was he as good a kisser as Apollo's son? I remember you talking about that first kiss for weeks." She sighs dreamily.

I mumble an answer, wishing she hadn't brought up Hector, wishing we were having this talk with two fewer parents in the room. Aphrodite *tsk*s. "If you think you're going to tell your parents anything they don't know, think again." She winks at them. "Judging by your blush, it was good."

My dad steps in at this point. Thankfully. "Deya, how are you liking your assignment? How are things progressing with the restaurant owner?"

She brightens. "Really well. I think I've found a promising match for her. I just want to check him out a little more to make sure I'm not overlooking anything."

"Excellent! There's so much at stake for this woman. I knew you were the right person for the job," he says proudly. My dad is always proud of Deya, even prouder than he was of me when she and I were competing for top probie. It used to bug me. Now that I know better, I'm glad she's the top in our class. Praise like this means a lot more to her than it does to me. Mostly.

"Oh, Eros," Aphrodite says, "you take these things too seriously. Ever since you and Psyche and your arrow fiasco, you've become such a stickler for getting matches 'right.'" She tosses her glorious hair back, looking skyward for drama's sake, no doubt, and completely ignoring the fact that she sent my dad to Earth to match my mom with a cursing monster. "The world needs more love! Why slow down the process when you could match everyone? Why hold back joy?"

My dad looks like he's talking to a child. "Mother, we've been over this a thousand times. We shouldn't involve ourselves any more than we need to. You know how powerful an arrow is. It can lead to destruction and hatred just as easily as it can lead to joy and love."

I shift, thinking of my epic mismatch. But Teresa looks interested at the mention of destruction and hatred. My girl can be so dark. "It can? How?"

"Well, it all depends on the strength of an arrow. Students have training arrows and are typically on low-risk assignments, so there's little potential for life-altering damage." He doesn't look at me when he says this. "And, of course, we monitor all matches and correct bad ones to ensure that nothing goes amiss. But with full Erote arrows, compatibility is essential. If a match isn't compatible, the couple will almost certainly stay together, but they will destroy each other. The strongest mortals may be able to break a bad match, while some few others may leave in a rare moment of strength. Those mortals must do everything they can to never see their match again, or the cycle will just resume. A bad match is like an addiction. You hate what it does to you, but you can't let it go."

"Not to mention the fact that if an immortal is pricked and separated from her match for long enough, she'll lose her mind bit by bit, whether it was a good match or not," Deya says pointedly.

Teresa points at me. "Sucks to be you." To my dad, she asks, "So if this self-destruction is such a risk, then why match at all?"

"Fair question. We match because people deserve happiness, and not all of them are strong enough to overcome their own fears or their own past. They need divine intervention. And, as my mother pointed out, the world needs more love. There's a lot more bloodshed when there's not enough love in the world. We help provide the universe with balance."

That balance is essential to mortals and immortals. Ares' department has been getting stronger and Athena's weaker for too long. If the pattern continues for generations, the Pantheon itself could be at risk of being absorbed by another pantheon, like we did with the Mesopotamians. You don't want to know what Zeus has had An, Ki, and Enlil doing for the last several thousand years.

Good thing the Romans just stole our religion instead of supplanting it, or we'd be screwed.

Teresa and my dad keep talking, and my thoughts turn to Ben. The Goddess of love knows this.

"He makes you happy, doesn't he?" Aphrodite says, as starry-eyed as if she were the one under the arrow's spell

Because it's Aphrodite, I don't filter myself. I let myself forget that this is contrived and just grin like a lovesick fool. She crawls down beside me. "So, really, between us girls . . . how *was* kissing him?"

I'm about to give a squealing answer when I see the hurt on Deya's face. Her mom just slid away from her to talk about a boy with me. So instead of gushing, I say, "It was great. Magical." I look over Aphrodite to my best friend and say, "Deya, why don't you come over and tell your mom about the match you're working on, though." I turn back to Aphrodite. "You should see the guy Deya has found for this woman. He's so gruff looking, but really sweet."

Aphrodite says, "Ooh, I love a little gruffness." Then to Deya, who's joining us on the floor, she says, "If you weren't such a prude, you'd know what I mean by now."

Deya looks like she was slapped. "What do you mean, prude? It's not like I've never kissed someone."

Her mother laughs. "Oh, what, that moon-eyed grandson of Hephaestus who follows you around everywhere? Hardly living on the edge, are you?" She sounds so sweet and innocent, but there's a distinct hint of scorn. If I can pick up on it, her own daughter sure as Hades can.

Deya turns a deep, hurt red. "Would you rather I take up with the next guy carrying a sword who comes my way?"

Her mom looks at me is if we're somehow in on this together. "She wouldn't know what to do with a sword, would she?"

My mouth falls open while Aphrodite laughs, like this whole conversation is a delight. Deya's eyes well with tears. She jumps up and runs from the room.

Aphrodite shakes her head, still chuckling. "How did I raise such a goody-goody?" she asks no one in particular.

My dad looks at me in concern. Then he flies after Deya. The truth is, Aphrodite didn't raise Deya, no more than she raised my dad. Aphrodite's children tend to find surrogate parents or go without. Deya's always had my parents, but it can't make up for everything. It can't make up for the fact that she's spent almost every night here for the last few years rather than go home to an empty palace for the millionth time in a row. Deya has more things at my house than she has at her own.

Aphrodite tries to pepper me with increasingly scandalous questions, despite the presence of my mom. I haven't done any of the things she's suggesting. I haven't even heard of some of them. Mercifully, my mom stops Aphrodite.

"Kali, weren't you and Teresa on your way to Hector's? I know he wanted to see you before you go back Monday."

"Right!" I say, jumping up. "Of course, come on, 'Resa." I blow my mom a kiss that I hope tells her thank you in huge, sparkly letters, and Teresa and I start running out.

Aphrodite calls out after us. "Kal, sweetie, will you ask Deya if she's seen my belt? I really need it back for my next—"

We're out the door before we can hear the sordid details of what Aphrodite needs a belt for. We cut across the emerald-green lawn to a path that will lead one tier up to Hector's home. And by Hector's, I mean Apollo's.

Teresa and I share "Did that really happen?" comments most of the way to Hector's. Until Teresa changes the subject.

"So, are you nervous to see Hector?"

I keep my head high. "What do you mean? Why would I be nervous to see Hector?"

"Oh, just . . ." She stops. Her eyes gloss over, and I'm about to snap her back to reality when she comes back on her own with a sweet sigh. "I gotta go. I'm on call, and it looks like my assignment's soul is about to be released. He's this sweet old man. His wife is already in Elysium, which I'm sure is where he's going, too. He'll be thrilled to see her." She gives me a rare hug. She only gets tender like this when it's a good one. "Assuming Charon is actually waiting with his ferry this time, I shouldn't be gone more than a day or two. But if you're not here when I get back, I'll be on Earth on assignment again next week. Text me with your progress on the prophecy, okay?"

I smile at her departing form. In these good reapings, I glimpse a merciful love in her soul that few immortals are capable of. It warms my heart to think of her giving this old man safe passage to his judgment and eternal fate.

Just as quickly, the thought leaves me cold. Fate. I wonder if this man really had any choices at all, or if the Fates had already decided what his eternal judgment would be. And if that's the case, how is that fair? If he chose badly all of his life because the Fates determined he would at his birth, then how can he be judged wicked? Aren't the Fates actually the wicked ones? And if he does end up in the depths of Tartarus rather than Elysium because the Fates decided so, then wouldn't it be better for him if he was never born?

These thoughts eat at me until I start stomping and jam my hands in the pockets of my chiton. I feel the thread the Fates gave me. How could it possibly be here?

I look around me and make sure that no immortals are near enough on their paths to see what I'm doing. Then I take out the thread. I focus on it, tuning out everything around me, until I think I catch glimpses of the same teeming life that I saw before.

"Kal, what are you doing?" My head flies up, and I stuff the thread back in my pocket before Hector can see what I was looking at. "Was that a thread?"

"Oh, that was nothing," I lie. "A thread came off my chiton, if you can believe it."

His eyebrows tell me that he *can't* believe it. Something made by Hestia, Goddess of hearth and home, isn't exactly going to lose threads.

Stupid, Kali. I can't think of what to say, so instead I take a few bounding steps and throw my arms around Hector. He hesitates for a moment, then puts his arms around me, too. It feels good. Despite his boundless muscles, Hector gives the best hugs.

A pinched *Ahem* sounds from behind me, and Hector and I break apart.

It's Ia-cursing-nira. "Sorry to interrupt," she says, clearly not sorry at all. I want to shoot the glasses from her face and make her fall in love with a cyclops. Not that cyclopes don't deserve real love, but because no self-respecting cyclops would be caught with a harpy like her. They have surprisingly good taste in women.

"Excuse me, Kali. Hec, I was really hoping to steal two minutes from you." And even though I'm standing right beside him, she manages to wedge between us, take Hector's arm, and start walking up to the Big Twelve tier. Before they reach the fork that branches off to his house, though, Hector removes his arm from Ianira's.

"I'm sorry, Ianira, but I haven't seen Kali all week. Can we catch up later?"

She shoots me a venomous look that Hector doesn't see, but to him, she's all smiles. "Of course. Thanks again." She stands on tiptoes and kisses him on the cheek. And he blushes.

When she leaves, I punch Hector's shoulder. "You and Ianira? Seriously?" I make a gagging sound, just in case my tone was too subtle.

He doesn't give anything away. Jerk. We take a smaller path that leads around his palace and into the gardens. Just when you think Olympus can't get any more beautiful, you come to the home of one of the Twelve, and it hits you all over again. Apollo's grounds are enormous. Thousands, maybe millions of acres of forests and springs and gardens and waterfalls dot the landscape. The purest air and most aromatic flowers I've ever smelled mingle and fill my senses. Like most immortals, I've only been up to Zeus' tier once, after the Oracle called me. It was so much better than even this that my mind actually blocked the experience. My dad explained that life would be too bleak if I were able to retain the memories of the sights and sounds and smells of Zeus and Hera's home. Styx, this is bad enough.

We walk over to an enormous lily, and Hector strokes a petal. Other petals drop to make a sort of couch, and Hector and I fall next to each other on the lily-chair.

"You're not saying anything, huh? Oh, Gaia. That means it's worse than I thought."

"Kal, you're currently spending your weeks with a mortal boy you matched yourself with. Why do you care what I'm doing?" The set of his green eyes is hurt and angry and . . . hopeful. It's the hope that makes me maddest at myself. Why do I do this to him? Why can't I kill his hope?

"Because you're my best friend, and you deserve better than a harpy like her."

"Is this why you're here? To tell me who I can and can't like?"

Part of me wants to yell, *See! You do like her!* But the other part of me is smarter. Thankfully. "No." I lean back in the lily. "I came because my mom said you were hoping to catch up with me before I go back to Earth."

"Huh. I'm glad to see you, but I didn't say anything like that to her."

I scratch my chin, covering a flash of disappointment. Not that I want him to want to see me, but still. "Must have been a diversion, then." I tell him all about the conversation with Aphrodite and what happened with Deya.

"I still don't get it, though. Where did I come in?"

"Oh, Aphrodite was asking me all sorts of questions about kiss—" The words stop in my throat, replaced with hot shame. At the same time, I see him wince. I can't believe I've just come up here, insulted Hector's taste in girls, and then thrown it in his face that I'm dating someone else. "Hec, I'm sorry. I shouldn't have said that. I should—I should just go." I move to stand up, but Hector grabs my arm and pulls me back down.

"All right, that's enough. Are we still best friends?"

"We are," I say nervously.

"Do we still talk about our lives?"

"We used to."

"We do," he corrects me. He closes his eyes. "I don't want to hear details about you and . . . Ben, but I do want to hear details about your life." He opens his eyes again, and intense green stares back at me. "Now what's going on?"

Where do I start? What can I tell him?

He drops his head. I've hesitated too long. "Look, Kal. I know something's going on. I saw the thread of the Fates that you stuffed in your pocket, and my sister is a guard for Heracles. She said she escorted you to a meeting with Thrax today." That guard was Hec's sister? I should have recognized the eyes. Curse the gods and their endless offspring. "I also know that Aunt Artemis is chaperoning you on Earth right now, though I can't imagine why." I want to interrupt, but he keeps talking. "I'm not going to push you to tell me, but I hope you know you can. I will always be here for you."

Relief encircles me like me like a hug. Nothing fills me with more peace than being with Hector, at least when we're not at odds. My mind works more clearly around him. Even the magnetic pull of Ben is more manageable in Hector's presence. I breathe more easily than I have all morning. "I know. I'll tell you everything eventually, okay? There's just some stuff I have to work through first."

"Do you swear?"

I swallow hard. Asking me to swear is serious. But what kind of friend am I if I can't even swear to tell him the truth? And what does it say about me that I'm glad he wants me to tell him, even now? "On the Styx, I swear it."

"Good." He leans back in the lily. "Now, if you'll keep that big mouth shut—"

"Hey!" I push him.

"I'll tell you about my assignment."

I lean back beside him and just listen to the sound of his voice. Well, for as long as I can, anyway.

"You didn't!" I cry partway through his story. "Hector, tell me you didn't convince Stone Savage to eat it!"

We are both laughing so hard, we're in tears. "I didn't have to convince him!" He breaks into chuckles. "I just told him that if he really wanted to eat meat fit for the gods, he couldn't cook it, because everyone knows the gods ate their meat raw after Prometheus stole fire from them. How was I supposed to know he'd try it?" Another wave of laughs. "With skunk?"

I can't breathe. "How much did he eat?"

"Every bite. He said because his arrow hit it, it was his job to eat it. 'Just like the gods.' He actually said that!" Hector's clutching his sides. "Kal, you would have died. Savage . . . when he gags, he actually . . ." He stops and explodes with laughter, which only makes me lose it again. "When he gags, he . . ." Tears stream down his face. "He farts. And then"—laughter—"Then . . . so . . . much . . . more." He fights for a breath through laughs. "It was like Mount Vesuvius blowing out one end"—chuckle, chuckle, chuckle—"and Mount St. Helens on the other!"

I fall out of the lily and crash to the ground, I'm laughing so hard. I look up at him through blurred eyes. "What's-what's the song . . . you'd set the scene to?" I ask through laughs, playing one of our favorite games.

He laughs, wiping his still crying eyes. "'I'm Coming Out'?"

"No, no," I cry. "'Smells Like Teen Spirit.'"

He wrinkles his nose, as if remembering the stench. "'Everybody Hurts.'"

I wince from laughing. "'Drop It Like It's Hot.'"

His whole body is shaking when he falls to the ground beside me. "'Push It'!"

We collapse into giggles.

Chapter Seventeen

When I appear in Flagstaff on Monday morning, Deya is already there. She waves at me from the kitchen, where she and Artemis are talking and laughing. Artemis waves me in. Am I imagining it, or is Deya avoiding my eyes?

"What are you two talking about?" I ask. Artemis grabs a golden apple from the air and tosses it to me. I catch it and sit on a stool across from Artemis, next to Deya.

"We may have stirred up a bit more trouble than we thought with our archery stunt at school," Deya says, looking at Artemis.

"What do you mean?" I ask, my eyes flying between them. "What happened?"

Artemis answers. "Tony Gunner stopped by."

"He stopped by? Here?" I cry. "Why? What was so wrong?"

Artemis holds out a hand, as if trying to steady me. "Nothing is wrong. He was just really impressed by your skill. He tried calling, but I forgot to keep that phone with me when I was hunting, so he stopped by."

"Okay. But why?"

"He wanted to talk to me about your training schedule. Deya swears neither of you talked to him about this. Is that right?" I nod violently. "Well, after your little stunt, Tony has had a change of heart about competitive archery. He's thinking about training again, and he'd like me to help." Deya pinches me under the counter. This is going to be easier than we thought! Artemis finding passion for life again, Mr. Gunner getting the inspiration he needs to compete—and win. It's perfect!

"That's fantastic!" I practically shout. "Good for Mr. G!"

"And he'd like you two to train with him."

Um. What?

"He says he hasn't been as inspired in years as he was watching the pure joy you two obviously have for archery. He wants that back, so he wants to shoot with you." She smiles archly. "Evidently, times have changed and now it appears that a handsome young teacher and two beautiful girls can't be alone together. So I'll have to be there. Every day. Thanks for that." Her sarcasm is not lost on us.

"Well, thanks, Artemis," I begin.

"Yeah, yeah," she interrupts. "Off to school with you."

We grab our things and go out to Deya's Jeep. The ride to school is oddly silent until we reach the parking lot and I decide I've had enough awkwardness.

"Dey, what's going on? Are you okay?"

"I'm fine. Why?"

"I'm just worried about you. I haven't seen you since that stupid conversation at my house, and I want to make sure you're okay."

"I'm fine, really. Why wouldn't I be? Oh, and before I forget, I talked to Thrax yesterday. He's going to look into Ben's dad and see if there was an unsanctioned match."

I hold a hand up to my heart. "Oh, for the love of Zeus, you are my hero! How did you convince him to help?"

She winks at me and steps out of the vehicle. Normally, I would laugh this off, but I can't. Not with that shadow in her eyes. I jump out and run around the car, grabbing her arm. "Deya, what happened? Did he do something to you?"

"He didn't use his 'sword,' if that's what you're asking."

I flinch at the word. "But did he hurt you? Did he try something?"

"Darling, I'm Aphrodite's daughter. I control the men in my life, not the other way around."

This is so vintage Aphrodite that I'm shocked to hear the words come out of Deya's mouth. I stare at her back as she walks into school.

Then I smell Ben's deodorant and my thoughts scatter with the wind. It's only been a weekend since I saw him, but the arrow has me humming with excitement. His hands cover my eyes, as if my senses didn't detect him across the parking lot. "Guess who," he says.

He twists me around and I kiss him. "Mmm, Shaggy. You taste better than ever," I say.

He laughs and gives me several quick kisses before slinging an arm around my shoulders. We walk like this into school, bumping hips. He tells me how much he missed me all weekend, and then tells me how the song is going. (Really well! Yay!) When we sit down in our first class, he looks like he wants to say something.

"Spill." I prompt.

He screws up his face. "So, feel free to say no to this, but Isa told my mom all about you. And, uh, she kind of wants you to come over for dinner. Tonight."

"That's great! I'd love to. Am I supposed to bring something? Should I wear something different? I feel like girls are always changing clothes a hundred times to meet a boyfriend's parents. Should I do that?" I'm painfully aware of the fact that I'm blabbering, but even more so of the fact that I referred to him as my boyfriend. I keep chattering faster, hoping to bury the word in a pile of conversation.

He grabs my hand on my desk and fixes his hazel eyes on me. "Kali, you don't need to bring anything and you don't need to change. Just come over at six tonight. In fact, if you want to come to band rehearsal at four, you can just come over with me afterwards."

I try to match his calm. "Perfect."

Like last week, we flirt all through class. By the time PE rolls around, even with my perfect recall, I struggle to remember what happened in class up to this point. But I know that Ben grabbed my hand and drew a wicked, smoky heart on my palm that the lovestruck part of me hopes will stay there forever. I keep peeking at it when no one else is looking. It's like he's telling me that I hold his heart in my hand. Which I kind of do.

I shouldn't love it. I really shouldn't.

Our archery unit will last for the next few weeks, and as soon as Deya and I walk into the gym, Mr. Gunner is already enlisting our help with the class.

"How would you two feel about being my aides for this unit in exchange for extra credit?"

We both nod. "Sure," I say. "And about what our aunt—"

He gives a tiny shake of his head. "Great. Why don't you two stop by my office at lunch and we'll talk about the particulars? Now, let's have you help out with a couple of groups."

After PE is over, we change and head into Mr. Gunner's office. I text Ben along the way to tell him I'll meet him at Paresh's after school. I hate missing an opportunity to be with him, even if just for lunch, but I have a prophecy to fulfill if I want my fate to be on my terms. Mr. Gunner is a big part of the prophecy. I just know he is.

"So, I'm sure your Aunt Cynthia told you I'm going to train with the two of you?" We nod. "Is that going to be uncomfortable at all?"

"No," Deya says firmly. "It'll be an honor, Mr. G."

"I'm not sure I deserve that."

"Why wouldn't you deserve it? You've come closer than anyone in the world to shooting a fourteen hundred. What could make you more deserving?" she asks.

"Beating it," he says.

"Our aunt will get you there if anyone can," Deya says, and I nod.

"That's the hope," he says. "See you later."

After three hours of following Delivery Guy around, we've learned that he lives alone, that he's a recovering alcoholic, and that his first wife left him because of his drinking. Cosmo digs up the majority of this dirt for us, but the reception he gives us is chilly.

"I've sent everything to your phone, Kali," he says.

"Okay, but could you give us an idea of his—"

"I'm actually really busy, so text me whatever you need, and I'll send it to your phone so you have access to it."

His voice disappears without warning. "That was weird," I say.

"Whatever. According to Cosmo's report, Delivery Guy went to therapy for a couple of years as part of his addiction recovery program." Deya pauses to skim the report, and then a hint of softness enters her voice. "He told his therapist his biggest regret is that he was too drunk to drive his wife to the hospital when she had a miscarriage." She holds a hand to her mouth. "He's never forgiven himself, even though the two are on good terms now."

"And I officially love him. Can we match them already?" I ask her.

"I don't know. Maybe we should just check to make sure that Restaurant Owner doesn't have a huge aversion to his past. You know, like if her dad was an alcoholic, it may be bad news. I'll see if Cosmo can run another check for me later."

"Okay," I tell her. I look at the time. "We need to get to the ranch. Archery lessons start in twenty."

We make it just in time to change and run out to the range that Artemis has created. Mr. Gunner is already there, and he's talking to Artemis. They look friendly, like they've known each other for years. How much did they talk this weekend?

"Ah, girls," she says, gesturing to us to come over and take mark. "I thought we'd do some speed drills, then move to depth exercises, then . . ." I stop listening, wondering how I'm going to get out of here in time to meet Ben at his band practice.

I don't. I arrive almost an hour late, and he looks disappointed when he sees me. No, he looks upset. And so does Paresh. He keeps shooting me dirty looks over his drums. When they finish a song, I rush over to explain about Mr. Gunner.

"Mr. G is training with you and your cousin? Mr. Gunner, the world record holder, wants to train with you?" He lets out a long swear and then mumbles in Spanish that I'm so out of his league. Too bad for him I'm fluent in Spanish.

"It's not like that," I say, though it totally is. "He wants to help *us* train. He thinks we could shoot professionally, and he wants to help."

"Cuz that's so much better," he says weakly. He's going to his unhappy place, and I put my hands on the side of his face to keep him with me.

"Ben, this is not a thing, okay? We've been over this. I'm good at archery. So what?"

He inhales sharply, but then nods. "You're right. Besides, it's totally hot."

I laugh and things return to normal while I admire him finishing his set. But a small part of me is getting tired of how often we keep having this same conversation. And a smaller, more traitorous part of me remembers that Hector was never threatened by me, and not just because he's a god. When my parents first invited Hec over for game night, we held chariot races in our backyard hippodrome, and I absolutely destroyed him. And when we moved on to wrestling and I pinned him in two minutes? His green eyes glinted with pride, his smile eclipsed the sun, and his laugh made my heart—

I stop myself before I can dwell too long on the past. I watch Ben sing and pull my head—and heart—back to the present.

In a business suit that says she won't be an admin assistant for much longer, Ben's mom insists I call her Marta, insists I hug her, and insists I'm too skinny and she'll change that. She calls me *querida* and orders me around like I'm a part of the family.

I love it.

"Marta, this was delicious," I say. I've had a handful of assignments in Mexico, and her tamales are among the best. I stand up to help her with the dishes, but she shoos me away.

"No, you and Benicio go, have fun. Isabella can help me." Ben and I start to leave the small dining room when Marta shouts out, "But don't have too much fun, *mijo*."

"*Ya está bien, Mamá,*" he calls back. Wicked laughter comes from the kitchen and echoes around the narrow hallway.

"Well, should I give you the grand tour?" he asks, his neck splotchy red.

"Yes, please!" I say, rather than what I'm thinking, which is *please don't wallow.* I know I'm overeager, but I hate it when he gets worked up about little things like this. So, his family isn't rich? So the walls have wood paneling and there are stains on the carpets? His dad's dad left them this house and a few acres of land rather than leaving it to his cheating son. If people at school call it "the Barn" because it's painted red, who cares? It was a gift from someone who loved them, given when they needed help. I wish he could see it that way.

The hunch in his shoulders lifts a little and he takes me down the creaky hall to his room. He opens the door, and it's like I've stepped into a time machine. The posters covering the walls of his cramped, but tidy, bedroom are all from forty years ago. The Smiths, David Bowie, Siouxsie and the Banshees, Blondie. He has a bookcase filled with vinyl records and a record player in one corner of the room and an acoustic guitar, acoustic bass, an electric guitar, and an amp crammed in the other. The small writing desk beside his bed is covered in notebooks and papers with guitar tabs and lyrics.

"Wow, where did you get all this vinyl?" I pull out a Stevie Wonder album.

"They were my grandpa's," he says. "He was a musician in the 70s and 80s at a time when there weren't a lot of Mexican

Americans in the punk or new wave scenes. You know the song "The Tide is High?" The mariachi part?"

"From the Blondie song?"

"Yeah. My grandpa was one of the trumpet players. He was legit."

"Wow. Your grandpa must have been so cool."

"Yeah, he was. He was the best." Ben's hair falls in front of his face. "I'm not allowed to have girls in my room, so, uh, do you wanna see the yard?"

Twenty minutes later, we're lying at opposite ends of a hammock between two ash trees, and Ben is strumming his guitar. It's not the most natural fit, but I could listen to him play all night.

"So your mom is pretty awesome."

I hear the smile in his voice. "She totally is. Since my dad split, she hasn't looked back once. Just picked herself up and us with her. Our last house was actually bigger than this one. She thought about selling this after my grandpa died, but we don't have a mortgage on this house and she thinks if she holds on to it for a few more years, she could sell it for a lot. So it just made more sense to move here. To the Barn."

"I like the Barn." He shifts. "I do. It has everything you need, doesn't it? You have a bedroom and a kitchen and bathroom. What more do you need?"

"Right, because you'd be happy living with Deya and your aunt in eleven hundred square feet."

Okay, so my bedroom in Olympus is triple that size, with a small flower garden in it. And maybe I did complain a little about the bathroom at the O-Ranch. And I'm sure there are social dynamics to living here that make Ben's life harder. But, and I mean this, "I'd be happy living anywhere if it was with the people I love. Especially if there was a Ziggy Stardust poster."

He lifts his head to look at me. "You like Bowie?"

"Yeah, I love him. Almost as much as I love Lou Reed."

"Lou Reed? You prefer Velvet Underground to David Bowie? You're crazy."

"Whatever," I tease. "You probably think the Rolling Stones are better than the Beatles."

"Yeah, because I hate the Beatles."

It's my turn to look at him. "You hate the Beatles?" I reach a bare foot up to nudge his ear. "We need to get these fixed."

"No, we need to agree to disagree."

I sit up on my elbows, making the hammock sway more. "Hey, I'm just playing around. Of course we're allowed to disagree. You can like whoever you want, and I'll respect that."

He rests his guitar on the ground against the tree and rubs a hand over his face. "You're right. Sorry. My dad didn't like my mom disagreeing with him on anything. He said it was a telltale sign that a relationship was falling apart."

"That's absurd."

"I know that now." He reaches for my hand. "If anything, the sign of a relationship falling apart is a guy running off with a teller half his age."

"Yeah, not sure how your dad missed that one," I say darkly. To my relief, Ben snorts. "We're allowed to like different stuff. Right?"

"You're right." He pauses. "I guess I'm just relieved you feel that way. I keep, I don't know, expecting you to realize I'm not good enough for you."

This recurring theme makes me wonder if Ben's trying to

get something from me that I can't give or if he's subconsciously pushing me to see if I'll leave.

Not that I would. Or could.

I squeeze his hand. "This can't keep being an issue between us, Ben. We're good at different things. We come from different worlds. We like different bands. The sooner we both accept that, the better. You see that, right?"

He tickles my palm. "Yeah, I do," he says. "And honestly, it makes it easier to tell you something I've been keeping back for a while now."

"You can tell me anything."

"Good." He takes a deep breath. "Because there's this guy named Justin Bieber that I just love. The dude is, like, OMG, so totally good."

I'm disappointed by how quickly the conversation has derailed, but it's better than the direction we were headed. I pinch his thigh, and he jerks, making the hammock rock perilously. "You secretly love the Biebs, don't you?"

He starts pinching me back. "It's not a secret if I just told you."

I squeal as he tickles my foot. "You know the words to every song, don't you?"

He starts singing Bieber's "Baby" through laughter, but stops abruptly when I tickle his knee. "Ack! No fair!" He wriggles around, trying to push my hands off of his knee, until the hammock flips him out and he lands on his back on the ground. I stay in, of course.

I peer over the hammock. "I win."

"Oh yeah?"

He grabs my arm, pulling me off the hammock so I land with a thud next to him. I get up on my elbows and kiss him softly. "Yeah."

In the back of my mind, I wonder what I'm thinking, building expectations of our relationship, getting emotionally invested like this when I'm actively trying to reverse our match. But as I lie beside him on the cool grass and listen to him sing a new song about a girl who stole across the stars, I marvel at his skill. I relish the fact that I've inspired such beauty to come into the world. And I set my concerns aside for another day.

Chapter Eighteen

I could almost think it's a trick of Chronos, but I've been here for three weeks already. Three perfect weeks, where Ben and I are already in a routine. After homework and archery every day, I go to watch his band rehearse, and once a week, I go to his house after dinner. Most nights we do mortie homework together then stargaze until it's time for him to go to work.

I'm in heaven.

Artemis and Mr. Gunner, on the other hand, are not. They fight every day about Mr. Gunner's use of sights, his draw and release, and, today, about stance. It never ends. The good news is that Artemis has never seemed more engaged in a task. The bad news is that Mr. Gunner is no closer to reaching fourteen hundred.

"Tony, if you will just angle that stupid foot forty-five degrees, you'll have more power."

"Cynthia," he counters, "power is not my problem. I need accuracy. And I get better accuracy with a more even stance."

When Deya and I are finished training on our own, we sit on the porch overlooking their training. They don't even pretend we're part of the process anymore, all the better for us. It's more fun to just watch them, anyway.

"So while you were off playing with your boyfriend last night," Deya says, "I popped back home and got the answer from Thrax about Ben's dad."

"You did? And?"

She shakes her head, looking down at our arguing teachers. "Nothing. Looks like he's just a run-of-the-mill horndog who couldn't keep it in his pants when he saw a hot younger woman."

I snarl. "What a pig."

"Yeah. Sorry. And I'm sorry for Ben and his family, too. I know you were counting on something more there."

"I was, but it was a reach. Besides, it means a lot to me that you cared enough to follow up with Thrax, of all people. Are you okay?"

She waves a hand. "I told you already, I'm fine." Before I can follow up, she continues. "Anyway, you know what this means, right? We're back to square one with the middle part of the prophecy." I hit my head on the railing. "Are you sure it couldn't be Ro?"

"No, I'm not sure. But it just doesn't feel right, you know? It's not like you were about to stick her with just anyone. You were messing with me to get a reaction. How are you doing with her, anyway?"

"Really good. I've given her a couple of nudges, and she's been a lot more open with him the last few times he's been there. He only delivers twice a week, but those deliveries are taking a lot longer." She smiles, and I think wistfully of a time when matches used to mean that much to me. I'm glad Deya has this, her calling.

"Well done, Miss Match," I say, meaning it.

A pink tinge blushes her cheeks. "So how are you feeling, not being on match duty? Your dad still hasn't sent you a new assignment?"

"No. I'm not complaining, but it's a little odd, isn't it? This weekend, he just told me to focus my energy on doing what I feel is right."

"Seriously? What does that even mean? Your dad is the king of parent code."

"I know. So I'm not worrying about it. Ben has been writing more songs than ever, and he says it's all because of me." My heart swells over the fact. Being a muse is so much more fulfilling than I ever thought it could be. "In fact, they're playing another show this Friday night. They're the first band opening up for an actual tour. It was a last-minute cancellation by another band, but it's still huge for them."

In fact, it's so big, that Zoe and her Amazon friend came up to Ben at school today and told him they'd heard his big news. Zoe and Ben have been avoiding each other lately, gym class aside. But not today. Zoe was thrilled, asking questions and congratulating him profusely. He blushed and beamed and stammered a thank you back, all while holding my hand.

I'm not going to lie: it was awkward.

"Speaking of Ben, I actually need to run to their rehearsal, and you should come. Ben likes you. He's always asking why you don't hang out with us."

She glances down at Artemis and Mr. Gunner. They're standing side by side, firing off arrows in rapid succession, and arguing the whole time. I've come home from studying at Ben's house to find them still arguing out there.

"Yeah, that sounds like fun. I'm in."

The guys are on fire at rehearsal. They can feel it, too. There's an energy to everything they play, and they've never sounded better. They're on such a roll that Paresh's mom and little sister actually come out to watch them play, bringing Deya, Isa, and me snacks. When they see the food, the guys suggest taking a break. Ben puts down his guitar and comes straight over to us, his eyes alive. He picks up Isa and twirls her around, then grabs the ball of spicy fried potato goodness from her hand and pops it in his mouth.

"Hey!" she protests. She walks over to the snack tray Mrs. Kapur left and grabs another *bonda*, as Deya and I do the same. Ben lounges on a couch in the garage, so I drop down beside him, slinging my legs over his legs. Shaggy and Paresh start talking to Deya about Mr. Gunner mentoring us, and Ben and I just listen as Deya makes up a story about how we got started in archery that has nothing to do with an Oracle.

The truth that Deya dances around is so simple, yet this is one of a million conversations I will never have with Ben, whether I fulfill the prophecy ten days or ten years from now. It hurts hiding my heart and my real life from him. The longer we're together, the harder this will get. Already, I struggle to remember that an arrow was ever involved in our match. It feels real. So real.

Shoot. What is he saying? They've moved on from archery and are talking about . . . quick memory check . . . got it. The influence of hip-hop on the musical *Hamilton.*

"I can't believe you don't know this, Kali," he says. "Notorious B.I.G.? The Ten Duel Commandments come straight from him."

"Lyrically, yeah, but the arrangement, the way the hi-hat is so persistent and almost aggressive? That's so Jay Z," I say without thinking.

"Dude, that's totally true." Paresh nods at Ben. "You just got schooled."

Red splotches climb up Ben's neck, and I want to rip my cursing tongue out. This is how I talk to Hector, not Ben. I try smiling, but I can see that he's upset. In the last couple of weeks, I've noticed he does *not* like someone knowing more about music than him. Which is hard, considering I know a lot more about music than he does. So I've found myself lying a lot. I hate lying, and it seems like I'm doing it to everyone around me these days.

I think fast. "In fact, I wouldn't have noticed it if you hadn't been listening to Jay Z the other night while we were studying. I remember you talking about how Jay Z has impacted so many artists, and then you were beating your thumb along with the hi-hat. I hadn't even noticed it before. You always seem to be able to pick out the layers in a song. Like, weren't you saying the horn part in 'The Schuyler Sisters' is from the Beastie Boys?"

None of this ever happened, but it's close enough to something he could say that I hope he'll accept it and let it go.

Paresh and Shaggy pull up the track and listen for the horn, and all the guys nod in unison when they hear it. Then they move on.

Thank Gaia.

A few minutes later, the movement of Deya's feet tells me she's bored with this conversation. She jumps up.

"Hey, I have a wild idea." Everyone looks at her. "Let's go do karaoke somewhere."

"Karaoke?" Shaggy asks. But he's only pretending to be skeptical. He's already breaking down and putting away equipment. The chance to spend more time with Deya is a chance he can't pass up.

"I don't know," Paresh says. "The show is tomorrow. I think we need run through our set at least once more."

"Oh, come on," Shaggy says. "We've put in enough time to do this show in our sleep. Let's go."

I look at Ben, who shrugs, and Isa, who begs to come with us. "I don't mind if you don't," I tell him.

"I'll see if my mom can pick her up at . . . Deya, where are we going?"

"The Pizza Box, just south of Heritage Square. They have all-ages karaoke from five to ten," she says. I smile. It's Restaurant Owner's place. She must have her match planned for tonight.

We all head over, and Ben and Isa join Deya and me in her Jeep. Ben white-knuckles it the whole way to the restaurant, despite Isa's wild laughter in the front seat. "She really is worse than you," he says when we finally reach the parking lot.

The restaurant is busy, but we only have to wait for a few minutes to get seated. The karaoke is already in full swing, although it's not even six, and there's enough alcohol being served over in the bar to ensure a line for the microphone. We put our names on the list and sit at one of the tables near the back of the main dining room.

We order a couple of pizzas and the guys and their sisters watch the karaoke while Deya and I watch for Ro. Isa gives me running commentary on the singers, occasionally holding her phantom microphone up to me to get my opinion on the performance.

Then Isa gets breathless. "OHMYGOSH!" she says, fanning her face. "It's Stone Savage! He won two Teen Choice Awards last year—one for best bone structure, and one for lips we most want to kiss! Stone freaking Savage!"

Um . . .

A voice I know almost as well as my own intrudes my thoughts. I look up through the dim restaurant in shock at the lighted karaoke stage to where someone starts singing Backstreet Boys' "Everybody (Backstreet's Back)" so flawlessly, I have to wonder if I'm dreaming.

"Ferry me to Hades, is that . . ." Deya starts.

"Yeah."

Hector, along with a couple of other guys. But he's the only one doing the actual choreography from the music video. I can't help it: I giggle.

"Kal?" Ben asks, pulling my attention from the stage. "Do you know that guy, or something?"

I nod. Isa turns on me, her eyes wide. "The super hot guy singing? You know him? He's with Stone Savage! I saw all these guys get up from Stone's table in the front!" She points to a table where an attractive Viking of a man sits with a bunch of people who seem to think he's important. Stone Savage. The megalomaniacal lead in the show Ben is musing for. But I thought they were in Phoenix. What are they doing here?

Hector and his crew finish to raucous applause and more than a few whistles from a table of college-aged girls at the bar. As a Muse, Hector has to be not only visible, but appealing to mortals. So his anti-glamour is something like what Deya consents to—it simply makes him super hot for a mortal rather than deadly hot as an immortal. I feel a pang looking at the little changes he's made to his face. It feels wrong to see him look different, not because I care that he's less hot, but because I don't know this Hector.

Beside me, Ben seems to grow in size. I swear, I can actually *feel* him getting jealous.

"How do you know him?" he asks.

"We're friends from home," I say, trying to act as if I'm not thrown by seeing him here. "He's a really good guy. He's a personal assistant for a TV producer."

Ben hunches over his Dr. Pepper. "Are you sure he's not the star of some reality show? Or, I don't know, a European model? That seems more in line with your past."

Whoa. Major brood coming on. "He'd laugh to hear you say

that," I say lightly. "You'd like him. You guys actually have a lot in common. He's a huge music fan."

Before I can hear his sarcastic retort, Deya tugs my arm. Thank Gaia. "It's our turn. Come on."

"Our turn?"

"Yes." She pulls me through the crowds and hefts me up to the stage. "What are we even singing?"

Extreme's "More than Words" starts playing, and in spite of myself, I smile. I know it's cheesy, but this is my jam. The lyrics flash on a tiny screen in front of us, but we don't need them. We look at each other and start singing, alternating lines and harmonies as if we've done this a thousand times. We're both good singers, but I suspect the reaction in the dining room has more to do with two pretty girls singing than the singing itself.

I look back at Ben, and he's still upset. A flash of irritation comes over me. Whatever, Ben. I'm having fun. Isabella and Paresh's sister are standing up and dancing as if we're rockstars. And as we work the room, I can't help but turn to Hector's table, where Hector's smiling up at us. If we surprised him by being here, he's not showing it. The punk. He's just shimmying in his chair to the music, enjoying the show.

We hit the final line, singing it in perfect harmony to wild applause. Deya curtseys to the room, and we leave the stage. Because they're right in front of us, we stop at Hector's table first. He stands up and hugs Deya and then me. I can't help but notice how quickly he breaks our hug. "Nicely done, ladies. Let me introduce you to my table." He does, and we smile and wave and thank them for their compliments. Stone Savage eyes Deya like she's his next prey. She looks closer to twenty than mortie sixteen, but still. What a titan-sized douche.

When Hector introduces us to his producer, a short, balding man, I shake his hand and tell him how highly Hector speaks of him. He thanks me and Hector escorts us away from the table before Stone can grab either of our butts. "What are you doing here?" I ask him as we weave through the crowd. Hector is about to put his hand on my elbow, but I take a big step forward. I know he's just being a gentleman, but Ben won't see it this way. I don't look at Hector. I don't want to see the hurt on his face.

"The show is going to be shooting here for the next couple of weeks," he explains, "I would have texted you, but I didn't know if we'd even run into each other. I should have figured."

"Well, now you can meet Ben!" Deya says brightly. She steps between Hector and me just before we get to the table. I stand by a now fully brooding Ben, who rises to meet me.

Ah, Styx and ferries.

Deya introduces Hector around, and when he gets to Ben, Hector stretches his hand out.

"Hey, man. I'm Hector. Good to meet you."

Ben shakes the offered hand. "Likewise. I'm Ben, Kali's boyfriend."

They keep shaking hands for a moment, and I hope to Hades that Ben isn't doing something stupid like trying to out-handshake a god. But Ben looks like he's ready to take on the world, including the bigger, infinitely stronger specimen in from of him. Meanwhile, Hector's jaw is tight—the only indication of how upset he is to hear Ben call me his girlfriend.

This is bad.

They drop their hands. Ben flexes his a little. Oh, Gaia. The Gorgon turd tried to out-handshake a god. This is worse than bad.

"So you're a musician," Hector says. I haven't told him, but

Hector has a sixth sense about these kinds of things (literally—it's part of his calling).

"Kali's told you about me, huh?" Ben says. "Funny that she hasn't told me anything about you."

"Ben—" I say sharply, tugging on his arm.

"That is funny," Hector says in a tone too easy to be real. "She probably didn't want you to worry."

"Why would I worry?" Ben asks with the darkly furrowed brow of someone who is worried.

"I'm sure you wouldn't. You two are adorable together. You have nothing to worry about," Hector says.

"And the gold medal in the head games goes to . . ." Deya whispers so quietly only I can hear. And Hector, judging by the small gleam in his eye. How dare he enjoy himself?

Ben puts his arm around my shoulders, and I'm annoyed enough I have to stop myself from breaking it off and smacking him with it. "No, I don't," Ben says. "You know, my band is playing tomorrow. You should come. We're opening for Tub Snacks."

"Wow, good for you guys," Hector says, the first genuine thing he's said to Ben. Maybe this night can be saved after all. "I'd love to come."

Maybe not.

"Are you sure you aren't busy with work?" I ask Hector in a super subtle yet obviously pointed manner.

"What kind of best friend would I be if I didn't make time to see your boyfriend in concert?"

Before I can answer—"the best kind"—we're interrupted by . . . Ia-cursing-nira.

"Oh, hey, Kal! Sorry to break up the party," she says in a sweetly apologetic tone that is just complete crap. "Hec, the food has arrived," she says, leaning in to him closer than she needs to. "I thought you'd want to know."

"Yeah, thanks, 'Nira." Because they have nicknames, apparently. He puts his hand on her lower back. My gut bubbles, and I could spit fire. How has this night become the absolute cursing worst? "I'm going to head back to my table. See you around, Ben."

"Remember about tomorrow night," Ben says, as if he actually wants him at the concert.

Hector smiles that same false smile. "I'll catch a ride with Kali and Deya."

He whispers something to Ianira so quietly, not even I can hear them. She laughs and says she'll see him back at the table in a minute.

He's walking away when I call out. "Hector, wait!"

What am I doing?

Ben's arm tightens, but I can't stop myself. My eyes dart around the table before meeting Hector's intensely questioning gaze. I feel like Python has been resurrected and is squeezing my insides.

"Um, the girls were really hoping to get Stone's autograph. Do you think you could hook them up?"

His eyes tear from mine. Then he's grinning at the bouncing girls. "Yeah, of course." Deya goes with him to take Isa and Paresh's sister up to his table, and I watch their wide eyes and glowing smiles as Stone wows them. Inexplicably, Ianira hangs back at our table. Even though I hate it, I introduce her to everyone. "Guys, this is Ianira, another friend from home." I don't even choke on the word friend. How's that for maturity?

"Lovely meeting all of you," she says, playing with her slick, high ponytail. The horrible, vindictive part of me that I keep buried deep inside is actually jealous that, in mortal form, Ianira is more beautiful than I am. It makes me want to shake off my anti-glamour and torch her with my glory.

"You're with Stone Savage's crew? What do you do, Ianira?" Ben asks more sociably than I would have expected. Is he batting his eyes?

"I'm a lab assistant for Dr. Chen at ASU—"

"The evolutionary biology guru?" Paresh interrupts, practically drooling. "But you're, like, our age. How?"

"I got my PhD when I was fourteen," she smirks. And, okay, this is technically true, but when you consider just how old our fourteen is to mortals, this isn't remotely impressive. There's a good reason I don't have a mortie Master's or PhD: I'm not trying to prove to Olympus what a colossal tool I am. Getting mortal degrees in things mortals know a tiny fraction about? Come on. "Dr. Chen has been asked to consult with Stone's television show, so they invited us up for the week."

When Hector returns to the table, the girls are so excited, they're only talking in squeals now. "Ready, Nira?" Hector asks her. She puts a hand on his chest and makes her goodbyes to our table. I want to end her.

"It was good seeing you," Hector says to Deya and me. He nods to Ben and the guys. Then he puts a hand on Ianira's elbow—her elbow!—and accompanies her back to his table.

No, *their* table. Because Ianira is with him. Gaia, I hate her. From her stupid leggings to her cute tunic to the fabulous embroidered gold belt that just ties the whole thing together to . . . to her stupid face.

"I like her," Ben says, smiling at their retreating forms. No doubt, he thinks they're a couple, which is why he's so happy. "She's cool."

"And wicked hot," Shaggy says. Paresh and Ben nod. "I mean, wickedly, tragically hot."

Deya and I just look at each other.

Eventually, Ben's mom comes to pick up the girls, and the guys' turn at the mic comes. They go up to the stage where the Beastie Boys are blaring from the speakers. Ben's swagger is back, and the guys do a perfect rendition of "(You Gotta) Fight for Your Right (to Party)." Hector and Ianira cheer as loudly as anyone.

When the guys return to their seats, they're triumphant. Ben gives me a sloppy kiss and says, "I'd like to see your boy top that."

It is everything I can do not to shoot him with an arrow. And not the love kind.

Chapter Nineteen

"**How was your** night?" Artemis asks us at breakfast the next morning.

"Fine," I grumble.

"Just super," Deya groans. Delivery Guy didn't show last night, so her match is still pending.

Artemis hums to herself while she throws together breakfast.

It's a few moments before I realize that she's humming. "Why are you so chipper?"

She adds dashes of herbs to what will soon be breakfast burritos. "No reason."

I bump Deya's leg with mine. "How are things going with Mr. G?"

"He has to be the most stubborn mortal I've ever met. Do you know that he refuses to try hummus? Who takes such a ridiculous stance about a condiment?"

When did they start talking about something like that? Wheels turn in my head. "That's funny," I say. "You should have him try some of yours. He won't turn it down after that."

She tosses her hands in the air. "That's what I told him. He said he'd try it, but only if I go hunting with him *and* use a rifle. I told him I'd never shoot one of those cursed things, and he called me a softie."

"You? A softie?" Deya asks.

"I know. Besides, I can hardly explain that I'm aware of the exact balance of animal life the Earth needs at any given moment and that I only hunt to maintain that balance. Trust me, if he'd been lectured by Mother Gaia for millennia on end, he'd do what she asks, too." She scrambles the eggs. "Anyway, what do you two have planned for today?"

"School. Deya's match, because he was a no-show last night. Oh, and Hector's in town. He'll be coming to Ben's gig with us tonight. You should come."

She gives an aloof shrug, but I know seeing her nephew is pretty good enticement. "Maybe."

Our chitchat lasts until it's time for school. As soon as Deya and I head out to the car, she says, "You're still thinking it, aren't you?"

I grin and climb into the passenger side, covering my mouth so Helios doesn't see. "Mr. G and *Cynthia*? Totally."

She sighs, but she doesn't argue. By the time we get to school, we're both in better moods. We climb out of the Jeep, and Ben isn't waiting for me in the parking lot like he usually does. He isn't by our lockers, either. I don't see him until I get into homeroom, where he's talking animatedly to Zoe.

When the bell rings, he smiles at me and takes his seat. But there's no flirting. No love notes. Just class. Which, let me tell you, is boring. We've moved past Ancient Greece to the fall of Rome and, although this is normally one of my favorite topics, my heart isn't in it.

By the time PE rolls around, it's obvious that Ben is still upset about Hector. The only time he talks directly to me, it's to make snide comments about things like how much cooler the Beastie Boys are than the Backstreet Boys. As if Hector wasn't being ironic and hilarious. But when we get out to the archery field, I turn my thoughts to Mr. Gunner. Deya and I head over to him before the rest of the class has filed in.

"Hey, Mr. G!" Deya says. "What's the story with you hating hummus?"

He shakes his head, grabbing gear. "She told you I hate it? I don't hate it. I just think it's overrated for a condiment. And she's one to talk. She's never even tried salsa before. Did you two know that?"

We look at each other, confused. "Yes, she has. She made us breakfast burritos this morning with homemade pineapple mango salsa," I say.

A smile creeps over his face. "That little . . ." he laughs. "She was messing with me."

Ben and Shaggy walk out to the field with Zoe. When she sees us, we wave to each other, and she steers the boys in our direction. "So, Mr. Gunner, are you going to support your students tonight?" Zoe ask as Mr. Gunner sets up the targets.

"In what?"

"We're the first band opening up for Tub Snacks tonight," Ben says. "You should come check us out, Mr. Gunner. You're not so old that you don't know how to rock, are you?"

Mr. Gunner snorts. "Please. I've forgotten more cool bands than you know."

We all laugh. "Then you'll come, right?" Shaggy asks.

He hems and haws. "Aunt Cynthia's even coming," I tell him. "You don't want to not like hummus *and* not like cool music, do you?"

The bell rings. "I'll think about it," he says.

Good enough for me.

It takes Hector swinging by the house to convince Artemis to come with us to the concert, but she finally consents. I'm annoyed that he's here, but glad, too. Artemis wouldn't have an excuse otherwise. I get ready in a snap, wearing a T-shirt of Ben's band with a big Sasquatch and several little ones following him. I concentrate on my hair for a moment longer than normal, so that the messy blonde waves are tamed prettily. When I walk out to the driveway and see Hector, I debate confronting him about deliberately baiting Ben last night. But a memory of him laughing with Ianira robs me of my voice.

"So. That was Ben," Hector says.

"Yep."

"And this isn't awkward at all," Deya says, pulling what I'm sure she thinks is an understated Hera. She hops in the passenger seat of the Jeep.

Hector and I share a tired glance, and I let my annoyance evaporate. Things may be different now, but he's still my best friend. "I like the face," he says.

I cock an eyebrow. "Yeah?"

"Yeah," he says. "I like seeing the mortal faces we immortals give ourselves. They say a lot about a person."

"What does your face say?"

"That I'm someone you can trust," he says. I squint, but I see what he means. His face is a little broader than normal, his features a little softer. His green eyes are less striking. He's still crazy hot by mortal standards, but it's a face you'd share your darkest secrets with. I shift, thinking about how I haven't told him my secret yet, despite swearing I would.

"And, uh, what does my face say?"

"That you like freckles."

A laugh escapes me. "I do. They're fun. Like a little puzzle on the face that I want to connect. You should get some freckles."

"I'll think about it."

Artemis comes out of the ranch looking showstopping. Her outfit is nothing special: jeans, a fitted white T-shirt, and sassy biker boots, but somehow, she is a force of nature. Her auburn curls frame her face perfectly, showing off cheekbones that could cut glass. Mr. Gunner won't know what hit him.

The concert is at an outdoor theater that seats a few thousand people. The area is beautiful, surrounded by pines and aspens. The frosty night air doesn't deter people from arriving early, but I'm still glad I brought Ben's jacket. When I get down to the roped-off stage, the guys are setting up.

"Hey!" I shout over the music. "Ben!"

He looks around, then spots me. His eyes light up, and I find myself both relieved that he's stopped pouting and annoyed by my relief, considering I did nothing wrong. "Kali! Isn't this amazing? We just met Tub Snacks, and they were so cool! I'll find you when we're done, okay?"

"Okay!"

When I turn around, it's to bump into Zoe and her friends. Amazon looks down her nose at me, but Zoe smiles. "Hi, Kali. Great turnout, isn't it?"

"Yeah, I think the show's going to be great!"

"Yeah, totally!" She fidgets with a lock of hair. "Hey, so did Ben's dad make it, do you know?"

Huh? I frown. "I, uh . . ."

She looks past me to Ben, misreading my frown. "Poor Ben. I know how much he was hoping his dad would come, for a change. Heaven forbid the guy tear himself away from his child fiancée to support his son." What is going on here? I nod, speechless. With a sad smile, she says, "Well, we're just going to go wish the guys good luck. See you later."

As she descends on Ben with her kind wishes and good intentions, I stomp back to my friends. My boyfriend is telling another girl intensely personal information without breathing a word of it to me. My heart hurts. My throat goes tight. I feel betrayed.

"So, that looks like it went well," Deya says under her breath. I drop onto the blanket beside her.

"This is a disaster, Dey." Tears fill my eyes, and I tell her about what just happened. People fill up around us, and soon Hector and Artemis join us on the blanket.

Deya drops her voice so I can barely hear her. "I'm not defending what he did, but they've been friends for years. He obviously relies on her for emotional support. And if it bothers you, get the prophecy fulfilled already. You do remember that an arrow caused your match, right? You two didn't just meet and fall in love like two regular morties."

Um. So, I may have forgotten that a little.

"Kali," Deya says in an exasperated huff. She looks at Artemis and Hector, making sure they're in their own conversation, before turning back to me. "You need to figure out this prophecy and reclaim your heart sooner rather than later. You heard what your dad told Teresa. You've known it since you were a first-year: a bad match is like an addiction. You and Ben have been fine so far, but it hasn't even been a month. If you're compatible, you can take your time fulfilling the prophecy, assuming you still want to." She continues over my protests. "If you aren't compatible, things will get ugly and uglier. If you don't leave before obsession takes over, you'll reach a point where you can't leave, even if you want to."

This sobering reminder is my last thought before Sasquatch and the Little Feet start their set and the noise blocks out everything else.

They start out with a peppy, hard jam that gets the crowd on their feet. I bury my hurt and try to enjoy the music. By their third song, all is forgotten. Deya, Hector, and I make our way over to the stage, bumping into Zoe and her friends on the way through the crowd. We edge up as close as we can to the front, cheering and dancing with abandon. I make a point, though, to stay far enough away from Hector so that I won't upset Ben. I keep my eyes locked on his, although I doubt he can even see me.

The farther they get into their set, the more the crowd responds to them. When they do a cover of the Smiths, everyone cheers. Ben sings this one, Shaggy's voice not having the right tone to pull off the cover. But Ben . . . his voice strikes my soul. Watching him, all of my frustration and sadness over the last twenty-four hours melts away, replaced with pride and awe. I didn't know he'd hoped his dad would be here, but knowing this, his overreactions and general edginess since last night make sense. This is one of the biggest moments of his life, and he wants to share it with the people he loves.

As they end their cover, they transition into Ben's new song, "Across the Stars." And, drown me in the Styx, it is beautiful. Just sweet and soulful and still edgy enough to be cool. Like something Death Cab for Cutie wishes they'd written. And the best part is that I inspired it.

Me.

The crowd goes absolutely wild for it, and when the guys leave the stage, they're called out for an encore. I scream louder than anyone. They come back and play "Lovestruck," and I forgive the arrow for matching us.

When the song ends and the guys leave the stage to wild applause, Hector cups his hand to my ear. His breath causes the hair on my head to stir, tickling my cheek. "You were right, Kal. They're good. They could be huge."

"Kali inspired those last two songs," Deya says.

The look in his eyes could turn me to stone. "I'm not surprised."

We return to our blanket to find Artemis talking to a lounging Mr. Gunner. I squeeze Deya's hand. Like Artemis, he's in a T-shirt and jeans. Without the hat covering his blond hair, he looks downright handsome. Artemis sees us, and grins. "Look who found us."

We plop down to the blanket. "Hey, Mr. G. Great set, right?" Deya says.

"I'm impressed," he admits. "And I'm relieved I won't have to lie to them on Monday." We laugh, and Hector takes the opportunity to introduce himself as a friend of ours. He seems uncharacteristically reserved. Hesitant, even. Through the next set, he watches his aunt and Mr. Gunner, who are laughing and fighting over the music.

Just before the main band is set to go on, Ben makes his way over to us. "Hey," he says, running over to me. I jump up and give him a big hug. "So?"

"You guys ROCKED!" I pull him away from my friends. "Everyone was feeling it!"

"I know, right? It's like a dream, how good it went! Tub Snacks' manager came over after the set, and everything. He said he loved our two new songs, and he thinks if we released 'Across the Stars' and 'Lovestruck' as singles, we'd blow up online." He grabs my shoulders and plants a kiss on me. "Kal, he wants to talk to us Monday. And I have you to thank for it!"

I flush, a nice, warm glow that makes my whole body tingle. "Me?"

"Yes, you! Kalixta Olympos, you beautiful creature, you are my inspiration. My muse! Everything I've written since I met you is gold."

The sounds around me fade away, and I catch a glimpse of him—not a soulgaze, but a peek of his struggle within. A fire burns inside of him, fiercely proud, roaring for approval, hungry to prove itself. If not checked, it will consume everything and everyone, including him. But if contained, it will make him stronger, refine him.

I put my hands on either side of his face, desperate to contain the flames. "You were incredible, Ben. You guys are going to be huge one day; I just know it. I am so proud of you; everyone here is proud of you. And anyone who doesn't support you can . . . I don't know, crap on a turd for all I care." He laughs, but his eyes are dancing. "I am so proud of you."

His smile reaches his eyes, and the fire inside of him swells. He wraps me tightly in his arms. As the music starts and everyone gets to their feet, he whispers, "Thank you. You can't know how much that means to me."

When Ben and I have our goodbye kiss for the weekend, it is so good and so real, I barely notice the weekend away from him. I smile through my conversations with my parents. I let Aphrodite gush about how she watched Ben's band and they were sooo good and she's sure anyone who plays with passion like that must be incredible at all sorts of things. I smile dreamily while I watch Teresa at sparring practice take down three opponents with a single sweep kick, and I don't even blink during my lecture from Cosmo about how hard we've been on our cars and how we need to better maintain our equipment. I hardly have the capacity to wonder where Deya is.

The kiss was just that good.

It isn't until Sunday night that anything can snap me out of my love daze. Hector shows up at my house unannounced, as usual. My parents are ecstatic to see him, inviting him to stay for dinner. He's a sucker for my dad's ahi tuna, so he does. They ask him questions about his current musing, and he entertains them with stories about the obnoxious Stone Savage.

When dinner is over, my mom sends Hector and me outside to "catch up." As soon as we're outdoors, Hector puts a hand on my shoulder.

"We have a problem, Kal."

"What?" Sometimes I think Hector is a little too even-tempered to be a god. I feel strongly about virtually everything. Like Canadian potato chips being vastly superior to American ones. I could go on about that for an hour. Unlike most of our kind, Hector isn't prone to hysterics or dramatics or even mild outbursts. If he says we have a problem, we have a problem.

He exhales forcefully. "It's Artemis."

"What? What do you mean? Did something happen to her? Hector, what's going on?"

His face turns to stone. "I should ask you the same question. What in Gaia's name are you up to?"

"I—I don't know what you mean. There's nothing going on," I say weakly.

"Don't lie to me, Kali. You swore on the Styx that you'd tell me what you're doing."

"I know, but . . . but why now? Why can't it wait until I've had a chance to fix everything? I'll tell you everything then! Why does it suddenly matter so much?"

I've never seen him this upset. His hands are balled into fists, and cords of muscle stick out in his forearms. "It matters because Artemis went out tonight. On a date."

A date? I want to squeal! "But that's perfect! What's the problem—" I throw my hands over my mouth. No. No, no, no. "Hector, how did you know that she went on a date? Did she tell you? Who told you?"

He leans down so our faces are almost touching. Torchlight flickers in his eyes, making his impossibly thick lashes look like they're spitting fire. "My dad."

Chapter Twenty

I tell Hector everything. About the prophecy, the players, and even, to my own shock, about the Fates. When I mention the old crones, he grabs my shoulders, forcing me to look into his eyes. He isn't just angry, he's terrified.

"Please tell me you didn't, Kali. Tell me you didn't tempt the Fates," he begs.

A shudder runs down my spine as I remember the sound of the scissors cutting the piece of thread. In my mind's eye, I see its thick, interlocked fibers glisten with countless sparks of life that I can't quite focus on. I recount my conversation with the Moirai to him in exacting detail. "I'm sorry I didn't tell you," I whisper.

"So you're doing all of this to . . . to reverse the spell?" I don't know how to interpret his tone or the look in his eyes. Hope? Concern? Regret? "No, don't answer that." He steps back, rubbing a hand over his face. "The Fates, did they say anything else? Did they do anything else?"

I give a weak, nervous laugh. "They told me they liked me."

He breathes out a curse in Ancient Greek, looking like he's holding himself back from hugging me. It wouldn't be the worst thing if he did. "Only you could tell the Fates that you don't like them and they'd like you for it. So they just gave you this thread? Whose is it?"

"I don't know. No one's. They said it was just a thread."

"Can I see it?"

I reach into my pocket and of course, it's there. But when I hold it out to him, I hesitate. It feels like I'm showing him something I shouldn't. Something so personal, that once he sees it, I can never take it back. He tenderly grabs it from my palm, his fingers grazing my skin, leaving a trail of heat. I watch him study the heavy thread, feeling oddly self-conscious. Then I study it, too. I focus on a single strand of the thread, and countless sparks of life flash before my eyes. So many sparks that I can't process anything that I'm seeing. I rub my eyes, then look at him. He blinks at it.

"It really is just a thread?"

"I don't know. The Fates gave it to me like it was the funniest thing in the heavens."

He narrows his eyes, concentrating harder. Then he shakes his head. "I don't know what to even think, but we can figure that out later. We need to let Artemis know about my dad."

"Okay," I agree. "Can you contact Deya? Have her meet us at the Port?"

He nods and closes his eyes. I really need to learn this trick already.

"She'll meet us there in fifteen minutes. Let's go."

We leave a note for my parents and get to the Port as quickly as we can. On the way, Hector asks me to repeat the prophecy.

"'To reclaim thy heart eternally, thou must complete these tasks three: heal the heart of a desperate maiden; restore to greatness a fallen champion; and save a soul from an unjust union. Should success be thine, thy destiny wilt thou find.'" I take a long, steadying breath before continuing. "'But beware the eye of the jealous son, lest thy quest for heart end in none.'"

Hector repeats the last line. "So you guys think it's Thrax?"

"I don't know. Deya does. I think I'm missing something. Again. Like I'm missing everything lately."

We arrive at the Port at the same time as Deya, though she looks flushed, as if she's been running. Or crying? I narrow my eyes, but she turns her head away from me. And it's then, when her caramel hair is flipping around her face, that I see a red mark on her neck.

It's a hickey.

Hector quickly explains the situation to Deya. When he mentions his father, though, no further explanation is needed. We get into position, grabbing our necklaces—Hector's thin gold chain bears a single scroll—then we vanish and reappear in the kitchen of the O-Ranch.

I'm about to call out to Artemis when I see movement outside on the porch. No lights are on out there, but with a full moon and immortal eyes, we don't need it. Clear as day, we see Artemis and Mr. Gunner.

Kissing.

Deya, Hector, and I look at each other, speechless. After several heartbeats, I have an idea. I drag them to the front door and open it, turning on the lights to make a show of us coming home. We stomp our feet on the mat and talk and laugh at nothing. But it's enough. Artemis and Mr. Gunner break apart and she shoos him down the porch stairs.

The three of us go into the kitchen and, a few moments later, Artemis walks in. She can't know that her face is red from all the kissing or she'd magick it clear. "Hey, what brings you three home early?"

Home? She's already referring to O-Ranch as "home"?

"Aunt Artemis," Hector says softly, "we know about Tony."

She tosses her head innocently. "What do you mean? That we went hunting today?" Hector doesn't answer. "Well, if you know anything, then you should know that guy couldn't shoot a deer if it . . ." She stops, looking at her nephew. Her façade crumbles. "Your dad—"

"You need to talk to him. Soon, Aunt Artemis."

Words tumble from her mouth. "Is he going to do anything to Tony?"

"I don't know. I haven't seen him this upset since my mom left. I tried to talk to him, but he wouldn't listen. You need to talk to him as soon as you can. Keep him from doing something he shouldn't do."

Heartbreak doesn't describe what I see on Artemis' face. It's torture. It's pure despair. It's the culminating hopelessness of eons. Her youthful, vibrant face has been stripped of everything. All that remains is a dark, endless, joyless pit where nothing lives or grows. I see this blackness overshadow her soul as plainly as the tears rolling down her face.

"Do I have time to say goodbye?" she whispers.

Hector can't meet her eyes. "I'm so sorry, Aunt Artemis. He's—"

She nods. "I know. I-I'll take care of your dad." The rawness in her voice can only come from millennia of crying. She grasps her Orion necklace and looks at me. "Please, watch out for Tony for me. Tell him"—she sobs—"tell him I'm sorry."

With a final hiccupping sob, she's gone.

Hector looks as devastated as I feel. "This is wrong," I say, my voice choked with emotion. "He can't just keep them apart like this."

"It's not just being kept apart that I'm worried about," he says.

He bends down over the kitchen counter, dropping his head in his palms. Deya paces, folding her arms tightly around herself.

I want to say something, to rally their spirits, to give us all hope. But nothing comes. I feel as lost and alone as they look.

The sound of a cell phone vibrating pulls me out of my head. I reach for my phone on the counter at the same time Hector does. It's not mine. He swipes at the screen then, after a pause, he half-smiles.

"Who's that?" I ask. Who could make him almost smile after something so monumental just happened? Other than me?

He waves a hand and stows his phone in the back of his jeans. "No one. But now that I'm on Earth, I should probably get back to my assignment."

I gape at him. He gives Deya a quick hug, then comes over to me, putting a hand on my chin to lift my face to his. He's so steady, so strong. I don't want to face whatever's next without him. "I'll be here for the next few weeks, so shoot me a text anytime, okay? I can be here whenever you need me."

He squeezes my shoulders and then, just like his aunt, he disappears. Just when I was about to tell him that I need him *now*.

I can't believe what's happening. If he had pulled Medusa's severed head out of a bag and showed it to me, I couldn't be more stunned than I am right now. I stumble over to the counter and fall onto a stool.

"What am I supposed to do?" I wonder aloud. I turn to Deya. "Hector just abandoned me in my time of need for someone else. And not just any someone: it's Ianira. It has to be."

Deya nods distractedly, still hugging herself. She's in a daze, staring off into space with a haunted look. "Dey? Are you all right?"

After a pause that feels like minutes, she forces her eyes to mine. "No."

"Is this about whoever gave you that hickey?" I ask softly.

Her hand flies to her neck, and she gives me a defensive look. "What, so you suddenly care about *my* problems?"

"What are you talking about? Of course I care."

"Like you cared when my mom humiliated me in front of my best friends? Like you cared when I ran off? You didn't even come get me yourself, Kali. Your dad did! What, did you and my mom just keep gossiping about me behind my back? How could you do that? With my own mother!"

Horror overcomes me. "Deya, no! That's not what happened."

Tears pour from her eyes. "Save it. Don't pretend you care now when you didn't care that I went to Thrax to get the information *you* needed about Ben's slimy dad," she snarls so intensely, I lean back. "Just like you didn't care enough to even wonder how I managed to convince Thrax to give us any information at all!" More tears, now. So many more. "You have no idea what I sacrificed, Kali! Did you even notice that Cosmo hasn't talked to me in weeks? That he refuses to answer me directly? Did you think to wonder why? No! Because you don't care that Cosmo caught me with Thrax! You didn't care what I was doing!" Her beautiful face is twisted in loathing. I barely recognize her. "Why didn't you care? Were you too busy worrying about whether Ben was flirting with his own match?" she screams. My stomach tightens. "You haven't cared about my life since you first laid eyes on Ben. Don't pretend you care now!" she cries. She runs out of the kitchen, shouting, "And don't you dare follow me."

I stare at her running form, my pulse racing, pounding in my ears. But I don't follow her.

I don't dare.

I lean back against the cool refrigerator door and slide down until I've dropped to the hardwood. My world is crumbling around me. I clutch my head, powerless to stop the bleak thoughts that crash against my mind like tidal waves. The dark waves rush over me, pull me under, and drag me down to the depths of my most hidden thoughts, to the last time I felt this low, to the event that set me on the path leading to this moment.

The Thunderclap.

It was months ago, and Deya and I were vying for the top spot in our year. We were doing better than some sixth-year probies. I was with Hector—the love of my life—and I was as happy as any immortal in history. I had just been assigned a match in a small town in France with a young French woman with a heart so kind, it was like she had a light on inside her. She was a primary school teacher with a troubled past, but she had fought valiantly to move past the abuse that had plagued her childhood. Her private nature made learning about her personality hard, so I was given permission to become visible. It's rare, but it happens, especially when a probie's track record is as good as mine was.

One afternoon, she was at a café preparing her lesson when my QM implanted a backstory in her head that included me at her summer art camp when she was a teenager. Elodie—the young woman—greeted me like an old friend, and we ended up talking for hours over espressos and macarons. She told me about her father—an alcoholic monster of a man—and the scars she had "earned" protecting her brother from him. In the course of my research, I had seen her visiting her brother, a young man with Down syndrome who lived on his own and worked stocking shelves at a local market. She talked about him with pride.

When we got on the subject of exes, she hemmed. I already

knew why: her last boyfriend was an alcoholic, just like her dad. They'd met their senior year of college and dated for four years, during which time he'd started drinking more and more. The first time he got rough with her, she moved out and he went to AA immediately. But he worked his way back into her good graces by convincing her that he was different than both their fathers. He'd messed up, but he was getting help. It would never happen again. He promised.

And it didn't happen again. Until it did.

By a stroke of mercy, after four years together, he left her for another woman. Elodie hadn't dated anyone seriously in a year. She'd been working on herself, she'd said. But I knew the truth here, too. She'd gone out with a handful of different guys, but the ones that kept drawing her attention were the ones who were damaged. The ones her subconscious wished she could fix. It was a miracle she hadn't gotten serious with any of them.

I loved Elodie. The more I spoke with her, the more I wanted to protect her and her broken heart. When she'd sent up her prayer for help, it had been an urgent plea to break her own dangerous cycle. She didn't know why she kept being drawn to the same type of man. She needed help.

And I was going to help her. Love was going to save her.

I poured myself into the match, devoting all of my free time to go beyond her neighborhood to research every person in her town. I must have soulgazed hundreds of potentials, and finally I found him: the manager of the *boulangerie* across town. He'd helped his brother get clean years earlier and now volunteered on weekends with a crisis center. His eyes turned dreamy when she came into his shop each week. I had prompted her to notice him, to talk to him, to go out of her way to get her brioche from him every morning before work. After two months, her heart was finally ready.

I was so eager to make the match that day in the bakery, so excited to bring her joy. My heart swelled as I watched them make eyes at each other in line. I took aim and fired. Impossibly out of nowhere, at the last possible moment, another man caught my target's eye. A charming, attractive, alcoholic monster of a man, just like her father. Exactly the type of guy she always went back to, the type of guy she hated herself for going back to. But while those past relationships had always ended, this one never would. They had made eye contact at the exact moment my arrow struck her.

The man flirted with Elodie in line and asked her out before she had even paid for her brioche. The manager watched it all unfold, looking heartstricken.

I was horrified.

I ported back home to my Dad, desperate for him to reverse the match. Because of course it could be reversed. I was using a training arrow. Training arrows were made to be reversed.

Except this one didn't work. After I tried, my dad tried. He tried again. Still nothing. Even Aphrodite was powerless to help. She told my dad that the woman's past had made her too vulnerable and that even the training arrow's spell was too powerful to overcome.

It was a snip of the scissors: a pairing so strong, the Fates themselves couldn't stop it.

I couldn't have done anything differently, my dad said. Some matches just didn't work out, he said, as if this made up for the fact that we had stuck Elodie with her own worst nightmare forever. But it wasn't my fault, my dad said.

He was right. It wasn't my fault, it was the Fates'. They were the very personification of destiny. The problem wasn't that the Fates couldn't stop this travesty, the problem was that they had *planned* it. I demanded that we talk to them, that we consult the Oracle and find a way to circumvent them, if necessary. I was willing to go to Hades and back, whatever I needed to do to reverse it. But my dad refused. It was over, he said. I had to accept that there was nothing more we could do.

She was lovestruck.

I'm sobbing at the memory, hunched over on the floor and grabbing my aching stomach. I squeeze my eyes shut, willing the vision to stop, praying for the memory to vanish from my mind. But it doesn't. Instead, the memory advances to the last thing I want to think of now—the one event that makes what happened even worse. I cover my face with my hands as I see myself running to the falls all those months ago. I weep remembering Hector's face as I told him that I couldn't be the Fates' plaything, that I couldn't love him anymore, that I couldn't give eternity to him, that it wasn't fair that I would never know if he really loved me or if it was just the magic of the arrow. A one-sided match. A snip of the scissors.

I can practically hear Hector shouting and crying over the sound of the water, begging me to just listen to him, to believe him that he loves me, that he'll always love me, arrow or no arrow. With my perfect recall, I watch me shaking my head, crying, falling to the ground where Hector holds me as our hearts break.

The memory eviscerates me. It breaks my heart all over again.

Eventually, my tears stop. I want nothing more than to port back home for the night and have my mom make me some tea and hold me and sing to me until I can fall asleep. But the truth is, I don't know if I deserve to be comforted.

Maybe I deserve my fate.

Chapter Twenty-One

Monday morning, Deya doesn't show at breakfast or at school. I see Ben in the parking lot, and we embrace like it's been two months since we saw each other instead of two days. I don't want to let go. He feels like my lifeline, the only thing keeping me from falling completely apart.

He puts his arm around me, and I rest my head on his shoulder as we walk into class. "Did you hear the news about Mr. G?" he asks.

My throat goes dry. "Uh-uh."

We step around students sluggish from the weekend. "He's entering the Global Archery Championship tournament!"

The despair I've felt for the last twelve hours lifts temporarily. "Seriously?"

"Yep. And check this: it's in Phoenix. This week! There were news vans here an hour ago and everything. Mr. G said teaching our class archery this semester has 'reinvigorated his love of the sport,' so when the Team USA coach called him up last week to ask him to participate, he said yes. Because of us! They asked him about his ex-fiancée, too, but he said he just wanted to focus on the future."

"Whoa, whoa, whoa." I stop him. "Mr. Gunner was engaged before? What happened?"

"Dunno. Paresh says he heard she died a few years ago. Said

he heard that's why Mr. G left the sport in the first place. Can you imagine?"

I can imagine, all right. I can imagine how crushed he's going to be to find out Artemis is just as gone from his life as his fiancée. Dread fills me.

When we get into homeroom and I see the spring in Mr. Gunner's step, I feel sick. I can't stand the thought of taking something else away from him. Artemis would kill me if she found out what I'm about to do. But I have to do it, and Deya isn't here to stop me. I drop my bag at my desk, take a deep breath, and march up to him.

"Well, good morning, Ms. Olympos," he says, removing notes from his leather bag.

"Uh, yeah, good morning, Mr. Gunner." I look around me and drop my voice. "Um, hey, so my aunt asked me to talk to you."

His eyes dart to the students, then to me. "Did she? About what?"

I swallow. Do it, Kali. Just do it. "Deya's parents are in Greece for work, you know, and late last night we found out they had a pretty bad accident—"

"Oh no! Are they okay?"

"We don't know. We think they'll be fine, but Aunt A-Cynthia"—I catch myself—"Well, as soon as she heard, she booked a red-eye out of Phoenix. She called me during her layover and asked me to tell you that she'd be gone for at least a week or two, and she won't have cell service." I see a flicker of hurt on his face, like he thinks this is all some excuse. So, even though I know I shouldn't, I say, "And she-she wanted me to tell you that last night was the best date of her life." My cheeks feel like they're on fire, I feel so guilty for lying. I hope he reads my blushing as embarrassment.

His lips twitch up in a smile. "Well, if you hear from her, tell her she has low standards. The next one will be way better." He stands up and resumes talking in a normal voice. "Now, if you'll return to your seat, we'll get started."

My week drags, with only school and the few hours a day I have with Ben to keep me company. I figure out how to watch television at the O-Ranch and tune into every moment of the GAC trials. By Wednesday, Mr. Gunner qualifies for the tournament with a respectable score. Only two archers place with better scores, and neither by much. One of them, to my shock, is the not-so-hapless-after-all Stone Savage. I know Hector said he was good with a bow, but I didn't see this coming. I text Hector asking him *"What the Styx?"* but he doesn't even respond.

Grrr!

Mr. Gunner leaves a voicemail on our house phone telling "Cynthia" how he knows she hated his stance, but he'll gladly listen to her lecture as soon as she's back from Greece and Deya's parents are okay. It hurts me to hear the hope and affection in his message, but not as much as it will hurt him to know he'll never see Artemis again.

In a second message—left because the first message was too long—he also explains his shooting schedule, in case she's checking messages: he'll have the first round of semi-finals Thursday and the second Friday, assuming he advances. At the end of those rounds, the top three cumulative scorers will compete for gold, silver, and bronze next Tuesday. He says he's the most excited he's ever been for a tournament.

I wonder if Artemis even knows.

Meanwhile, Sasquatch and the Little Feet met yesterday with Tub Snacks' manager. Ben didn't tell me what happened in the meeting, other than to say that the manager is a slimy, two-faced douchenozzle, and he wouldn't sign with him if his life depended on it. Needless to say, my boyfriend hasn't been the most pleasant person in the world since then. And nothing I do seems to help. I've tried talking to him about it, changing the subject to take his mind off of things, Styx, I've even tried making out. Nothing seems to work. It's like he's determined to sulk.

And while I love him more than Heaven and Earth, I also want to punch him. Hard.

And because the Fates don't hate me enough, Deya is actively avoiding me. She's still staying at the house because she's dedicated to her match, but she won't leave except to follow Ro or Delivery Guy. So I just get to wallow in my guilt over her botched love and home life, over my failed attempt to match my favorite teacher with a man she actually loves, and over my downwardly spiraling relationship. Yippee!

At least I've managed to talk Ben into hanging out at the observatory before his shift. We're on the "Pluto Walk" right now, a meandering outdoor path between the different buildings on Mars Hill meant to show the distances between the planets in our solar system. He finally holds my hand, and I breathe out a small sigh of relief. We have a couple of hours left before his shift, and if he's in a good mood, that will make the rest of our tour and "The Sky Tonight" presentation in the theater so much better.

We reach the dome that holds the Pluto Discovery telescope and start the spiral climb to the top. Ben points down to the floor.

"You see that step there? How it's lighter than the others?" he says in a hushed voice. I look to the discolored step.

"Yeah?"

"The Great Human Waste Debacle of last July," he says. "This five-year-old kid had been freaking out all day, demanding everything in the gift shop, eating all sorts of crap and just chucking the wrappers. His parents didn't do anything to stop him. When he got here, he was so hopped up on candy, juice boxes, and hot dogs, it started coming out both ends." He shakes his head. "That suuucked to clean up, I tell you."

My mind wanders to a similar story I heard recently, the one about Stone Savage. The memory makes me chuckle.

We reach the top of the stairs where the closed wood-beam roof encircles a massive telescope. The tour guide explains about the discovery of Pluto while Ben tells me more stories that definitely aren't tour-appropriate, mostly involving kids puking or teenagers getting caught making out. Now, don't get me wrong, I like a good vomit-slash-caught-in-flagrante story as much as the next girl, but I happen to love astronomy. So while I smile at my boyfriend telling me yet another story about a kid crapping his pants, I kind of just want to hear about the mortie's discovery of Pluto. I'm about to beg him to stop when a loud voice coming up the stairs overpowers mine.

". . . and I had to explain that I said we should be platonic, not plutonic," the loud girl laughs. "Last time I date a geographer."

I look at Ben, about to roll my eyes, when a couple comes into view.

No, not just a couple. Hector and Ianira.

Un-cursing-believable.

Hector's hand is on the small of Ianira's stupid back, and they're both smiling. At least until they see us. Hector's smile doesn't even falter. How dare he?

"Oh, look," Ianira says.

She's dressed up like she's going to a cocktail party, wearing a little black dress with a thick, elaborately twined gold belt that makes me feel like maybe I should branch out of the T-shirt and jeans department. It's that fabulous. And . . . familiar. I narrow my eyes at her waist. Why do I know this belt? Of course! It's the same belt she wore at karaoke. I snort to myself. Get a new wardrobe, harpy.

"It's Kali and . . . Ben, wasn't it?" she asks. Ben nods. "It's a pleasure to see you again."

"You, too." He smiles at her, then nods to Hector. "Hey, man."

"Hey," Hector replies. His hand is still on Ianira's back, and they're standing closer together than you stand with a friend. I grow cold. "Funny running into you guys again." Why is his smile so effortless? Why isn't this awkward for him? He's in *love* with me, for Gaia's sake! He stuck himself with an arrow and will never get over me. Did he just . . . forget?

"Yeah," I say, wishing I could think of anything other than them touching. Ben's hand tightens around mine. He's wearing a stupid smile. "Um, anyway, we're going to keep going so we can catch the night sky presentation. You two have fun on your date," I say, testing Hector.

Hector just smiles. "Thanks. You, too."

Wait, what? Hector and Ianira walk past us, and my head swivels on its own accord, following them. He just said it! They're on a date!

"I really like that girl," Ben says, still looking at them, too. In fact, as I look around the observatory, a lot of eyes are on them. "There's something about her that's, I don't know, different. Like not just how gorgeous she is. She's—"

Is *my* match talking about how hot Ianira is? I grab his hand and yank him down the spiral staircase, away from her clutches. She's already stolen one boy away from me. She can't have Ben, too.

I stomp down the stairs, fully aware of how unfair I'm being. If Hector's found a way to get over me, who am I to begrudge him that? But begrudge I do.

"It's like, she's so cool and smart. And she's funny and stuff. You can just tell."

Styx, is he still going on about her?

We're outside now, and I wheel on Ben, grabbing his shoulders and shaking him. "Enough, okay? Enough about how incredible Ianira is! I'm right here!"

Ben closes his eyes and blinks several slow, long blinks. It's like he's coming out of a daze. "Wow, I'm really sorry, Kali. I don't know what got into me."

"Ianira, obviously," I say, not bothering to check my waspish tone. I storm away from him, and he's right on my heels, grabbing my arm.

"Kali, wait, I'm real sorry. I can be such a dink. She seems fine, but she's no you. I honestly don't know what I was going on about."

Something about his earnestness strikes me. I've been with Ben for almost a month now, and I've never seen him act like this, not even around Zoe. My brow furrows. "Are you serious? You really didn't mean to go off like that about how hot and awesome she is?"

"No!" he says, putting his hands on my face. "You know that's not me. Honestly, I can't even remember why I said all that crap. I wasn't thinking straight. You gotta believe me."

My brows knit further together. I believe him, but then why was he saying it?

"Full disclosure, though, her belt was pretty hot. You gotta get one of those."

I gasp.

That thieving, Gorgon-loving harpy.

I'm too distracted the rest of the night to enjoy my date, which sucks, because Ben is on his best behavior. He's out of his brood, he's whispering new lyrics to me, and he's flirting his pants off. I should be overjoyed, but I'm too upset. As soon as the night sky presentation is over, I make up some lame excuse about Deya needing me, kiss Ben just long enough to remind me how much I love kissing, then run to my SUV. As soon as I'm in it, I clutch my necklace and summon my quartermaster.

"Cosmo?"

No answer.

"Cosmo? Are you there? Hello? Is anyone on duty tonight?"

Still nothing.

"Cosmo, you brilliant jerk, you, answer me!"

"Brilliant jerk?" the voice over my ear asks. "You're obviously trying hard to win me over." He doesn't sound sarcastic so much as hurt.

I feel sick with guilt. Whatever happened with Deya and Cosmo is at least partly my fault. If I'd been a better friend, I could have slapped some sense into her gorgeous brain before she even thought about talking to Thrax. And as for what Aphrodite said . . . I cringe. If I could go back, I would have left Aphrodite to her skeezy thoughts and chased after Deya.

So, yeah, I feel guilty. I feel awfully, horribly guilty. I feel like my shame-coated insides are trying to claw their way out of my chest and leave me used up and worthless and empty.

But I also feel really, really annoyed. Everything is falling apart around me, and I'm tired of just sitting here and letting it all happen. I need to do something.

"Listen, Cosmo, I don't know all that happened with you and Deya, but if you're so upset by it that you can't work with us, then I get it. Ask for new probies and we'll ask for a new QM. But until that happens, we're partners in all this, okay? If I need something, don't hold it against me, and if you need to correct us, just correct us. This mortie high school drama is starting to piss me off." Righteous indignation feels a lot better than guilt.

Silence.

"Cos, come on."

He huffs. "Fine. What do you need?"

"Everything about Aphrodite's belt."

"Her cestus? The one my grandfather made for her?"

"That's the one."

"There's really not much to know. Hephaestus made it for Aphrodite when they were married as a sign of his love for her. It makes her even more irresistible to men than she already is. It comes in handy when she's among mortals, considering her immortal glory would incinerate anyone who gazed upon her true form." He pauses. "Yeah, not much else to say."

"What does it look like?"

"It's a thick, intricately embroidered gold belt. Close your eyes and I'll send you a flash."

"Send me a text, Cos. You know I suck with flashes."

"I'm not sending you a message on that cursing device," he says. "I don't know everything you're up to, but you're a goddess, Kali, not some mortie-loving nymph. Clear your mind, let down your walls, and close your cursing eyes."

"Ugh! Fine."

I pull over and close my eyes. I try to clear my mind, but a million images pop up every time I kick one out of the way. And those walls aren't getting any lower.

"Kalixta, for the love of Mother Gaia, stop it. Think about, I don't know, the last place where you were perfectly happy. The sights, the sounds, the smells. Focus."

I let my mind wander, remembering times with my family, with Teresa and Deya. I think of my house, of game night with my parents, of watching Ben onstage. "Okay, send it."

I feel a flickering in my head, see quick images, but it doesn't stick.

"Focus, Kal," he repeats.

I take a deep breath, and for a moment, I smell water, fresh, clean and mystical. I hear a roar and can almost feel mist sprinkling my face. But then I see Hector's crying face. I hear him yell that he loves me. I see my heart shatter and scatter across the skies.

"It's no good, Cos," I admit, feeling as defeated as a first year on the archery grounds. "I can't do it."

He growls before going silent. For a minute, I think he's left the conversation. But then my phone buzzes. I look down and see a picture of a gorgeous belt that looks like it's made of braided gold.

It's the same belt.

"Thank you," I exclaim. "Do you know where the cestus is now?"

"I assume your grandmother has it."

"You don't keep tabs on magical items like these?"

He actually laughs. "Kali, who would steal from a Big G?"

So trusting. Immortals like Cosmo don't come around often. I see why Deya—who's constantly exposed to the seedier element of Olympus—likes him.

"Yeah, I'm sure you're right. Thanks, Cos. And, hey, you really need to talk to Deya. She . . . she misses you."

He pauses again. "My liver's been eaten enough. Someone else can steal fire for her."

"Okay, Prometheus. But you don't know the whole story. You should—"

"The whole story? She came to 'watch me work' one night, told me she was falling for me, *kissed* me, and then next thing I know, she and Thrax are . . . " He clears his throat. "I know as much of this story as I need. Do you need anything else?"

"Yes, actually. Can you look up information about a mortal for me? Anthony Gunner? Mid to late-twenties, lives in Flagstaff, Arizona? World champion archer? I'm looking for information on his fiancée."

He sighs. "Kali, I'm a QM, not your personal information service. Is this for a match?"

"Yes," I say, though not in the way he means. "And besides, whether you want to believe it or not, you broke my best friend's heart, so you owe me."

Longest pause yet. His voice is low when he answers. "Melanie Sonne. She died in a car accident a little over three years ago."

"Son? Like a child?

"No, S-o-n-n-e."

"Melanie Sonne," I whisper. "Sonne." For some reason, her

name sticks in my mind. "You said it was three years ago? When, exactly?"

"Looks like it was . . . oh, Gaia. It was during a Global Archery tournament. He shot a world-record thirteen ninety-four, then got the call ten minutes later. She was pronounced dead at the scene."

"Ouch," I whisper, for Tony even more than Melanie. "One last favor. When was Mr. Gunner's last match?"

"That was it."

I want to cry for Mr. Gunner. First Melanie, now Artemis. I clear my throat. "Thanks, Cosmo. I'll tell Deya you said hi."

"But I didn't."

"No, but you should. What happened with Thrax is sort of my fault. You need to forgive her."

I let go of the necklace before Cosmo can say anything else.

Chapter Twenty-Two

On Friday afternoon while Ben is at school, I watch Mr. Gunner's final cumulative round, which I recorded this morning. I know I could just check the score on my phone, but it's more fun to pretend it's live. Mr. G is absolutely crushing it. In yesterday's match, he shot a thirteen seventy-seven, beating the next closest archer—Stone cursing Savage—by over twenty points! Mr. G has the top combined score so far, followed closely by Stone, followed by the third-place shooter—a full eighty points behind Stone! Mr. Gunner's already guaranteed to compete in the medal round.

With six arrows to go and Mr. Gunner sitting at twelve ninety-eight, the door opens, and Deya comes in, almost stumbling when she sees me. "Oh, hey. I didn't think you'd be here. I was just—"

"Leaving?" I ask. The word is hot and sticky in my throat. She left a note this morning. She must have planned to be gone before I'd see it.

She nods. "Ro and Delivery Guy are officially matched. Her kids asked if they could see him again, so she brought them during lunch today, when he was conveniently making a delivery. They loved him. He was so sweet, too. Ro got teary-eyed when she saw him playing with them and teasing them, and stuff. I matched her right then, and she asked him out two seconds later. They're going to be an awesome couple."

My chest grows tight. Hearing Deya's love for this match tugs at my heart. I remember caring this much about a match. Styx, I cared this much and more about Artemis and Mr. Gunner. "I'm glad. She seems like she could use someone like him. Someone who can weather the storm with her." I wish I could have been there to see it.

"Yep. He'll do it. I've never been so sure of a match." Her eyes flit to the TV, and she frowns. "Anyway, I should—yikes, Mr. G. That was awful."

I look at the screen and see Mr. G cursing. He shot a five. A five? I bet he hasn't shot so low since he *was* five.

I pull my eyes from the TV and look at Deya. "Can we talk before you go?"

"What's to say, Kali? Your dad asked me to come keep an eye on you while I made my match. I made it. You asked me to be patient with you and your situation with Ben while you try to figure out the prophecy. I did my best."

"Having you here has meant everything to me, Dey."

"Yet I'm leaving, Artemis is gone, Mr. G will probably get blasted by Apollo, and you're still sticking around."

"It's not like that. I have to be with Ben while I figure out the prophecy or I'll go mad. You know that!"

"Right, and you're trying so hard to figure out the prophecy these days." I wince at her words as she winces at the TV. Holy Hades. Mr. G just shot a four. A four! Anything below a five doesn't even count, so he's still sitting at a thirteen oh-three. "Well, I have a real life to get back to. Your dad talked to my mom; I'm moving in with you guys. Well, with your parents. So I guess I'll see you on weekends." Her voice is thick but firm.

Meanwhile, my voice is thin and mushy. Emotion makes my

throat ache. "Deya, I screwed up. I've been so absorbed with my own problems that I forgot about everything else, and I know I started doing that before we even got here. I'm sorry. You can't know how awful I feel. Please forgive me. I can't do this without you."

"This?" she says with a disbelieving laugh. "What, date a mortal? Fulfill the Oracle's prophecy? I can't just be your backup for the rest of my life! I have my own crap to deal with!"

"I don't mean Ben or the prophecy. I mean . . . life! We've done everything together since we were babies. I don't want that to just stop now. Please don't leave."

"Kal, don't you get it? You're the one leaving *me* behind! You've moved on. You chose Ben over all of us. Forgive me if I don't do the same."

I cover my throat with my hand, feeling sick and vulnerable. Is that really what everyone thinks?

Worse, is it true?

A sad smile forms on Deya's mouth. She clutches her necklace. She's about to vanish when a heavy knock sounds at the door.

"Hello? Cynthia? Please be here!" Mr. Gunner calls through the thick wooden door. "Cynthia? Kali? Deya? Please!"

Deya and I glance at each other. She's still grasping her necklace. I plead with my eyes. Then with my mouth.

"Please, Dey. I can't do this without you."

She exhales and drops her necklace. "Fine, but I'm just helping Mr. Gunner," she says. She strides to the door and throws it open.

He sinks in relief. "Thank all that is holy. Please tell me Cynthia is here, too."

"I'm sorry, Mr. Gunner," I say. "She's still in Greece. She won't be back till next weekend at the earliest."

He shakes his head. "I'm sorry, Deya. How are you doing? Are your parents okay?"

Deya looks at me in alarm. Oh, right. I didn't get around to telling her about my lie. If only I could speak telepathically!

I give her a quick, pleading look. Her slow, long-suffering blink is all the agreement I need. "They're going to be fine, Mr. G," she says. "Thanks for checking. But are you okay?"

Mr. Gunner sweeps into the house, holding his head. He drops down on a leather armchair across from the TV, muttering a string of curses mingled with moaning.

"No, I'm not okay. I knew it," he mumbles. "I knew she hadn't forgiven me."

Deya frowns. "Who are you talking about, Mr. G?"

He bends lower, still grabbing his head. "Melanie. My fiancée. She hasn't forgiven me, or none of this would be happening."

Vengeful fire roars in Deya's eyes. "You're engaged?"

I look at her, moving my hand across my throat in a "cut it out" gesture. "Mr. Gunner, didn't Melanie pass away?" I ask delicately.

"Yes. I'm not delusional, Ms. Olympos." He moans. "I'm cursed."

"Cursed?" Deya says, looking at me like she definitely thinks he's delusional.

His eyes are pools of despair. "Melanie Sonne. My first love. She was the kindest person I ever met, but, boy, was she jealous. She told me that if anything ever happened to her and I tried to move on, she'd haunt me from beyond the grave. I always thought it was just a joke, her way of telling me how much she loved me and that she couldn't stand the thought of me being with anyone else. We had a saying: 'I want the stars and more for you,' we would tell each other. I meant it. But after we'd been together for a few years and the engagement kept getting pushed out, we started fighting a lot. Neither of us was really happy anymore. She was talking about moving out, and I was planning to end things, no matter what happened with the tournament. She called before my match and said we needed to talk. I just assumed she was going to break up with me then. If anything, I think I shot so well because I was so relieved. But then . . ."

"The accident," I whisper.

"I haven't entered a single tournament since then because I felt so guilty. And I haven't gone on a single date until Cynthia. I can't explain it, but it's like the moment we met, I felt alive again. I've never felt this way about anyone, including Mel. I know it's stupid, but your aunt . . . I love her. Since that first day that we shot together, I've been asking Melanie to give me a sign if she forgives me." His voice hitches. "Well, I got a sign, all right."

"What do you mean?" I ask.

He looks at the TV, his face twisted. "Haven't finished the recording yet, huh? Well don't bother. I don't hit another target."

"No tens?" I ask, referring to the bullseye.

He laughs bitterly, looking as forlorn as Artemis looked when she left. "No, I'm not saying I just missed the rings. I stopped hitting the actual target. The bale itself. By my last shot, I didn't even hit the ground around it. I ended with a thirteen oh-three. If I hadn't been up so much on the other two, I'd have been eliminated with a score like that. But as it is, I'm in third place. Third place with no hope."

"No, Mr. Gunner, it's just a slump. You just need a couple of days to recover."

"Kali, I shot over a hundred arrows in practice after this . . . this nightmare." He points to the screen. "And I got over a hundred zeros!"

A hundred zeros? That isn't just bad, it's nonsense. Even kids playing with their first bow and arrow can hit the target sometimes. But Deya has caught on to something else.

"So what does this have to do with Melanie?" she asks.

"It's her sign. She doesn't forgive me. She'll never forgive me." He draws a sharp, pitiful breath. "I'm cursed."

I shoot off a quick text to Ben.

Can't go out tonight. Family emergency. Be in touch as soon as I can.

I hit Send. Deya and I arrive at the Port a moment later.

"Melanie Sonne? 'The jealous Sonne?'" Deya says. "Could she really be the one the Oracle told you to look out for? Is it even possible to curse someone from beyond the grave?"

"I don't know," I admit. We walk by countless immortals popping to and from Earth to get to the path that leads to the Big Twelve's tier. "If she worshipped Hekate, maybe? But why? Cosmo said she's in Elysium."

Deya's breath catches. "You, uh, you talked to Cosmo?"

"Yes, and please don't freak out, but I told him he was being stupid avoiding you and that if he wants to avoid you forever, then he can request new probies, but otherwise, he needs to suck it up and just help us out."

She fiddles with her necklace. "You said that to him?"

"Yes and, okay, don't freak out again, but I told him that there was more to the story with Thrax and that this is all my fault and he needs to talk to you and forgive you and I might have said he broke your heart a little. Please don't smite me."

She stares at her sandaled feet hitting the path. Her expressions change too quickly for me to know what she's feeling. The rapid pulse in my ear blots out the chorus of creatures and sounds of parties and festivals and fights happening all over Olympus. She settles on a frown. "I don't hate you," she says. "I hate that you're gone so much now. I hate feeling like I need to babysit you to protect you from yourself."

"I'm sorry I've turned you into my babysitter. I've been so absorbed with my problems that I haven't paid attention to yours. You put your life on hold to help me. You've done everything for me, and I've been a terrible friend. I'm sorry, Dey. I've made everything harder for you."

"Not everything. That distinction belongs to my mom." Her voice is low, but she doesn't cry. "I hate her. I hate how badly I want her approval, and I hate that I idolize her when she doesn't deserve it. I hate that I acted like her to impress her and lost someone I care about in the process. I can't keep doing this to myself."

"You haven't lost anyone," I say, because I'm not sure if she's talking about me or Cosmo, but I know I'm speaking the truth either way. I link my arm in hers. "How can I help? Do you want me to tell off your mom for you? Wanna get some spray paint and vandalize your house?"

"*Her* house, you mean. I'm moving in with my real family. And I'll still be there whenever you fix your mess of a life." I laugh, but my heart swells as we walk together. "But tell me more about this spray painting thing."

We've reached Olympus' second tier, and suddenly I'm not sure what I'm doing. Am I really planning to just go up to Artemis' house and tell her about Mr. Gunner? Should I announce myself first?

"I thought I'd find you two here," Artemis says from behind us.

"Artemis!" I cry. "How did you know we were looking—" Her flat look shuts me up. Goddess of the hunt. Right. "We had to see you." I look around, making sure we're alone. "It's Tony. He can't hit anything, and he's competing in the medal round for the Global Archery Championship on Tuesday! He thinks his late fiancée cursed him and he's a mess without you. Artemis, he *needs* you."

"She's right," Deya adds. "The last thing I want to do is piss off Zeus or Apollo . . . but you should have seen his face, Artemis. He said he loves you."

Pain floods her eyes. "What do you want me to do? I'm the *maiden goddess.* I can't be with him. Don't you get that?"

"Why, though? Because of some promise you made to Zeus when you were three years old? Artemis, you didn't understand what you were promising! Surely he won't hold that against you!"

"Of course he wouldn't. He was thrilled when I met O—" her voice catches and she looks skyward. "When I met Orion," she whispers. "I was still so young when we met, but, oh, I fell hard. He was so bold and cocky and fearless. Like a god, but with all the little mortal quirks that make them so fascinating. I was obsessed with him. My father was excited to see me finally understand what love is. But . . ." she shakes her head.

"But what? If Zeus doesn't mind, then why does it matter?"

"What's the point?" she demands. "These aren't the days when the Earth was young and the gods were few. If you haven't noticed, we're swimming in gods here. Zeus won't give ambrosia to another mortal. So if I have sixty or seventy mortal years with Tony, what good does that do me when he's gone?" Her expression is fierce and desperate.

"What would sixty or seventy years with Orion have meant to you?" I ask.

Artemis' eyes water, and her voice drops to a whisper. "Everything. It would have meant everything."

"And do you feel for Tony what you felt for Orion?" Deya asks, glancing at me.

"More," she says, holding her Orion necklace. "Orion is the stars, but Tony? He's heaven. A heaven I'll never know."

"Artemis, there has to be something we can do," I cry.

With dead eyes, she says, "I'm sorry. It's over."

She walks away, and I stare at her back for a moment before remembering something. "Well, can you at least help us uncurse Tony? Is it even possible that his fiancée cursed him when she died?"

She turns around. "Yeah, it is. But the only way to get her to release him would be to travel to her home in the afterlife. And Hades has forbidden Olympians from traveling to the underworld. I'm sorry about Tony. More than you can possibly know. But his life is more important to me than his archery career. The best thing I can do for him is stay away."

Deya slumps down to the grass, and I follow, batting at fireflies.

"How is it possible that the only Big G in the history of Olympus to follow the rules is the one who needs to break them all?" I cry.

"I know. What are we gonna do?" Deya moans. "She and Mr. Gunner deserve happiness. They deserve each other! I'm halfway tempted to just shoot them both, and force them to be together, whether they like it or not." She half-grimaces, half-smiles. "Sorry about that. Too soon?"

"Ha ha," I say, though she's not wrong. I don't want to admit this to Deya or my dad, but I'm afraid that their warning about bad matches might be true of Ben and me. I want to be with him, but when I am, it feels like we fight more and more. And it's only been a month. What will it be like in a few years?

I shudder. I have to break myself of the arrow's spell, for both of us. If not, I'll love and hate and follow him until he dies.

Wait.

"I know how to talk to Tony's fiancée."

This is why I love my best friends: no matter how harebrained my schemes are, they support me. Sure, they'll tell me if something's flat out wrong or just plain stupid, but they still care enough to help.

"You're flat out wrong," Deya says. "This is just plain stupid." She turns to Teresa. "Right?"

"Actually, for a Kali plan, this isn't half bad."

I know better than to protest.

We discuss the particulars as we pass our backyard hippodrome and arena to reach the prehistoric woods on my parents' grounds. The nature here is messier than most parts of Olympus. My parents like it. They say it feels more authentic. I say it feels more like a venomous four-foot spider is going to pounce on me at any moment. Good thing Olympus doesn't do spiders. (Little known fact: Athena will absolutely turn you into a spider if you say you can weave better than her. Arachne learned that one the hard way.)

Slowly, Deya starts to come around. Sort of. "I think it's a suicide mission, but it's your call," Deya tells Teresa.

Teresa puts a hand on her hip. "Artemis was right: Olympians can't go to the underworld. Good thing for all of us that I'm not only an Olympian. Psychopomps are conductors of souls, which means we belong to both worlds. Besides, Hades is my grandfather and death is my dad. The underworld is my home as much as Olympus is." Her eyes are flinty.

Deya wheels on me. "See? This is dangerous!"

"No," Teresa argues, "it's not. It's actually pretty easy. I can have an answer for you tonight."

"That isn't what I mean," Deya says to Teresa. Then to me: "Kal, you know there's more danger to this than Teresa's letting on. The more time she spends in the underworld, the more it pulls at her, *especially* when she's not under Hermes' protection," Deya says. "Her calling takes her to Charon's ferry, not beyond. Don't ask her to do this."

I crumble. "Maybe Deya's right. 'Resa, maybe you shouldn't."

"Will you two stop being babies and just get moving already?" Teresa interrupts. "I'm not going to stay in the cursing underworld, all right? Let's go."

I grab her hand, more grateful than I can say. "Okay. But there's just one, tiny thing . . ."

"No," Cosmo says. "Absolutely not." We surround him in the QM vault, cool gadgets and aqua screens and caches of weapons all around us. "You don't think I know about that little trick you played on me so you could visit—" he hushes his voice all the way down, "the *Oracle*? Because I know." He glares at me, avoiding Deya altogether.

To my surprise, Deya speaks up. "Don't pretend you minded."

He slams a considerable arm onto his desk. Immortals overlook his strength because of his limp. They shouldn't. "I *did* mind! I thought you liked me!"

"Yeah, because I do!"

Teresa gets in the way of the lover's quarrel, planting her fists on the desk across from Cosmo. "Cosmo, we both know I don't need permission to get into the underworld. It's not just my calling, it's my birthright. All I'm asking is for you to put it on a screen for Kali and Deya, okay? That's all."

"That's all," he mutters under his breath. "As if I won't have to bypass a thousand different layers of security to do that."

"As if you couldn't do that in your sleep. You're the first QM to graduate at sixteen in a millennium," Deya says, gesturing to his necklace.

He tries to hide it, but the compliment clearly pleases him. "All right, fine. But I'll only screen you for thirty minutes. Anything longer than that will set off the hounds."

"Cosmo, what part of 'it's my birthright' don't you understand? Hades won't release his hounds on me," Teresa says. "I'm a reaper. I'm family."

"And I'm not. You have thirty minutes."

Teresa huffs, but agrees as Cosmo drips a solution into her eyes and ears. We look into the aqua screen and see ourselves reflected back between blinks. Weird. She nods at us, then takes a deep breath. Hades' and Poseidon's realms are both connected to Olympus, so Teresa doesn't have to go to the Port to jump. Only reapers can go to the underworld, where they meet Charon at the docks of one of the rivers that leads to Hades. Sometimes, they accompany the soul across to the gates.

They never go beyond unless invited by Hades himself, because they can only return if Hades lets them.

Which he doesn't.

And this is why our plan hinges on Teresa. Her unique heritage means that she has an open invitation to the underworld. She has a room at her grandparents' palace and everything.

But Deya is right: It's common knowledge that going to the

underworld is seductive to a psychopomp for reasons I cannot possibly understand.

I have to trust my friend, though. She wouldn't offer to help if she couldn't come through. With a nod to us, she vanishes. Instantly, she reappears, and it's like we're right with her. She's bypassed the docks entirely and is standing at the magnificent, if creepy, adamantine gates of the underworld.

Where an enormous, snarling, three-headed dog is about to bite her head off.

Ferry me to Hades.

Chapter Twenty-Three

"**Abort!**" **I scream** into the water. "Abort!"

"She can't hear you!" Cosmo shouts at me.

"We have to do something!" Deya shrieks.

We stare, helplessly, as the vicious monster bends down, one of its mouths open, showing rows and rows of jagged teeth.

"Oh, Gaia," I whisper.

The monster gives a ferocious growl that shakes me to my very soul. How much more terrifying must it be for Teresa? I whimper. I can't believe I sent one of my best friends to her death. How could I do this?

The ferocious creature gets closer, and saliva drips from its foaming mouth. Fangs as big as Teresa's face descend upon her. Like a coward, I slam my eyes closed and whisper, "No."

The growling stop abruptly.

No.

I brace myself for crunching, but instead . . . is that panting?

"Who's a good boy? Did you miss me, Cerby?"

My eyes pop open. "*Cerby?*"

We stare at the aqua screen, where Teresa is rubbing the beast behind two of its six ears. One of the heads smashes another head out of the way for her to pet it.

"Okay, okay," she laughs. Teresa laughs? A massive tongue wipes across her face, blotting our vision. "I have ear scratches for all of you." Her voice is so playful, I almost don't recognize it. No, I don't recognize it. I don't remember the last time I heard her laugh like this. "Big, bad Cerberus. You don't scare me." More licks and laughs. "Do you want to take me to the Elysian fields, boy?"

Cerberus pants with one head, yaps with another, and keeps licking her face with the last. I take that as a yes. Cerberus crouches down so she can grab his fur and climb onto his enormous back. She puts her arms around the middle neck and the beast starts running.

It is shockingly fast. I'm getting windswept just watching the rivers and aimless souls blur by. But I'm also intrigued by what the underworld looks like. Like Olympus, there are tiers, so to speak. Through Teresa's vision, I see pools where souls bathe themselves, sobbing and begging for the waters to erase their memories. I see souls that have faded into shadows, writhing on the ground in despair. Cerberus flies over bleak hills where other souls labor in endless futility. He bounds over swirling rivers that lead towards light and darkness. I catch a glimpse of a river that looks like it's flowing downward, deep below the underworld. The water turns a thick, oily black the lower it gets until it's too dark and far down for me to see. It's slick with evil. Tartarus.

From the corner of Teresa's eye, I see arms reaching from the river. My throat catches. A soul is pulling itself out of Tartarus. Vileness rolls off of this being in waves. It's a moment before I realize that Teresa is pulling on Cerberus, turning him around to the river. The soul's head is out now. I shudder. Full body. Its face looks like it has melted. The sockets of its hard, wicked eyes peer directly at Teresa as she jumps off Cerberus.

Holy Styx, another soul is crawling out beside this one. I shiver so hard, I fear my teeth will break.

Teresa looks over at Cerberus. "You got that guy?" Cerberus

growls. With a single bound, he jumps to the second soul and catches him in the teeth of one mouth. The other two mouths start shredding the now shrieking soul. The sound shakes and pierces me like I'm being stabbed. Then it stops. Cerberus has bitten through the soul, and it bleeds out, the same thick, oozy black of the river.

The soul has ceased to exist.

Teresa bends down to make eye contact with the first soul. "You going back down, or do I have to send you there?"

The soul's eyes flash from Cerberus to Teresa. But a mean glint is all the answer Teresa needs.

She stands up. With a shake of her head, she reaches her foot back.

And kicks the soul's head. Off.

It explodes into fleshy, oily drops that melt into the river and flow back down into Tartarus. Teresa spits in its direction and climbs back on Cerberus, rubbing his neck.

"Good boy."

I can't breathe. I can't blink. I can't believe what I just saw.

I was wrong not to be afraid of the underworld. Very, very wrong.

Cerberus resumes his dizzying pace. More joyless, wretched souls breeze by my eyes. I finally shake off my shock when the monster passes by a breathtaking palace and grounds that could belong on the highest tier of Olympus. He keeps running and occasionally snapping at wayward souls until he reaches the Trivium, where three roads meet. A glance shows me where each leads: Tartarus, the home of the damned, the Fields of Asphodel, the final home of those who did neither true good nor true evil in life, and Elysium. Three judges sit at the crossroads. Teresa bows low to them, and they nod their heads in return.

"I seek to visit a soul in Elysium," she says.

"For what purpose?" one of the judges asks, a kind-looking man wearing a crown.

"To help a mortal regain his heart."

Another judge with a beard and curly hair under his crown frowns. "You? You would care to help a mortal in this manner? Or is this perhaps for a friend?"

Teresa nods, but my heart stutters. How do they know?

"And you would seek to return to Olympus with the soul?" another, who looks like he was born directly from the Earth, demands.

"Not with the soul, only with information. But I seek return for myself."

The judges look at each other, and for a moment, even the kindly face looks stern. "You seek the 'jealous Sonne,'" the kind one says. Teresa nods. "This is not an easy quest. I fear you will not find what you seek. But you will find answers. Search for her beneath the pomegranate tree."

She nods. "Thank you."

The bearded judge tuts. "Oh, you know you need not thank us, dear. You are a credit to your father."

Beside me, Cosmo gives a nervous, breathy laugh.

"Next time you're visiting Hades, would you sneak us some of your father's cheesecake?" the Earthen judge asks.

"You know, Aeacus," Teresa says, "if you'd just come to a dinner party when you're invited, you wouldn't have to beg for treats like Cerberus."

"Oh, right," Aeacus says. "And let the Elysians slum it in Asphodel for a night? I think not."

They all share a laugh. "Thanks for your help," Teresa says, slapping Cerberus' back to spur him forward.

"Don't forget about my cheesecake!" Aeacus calls after her.

Cosmo, Deya, and I all rock backward, exhaling. But then a vision like nothing we've seen before fills the screen, drawing us back in.

It's Heaven.

Elysium. It's better than anything I could imagine, and I live on Olympus. Although I can't remember Zeus' or Hades' palaces, I know this is infinitely more beautiful. A sharp longing in my chest pulls me forward until I'm almost falling into the aqua screen. I bump shoulders with Deya and Cosmo, who are trying to dive in, too.

Music so beautiful it brings tears to my eyes seems to come from the air itself. The sound is so rich and moving I feel like I can taste it. I can't describe in words what I see, only what I feel. Bliss. Joy. Safety. Nirvana. Euphoria. Total clarity. I feel a hunger to learn everything of worth; a desire to be my best self; a happiness so deep and contented, my heart can't contain it. I feel like I'm wrapped in a warm embrace by everyone I love most: my parents, Deya, Teresa. Hector. I want to melt into the embrace and never let go of the depth of this perfect, powerful love.

A hand comes up to rub my eye, and I realize it's Teresa's hand rubbing Teresa's eye. I bring a hand up to my cheek and wipe the tears from my face, too.

I can't stop crying, I'm so happy. I don't understand how I can get all of this from just seeing this perfection, but I know being there must be unimaginably, unbearably better. How Teresa is even conscious in the presence of such exultation is a mystery.

Now that I realize I'm not there, it's easier for me to notice things, like the delighted souls singing, painting, gardening, creating. Some play games, others compete, while others read and write and debate. Through Teresa's eyes, I see Homer telling stories, Shakespeare directing a play, and Marie Curie performing an experiment in front of a large group. I see parents laughing and playing with children who I suspect have been born here.

The Elysian fields are endless, its sublimely happy inhabitants countless. All of them are still discovering and mastering the subjects they enjoyed in life and learning new ones in eternity.

Teresa eventually finds the pomegranate tree, under which a pretty young woman reclines, reading Plato's *Republic* with the man himself. Teresa climbs down from Cerberus while children run to the giant dog, petting him and begging for rides.

"Excuse me, are you Melanie Sonne?" Teresa asks.

Melanie looks up, her bright brown eyes inquiring. "Yes!" she beams. "And you are?"

"A friend of Tony Gunner's."

Melanie's face brightens even more. She holds a hand to her heart. "Oh, dear Tony! How is he?"

"He's been better," Teresa says, explaining Tony's archery predicament.

"I'm so sorry to hear that," she says. "But if he believes in himself, I know he can do it. He's the most talented man I've ever known."

I can't tell if Teresa's frowning, but I sure am. What's going on? Why is she being so nice about Mr. Gunner?

"Well, that's actually why I came," Teresa continues. "Tony thinks that he can't shoot anymore because you haven't forgiven him."

Melanie's laugh is the sound of a breeze on a summer day. "Haven't forgiven him? I'm in paradise. How could I hold a grudge here? What would I even hold a grudge for? Tony is a wonderful person."

More frowning.

"He seems to think that you planned to haunt him from the grave if he ever tried to move on."

Her smile fades into something regretful. "In life, I wasn't a confident person. I clung too hard to people to compensate for not loving myself enough, and I clung harder to Tony than anyone. He and I were over long before I died, but we were too afraid to admit that to each other. I will always love him dearly, but we were never meant to last. I wish he could know that. I want the stars and more for that man. If he only—"

The aqua screen goes blank.

I wheel on Cosmo. "Get it back!"

His face turns a brilliant shade of red. "I-I'm sorry, I can't."

"Of course you can!" Deya yells. "Come on!"

His red face deepens. "I'm sorry, I can't risk it. Just because Teresa can go there unnoticed, it doesn't mean that Hades or Heracles won't be on the lookout for screens. You'll have to get the rest of the conversation from Teresa."

"Cosmo!" I cry, but he shakes his head.

I want to scream and argue and maybe punch him a little, but deep down, I know he's right. Teresa can fill me in on everything else, and we already know what we need to know: Mr. Gunner's fiancée didn't curse him.

No, when I think about it, the reason I'm so upset that the screen went blank is because of the intense joy that was sucked out of me when my vision of Elysium ended. And worse still, I can remember every single detail, every thought and feeling and epiphany, but without the surety of the love and elation that surrounds you in Elysium.

Deya's rubbing her eyes, mourning the same loss. "What do we do now? How are you supposed to fulfill the prophecy?"

"I don't know." I put my elbows on Cosmo's desk and prop my head up with my hands. "I thought for sure that Melanie was 'the jealous Sonne.' But the judge told 'Resa she's not the one we're searching for." I cover my face.

No one speaks for a moment. "Have you considered," Cosmo finally says, "that someone else has cursed this guy?"

"Who else would curse him? Didn't Zeus put a ban on cursing morties?" I ask.

Cosmo just raises his eyebrows. "Don't tell me you believed that."

"Says the guy who thinks no one would steal from a Twelve . . . oh my ferries and Styx," I say, spinning to face Deya. "I forgot to tell you the most important thing! I know who the 'unjust union' is between."

"What? Who?"

"Hector and Ianira! She stole your mom's belt—the one from the karaoke night. She was wearing it the last time I saw her, too. Ben went totally gaga for her, then two minutes later, he couldn't even remember what he was saying. That harpy's trying to break Hector's self-sticking with Aphrodite's cestus!"

Cosmo blinks rapidly. "Ianira? The genius muse? She *stole* from a Twelve?"

Deya's flexing her draw hand. "Oh, I could shoot her in the face for this."

I nod. "Get in line."

Teresa returns later than expected looking wistful. I've never seen her wistful, but after seeing Elysium, I know how she's feeling. She tells us her conversation with Melanie ended only a few moments after the screen ended, so we didn't miss much. We're back to square one. As we strategize about each part of my prophecy, the progress report looks something like this:

Heal the heart of a desperate maiden: colossal fail.

Save a soul from an unjust union: in process, pending a slap to Ianira's skeezy face.

Restore to greatness a fallen champion: see the aforementioned colossal fail.

Beware the eye of the jealous son: is there a failure more colossal than colossal? Because that.

As for the last part of the prophecy, my quest for heart possibly ending in none, I feel like that threat looms ever closer. Ben has texted asking about my family (I told him I had to disappear for an emergency, after all). He texts to ask if I'm okay, if I need anything, if he can do anything. My lack of response leads him to ask if Hector is with me and if he's the one who gets to comfort me through this crisis.

I don't respond. I also don't blast him off the face of the Earth, so my restraint is admirable, really.

An hour later, he sends me a video of him singing a new song that he's writing—an apology song. It's just a single verse, but he sings of sorrow and longing. His regret is tangible, and the song is enough to soften the hardest heart. I want to swoon, and not just because of an arrow, but because he's so unbelievably talented. The fact that I could incite such fervor and fear and beauty is overwhelming. In these bursts of raw, inspired talent, he refers to me as his muse, for Gaia's sake. It's everything I wanted.

So why does the thought of returning to Earth in twenty hours make me want to cry?

I wander from my room downstairs to the kitchen, desperate for something to take my mind off of my predicament. My mom is there, heckling my dad while he bakes. Mortie appliances are everywhere: refrigerators, freezers, ovens, mixers. For a second, I stop and look around me to make sure I am, in fact, on Olympus.

My mom says something that, judging by my dad's reaction, must be sarcastic.

"You're not helping," he grumbles.

"Monster," she says, "you're the one trying to compete with Hestia in a bake-off. It is my duty as your wife to point out how ridiculous you are to think you can beat the Goddess of domesticity."

My feet shuffle on the marble, and I sit at the counter next to my mom, putting my head on her shoulder. "What's going on?"

My dad clangs pots and pans, keeps accidentally jamming his finger in the mixer, and tries to start the oven. The gas stove flares on instead, charring his chiton. He spews a string of curses in Greek and magicks the fire out.

"Uh, Dad?" I say, pointing to his singed eyebrows.

"Styx!" he yells. He fixes his eyebrows.

I look at my mom, who's barely concealing her enjoyment. "So?" I prompt.

"Apollo's party tonight is mortal themed, thank Gaia. If I have to attend another one of his parties where he challenges people to play his golden lyre, I'll melt the cursing thing down," she says. I snicker. "So, for tonight's party, not only do we have to dress as mortals and bring mortal dishes, all of our preparation has to be done the way mortals would prepare them. Anyone who didn't have mortal clothes, which includes most of us Ancients, has had to go down to Earth and shop for them. Isn't that ridiculous? A few of your sisters and brothers took me shopping yesterday so I wouldn't stand out too much."

This bothers me. I don't know if I feel like she should have invited me or if she shouldn't have had to. But I was gone—what can I expect?

"And the food is . . . what's the word, Monster? Lucky pots? Where everyone brings food to share?"

"Potluck," I say.

"Right, potluck. Every family has to bring potluck food that's been homemade in our own kitchens with these funny instruments." She gestures to the out-of-place appliances. "Of course, your ridiculously competitive father has decided to try something called 'Baked Alaska.' It's supposed to be very hard to make, but, because he's 'very smart' and 'a god,' he just knows he'll have no problem making it perfectly." She smiles sweetly at my red-faced father. "Is that about right, dear?"

He answers in a form of Greek so ancient, I don't know it. Judging by my mother's throaty laugh, though, she does. She responds in the same form. Though my dad's nostrils flare, he's fighting a smile.

"Oh, Gaia, are you two flirting? Gross," I moan, dropping my head to the marble counter.

"We weren't flirting," she says, giving my shoulder a little push.

"But we weren't fighting, either," my dad says. I lift my head in time to catch him wink.

The ease of their banter causes something in me to snap. "How do you guys do it? How are you still so in love after so cursedly long? I know, I know, the arrow made you fall in love, but you've been together for millennia and are still stupidly, grossly in love, while I've been with Ben for a month and I seriously worry that I'm going to punch him in the throat half the time. How do you do it?" I demand.

My parents look at each other. I probably shouldn't have admitted how things are going with Ben, but I'm at my wit's end here. If my dad can make Baked Alaska, I can scrounge up some humble pie.

My dad sets down an oven mitt (that he was using upside down). "Kali, you should know better than anyone that an arrow doesn't guarantee a perfect relationship."

"Then what's the point?" I ask, crying. "Why use arrows at all if people can get stuck by them and still be so miserable?" I sniff. My mom's arms wrap around me.

"Sweetie, what's going on?"

Once I open my mouth, the words just pour out of me. "Everything's a disaster. Ben is driving me crazy and he's so hot and cold. But he said I'm his muse and that he needs me, and even though I thought I wanted to be a Muse, which would be perfect seeing as we're lovestruck, I don't know if I can take it anymore. And I tried to set up Artemis with Mr. Gunner and she fell in love with him, but Apollo found out and she can't be with him anymore and now Mr. Gunner thinks he's been cursed because the Global Archery Championship round is in two days and he can't hit anything. And Ianira's tricking Hector into loving her, and I don't know how to tell him without hurting him and I hate her stupid face and I just . . . everything is a mess and I don't know what to do!"

I'm crying so hard, that no matter whose granddaughter I am, I look ugly. Red, puffy, snotty ugly.

"What can we do?" my dad asks from beside me, now. He rubs my back while my mom hugs me and smooths my hair.

"Reverse the arrow!"

My mom's hand falters in my hair. Her sigh puffs against my cheek. "Oh, sweetie, there's nothing to—"

"Nothing we can do," my dad says over her. "You have to work through this on your own."

"Then convince"—I cover my mouth—"Apollo to stop being so overbearing!"

"The sun God has always jealously guarded his sister's affection," my dad says, a hand over his mouth, too.

"What did you say?"

"That Apollo has always been—"

I wipe my eyes. "No, you said the sun God."

My dad looks confused. "Yes, of course. You know that Apollo is the sun God." My mind is going a million miles an hour, so I don't answer, and he continues. "Kali, come on. Apollo, the sun God? The God of music, arts, prophecy, healing? Apollo of the obnoxious golden lyre? Apollo of the silver bow? Stop me when I hit one that sounds familiar."

My brain catches up. "All right," I sass. "If this is a test, I'll point out that his bow was gold. Artemis' was silver."

My dad snorts. "Good to know you were listening to something." He looks at my mom. "This is your fault."

"My fault?" she cries. "How?"

"Your mortal blood runs through those veins."

"My 'mortal blood' was burned out by ambrosia thousands of years before Kali's veins were conceived. Besides, you run the department that instructs her. If she doesn't know something as basic as a god's responsibilities, it's your fault."

They keep bickering, but I tune them out. "The jealous sun," I whisper, hitting my head with my palm. "The jealous, cursing sun."

I am such an idiot.

"Dad, could, um, *he*, curse Mr. Gunner?"

My dad suddenly looks uncomfortable. "I don't know who Mr. Gunner is, and technically, mortal cursing has been banned."

"But?"

His eyes shift around the room and he magicks a huge canopy over top of us all. I blink to adjust to the sudden shade. "Don't you tell a soul about this, Kalixta. I'm telling you this out of concern for Artemis only. Zeus doesn't monitor the Twelve, or any of the Ancients, unless something is a direct threat to Olympus." He taps his fingers fast on the counter. "So, yes, Apollo could have cursed the man. And if he and Artemis were really in love, Apollo probably did. It wouldn't be the first time."

Resolve hardens my spine.

"Thank you," I say, kissing my parents and squeezing them tightly. Then I run up to my room to get ready for the party.

Apollo, you jealous, Gorgon-loving son of a harpy. I got you.

Chapter Twenty-Four

Apollo's palace is generally the paragon of taste and elegance even for a Twelve.

Right now, though, it's a shrine to all things mortie, ranging from straight-up ironic to kitschy to cool. He has kitten calendars hanging on walls, motivational posters that say things like "Reach for the Stars," and paintings of wolves howling at the moon. Actual televisions sit throughout the expansive room, playing movies like *Friday* and *Sharknado* and *This Is Spinal Tap*. So far, the music I've heard in the background has been Son House, Led Zeppelin, and Prince.

Apollo is so freaking cool.

It is immediately obvious which immortals have spent time among morties in the last, oh, ever. Demeter, Goddess of the harvest, looks like an infinitely hotter Beyoncé in an outfit that clings to her every curve. On her arm is a gorgeous mountain god with a shaved head and a leather jacket.

Meanwhile, Athena looks like a horrible cross between a librarian, a nurse, and a hobo. And she's wearing Crocs. Crocs! I shudder. The Goddess of wisdom doesn't know crap about fashion.

I don't see my friends anywhere, but as I crack open a Shasta, Cosmo joins me at one of several dozen refreshment tables, looking like an iteration of Doctor Who.

"Geek chic looks hot on you, Cos," I say.

With a cheeky grin, he plucks at his bowtie. "Thanks, Kali. Um, you haven't seen Deya, have you?"

I arch an eyebrow. "Why? Have you had a change of heart?"

He blushes and mumbles. "It's just, after seeing Elysium . . ."

I know what he means. Seeing true Heaven has a way of putting things in perspective for you. Like everything from your soul to your world view has been scrubbed clean.

At least, that's how I feel until I hear Thrax behind me. "Mmm, everything at this table looks good enough to eat."

And I need a shower.

I wheel on him, but Cosmo spares me from having to say anything. "Gee, Thrax, I was hoping you'd notice," Cos says, pretending to twirl his hair.

I cough a laugh. Thrax snarls. "Funny. All this time, I thought you were jealous of me for hooking up with Deya. I should have known you were really jealous of that slut for hooking up with me." Thrax gets right in Cosmo's face. "Keep dreaming, demi."

Cosmo's face doesn't change in the slightest. But his hand darts up to Thrax's neck. And squeezes. And lifts. As Thrax's feet rise off the ground, his eyes bug out. His legs flail and he struggles, in vain, to break the unforgiving grip Cos developed growing up in his grandfather's forges. "You're right about one thing, Thrax. I have dreamed about doing some seriously messed-up things to you. I'm sure Deya would be jealous of what I have planned."

Something pops in Thrax's face. Maybe a vessel, maybe an eyeball. But when Cosmo lets go, the taller boy drops to the floor, unconscious. Huh. Looks like we do need oxygen.

Cosmo smiles and adjusts his tie. "I'm gonna go talk to some friends. Tell Deya I said hey, will you?"

I wave at Cos as he walks away. That was awesome. I have to

tell someone! I glance around the room and finally spot Hector with his dad. I step over Thrax's body and head through the crowd, nervous at the thought of seeing the sun God.

Apollo looks like he's competing at the X Games. To my surprise, Calliope, Hector's mom, is with him. She looks like she's about to headline a set at a music festival, with her glorious black waves free around her face. With them is a smiling Hector who looks, well, perfect. Unselfconscious indie without crossing the line into hipster. And he's just so painfully hot.

Someone blocking my view of Hector's full glory shifts, and my gut clenches. Ianira is with him. His arm is around her. They're talking and laughing with his parents. I. Want. To. Die.

Two arms loop in mine. I look from my left to my right, seeing Teresa and Deya. They look amazing. Teresa is all leathered-out and has applied some mortie makeup to play up her soulful eyes. She must be in a good mood to put her arm in mine. That's usually more of Deya's thing. Meanwhile, Deya's in high-waisted, wide-legged pants that show just how long her legs are.

"You guys just missed the most amazing thing!" I say.

"You mean Cosmo?" Teresa asks. I nod.

"We saw!" Deya says, squealing. "It was hot, right? I mean, it was super hot," Deya says, and we have no problem agreeing. As she gushes, we agree with every word. She looks happy talking about Cos. Those two are going to be okay.

"Anyway, Kal, why didn't you tell us you were planning to look so good?" Deya asks.

I give them a little curtsy, laughing. I'm wearing an oversized cable-knit cardigan with leggings, ankle boots, and a chunky belt that shows off my curves. The fact that the cardigan is one I stole from Hector makes it that much better.

When he sees me out of the corner of his eye, I feel a stab of pleasure. His eyes widen and linger on me in his sweater. He's mid-conversation with Ianira, but a small smile forms on his lips.

I can't take this. I can't take seeing him with her. I whisper to my friends. "What do you want to bet she's wearing the belt underneath her clothes so Aphrodite won't notice?"

"Oh, I guarantee it," Deya says, studying the girl's silhouette. Deya has fire in her eyes. "Wait here."

She runs over to her mom, grabbing her from the midst of literally dozens of admirers. Teresa and I both groan. She's dressed as a Victoria's Secret model.

"At least she's not naked," Teresa says.

Deya casts us a glance and gestures for us to follow her. She drags her mom over to Apollo and Calliope, Hector and Ianira. Teresa and I get close to the conversation without being directly involved. We watch the color drain from Ianira's face.

"Apollo, this is such a cool party. Thanks for inviting us," Deya says.

Apollo smiles. "You're welcome." He looks Aphrodite over, but to his credit, he doesn't leer. "You look lovely, Aphrodite."

She smiles and flirts and he doesn't seem to care. That's one of the good things about Apollo. Looks alone don't do it for him. He likes a little substance. Oh, and he likes cursing and possibly killing his sister's boyfriends. So, you know.

"Mom, have you met Ianira?" Deya asks.

Aphrodite touches Ianira's shoulder. "I haven't, but you are stunning, girl. And hilarious! You have the 'pretentious mortal' look down perfectly." She leans in conspiratorially, ignoring Ianira's flush of embarrassment. "Can you imagine if you had to wear those ridiculous glasses outside of a party like this?" Aphrodite laughs, and Teresa and I turn our backs to hide our giggles. This is the greatest moment of my life.

"Yes, well," Ianira gestures to the mortal-themed party all around her as if she doesn't wear those stupid things every day, "When in Rome . . ."

A record literally scratches. Everyone but Ianira stiffens at the colossal, egregious insult. It takes her a moment to realize what she's just said. Her already-pale face goes pure white. "I am so sorry, Apollo!" she cries. "I've been in the mortal world so much lately, I didn't think about what I just said. It just came out! Please, forgive me," she begs.

"Not such a genius now, is she?" Teresa mutters, causing me to shake with laughter.

Hector grimaces. "It's an honest mistake," he says to his parents. "Right?"

Apollo smiles tightly. "Right. Now, if you'll excuse us." He and Calliope nod to their son and step away to make their rounds.

An awkward pause extends to an awkward eleven seconds. Deya milks it, speaking up just when it looks like Ianira's going to run . . . or collapse from shame. "So, Ianira, I've been meaning to ask you. When we ran into you at the karaoke bar, you had the most *fabulous* belt on!" She turns to her mom. "It was chunky, kind of like the one Kali's wearing," she says, pointing to me. Quickly, Teresa and I pretend to laugh at the movie playing in the corner: *Terms of Endearment.*

"Ooh," her mom says.

"Yeah, and Mom, it was gorgeous. It looked like embroidered gold. And I noticed more than one guy drooling over her in it." She turns back to Ianira. "Where did you get it? I'd die to get my hands on something that yummy."

Ianira squeaks out something about not being sure, but Aphrodite realizes exactly what's happening. Rage flickers off of her in actual sparks. Immortals all around notice and take a step away. Her unspeakably beautiful face is still smiling, but it's a sociopath's smile. The smile of someone about to do serious violence. Deya puts a hand on her mom's arm.

"You know," Aphrodite says, "I had a belt like that myself once. If you ever find one like it, I'd *kill* to get it back."

I swear I'm not making this up: Ianira pees her pants. It's just a trickle down one leg, but she has undeniably peed her pants. Her jeans slowly darken down the pee path. Teresa and I double over, laughing so hard we can't breathe.

Ianira doesn't make any excuses or apologies or anything. She just runs.

Aphrodite mutters something in the same extra-ancient Greek that my parents use, and I can't help but wonder if she's just cursed the fleeing girl. The thought sobers me a little. But then I remember the pee stain, and I double over again.

Moments later, Deya joins us, also in hysterics.

"Did you see—"

"The pee?"

We fall onto the floor, all three of us. Immortals and Twelve alike are looking at us, but we don't care. We can't care. *Ianira peed her pants.*

A few minutes later, we're all wiping our eyes, still on the floor when a hand reaches out to pull each of us up. "It's the oddest thing," Hector says over our laughter. "I find myself very suddenly dateless."

Deya and Teresa step around us. "Take ours," Teresa says. "She may not be as smart, but she's not as stupid, either."

Deya bursts out laughing again. "And she's never peed her pants!"

My friends howl with laughter and walk away, leaving me giggling with Hector. He pulls me up and lets me fall against him, still laughing. But when the music changes to a slow song, Hector's hands shift, and he's guiding me on to the dance floor. My giggles fade and my pulse speeds up.

The feel of his warm, strong arms around my back does funny things to my stomach. I put my arms around his neck, and it takes every ounce of willpower not to twist his hair around my fingers.

Hector looks amused. "Did Ianira actually steal Aphrodite's cestus?"

"Yep."

"Is Aphrodite going to obliterate her?"

"Meh, that's not her style. She'll definitely curse her, though."

"Why?"

"Because Aphrodite is—"

"No, I mean why did Ianira steal the cestus?"

"Hector," I say. "Come on."

"Come on, what?"

"Are you kidding me? You know exactly why she stole it."

"Tell me."

"Are you trying to say you don't know?"

"No, I'm trying to say that I want *you* to say it." His hands adjust on my back and pull me in ever so slightly.

"She was trying to break the arrow's spell," I say, not sure why I'm blushing, "so you'd move on from me."

We don't need to be anywhere near this close to hear each other speak. But with my immortal ears, I can hear the ichor coursing through his veins. I can hear the rhythm of his heart, how it's speeding up.

Mine is, too.

"So why did you step in?" he asks. "Why involve yourself in this at all?"

I go white hot, and the urge to kiss Hector almost overtakes me. I stare at his lips, wanting to lean in so badly. I move my hand so I'm playing with the nape of his neck. My heart is hammering a plea to get closer, to hold him tighter. "We've had enough Olympian interference in our love lives. I couldn't stand the idea of her tricking you." My eyes jump from his mouth to his eyes just for a moment. They're twinkling.

"Are you sure that's all it was?" he says, dropping his voice so low that my knees threaten to give out. "Are you sure it's not that you can't stand the idea of me moving on?"

My eyes close in spite of me, and I feel myself nod. I'm aware of every single place where our bodies are touching, and I'm aware that it's not nearly enough. I crave his mouth, and I tilt my head towards his.

In the back of my mind, I hear the song end and a fast, heavy beat takes over. It's nothing compared to my beating heart. But why aren't we kissing?

I open my eyes, and Hector's face is at war with itself. He's staring down at me like he doesn't know what to do. But his hands are locked around me. I couldn't wiggle free if I wanted to. I mean, I could.

But I don't want to.

"Hector?" I whisper. "Are you okay?"

"Are you still with Ben?"

It's like a bucket of ice water has been thrown over me. I clear my throat and look away. "Yes, but—"

"Are you working on the prophecy?"

"Gaia, yes. I'm doing everything I can. But you know the *complication*. I don't know how to fulfill it now." I can't mention Artemis, but I know he understands. How could he not? "Things with Ben . . . they're not right. We fight a lot, and even though I've inspired his music—I'm his muse—I don't like it like I thought I would. I don't like us."

The muscles in his jaw tense. "So what happens if you manage to end things with him, Kali? Where does that leave us? Are you going to be with me after we've both been stuck by arrows? Can you trust what I feel for you? Can you feel the same way for me?" The questions are coming so quickly, I don't know which to answer. But I can't lose him. I can't lose this moment.

"I don't know, okay? I don't know what I'm doing, and I don't know how to end things with him, or if I even can. I don't understand any of this, Hector. I don't know what's real or what's an arrow, and it's making me sick. I just really need my best friend right now."

His face crumples underneath my plea, but he doesn't stop. "So you can't say if you're ready to be with me, but you can't stand the thought of me moving on?"

My insides churn at the thought. "No."

He lets go of me now, rubbing his hands over his face. "Do you have any idea how unfair this is, Kali?" I have a knot in the pit of my stomach the size of Olympus. I nod, tears welling in my eyes. "You can't have it both ways. You can't have *me* both ways!"

"I know, but I can't not have you at all, either! Hector, I don't know what more to tell you. I need you! I can't stand the idea of you being with anyone but me."

"But you can't stand the idea of being with someone who's compelled to love you? Like you're compelled to love Ben, right?"

I grab his hand. He doesn't pull away. "I don't know! The longer I'm on Earth, the less I understand about this whole thing. But I know an arrow doesn't guarantee a perfect relationship," I say, quoting my dad.

He lifts my chin with his hand, and his eyes bore into mine. "Then what does?"

Us! I want to shout. I want to grab his face and yell it for all the heavens to hear, for him to hear. But I can't. Because while I'm being irrational and unfair right now, I won't be purposefully cruel. I can't make a promise like that, no matter how badly I want to. Because I'm not free yet, and neither is he. Maybe he never will be. And I have to figure out if that will matter.

I stand on my tiptoes and put my arms around him. "Can we just agree for one night that it's okay not to have all the answers?"

He hesitates, but his arms wrap around me, too. "I don't know if I can do that, Kal."

"Please," I whisper in his ear. I know he wants this as much as I do.

His heart beats against my chest. "Okay."

When the music turns slow again, we're still hugging each other on the crammed dance floor. We sway to the rhythm, our hearts beating as one.

Chapter Twenty-Five

Hours into the party, Hector and I agree to take a break from holding each other. I feel naked without him. I see my friends talking with a group of people, and I slip in behind them.

"Do you guys have a sec?" I ask.

They nod, making excuses to step away. We congregate in a corner of the room.

"What is going on with you and Hector?" Deya demands.

My cheeks are bright red. "I don't know. But I like it," I admit. "But more importantly, have you seen Apollo?"

Teresa nods. "He and Artemis are outside, actually. They went for a walk about fifteen minutes ago."

I take a deep breath. "Okay, wish me luck." I start walking outdoors, but then I hop back to them. "And if Apollo curses me into oblivion, tell Hector that tonight was the best night of my life."

I walk through the partygoers, smiling and saying hi to people I know as I make my way outside. It's a beautiful night, and the stars are as bright as ever. But I'm not looking at the stars. I'm looking for the sun.

My walk leads me past fountains and gazebos and sculpture gardens. I'm about to turn into the maze when voices stop me.

"Swear to me, 'Pollo. Swear that you didn't curse him," Artemis begs.

"Art, I swear! Of course I didn't curse him. Why would I do that?" Apollo asks.

"Because you always have! Hippolytus, Orion—"

"That's not the whole story, and you know it."

"All I know is that anytime I've gotten close to a man, you've conveniently interfered."

"None of them are good enough for you!"

"Good enough at what? At being moral, kind, decent people? Tony is! I've done all the same checks you have! He doesn't lie or steal or cheat or make himself out to be anything that he's not. He doesn't think he's better than me—"

"Because he's not," Apollo snorts.

"At archery? At hunting? At tending to animals? Of course not! Neither are you!"

"I'm better at archery than you are."

"No, you're not. Not even with your golden bow. And if you were mortal, you wouldn't be better at archery than Tony. But that's not the point. I love him. He makes me feel stronger and more alive than I've felt in millennia. He challenges me and he's not afraid to be challenged *by* me. Do you have any idea how rare that is? Even Orion hated that I was better than him. His bravado was nothing more than his being threatened. But Tony isn't like that! He doesn't care that I beat the pants off of him at anything. To him, it makes me *more* attractive, not less."

"He may have tricked you into thinking that, but he's lying. I've seen too many mortals to believe it."

"I *love* him!" Artemis cries. "Don't I deserve love? Don't I deserve happiness?"

I peek around a tree to see Apollo pull his sister into a hug. "Of course you deserve happiness. But why can't you just be happy being with your brother and being a great aunt and teacher? Why does it have to be with this guy?"

Artemis' reply is muffled. "And why do you always go back to Calliope, no matter how many times she leaves you?"

Apollo hisses. "Ouch. Not fair, sis."

"No, and neither is cursing the man I love."

He holds her out at arm's length. "If I'd cursed him, you'd know. You have that weird tracker sense that tells you this sort of thing, right? Have you seen any trace of a curse?"

"No, but you're clever. I know you did something. Apollo, keep us apart if you have to. Dash my heart into a million pieces and scatter them across the sky again. But please, do not harm him." A sob escapes her. "Please."

She disappears before Apollo gets the chance to answer her.

I stay, watching him stare at the sky for a moment that becomes several minutes. I start to creep away, when I see Apollo standing two feet in front of me.

"Going somewhere?"

My heart has just seen Medusa's head and turned to stone in my chest. "Um, oh, hi, Apollo," I say, trying not to choke on fear. "I was just—"

"Spying," he says. His golden hair, bronze skin, and bright green eyes reflect the moonlight. "Hear anything interesting?"

"No, that's not—I wasn't, I mean . . ."

He puts his hands on my shoulders, turns me around, and directs me toward the house. "Kali, how long have I known you?"

"Since the day I was born," I answer weakly.

"Right. So let's be honest. You think I cursed Artemis' boy-friend—the boyfriend you helped her acquire—and you came here to try to talk me into letting up on the curse."

I understand how Ianira must have felt when she wet herself. "Um."

"Listen, I know you think I'm a—what is it you're always calling people—a giant Gorgon turd for being so overprotective, but you don't know Artemis like I do. I promised our father when we were young that I'd watch out for her and that I'd never let her get hurt. Hippolytus? Orion? Those guys were all charm and swagger and competition. They didn't care about her as much as they cared that they had her."

He stops and turns me to face him. "I know you've been digging for answers. Do you want to know what really happened with Orion? He bet me he could swim so far out, that neither Artemis nor I could reach him. I laughed at him. Then he told me that he could catch our arrows before they hit him, because he was the greatest sportsman and athlete and hunter and swimmer and everything you can imagine. He insulted both my sister and me to the point that I agreed. When Artemis returned, he was already so far out, she didn't realize what we were shooting at, and neither of us know whose arrow actually hit him." He looks tormented, but his words are fierce. "Do you know how much I've regretted that moment? Can you imagine what it's like to hear the pain in my sister's voice haunt my nightmares every night for thousands of years?"

I shake my head.

"I have to protect her from that pain," he explains. His voice is almost pleading. "Can you understand that?"

"Do you really think the pain she feels right now is better?" I ask.

He opens his mouth, then closes it. He starts walking again, and I follow. "I can't expect you to understand when you haven't been able to see what's right in front of your face for all these years."

I frown. "What's that supposed to mean? Hector was struck by an arrow! Why is it so hard to imagine that I want someone to *choose* to love me instead of being compelled to love me? You're the God of prophecy, right? Doesn't it get old? The Fates already having decided someone's entire life before they're even born?"

His eyes pierce me as easily as his son's always have. "You don't believe that."

I laugh wryly. "I've been railing about this for a while now. Ask anyone."

"Oh, you may have believed that at one point, but I suspect you've begun to realize there's more to Fate than that."

"Or maybe the Fates already determined we'd have this conversation," I counter.

"Sure. Or maybe you're getting a little too familiar with a God because you don't always make smart choices."

I stop. My eyes and mouth are as open as they can be. My heart is as stopped as it can be without being dead. My brain is screaming every curse word I know in every language I know all at once.

Apollo steps toward me, leaning down so our eyes are inches apart. "Wow, Hector's right. You really are a dramatic little thing, aren't you?" He chuckles. "What do you think I'm going to do to you, Kali? You're practically family." He puts his hand on my cheek. "Breathe."

I do. I gulp in air.

"I'm going inside," he says. I hadn't realized we were back at the party. "I trust you'll keep our conversation—and the other one—between us."

I nod. "Yeah, of course. Um, and Apollo, thank you for not smiting me."

He laughs.

"But—and please know I say this with nothing but respect for you and how infinitely more powerful you are than I am—I still think you're wrong about Artemis. I think she's so miserable, she may join Orion in the heavens. And I'm not being dramatic. I'm being honest."

"Thank you for being honest. And I trust you'll believe me when I tell you—honestly—that I didn't curse that man. And that I know better than anyone what's best for my sister."

He turns away from me without another word.

After several thousand heartbeats, I've recovered sufficiently to return to the party. Apollo and a dozen of his children are scattered near the front of the expansive main room as he announces the winners of the mortal bake off. No surprise, my dad's Baked Alaska didn't make the cut—my mom and Calliope are laughing about it in the corner. Also no surprise, Hestia and Thanatos won first and second, respectively.

"Next, while I hadn't planned to do this tonight, several of you have asked me if we could play my favorite little game." He waves his hand and a beautiful, gilded lyre appears. He holds it up for everyone to see. I catch my mom's eye as she makes a gagging face. I don't dare to laugh. I just glance back to Apollo. I don't know much about the lyre, other than that it's like a harp and you pluck the strings to make it play. This lyre is perfectly symmetrical. The base is sculpted beautifully where it's partially covered by what appears to be a tortoise shell. Its limbs curve upward and then flare out at the top where a gold pin fits into holes at the tips of the curved limbs, holding them together.

"The game is simple: this instrument can only play a single note. All you have to do is play it." He grins, as if this is a long-standing inside joke. Neither Calliope nor any of Apollo's children, including Hector, seem to be in on it. "Anyone who plays the note can have any one thing in my possession. But you only get one attempt each," he says, pointing at everyone.

"It's rigged," my dad yells out to laughter and applause.

Apollo laughs. "I assure you, Eros, it's not. This instrument is very special, but it does play. I swear on the Styx."

Eyebrows rise among some immortals, while some of the Twelve and the Ancients scoff.

Apollo passes the lyre around the room, and immortal after immortal tries to play it. When they tug on any of the strings or all three of them at once, nothing happens. Not even a twang. As the lyre approaches, I study it. From tip to tip, it looks like a single piece of gold. It has notches along the limbs where the three strings fit in. No, one string, I see as it gets closer. It's one string wound from notch to notch to make three lyre strings. I feel like this is significant, but I can't put a finger on why.

When the satyr next to me tries to hand me the lyre, I'm badly tempted to grab it. If I could study it closer, I may be able to figure out what the trick is. But I need some leverage over Apollo if I'm going to fulfill this prophecy, and I can't risk it yet. I hold my hands up and let the nymph to my left grab the lyre so I haven't touched it. I keep studying it, the symmetry of the long limbs, the outward curve of the tips. If not for the tortoise shell and the gold pin holding the limbs together . . .

My breath catches.

No. It couldn't be that simple.

Could it?

When the lyre reaches Apollo again, no one has been able to make it play. He looks pleased with himself. "Well, better luck next time." I notice him holding the lyre by the sculpted base, rather than by one of the limbs. His hand fits there perfectly. "If no one else would like to try—"

"I would!" I yell out.

Every face turns to me. My breath comes rapidly. My stomach is rolling and flipping, and my mouth is totally dry. It's probably my hyper-freaked out imagination, but a nervous energy seems to buzz all around me, too. Apollo looks interested, but not worried. Nowhere near it. "Come up, Kalixta," he invites pleasantly.

I walk past my friends, past my parents, who *do* look worried, and stand by Hector. I need his calm strength right now, because my hands are shaking so badly, I know even morties would be able to see it from across the silent room. Apollo hands me the lyre. As soon as I touch it, a loud clang sounds from the kitchen. I jump, along with half of the immortals. Anxious titters sound from around the room.

I grip the lyre. It's gold all right, but as I tug on and squeeze the limbs, it's also springy, like wood. I inspect the limbs and the base. Like I suspected, the base isn't a base at all; it's a handle. I grab the tortoise shell and pop it off from around the lyre. Immortals *ooh* and gasp. My eyes flash to Apollo. The corners of his eyes are tensed. Swelling with courage, I move my hands up the lyre to the golden pin holding the limbs in place. I inspect how the pin fits into the limbs, and try pulling and twisting until I notice small golden caps on the outsides of the pin. I unscrew these caps, and the pin slides out easily from both sides.

The limbs bounce out, but then get caught by the string, which is still held in place by the notches. I put the limbs between my knees and slowly pull the string out of each notch. Holding my breath, I pull the lyre from between my legs. It springs perfectly into place.

"It's a bow!" someone shouts.

Hushed conversation overtakes the room. I'm so nervous, every part of me is shaking. But when I grab the handle and draw on the string, a calm comes over me. The room falls into a dead silence. I close my eyes and release the string.

THWONG.

The room erupts in cheers, and I slump against Hector. His hand on my back steadies me. A crowd runs up to congratulate me, hug me, give my high-fives and fist bumps. I feel like I've just sprouted wings. I could be flying, for all I know. I turn to Apollo over the heads of the well-wishers and laughing immortals. He looks upset. Not angry, but troubled.

Eventually, a path clears between us, and I step forward. "Name your price, Kali. Anything I have," he says, his voice stiff.

"Can I trade it for a favor?"

"No." His refusal is so swift and final, I get the feeling he knows exactly what I was going to ask him. And that can only mean he actually did curse Mr. Gunner. Somehow.

"Can you give me a bit to think about it?" I ask.

"You may look over what I have, but this offer expires with the party."

He stalks away, and I try to find my way back to my friends and family. My parents manage to pull me through my eager new fans.

My mom is elated. "Do you realize what this means? We never have to play that cursing game again!" She hugs me hard and kisses both of my cheeks. "You brilliant girl, you!" I laugh.

Unlike my mom, my dad looks concerned. This is typical.

Although my mom has been on Olympus longer than the vast majority of immortals, he thinks her twenty years on Earth before she became immortal sheltered her from the darker side of the mountain. He grabs my shoulders. "I'm proud of you, Kali. Do you know what you're doing?"

"I don't know. Apollo swore to me that he didn't curse Mr. Gunner," I say openly, albeit in a low voice. Now that Apollo has admitted to knowing my plan, there's not much point in being secretive.

"I wanted to ask him for a favor instead of a possession, but he refused. But if he didn't curse Mr. Gunner, why would he refuse?"

"Don't even think about asking him," my dad tells me. If he knew that I already had, this would be a very different conversation.

"So what should I take, Dad? Mom?" I ask. "Are there any artifacts that can unbreak a curse?"

My dad shakes his head.

"Kali," my mom says. "My only advice is that you don't choose an object of power when you could choose an object of meaning. Power doesn't grant happiness. Choose something that will make you happy."

Despite my mom's advice being such "Mom" advice, as Hector takes me around his home for the next couple of hours, it starts to make sense.

Apollo undoubtedly has scary-powerful objects in his possession. But I don't want scary-powerful. I wouldn't know how to use scary-powerful.

We find our way back to the main room, stepping over immortals passed out or asleep. Some are talking or watching the movies that have played on repeat all night, and others are still playing mortal board games. The sun is close to rising, signaling the end of the party.

"So what's it going to be?" Hector asks.

We haven't touched at all since I figured out how to play Apollo's bow. It's like everything we said has been put back in a box, and we're just friends again. So while I badly want to grab him and say, "You," I can't. That arrow has already been shot.

"I just wish there was something that could help out Artemis or Mr. Gunner."

He looks at his feet, so I can't read his face. "You're pretty intent on fulfilling the prophecy, huh?"

"It's not just that. It's that I've seen how happy they are when they're together. Hec, I saw into their souls. They're as perfect a match as I've ever seen."

Hector's eyebrows arch. "I thought you hated this sort of thing. Yet, here you are, talking about matches and souls and happiness." He puts a hand to my forehead. "Are you feeling okay?"

I playfully swat away his hand, though as soon as it's gone I wish I hadn't. "They deserve love. They deserve each other."

Hector grabs my necklace, fingering the heart, the wing, and the arrow. His parents walk into the room, arms around each other. Calliope looks tired, but happy. Apollo kisses the side of her head. Something about the way he's holding her tells me he doesn't want to let her go. A hint of sympathy tugs at my heart. I see in him the man who's been abandoned by the love of his life for generations, and yet who always opens his heart back to her when she returns. And underneath that man, I see the little boy desperate to keep the one person he can always count on beside him: his sister.

But that abandonment isn't Artemis' fault, and this isn't her burden to bear.

"What have you decided, Kali?" Apollo asks me.

"Everything in your home is phenomenal, Apollo," I say, and my eyes turn to Hector. Yearning and regret surge through me. I wish things were different. I wish I had never stuck myself with an arrow. I wish Hector had never stuck himself—

My thoughts stutter. Do I wish that? Being with Hector was the happiest I've ever been in my life, even if it was a lie. The memory of that joy haunts me, but it comforts me, too. It reminds me of what I want more than anything, both for me and for the people I love. It's the closest I've ever come to Elysium.

I will do everything in my power to feel that way again. And when I fulfill this prophecy and choose to love again, it will be with someone who chooses me back.

I tear my eyes from Hector to look at Apollo. "The only thing that holds any meaning to me is the bow."

His jaw clenches the way Hector's does when he's upset. "What bow?"

"The one I just played. Your bow."

"Why? Of everything I have, why that?"

I know he's angry, because it's obviously important to him. But it's important to me, now, too. "Because of what it represents."

"That you beat a God," he states, his voice harder than diamonds.

"No," I say. "That I cared enough about a match to try."

Chapter Twenty-Six

Only two hours after leaving Apollo's party, I find myself shuffling into school, fighting off sleep. I'm still wearing the mortie outfit I wore to the party, but I fortunately remembered to change my appearance in the car on the way over. I spot Ben up ahead talking to Zoe. When they see me, they both rush over.

"Are you okay?" Ben says, giving me a tight hug. I make eye contact with Zoe, who looks physically pained. Ben's arms around me feel . . . wrong.

"I'm fine," I say, hiding my confusion as he releases me.

"How is your family?" Zoe asks. "Ben told me there was an emergency and that you weren't answering his messages. We were looking all over town for you! I hope everyone is all right."

"Oh, yeah, everything's fine." I say. "Deya's parents were in an accident, but they're going to be all right. I forgot my phone at the house or I would have updated you," I tell Ben. "Thanks for caring," I say to Zoe.

She smiles and pats my arm. "Of course. I'll let you guys catch up." Her smile is only a little tight as she turns around and walks away.

Ben hugs me again as I'm watching Zoe leave. The hug feels nice, and he smells good, and his arms are warm and caring. But I don't sink into it the way I should. If anything, I want it to end.

"So, I watched the video you sent of the guitar part for your new song. How's it coming?" I ask.

Excitement bubbles up in him. "I don't think I've ever written as much as I did this weekend, and the lyrics? They feel good. I was worried about you and I felt bad about how things have been lately, and that channeled into—" He quietly sings the lyrics as we walk into school. He's not wrong; they really are good. Poetic without being cheesy, thought provoking without being needlessly enigmatic. I can hear how the different parts will fit together, and I'm happy for him. I really am.

He holds my hand on our way to class, and the whole time we touch, I feel like I'm cheating on Hector. It doesn't make any rational sense, considering Ben is the one I was matched with against my will. And that makes me feel worse. But try as I may, I can't get my mind off of every touch and whisper from last night. I can't stop thinking about Hector and the feel of our hearts beating together.

I shake off the sentiment. That heart isn't mine to think about. It belongs to an arrow.

But so does Ben's. How can I keep letting him be with me?

A substitute teacher walks into the room, pulling me from my thoughts. "Mr. Gunner is still unwell, so I'll be substituting today," she says. "If you'll all turn to page—excuse me, where are you going?" she asks me.

I hadn't even realized I was standing up. "Um, I'm sorry, I don't feel well." I glance at Ben, who looks concerned. Then I grab my bag and run from class.

I jump into my SUV, calling up Cosmo. "Kali! Great job on the bow last night. Man, that was a huge surprise—"

"Cosmo," I interrupt, "I'm sorry, but I don't have time for

chitchat." I'm already pulling out of the parking lot. "I need an address for Tony Gunner."

"Oh, yeah, sure. Sending it to your phone's map now."

"I owe you. Give my love to Deya!"

His voice squeaks. "Deya?"

"She left early last night, didn't she? Conveniently at the same time as you?"

More squeaking. I laugh and let go of my necklace.

I pull into Mr. Gunner's place ten minutes later. It's an old ranch-style home built on a couple of acres. I run up to the door, slamming my fist against it. A dog barks from inside the house.

"Mr. Gunner! Open up! I know you're in there!" I can practically hear the despair in the beating of his heart. I pound the door again, yelling over the dog. "Mr. Gunner!"

The dog's barking ceases, and the door cracks to show Mr. Gunner looking like "The Dude" with a shaggy beard and a bathrobe over a T-shirt and boxers. The stale smell of pizza and beer and guy waft out of the door. I wave a hand in front of my nose.

"What are you doing here, Kali?"

"How long have you been holed up like this?"

He rubs his eyes. "When did I last see you?" I shove the door open and move past him. "Do you have any idea how much trouble I'd be in if someone knew you were here?"

I pull a Hera. I spot his gear on the kitchen table and grab it. "Get dressed, then meet me outside," I say.

He grumbles.

"I'm not asking." I go out the back door, slamming it behind me.

It takes a couple of minutes, but Mr. Gunner appears shortly after wearing pants and—hurray!—no bathrobe.

"You have a bale back here, or what?" I ask. He points through some pines farther into his yard. I eye him on the walk over. "I didn't peg you as the self-pity kind of guy."

He spits out a morbid laugh. "Hey, I've earned it. I've had my share of shi—sorry, I mean crap."

"Right, your fiancée."

"Yeah, and my parents before that. I've earned some mental health days." His eyes are bloodshot and haunted. I didn't know he'd lost his parents.

"So what are you going to do about it?" I ask.

"What do you mean? What am I supposed to do?"

"Suck it up! Crap happens, right? But you can't let this define you. You hold the world record in archery. Now prove it!"

We've reached his homemade target range and now I see what he meant last week. Arrows are scattered everywhere except near the target. He didn't even bother to retrieve them, which is un-characteristic of any real archer. "I've been cursed, Kali."

He grabs his bow from my hand and pulls out an arrow from the quiver I've dropped on the ground. He doesn't bother stepping up to the line. He just nocks an arrow and draws. He holds it for a moment, mouths, "Forgive me," and releases. It's not the best form I've seen from him, but it's good enough to hit the target.

It flies a dozen feet over the bale.

He nocks another arrow, draws, and releases. Then another. And another.

Nothing but air.

He looks at me in defeat and drops his bow on the forest floor.

"No" I say, shaking my head to clear it. "No, this doesn't make any sense. You can't be cursed. I checked!"

"Huh?"

"Nothing. I just mean, there has to be something else." I walk towards him and scoop up the bow. "Have you re-stringed it? Checked the sights?"

He looks at me flatly. "Seriously?"

I nock an arrow, draw, and release. My arrow flies and hits hard . . . in the middle of a tree ten yards from the bale.

"What the—?" I shoot again and again, just like Mr. Gunner, and like him, I miss every time. He looks at me like I'm cursed, too.

But I realize now what the problem is: Apollo was being honest when he said he didn't curse Mr. Gunner. He just failed to mention that he'd cursed his bow.

"Where are your other bows?"

"Kali, do you really think I wouldn't have tried my other bows? I've gone to three different stores and bought a dozen new bows! It's the same thing with every one of them. *I'm cursed.*" He tries to walk back to his house, but I run in front of him.

"Are you willing to try one more bow?"

Hours and hours later, Mr. Gunner thinks his curse has been lifted, at least temporarily. He's in good shape, and the longer he shoots, the better he gets. Not his personal, world-record-holding best, but more than enough to make tomorrow very interesting.

"Let's just hope my luck holds," he says as we collect his arrows.

"Don't say that," I tell him. "This isn't about luck. It's about rewriting your own fate."

"Rewriting it, huh?" He drops arrows into the quiver I'm holding, avoiding my gaze. "Do you think that rewrite will include your aunt when she gets back from Greece?"

I swallow hard. I don't have the heart to tell him the truth. Not yet, at least. "That's not my call. But if it's up to her, yes."

He frowns and smiles simultaneously, which ends up looking like a weird dance on his face. "If it's up to her, huh? What has she said?"

I smile, but I want to cry. A weird dance for my emotions. "She likes you, Mr. G. Don't push it."

When we get back to his house, I hand him the quiver. He grabs my shoulder. "I don't know how to thank you, Kali."

"Win tomorrow."

"Are you sure you're okay with me holding onto this until tomorrow? This sucker is quite the good luck charm," he says, hefting Apollo's—correction, *my*—golden bow. Which just so happens to be curse-proof.

"Yes, please. Hold on to it. In fact, sleep with it. Don't let it out of your sight."

"Deal," he smiles. "See you tomorrow."

I get into my car and hear my phone chime. I hadn't realized I'd left it in the car. I swipe the screen to see thirty-six texts from Ben.

Thirty-six.

I'm so annoyed, I don't even bother reading them. I just pick up my phone and call him.

He answers on the first ring. "Are you okay?" he blurts out.

"I'm fine. Why?"

He curses. "You ran sick out of class twelve hours ago, and I haven't heard from you since! I thought something seriously bad had happened to you, and no one's at your house. I've called the hospital and the police about a dozen times each."

I groan, feeling like a huge jerk. "I'm sorry, Ben. I just . . . slept it off in my car. And my phone died, so I didn't get your messages until I plugged it in a minute ago. I'm fine."

"I'm so relieved. My mom has been lighting candles for you, and everything. You can't just leave on me like that, Kal. I . . . need you."

My throat tightens. "You do?"

"Yeah, and I'm coming over, okay? I'll be there in ten."

He clicks off and I sigh. It's sweet, his concern. How he cared enough to go to such trouble for me. But the pang in my heart is less about how sweet he is and more about how I wish he weren't coming over.

I pull into the ranch and just sit in my car, grabbing my head. I feel . . . different. My feelings for Ben are different. I don't have that inextricable pull that I had only a month ago, or even a week ago. When I think about him, I see the hair in front of his eyes, I see him looking down at me from the stage, alive with talent and energy and passion. I remember hundreds of grazes and kisses and love notes. I hear his voice telling me about the stars, singing just for me.

But I don't feel butterflies. I feel nostalgia.

Lights flash at me as a vehicle pulls into the driveway. I turn off my car, the thuds of my heart sending waves of panic through my body. I have to do something, now. I can't keep feeling like this: stuck and sad and done. It's not the raging madness of a bad match. But it's not love. For days, I've had a question bouncing around in the back of my mind that I couldn't quite put my finger on in the midst of all of this regret. But it's finally surfaced.

How is it possible that I feel like this at all?

I take a deep, ragged breath and step out of the car to meet Ben. But it's not Ben stepping out of the car, it's Hector.

"Hec, what are you doing here?"

He slams the car door and runs over to me. "I just had to see you, Kal. I haven't been able to stop thinking about last night."

The sun rises in my chest, and I struggle to stuff it back down. "Me either."

He grabs my hands. Warm, pleasant, tingles run up my arms, and without thinking about what I'm doing, I interlock our fingers. "When we were talking at the party, you said you didn't know what was the arrow and what wasn't," he says. "Here you are doing everything you can to break your spell, and I'm going out with Ianira to make you jealous—"

"Wait, what?" I demand. "What do you mean, make me jealous? She was using the belt to get you to fall for her!"

His hands squeeze mine. "The belt must not have been strong enough to overcome how I feel for you."

"It wasn't stronger than the arrow, you mean," I tell him, and the thought makes me drop my hands. I stuff them in the pockets of Hector's oversized cardigan. The thread from the Fates is there, of course. The hags just love taunting me.

Hector runs a hand through his hair. "That's why I'm here. I don't know what's the arrow and what's not either, Kal. But I can't handle the arrow getting in the way of everything that we could have. That we *should* have. You're everything to me. When I'm happy, you're the first person I want to share it with. When I'm upset, you're the person I want to make me feel better. When I hear something that moves me, I have to listen to it with you and see you love it before I can love it. I fall in love with the world *through* you, Kali."

Tears spring to my eyes. I feel like his every word is setting me on fire, and the feeling of the thread in my pocket is the ice that's dousing the flames. "I haven't been fair to you," he says. "How can I resent you for being with Ben instead of me when you're compelled the same way you think I am?"

"You *are* compelled, Hector."

He wrings his hands, and I'm filled with a desperate need to hold him tight and never let him go, a need I can't give in to.

"Not for long. That's what I came to tell you. I'm going to the Or—"

The sound of tires spitting gravel in the driveway interrupts us. Ben's old truck skids to a stop a few yards away from us, and he jumps out of his truck, running to me. My eyes dart to Hector's in time to see shock. Shock and pain.

Ben pushes past Hector and grabs me in a tight hug. "Oh, Kali. I'm so glad you're okay. I don't mean to freak, but after this weekend and then today, I just—" He kisses me, and I go stiff. Then he holds me out just enough to study my face. "Please don't disappear on me again."

I back up, removing his hands from my face. "Ben, can we talk about this?"

But he isn't listening. He looks behind him to see Hector. How he missed a 6'2" Greek god on his sprint over here is anyone's guess. Ben goes all tough-guy. "Hey, man. What are you doing here?"

"Ben," I say before an incredulous Hector can respond, "we have to talk."

"No, you don't," Hector says, looking right at me. The pain on his face is so deep, I feel it in my gut. But worse than the pain is the betrayal in his eyes. It's as if I lured him in just to stab him when his guard was down. "She's lucky to have you, Ben."

With that, he turns around and just walks to his car. Ben tries to put his arm around me, but I shrug him off and run to Hector.

"Hec, wait! Don't go!"

His heart has been dashed to pieces, and the painful aftermath shows on his face. "I am such a fool, such a complete and utter masochist." He throws open his car door, heedless of the tears welling in my eyes. "After everything last night, you're just with him? *Kissing him?*" His voice drops dangerously low. "I can't believe I let myself think you were really trying to break the arrow's spell! You're too afraid to let this end, aren't you? Or is that you're just too afraid to let this," he says, pointing back and forth between us, "begin?"

"How can you say that?" I cry as he opens his door. "You just told me that you understood about the arrow. How can you just turn around and blame me?"

"I don't blame you. I blame myself for hoping."

I want to scream and cry. I stomp my foot on the ground, the force of it causing the earth to tremble. I'm not even a little sorry when I see Hector stumble against the car door. He drops into the driver's seat. "Stop it! What were you going to say? Just before Ben arrived—what were you going to say?"

"That I've finally reached my limit, Kal. I'm done."

He slams his car door, his engine roars to life, and he's gone.

I cover my face with my hands, wanting to break down completely. No, wanting to jump in my car and chase him down to get some answers. No, wanting to curse him into—

"What was that about?"

Styx. I forgot about Ben.

"Ben, I'm sorry." I don't know what to apologize for first.

"No, I'm sorry. I'm not accusing you of anything, Kali. The guy clearly has feelings for you to leave so upset." To my surprise, he chuckles. "I should have guessed that the first time I'd come to your house, I'd have to get in line," he teases.

I can't believe he's actually talked himself out of a brood. I'm not sure how to respond. But something he said clicks in my mind.

"Wait, you said that when you were checking all over for me earlier today, that no one was at my house. But you just said this is the first time you've been here. How did you know no one was around if you've never been here?"

His gaze shifts. "Oh, I had a friend check."

Why won't he look me in the eye? "Who?"

"Come on, Kal. Who cares? Why does it matter?"

"Because it does. Who was it?"

His nostrils flare. "It was Zoe, okay? She was asking about you in PE, and when I told her about this morning, she asked me to keep her posted, all right? It's not a big deal. She was being nice. When I told her you were still MIA a few hours ago, she volunteered to drive over here and check."

I can't believe how stupid I've been. And I don't blame him for a second. "Did you guys have a good time together this weekend?"

He jams a hand in his pocket with his phone. Is he protecting it from me? "What is this? Do you think I'm *cheating* on you? After Mr. Male Model shows up here, freaking out about seeing us together? What right do you have to be jealous?"

"Absolutely none. You're right. I've been the most colossal hypocrite." I rub my temples, exhausted. "Ben, why are you with me?"

"Are you kidding? Kali, you're cool and you're fun and you're beautiful."

"Okay, but so is Zoe. Probably a lot more fun, and certainly a lot more compatible with you."

He throws his hands in the air. "There's nothing going on with Zoe."

"I know," I say honestly. "But I want to know the reason you're with me, specifically. We fight a lot. Don't pretend we don't. You wrote an apology song for a fight I wasn't even a part of this weekend, Ben! And you were right. I was with Hector, and he did comfort me, and I should feel a lot worse about this than I do."

He doesn't answer.

"Don't you think it's strange that we're together but keep seeking out other people? Two people in particular?"

The annoyance fades from his face, replaced by softness. "I care about you. I need you. You just . . . do something to me. It's like you make me tap into this deep part of myself and pull out all the dark bits of my soul. I've never been as in touch with myself and my music as I have been since you came into my life. You've done this to me, Kali. I don't know what I'd do without you."

This should be music to my ears. It would be if being a muse was my true calling. I am Ben's muse. But—compelled or not—should the first thought that comes to Ben's mind when he thinks of me be that he's more in touch with his personal darkness?

My head aches from how deeply my brow is creased. "Ben, tell me about your dad."

"What?"

"I know you were hoping he'd come to see your band play. Zoe told me. It was unforgivable for him not to come. How did you feel?"

His body is tight and his shoulders hunched. "Whatever. It's not that big a deal."

"Don't you think we should be able to talk about this together?"

"What's there to talk about?" he asks, grinding his foot into the driveway.

I wait for him to say something more, to curse or yell or break down. But nothing comes. The wound is too fresh to expose, at least to me. He's so hurt, this boy who doesn't know how to control his pain or his fear. He has let me in over the last month, but just enough for him to tap into his poetic side. Just enough for him to create but not heal. I've given Ben inspiration, but not what he really needs.

Love.

And I've been keeping him from it this whole time.

The truth hits me like a bolt from Zeus: the unjust union the Oracle told me about wasn't Deya's restaurant owner; it wasn't Ben's dad; it wasn't Hector and Ianira, with her stolen belt.

It was Ben and me.

A mixture of sorrow and regret and self-loathing fills me. I did this. I caused Zoe and Ben this grief at not being together. I distracted Ben from what could bring him healing and—more importantly—real, lasting happiness.

And I caused Hector a world of pain and betrayal that I can't even stomach thinking about.

For the first time since knowing him, since even seeing him, I focus hard on Ben, beyond the cute, brooding, bass-playing boy, and I peer into his soul. Through a hazy concert hall, I see an orchestra. The string section is playing, intent and passionate, but the sound coming from them is dissonance. While each performer plays with exceptional skill, some of the violins are out of tune and the cellos are all playing at different paces. It's a mess, disorganized and discordant, but with remarkable potential. It just needs a conductor.

A deep, heart-wrenching ache settles into my bones. This poor boy has all the talent in the world, but it's not enough to make him happy. *I'm* not enough. And he's not enough for me, either. If I'm painfully honest with myself, I've known that for a while now. And I know what I need to do about that.

My mind is made up when Ben's phone chimes, yanking me from my epiphany. He pulls it out of his pocket.

"It's a text from my mom," he says, showing me his phone. "She wants me home thirty minutes ago." I nod. He leans in, and every sense in my body revolts. I can't kiss him. Not now. He seems to understand, because at the last minute, he turns his head just enough to kiss my cheek. "See you tomorrow."

I watch him go, relieved, yet anxious.

It's not enough to know that I've made this mess, now I have to fix it. And for once, I know how.

Chapter Twenty-Seven

BEEP.

"Artemis, I know I shouldn't be doing this, and I know I'm thanatotic for talking to you like this, but I'm really disappointed in you. You're the strongest, bravest immortal I know, yet you're too afraid of getting hurt to go after what you truly want. You're the only Goddess out there who follows all of the rules, but those rules were made in a different age when Zeus was young and the world was younger. Times have changed, Artemis, and you need to change with them. So Apollo doesn't want you with Tony? So you're afraid of something happening to him? The Artemis I thought I knew wouldn't be a victim like this; she wouldn't just be a martyr when she could be happy. And she sure as Styx wouldn't let her brother or anyone else threaten someone she loves." I sigh. "I figured out how to break Tony's curse, and I'll be at the medal round today. I hope you come. You should at least watch, because Tony's going to smash the Hades out of that record."

I press End on the call and hope to Gaia that she's still checking her voicemail.

In a show of pride, the principal has given Mr. Gunner's students the day off to see the medal match in Phoenix. And in a show of support, Deya and Teresa have taken the day off to keep me from having a nervous breakdown. Teresa drives us down to Phoenix, which turns out to be a blessing because she's a way better driver than we are. Cosmo hasn't had to yell at us once.

"So that's his only text since last night?" Deya asks.

"Yep," I say, handing my phone across the console to her in the passenger seat. Her eyes scan the same message I've avoided answering all morning.

Sorry about last night. Are we okay?

"Do you know what you're going to say to him when you see him?"

I tell them.

"But what about the arrow? The prophecy? After everything you've done—*we've* done— you're just going to give up your quest?"

I reach into my pocket and run a finger over the thread I knew would be there. "I don't know if any of that matters anymore."

"Are you being fatalistic again?" Deya turns around to study me.

"No, realistic," I say with a hard-won smile.

Teresa looks at me in the rearview mirror. "What's changed?"

"Me."

We pull into the overflow parking lot at the range, and I'm a bundle of nerves. I follow my friends to where they're lining up behind tourists and students, but then I see Mr. Gunner running from the range towards us.

"Kali! Deya!" Mr. Gunner yells, wearing shorts and a navy polo shirt. He talks to the range security guards, and they unhook a rope to let us out of the line. We introduce Teresa to him as a friend, and he says, "The more, the merrier. I need as many good luck charms as I can get."

We follow him through the facilities and past the spectator-filled stands to the outdoor target range. He explains that the officials already checked over his equipment and, while they were fascinated by the golden bow, it was technically up to standard.

"So, tell me about your competition," I say.

He points across the range to a stocky man. "Jens Bjorkman, who passed me up in the cumulatives after my train wreck last round. He's good, but he's not the real competition." His hand moves to point out a bear of a man with pale blond hair.

"Ugh, Stone Savage. That guy is such a tool," Deya says. "You have to take him down."

"That's what I'm hoping," he says.

Stone's entourage is huddled around him. They part, and he walks by them to the shooting line. I lose sight of what he's doing, though, because Hector is twenty yards from me, standing with Stone's people. His eyes skip over me as if I'm a stranger. My heart throws up.

"I can't stand this," I tell Deya and Teresa. "I need to talk to him."

"No," Teresa says. "You need to keep it in your pants long enough to end this."

She's right. I don't get to talk to him. Not yet. We watch Jens and Stone take practice shots. As long as Mr. Gunner's head is in the game—and he doesn't get cursed again—Jens doesn't stand a chance against him. He hits more eights than nines.

But Stone. Holy Hades. Hector said he had skill, but how did this Gorgon get to be so good at something that requires so much discipline? He's hitting tens like the bale is seven meters away rather than seventy.

Mr. Gunner turns to us, looking green. "I can't do this. I'm not ready for this. I haven't competed in years. What am I thinking, competing now?"

Teresa grabs the collar of his polo shirt. "Get it together, man.

There's nothing at stake here. You're winning a medal *no matter what*. So, you stink it up and get bronze? Isn't that better than the big fat nothing you'd get if you were home on your couch, scratching yourself and eating Cheetos?"

I choke on what I wish were a laugh. There's so, so much more at stake than either of them realize. But Teresa's words do the trick: Mr. Gunner's face clears. "I get your point," he says, straightening his shirt. "But don't knock Cheetos. They're delicious."

"Shut up and show us what you got, Mr. G!" Deya says.

Mr. Gunner goes up to the shooting line and straddles it. Then he fires off half a dozen bows, sinking each into the bullseye like this is his regular Tuesday routine.

He struts back to us and slaps our hands in high-fives. Stone shoots him an icy glare. When a bell sounds, indicating that the match will begin in five minutes, Mr. Gunner says, "I should go wish them both luck. I'll be right back."

"I'll go over with you," I say. "I have a friend I want to say hit to, anyway."

Mr. Gunner goes to Jens first, and the two shake hands and start talking. I pass them to go straight to Hector, who steps away from his group.

"Hey," I say, following him. He doesn't look at me. "What are we, five? Look at me!"

He does. It is not a happy look.

"Are you ready to tell me what you were trying to say last night?"

He shakes his head. "It doesn't matter, Kali. I deluded myself into thinking that we could happen, but we're never going to happen. You're never going to get over the arrow, and you're never going to trust the way I feel because of it. And even if you do fulfill the prophecy, you're always going to find a reason for us not to be together. You decided too long ago that you couldn't have a love story like your parents, not because of the arrow, but because you're terrified of a love so strong, it could shake the heavens." Behind the sadness in his eyes is resolve as firm as stone. "So I'm out."

"I was wondering when you'd finally go full Greek god on me."

"What is that supposed to mean?"

"It means you're being an immature, overdramatic—" A glint of light hits me in the face. I look past Hector to see something being angled to reflect light directly in my eye. What the Styx? I squint, raising a hand to block the light, and I see three robed and hooded old crones.

My eyes widen. "Hector, I know I just told you what a brat you're being, but I need you to wait for a minute." I run backwards for a moment. "We're not done here."

The Fates are standing up against the bleachers, and I sprint to them.

"Kalixta Erostos," Scissors says.

"We have to stop meeting like this, ladies," I say carefully. "I thought you didn't get out much."

"We get out when there's a show," she says almost casually.

"I get the feeling you're not talking about the new Marvel movie," I hazard. "So why are you here?"

"To watch you try to beat fate," the one with the staff creaks.

"But that's just it, isn't it?" I say. "There's nothing to beat."

The Moirai with the spindle of thread narrows her eyes. "What do you mean?"

I pull out the thread they gave me, the thread that's been in my pocket no matter what I'm wearing since the day they gave it to me. "I was wrong about this. It isn't just a thread."

"What is it?" Staff asks.

"It's a blank slate. It's potential." I point to one end of the thick, iridescent thread, where the tiny fibers wind together and around each other, like an elaborately wrought licorice. Hundreds of interlocking fibers make up that thread, but each of those fibers is made up of hundreds of other fibers. "This thread may have a beginning and an end, but there are countless endings and millions of paths I can take to get to those endings, aren't there?" I gesture to one thread that has a tiny break on it. "Like if I go up against a god, I could continue along or I could hit a very early end." I stop at the break. "And if I stick myself with an arrow, I could choose to follow that through," I follow a fiber as it circles the larger thread all the way up, "or I could just cross an intersecting path." I veer off of that fiber to an interlocking one and follow it up the thread.

Scissors, Spindle, and Staff smile at me, showing their gap-toothed, black-hole mouths.

"A couple of errors," Scissors says.

"A jump or two in logic," Staff says.

"But you've figured it out, have you?" Spindle says.

I nod. "This whole time that I was mad at you, I should have been mad at me. I was the only one keeping myself from the fate I wanted."

"So why are you still here?" Spindle asks.

I look back at Mr. Gunner and Hector and my friends. I turn back to the stands and my eyes hunt for Ben, who's looking at Zoe two rows in front of him. "Because I have a calling to answer."

They cackle, like this is the funniest thing they've heard in eons. Then Staff points back toward Mr. Gunner. Or maybe Hector or Stone. "Be that as it may, you also have a prophecy to fulfill."

I frown. "What? What do you mean? I thought you said—"

"Oh, you're correct that your fate is in your hands," Scissors says, "But right now, so is theirs. What was it the Pythia said? That your quest for heart could end in none?"

My head whips over to Hector, and I stop listening to them altogether. I just run. I risk a glance behind me, but the Moirai are gone. In the stands, Ben looks at me with the same betrayal I saw on Hector's face last night. *I'm sorry*, I think. A moment later, my phone vibrates with what I'm sure is a text from Ben. And another, all of which I have to ignore for now. I get to Hector, and I grab him.

"I wasn't planning to do this yet, but you need to know I don't care about the arrow anymore, okay? I care about you. I want to be with you, but I have a lot of crap to get done and not a lot of time." He opens his mouth to argue, and I put a hand over his lips. "Don't give up on me now. Let me fix this."

"I can't keep doing this. I meant what I said, Kali. I'm done," he says, turning from me.

I want to scream at him. *I love you, you son of a harpy!*

Hector spins around, gaping at me. "Did you just . . . did you just insult me? Telepathically?"

My mouth falls open. I did it! "Yes," I exclaim. "I did. And I meant every word."

"You called me a son of a harpy!"

"Yes, and I also told you I love you," I say. Beyond Hector, Mr. Gunner is approaching Stone, who's staring him down. I take two steps toward Hector until we're close enough to kiss. "Now, can we resume this conversation later? I have a prophecy to fulfill before your dad ruins everything."

"My dad?"

"Later." I grab his considerable shoulders and peer into bright green eyes with golden sunbursts around the pupils, eyes I know better than I know my own. "I love you. No matter what happens today, I need you to remember that."

I push off of him toward Mr. Gunner, but Hector grabs my arm. The intensity of his gaze could turn me to stone. "Finish this now. Then we'll talk."

I nod and race over to Mr. Gunner, where he's talking to Stone.

Stone's slimy eyes roam over me. "So this is how you got your groove back, eh Gunner?"

"Don't embarrass yourself, Stone, and don't you dare insult this girl," Mr. Gunner says. "I just came over to wish you good luck."

Stone laughs. "Like I'll need it! You're the one with the historic choke on your record, not me."

Mr. Gunner just nods. "Yeah, you're right."

Stone folds his arms in a way that makes his biceps look even bigger. Ugh. "That's all you have to say for yourself? No explanation? No excuses? I thought you were telling everyone you were cursed."

"Maybe I was, maybe I wasn't. But it's time I moved past that." Mr. Gunner's face lights up, eclipsing the sun. I follow his gaze.

Ferry me to Hades, it's Artemis.

I break into a grin as she steps around TV cameras and reporters and coaches to get to us. She's wearing a "Team Gunner" T-shirt.

Stone's face goes as hard as his name. "How many women do you have in your little harem?"

Mr. Gunner puts a finger up to Stone's face. "You insult the woman I love or anyone in her family again, it'll be the last thing you ever do."

Stone slaps his hand. "Why, you gonna stop me?"

With a laugh, Mr. Gunner walks by Stone to get to Artemis. He calls back, "No, she will."

I hold back while Mr. Gunner and Artemis have their reunion, though there are plenty of eyes on them as they kiss. Plenty of *ooh*s, too. Stone looks like he could break things, he's so angry.

"Can I ask you a question?" I say.

He clenches his jaw and turns to me, his bright green eyes hard. With golden sunbursts around the pupils.

"Apollo," I whisper.

He looks all around us, then at me. "Breathe a word of this to my sister—"

"And you'll end me, I get it." My pulse is like a runaway train. "What are you doing here?"

"I've come to see if that man gets to live."

"*Live?*" I whisper-shout. "Apollo, you can't—"

The rage of a God bears down on me. I shrink. His voice is so low and menacing, I don't hear it with my supernatural ears; I hear it in my soul. "I can do whatever I want. If this man doesn't deserve my sister, he doesn't deserve his life."

The iridescent thread in my pocket seems to go heavy. Like I'm at a crossroads. Like the thread is ready for me to see this fiber through to the end or jump paths. I'm not sure myself.

"So what's the plan? Beat him and then kill him? Will your sister ever forgive you?"

"She always has," he says, turning my legs to jelly. But the way his forehead creases makes me think there's a bit of bluster behind his words.

"I have a counterproposal," I dare in a shaking voice.

"Go on."

"I want to challenge you."

Incredulity explodes across Apollo's face. But he's interested, too. Of course he is. "You want to challenge me? A God? Why would I agree?"

"Because you love a contest more than anyone. The rest of the Big Gs get offended. You get excited."

He looks at me shrewdly. "I'm listening."

With all the courage I can manage, I say, "If Mr. Gunner beats you, not only does he keep his life, but he gets Artemis, too." His body language shifts, and I'm positive he's about to walk away from me. "Remember that Mr. Gunner is mortal—that's, what, sixty mortie years he'd get with Artemis? You're eternal. You've taken vacations longer than that."

He looks almost amused. "You're right. And if he loses, do I have your *permission* to smite him from existence?"

"No," I say. My pulse throbs in my neck. "Smite me."

"What?"

"Artemis means a lot to me, too. I want her happiness as much as I want my own. And just consider what Artemis is saying by just being here, by kissing Tony in the middle of a cloudless day: she doesn't care who's watching. She's choosing him over everything. So yes, maybe you'll have to watch them together for a few decades, but at least if he loses, you can take your wrath out on me."

Apollo's green eyes focus and I get the feeling that he's reading my soul. Or that he's looking forward to squishing my life force out of existence. "You have a deal."

I'm half-relieved, half-petrified. "Excellent. But only if it's a fair fight."

He looks like he wants to spit. "Of course it's fair. Stone's mind is taking a little vacation, but this is still his body. And while I'm in his body, I'm confining myself to his mortal limitations."

My eyebrows jump. "Do you swear on the Styx?"

His brilliant green eyes flash red for a moment, but he nods.

I study him for any sign of a trick, but breaking an oath sworn on the Styx comes with a fatal penalty, and Apollo's anything but thanatotic. "And you haven't done anything to Mr. Gunner or his equipment? Or my equipment? Or, I don't know, his target? Or asked the wind to flare up every time he shoots? Or Helios to blind him? Or—"

"Enough, Kali," Apollo says. "Even had I wanted to, my sister has now put him under her protection. He's been Olympus-proofed." The aggravation in his voice is evidence enough for me.

I stop talking and watch Mr. Gunner and Artemis through Apollo's eyes. The way they laugh and tease each other. The way her eyes dance when she talks to him. The way he listens to her and pauses to think about what she said before he responds. I would think a brother would be thrilled to see such respect and adoration for his sister. But Apollo's face shows jealousy. And I doubt he even knows who he's jealous of.

A buzzer sounds, and the archers are asked to take their marks. The match has begun.

Chapter Twenty-Eight

The archers have one hundred and forty-four arrows to shoot and one minute per shot, regardless of how the wind blows or how tired they get. That means that a match where they take the full minute each time could take over seven hours.

This match won't take more than three.

Apollo and Mr. Gunner are shooting fast and with deadly accuracy. By intermission, after the hundredth arrows have been shot, Apollo has a nine eighty-six and Mr. Gunner has a nine eighty. The scores to this point are unprecedented, but the Phoenix sun is hot and everyone is feeling the effects.

I've been trying to get Hector's attention and Ben's been trying to get mine. The archers stretch and rehydrate. Artemis talks to Mr. Gunner, giving him a pep talk, or maybe a lecture, while Deya puts her head on my shoulder.

"Is there something weird about Stone today, or what?" she asks. Apollo stares at Artemis and Mr. Gunner with the straightest posture I've ever seen. It's so formal and godly, I almost pull a Hera.

"Stone Savage is a nutcase. Nothing that dude does makes sense." I take a minute to tell her and Teresa Hector's story about the skunk, laughing hysterically by the end of it.

Intermission ends and Artemis returns to her seat by us on the sidelines. "What are you guys laughing about?" she asks.

"Stone Savage's gastronomical pyrotechnics," I say.

"The skunk story?" she asks.

"That's the one."

"Good."

The archers resume shooting, with Apollo shooting first because he had the high cumulative score going into the match. Over the next hour, Apollo shoots a dozen straight tens followed by a handful of nines, with Mr. Gunner matching him shot for shot. Jens, however, is starting to falter. He's so far behind the other two, now, he'll be lucky if he breaks thirteen twenty.

With ten arrows remaining, the crowd is perfectly silent. Apollo has shot several nines in a row, and Mr. Gunner is only a single point behind him now. The silence in the arena extends to the shooters. Apollo has stopped making snide comments and Mr. Gunner has stopped flirting with Artemis. The only sounds are from the announcer and a moaning Jens.

Jens straddles the shooting line and draws, but his draw arm is shaking. The wind has picked up to ten miles an hour, and he holds the draw, waiting for the wind to die down. Thirty seconds pass. Forty-five seconds. His arm is shaking so badly, he's sweating. At fifty-eight seconds, I hear an audible *pop*. Then Jens screams. He writhes, flails. And the arrow releases.

It shoots straight for Mr. Gunner. And he has no idea it's coming.

"No!" I scream. I lunge toward Mr. Gunner, but I'm not fast enough. The arrow is blasting toward him, aiming straight for his heart.

But something even faster zooms past me. With impossible speed, I see Artemis bolt to Mr. Gunner, covering dozens of yards faster than the blink of an eye, gaining on the arrow. At the last moment, she leaps. She crashes into him and they slam into the ground. The arrow whizzes right over them. Artemis is covering Mr. Gunner like a mother bear covering her cub.

He's safe.

He's safe, and I can breathe.

The crowd, the immortals, Mr. Gunner—everyone reacts at once. There's screaming in the stands. People are accusing Jens of trying to kill Mr. Gunner. Artemis is holding Tony, scanning him for any signs of injury. When she's satisfied herself that he's fine, she jumps up, Old World rage on her face. She takes one look at Stone, and I realize she knows.

She marches past me, and I grab her arm. "Artemis, you should know—"

"This isn't your fight, kid."

"Um, I sort of made it my fight when I challenged your brother to a contest."

"You what?" She curses. "It doesn't matter. I'm done playing by their rules, Kali. I don't care if you swore an oath to my father on the Styx," she says, the power of a full Goddess rippling through her. "This. Isn't. Your. Fight." She grits her teeth, shakes off my grip, and marches toward Stone.

I watch her stride, dimly aware of my friends surrounding me. "Holy Hades, Artemis is terrifying," Teresa says appreciatively.

I just nod.

"I think someone wants to talk to you," Deya says, pointing across the range. Hector is pacing, his arms folded, chewing on the inside of his cheek. I've never seen him look so nervous. "No, another someone," Deya says. I look past Hector to where Ben is trying to fight off a security guard to jump the fence. In the chaotic stands above, Zoe looks heartsick.

"Wish me luck," I say, already walking.

"You'll need it," she calls after me.

Hector stares me down the entire distance between us. He's shaking his head and scowling. When I'm about to pass him, I reach out to grab his hand. Instead, he pulls me close in an embrace that makes my knees tremble.

"Don't do anything dangerous like that again," he whispers into my hair.

"Like what?" I ask against his neck. "And why are you shaking?"

He kisses my head, and my heart soars. "I heard you talking to my aunt. You challenged my dad? What were you thinking?"

I don't answer. I just settle into his chest and breathe until I want to cry. I want to grow roots here and stay in his embrace forever. Well, almost. I pull myself off his chest. "I need to go settle things with Ben." He winces just hearing the boy's name. "But I'll be right back. Don't move, okay?"

His eyes lock on mine. "Kali, what you said earlier. You're serious about this, aren't you? About us?"

On the Styx, I swear it, I think to him.

The look on his face reminds me of Elysium.

I jog past reporters who want to know what happened, who that was who saved Mr. G, who I am, if I think Jens was trying to kill Tony, how I know Stone. I ignore them and stop at the fence where Ben stands on the other side. His ash-brown hair is pushed back where he's been running his hand through it.

"Holy crap, Kal, what happened out there? Is Mr. G okay? What is going on?"

"He's fine," I say. "Everything's going to be okay."

His hands twitch on the fence, and as a silence stretches out between us, I know the time has come. I put a hand on his.

"Ben, it means a lot to me that you care about me. This

relationship, dating you, it's meant more to me than you could ever know. You came into my life at a time when I felt lost, and you helped me find myself again. I'll never forget that. You've given me so much, and now I want to give you something."

"What?"

"Your heart." At his confused look, I say, "I don't think either of us are as happy as we deserve to be. I know: I'm your muse. In a way, I'm glad I could be that for you, but it's not enough for either of us. I'm no one's sidekick, and you're no one's second choice. You deserve better than what we have."

"No, Kal, you're incredible."

"Thanks. I think you're incredible, too. I just don't think we're incredible together. I think there's someone else that you could have forever with, and I want that for you, truly."

"Is this about Hector?"

I smile, and I hope he can feel my sincerity. "No more than it is about Zoe."

His walls fly up so clearly, I can see them without even looking in his soul. "Zoe? Kal, that's never going to happen. She's my friend."

"Yeah. Your best friend, right? The person you tell your deepest secrets to and the person you want to talk to when something amazing or terrible happens? I'm not saying you're in love with her right now, but I'm saying that you shouldn't hold back because you're afraid to ruin your relationship. You won't, Ben. I promise you won't."

His brow wrinkles, and he doesn't speak right away. When he does, he looks resigned. "You know, I was waiting for this. I knew something was off with us, but I just didn't want to be the one to leave, you know? I didn't want to be like my dad." He clears his throat. "I didn't want to be the bad guy."

"Ben, you could never be the bad guy. You're a good guy. You're the best guy."

He breathes out a laugh. His eyes are wet. "So this is it, huh?"

A lump forms in my throat and I blink through blurry eyes. "Yeah. I think this is it."

"Then come here." Over the fence, we hug each other one last time, and when we let go, I feel a piece of my heart go with him.

With a wave, Ben returns to the bleachers and I walk back to Hector. He holds out an arm for me and I sink into his embrace, tears rolling down my cheeks. When the wetness soaks through his shirt, Hector says, "You okay?"

"Yeah. Just really, really happy." He looks down and tips my face up to his.

"And Ben?"

I point to the arrow on my necklace. "He will be."

"Good." He grabs my hand from my necklace and wraps it back around his waist. I smile against his chest.

Officials have been interviewing the archers while medics check out Jens. Hector and I move a little closer to hear what's going on. Deya and Teresa approach, grinning stupidly at us. I stupid-grin back.

"So, Jens has 'archer's shoulder.' The strain of long draw after long draw was too much after repeated stress injuries, and he dislocated it," Teresa says.

"So he wasn't trying to kill Mr. Gunner," Deya says.

No, but someone was, I think but don't dare say aloud. I look for Apollo in the crowd of security guards and tournament officials. I spot "Stone" beside a tall banner next to the water and Gatorade station with Artemis. They're only maybe a dozen yards from us, but with all the clamor, it's hard to hear what they're saying, even with immortal ears. I tell Hector I'm going to check on Artemis, and he nods. But when he spots them himself, his eyes narrow.

I take a few steps towards them, but Artemis glares at me with eyes of fire. "Kali, get your butt away from here or I'll destroy you after I destroy my brother."

I run back to my friends and tuck myself under Hector's shoulder so I can't get zapped. "Artemis and my dad fighting?" Hector asks.

My head jerks up. "You knew?"

"Kal, seriously? You don't think I'd recognize my own dad? Or that Stone suddenly has the posture of a Hephaestian automaton?" I frown. "I've been trying to keep an eye on him. I hoped I'd be able to intervene if he did anything that would hurt Artemis." His green eyes look stormy. "I wasn't fast enough—"

"You didn't need to be."

He bumps the side of his head against mine. "You've spent the last month looking for a way to overcome your fate, and I've just sat in the clouds and watched my life happen. You're my hero, Kal."

A roar more powerful than the falls swells within me. "Really?"

He gives me a look that sends shivers down my whole body. "Really."

I want to melt under the heat of his gaze, but the bustle around us pulls my attention.

The officials have taken everyone's statements and the medics have carted Jens off. A voice announces that Jens has been awarded the bronze medal and that Mr. Gunner and Stone will be competing for gold in ten minutes. The crowd cheers, and the archers wave. But Mr. Gunner looks pretty shaken up. I get it.

When Artemis and a very badly chastened "Stone" return, I catch her eye and nod over at Mr. Gunner. She takes the hint.

"How are you holding up?" she asks him.

His hands cover his face. "Not good, Cynthia. I don't think I can do this. It's Melanie's curse, all over again. She doesn't want me to shoot and she doesn't want me to move on. How am I supposed to compete now?"

"Tony, there's no curse—"

"You know I just almost got shot, right?"

"Yeah, I do know. And watching it was one of the worst moments of my life." She puts her hands on his face. "I don't care what you do today, as long as you give it your best. Because your best is all I want. Your worst, too." She wrinkles her nose, and I realize she's tearing up. Artemis! "I love you. I know we've both lost and we've both been hurt by it. But I'm not going to let that keep me from you. I had a love written across the stars once." She clutches her Orion necklace, and her voice cracks. "But you're more than the stars to me, Tony. You're my universe."

Mr. Gunner's eyes squeeze shut. Tears stream down his face as he wraps Artemis in his arms and just holds her. When he finally opens his eyes, he looks heavenward. "Thank you, Mel," he whispers. "Thank you."

"What am I missing?" Artemis asks.

"I just got my sign." He kisses her firmly on the lips. "You're my universe, too, Cynthia." The buzzer sounds. "Now it's time for me to crush this douchebag."

Artemis laughs. Hard.

Apollo passes me to return to the line. "This isn't over," he tells me. "I don't care what my sister says. Our deal stands."

I look at Artemis giving Mr. Gunner a pep talk, and the faith I thought I'd lost blossoms in my chest. "Apollo, there's only one thing I'm better at in the universe than you, and that's matching.

I have the ability to see into a soul and understand the love that can complete them. I wish you could see what I see when I look at Mr. Gunner and your sister. It would take your breath away."

He looks at them, and that glimpse I got of his soul comes back to me. Fear of abandonment eats away at him. He walks away without another word.

Apollo and Mr. Gunner approach the line at the same time.

"There's a lot riding on this tournament," Apollo says. "Do you really think you can beat me?"

"I'll do my best. If that's not enough, I'll just train harder."

"Because you want to beat me so badly?"

"That wouldn't be the worst thing," Mr. Gunner says with a smirk. "But I'm just trying to be the best *I* can be."

I expect Apollo to pull a Hera, but he doesn't. If anything, he looks bewildered.

"Good luck, Stone," Mr. Gunner says.

"Same to you, Tony."

Chapter Twenty-Nine

Both archers move swiftly, hitting tens on their first few shots. But the adrenaline quickly wears off and exhaustion starts to set in. With four arrows to go, Mr. Gunner sinks a bullseye to reach a score of thirteen seventy-six. For the first time in the match, he's tied with Apollo.

I might die of anxiety.

Both men will break Mr. Gunner's world record today, but beating the record means nothing if Mr. Gunner loses to Apollo, at least not for me. As much as Apollo has been acting civilized since they returned to the line, he's gone Old World. The only way Mr. G and Artemis get to be together is if he wins. The only way I live to see another day is if he beats Apollo. Yet the few mortals in history to beat the sun God at something ended up with donkey ears, strung up and flayed, or just straight killed. I pray to Zeus for donkey ears.

I squeeze Hector tighter. Three more arrows apiece.

Ten for Apollo.

Ten for Mr. Gunner.

Two more arrows each. Apollo straddles the line, looking beat. He draws, the wind at four miles per hour. He pauses. And pauses. At forty-one seconds, the wind drops to a mile per hour. Apollo shoots.

Eight.

My jaw drops. Gasps circulate in the stands. Apollo has just shot an eight. The lowest either he or Mr. Gunner has shot yet today. Even mortal, Apollo couldn't have expected this. As he turns from the bale, he looks more shocked than anyone. Tears sting the back of my eyes. I challenged a God so that someone I love can have a chance at real love for the first time in her life. And seeing Artemis walk over to Mr. Gunner, I know I did the right thing.

"This changes nothing," she tells him. "Your goal is to knock back two more tens, okay?"

"You got it, boss," he grins. She slaps his butt.

Apollo's eyes look like they're going to scorch this entire arena from the face of the Earth.

Mr. Gunner steps up to the line, hefts his bow and nocks an arrow. The wind has picked back up again, blowing eight miles an hour. Like Apollo, Mr. Gunner waits for more favorable wind. He holds his draw expertly, as if he doesn't feel the strain at all. With only seconds to spare, the wind is still blowing. Mr. Gunner adjusts his aim. Exhales. Releases.

Nine.

A collective exhale sounds from our group. Mr. Gunner is sitting at thirteen ninety-five, Apollo at thirteen ninety-four.

Apollo wears a stunned expression. He's losing to a mortal for the first time since he was the youngest, brand-newest God on Earth. He steps up to the line one final time, putting one foot in front and one foot behind it. He couldn't have expected such a fierce competition. Until this week, Apollo has never shot for so long with mortal frailties. He's never felt a burn in his muscles or the sun beating down on him. He's never had his hands cramp or had a headache from squinting at the same spot one hundred and forty times in a day. He's never been so close to losing his sister. But he's not going down without a fight.

He pulls an arrow from his quiver, nocks it, and raises the bow. He draws with every ounce of power in him. The muscles in his back look like they're straining, not just from the exertion, but from the effort of containing the God within. Apollo takes aim and fires.

Dead center.

The Stone contingent in the crowd screams and cheers. The ichor in my veins feels like it's curdling. Mr. Gunner needs a perfect ten to win. A perfect ten, or else this is my last moment with Hector, with my friends. A perfect ten, or I'll never see my family again.

But I can't dwell on my fears, because this may be the last opportunity I have to fulfill the prophecy. To save Ben.

I stand on tiptoes and whisper in Hector's ear, "No matter what happens, Hec, I need you to know that I love you."

His brow tugs into a deep *V*. "That sounds oddly final."

"Hopefully it's just the beginning. But either way, I have a job to do. I hope I'll be back."

Hector's eyes glint, like an emerald on fire. "You *will* be back, Kali. We're not done here."

I flash him a tight smile before clutching the wings on my necklace and going into stealth mode. I slip over to the stands as Mr. Gunner takes his mark. I look for Ben. Like the rest of the crowd, he's intent on Mr. Gunner. Well, like most of the crowd. I see a girl twirling a red curl around her finger, stealing glances at Ben's nervous face two rows behind her.

As Mr. Gunner reaches into his quiver, I clutch the arrow on my necklace. I sigh as my gear shimmers into existence for only me to see. Hefting my bow is like saying hello to an old friend. I can hardly believe how much I've missed this feeling: the studying, the careful observation and meticulous calculations, the satisfaction—not of shooting, but of matching. I doubt I'll ever get over the match that broke my heart, assuming I live long enough *Please, let me live long enough.* It's still a Thunderclap, but not in the way I thought. Everything has meaning. Each match matters. If Mr. Gunner wins, this knowledge will make me study and plan and work harder than ever for every single match. It will make every success that much sweeter. Hope soars in my heart.

This is my calling.

With a glance back at Mr. Gunner, I grab an arrow and nock it at the same time he does. I mind his every movement, sensing the way his muscles strain, waiting for that exact moment he releases so that I can time my strike with his. When we both release our arrows, Ben will be freed from our unjust union, whether because the prophecy is fulfilled or because Apollo has blotted out my existence.

Gaia, I hope the prophecy is fulfilled.

I line my target up in my sights, waiting for Ben's eyes to fall on Zoe. It doesn't take long. He looks down to see her gazing up at him, bouncing and crossing her fingers. At her smile, the orchestra that makes up his soul explodes with an urgent desire to get this performance just right. But nerves and fears and old wounds keep the strings on different pages. He needs someone to guide his performance.

And here she is, a steady, even conductor who can sense when the performance is about to take a bad turn before it happens. Here stands the one person with the patience and commitment to be able to raise a finger and get the strings on the same notes, on the same page, in beautiful harmony. Here stands someone bold, but not fearless. Someone with mounting pressure to be someone she doesn't want to be. I see the expectations others place on her to follow a different path, one she's afraid she'll be forced into if she can't find the strength to break free.

When she looks at Ben, the strength of Atlas swells in her. With him, she can be anything. With her, he can finally be himself.

They need each other.

I draw, pulling with all my heart and might, not breathing so I don't miss a beat. The crowd is totally still. They await that perfect shot that will make history. A shot that will change a champion's life and heal a Goddess' heart. And I await a shot that will give two mortals a forever they can't create on their own.

Everyone has waited long enough.

I fire. Mr. Gunner fires. Our arrows fly. In perfect trajectory, two arrows strike their targets. The walls crumble and Ben beams, his symphony playing in perfect harmony just as the audience erupts into thunderous applause.

Two perfect tens.

The entire crowd stands and jumps, with resounding yells and ear-splitting cheers. Beneath it all, though, is a sweet, joyful melody playing from one heart to another. Ben and Zoe push through the throng towards each other. When they embrace, jumping up and down, it's for more than a world championship. It's for their personal forever. Ben's eyes search the range and find me, and for a second, I panic. But he gives me a smile that looks older. Wiser, somehow. I point to Zoe and wink, and he waves me off. He gives her another hug, and with my extra-supernatural hearing, I hear her ask him if he's doing anything after the match.

I grin. They're going to be just fine.

I turn from them, feeling like my joy is full. Well, almost full. I have a pair of lips that I need on mine. Right now.

I navigate through the crowds and the media, ready to go Old World on these fools, when I see Hector. I pull him in for a hug and I whisper in his ear, "Wanna get out of here?" When my lips graze his neck, I feel his knees go weak. I hold him up, grinning against his chest.

"Kali," he says. "There's nothing in the heavens or on Earth that I want more. But I can't."

"What?"

"I have to see the Oracle."

I want to smite things. Many, many things. "What? Why now, Hector?"

"You know why." His eyes hold mine.

I growl. "Fine! But I'm taking you there myself. Now."

He lets me grab his hand, and we race for an exit. I try to push him into a secluded corner for just a minute, but the mob of fans pushes us instead toward Artemis and Mr. Gunner, who are shaking hands with Apollo.

"Good match," Apollo says, the words sounding clipped and positively venomous.

"You, too," Mr. Gunner says, ignoring Apollo's tone. "Do you want to go out, grab a drink after the circus dies down?"

Taken aback, Apollo glances at Artemis.

"We can't, Tony," she says. "I was actually hoping to introduce you to my brother. He's a colossal jerk sometimes, but he's my best friend. I'm pretty eager for the two most important people in my life to meet."

Apollo takes a step back, but there's no way he's not listening as Mr. Gunner nervously asks, "Do you think we'll get along?"

Artemis chuckles. "No, not a bit. He'll probably want you dead for a while. But I'm tougher than he is," she says, smiling fiercely. "Besides, once he really gets to know you, he'll love you almost as much as I do."

"Kinky," Mr. Gunner says. Artemis laughs and kisses him, a long kiss that tells me I'm not the only one desperate to get the love of my eternal life out of this cursing maze.

"I'm going to start blowing things up if we don't get out of here," Hector says.

"Join the club."

Artemis and Tony break apart and spot us as we're just about to make a fast break. "You two. Here. Now," Artemis says.

Not one to defy a Goddess, I step forward, but Hector holds me firm. "We'd love to, but we have somewhere to be. Congratulations, Tony!" he yells. His eagerness makes me giddy. "Outstanding job!"

"Yep, congrats, Mr. G! You did it!" I say as we back up. "Fourteen oh-five!"

Instead of letting us leave, Tony runs through the crowd, which parts easily for him. He gives me a quick hug. "Thank you for everything, Kali." I allow myself to pause and really smile at him. Olympian rules aside, something tells me I'm going to see a lot more of Mr. Gunner for a long time. Zeus loves a happy ending. "Now go, your boy here looks like he's about to break me in half."

With a wave to Deya and Teresa and Artemis and Tony, we run for it.

We dart around corners until we find a part of the arena that's totally empty. We're in the clear.

"Not so fast."

The force in the voice stops us abruptly. It's Apollo. Not

Apollo-wearing-Stone's-body. Apollo in his full glory, the power of the sun radiating off of him, burning my eyes. I squint.

"That was a game well played, Kali," he says. The air shimmers around him. Heat rolls off of him in powerful, painful waves. I feel like my skin will be charred to ash.

Hector steps in front of me, blocking my trembling, scorching body from his enraged father. "No more, Dad. No more deals with Kali, no more threats, no more destruction." He looks back at me. "Besides, she won when Tony won. This is over."

The muscles in Apollo's jaw tense, but he smiles. "Of course, son." He looks past Hector to me. "I hope you've found what you're looking for."

I step out from behind Hector and slip my hand in his. "I have."

"At least something good has come from all this," Apollo mutters. A hint of amusement is visible beneath the fury sparking from his eyes. "Now it looks like I have to meet my sister's boyfriend over drinks. Maybe Dionysus will give me some of the good stuff so I can endure this." He groans and then vanishes. I laugh weakly and almost sink into the ground.

"Your dad's going to become an alcoholic."

"Drinking is better than smiting," Hector says, turning to face me. He takes a deep breath then gently grabs my necklace instead of his, which I know is his way of getting to touch me without breaking his no-kissing-until-the-cursing-arrow-is-reversed rule. The soft touch of his hand against my skin makes me shiver down to my bones. "Cosmo, we need to port to the Oracle at Delphi ASAP. Can you hook us up?"

"Um . . ." Cosmo starts.

A moment later, we hear a distinctly non-Cos voice say, "Actually, kids, you're due home."

It's my dad.

I can't believe I thought the Fates liked me.

My dad—who was doing quality control at the time—has instructed Cosmo to port us directly to my house. We're standing awkwardly in my parents' room, which is roughly half the size of the arena we just left. I don't know what kind of a lecture I'm in for, but at least my parents' roof is finally coming in handy. Helios won't be able to report anything that happens here, the old gossip.

My mom is lounging on a divan, smiling at us, which feels out of place compared to my dad. His arms are folded tight, and his wings are high behind him. It could be terribly intimidating, but I've faced down the Moirai and a God and lived to tell the tale. This is a stroll through an Olympian rose garden.

"What is it now, Dad?"

"You went to the Oracle to figure out how to reclaim your heart? Is that what I'm to understand?"

"What else was I supposed to do?" I cry. "I had to be free of the arrow's spell, and I am. I rediscovered my true calling and made the best match of my life. I helped Artemis find real love and—"

"And she saved a mortie's life," Hector adds. He looks anxious. Whether it's fear of what my dad will do or because he wants to get to the Oracle already, I don't know.

My dad gives us a long, measured look. "Hector, if Kali already saw the Oracle, why do you want to go there?"

Hector grabs my hand, his touch not giving me strength as much as it makes me want to kiss his face off. "To reverse my arrow. I love your daughter, but I don't want the arrow to get in the way of anything we could have. I want to reverse the spell so I can prove that we really do belong together."

My mom's still smiling, her legs kicked over the arm of the divan. She's swinging a sandal lazily off of one toe. "Hector, how long have you loved my daughter?"

"Since the arrow. Since I was twelve."

"I want you to think of the first time you felt like Kali was special." He cocks his head, so my mom continues. "Do you remember Teresa's tenth birthday? I only remember it because I was talking to your mother at your dad's last party. She saw you and Kali dancing together and reminded me of a story I'd forgotten. You told her that most of the immortals refused to go to Teresa's party because they were afraid of her, so Kali threatened to steal her dad's arrows and match each of them with a different head of a hydra if they didn't shut up and get to the party. You're a little older than the girls, so you were maybe eleven when this happened. Am I right?"

Hector looks like he's having a Thunderclap of his own.

"What am I missing," I ask my mom. I clutch Hector's hand tighter.

"Kalixta," my mom says. "You started out so happy with Ben, but things were rough near the end, weren't they? You seemed exhausted and miserable. Is that a fair assessment?" I nod. "Why didn't you break up with him?"

"I wanted to, but the arrow stopped me."

"So you tried and were unable to?"

"No . . ." I shake my head and keep shaking it. I look at Hector, whose eyes are wide. He starts laughing.

My mom sits up straight. "You didn't break up with Ben because you'd been told that an arrow in an immortal match is unbreakable.

But if you'd been told that, with enough effort, it would be possible to break an arrow's spell, would you have ended things with him?"

"Yes. In fact, I think I was about to—"

Mom conjures up a towel and throws it at my dad. "See, Monster? I told you that's the lie we should have gone with."

"What?" I look at my parents in turn, emotion crawling up my chest and into my throat and spilling out my eyes. "What are you saying? What the Styx are you saying?"

"They lied," Hector says, looking happier than a sailor with a siren. He tugs me closer, throwing his arms around me. I'm shaking too much to reciprocate. "They lied about the arrows, Kali."

"No, they couldn't have," I say. "They were both stuck!"

"Hector's right," Dad says. "Arrows don't work on immortals. When Aphrodite gave me the assignment to match your mom with a monster, I watched her, like any good Erote. The more I watched her, the harder I fell. And your mom and I were already happily married and living together when she finally saw my real face. Didn't you think it was strange that she only pricked herself after we were happy? After I "accidently" let her see a glimpse of my glory? We were already in love, but we had to tell Zeus it was the arrows so he'd give your mom ambrosia and let us stay together. You know what a romantic he is."

I bump my forehead against Hector's chest. My world has been rocked. Up is down, white is black, Aphrodite is a virgin. Nothing makes sense anymore. "But what about Ben? Obviously the arrow worked on him."

"No. The power of the arrow was nullified. If you had struck him with the arrow instead of yourself, he would have been compelled to love you. But we'd have been able to reverse it, because it would have been *his* match. Instead, this was your match. Or non-match, rather. When you pricked yourself, nothing happened except that you were honest about your crush. I suspect, too, that this forced you to confront some truths about your feelings about Hector that you'd buried," Dad says as sagely as any Oracle. I'm sputtering. Literally sputtering. "I know what you're thinking. What about all the immortals who pricked themselves: Dionysus, Zeus, Aphrodite, even Apollo in his youth? They ultimately did exactly what they wanted under the guise of being magically compelled. Look around Olympus. Is that really so surprising?"

Hector gives a low, disbelieving chuckle. It reverberates through me.

"I watched the screen of your match, Kali," Dad says. "Ben saw the girl he couldn't let himself like—Zoe—wearing a look that said she was going to ask him out. He panicked. He looked at you and saw the perfect out: a beautiful girl with similarly esoteric tastes in music. Why wouldn't he approach you? Why wouldn't he fall for you?"

My mom butts in. "And I think if you were to reexamine the weeks leading up to your accidental sticking, you'll realize that you had a crush on him before the arrow. Taking five weeks on an assignment. You?" Mom asks, echoing Deya's sentiment from all those weeks ago. "And how did you somehow go visible to him at the last possible moment before Zoe could ask him out or before you could make the match? You had a crush. You conveniently stuck yourself with an arrow."

Ferry me to Hades.

I magick up a chair and slump from Hector's arms down into it. Hector rests his hands back on my shoulders. They're trembling.

"Why didn't you tell us?" Hector asks, the words sounding raw, like the shock and relief is fading, replaced with the pain of all those months we were apart. "We were torn apart. What would have happened if we hadn't figured out the lie? Would we have just been separated forever? How would you have lived with that?"

"If an arrow does anything for immortals, it makes them honest," Dad says gently. "I soulgazed the two of you when you were, oh, five or six years old. You were as right for each other as any two souls I've ever seen. You're only more so now. So when you told us that you pricked yourself, Hector, I knew you were just sharing your real feelings," Dad says. "And, not to get too full of myself, but I'm the god of love. I may not have foresight like your father, but when you've seen trillions of matches play out, you come to know the moves by heart. The day after you two broke up, I predicted that you'd be back together, well, yesterday, actually. I'm embarrassed to admit I may be slipping."

"Monster!" my mom yells at the same time that I shout, "Not helping!" I incinerate an antique vase with my smiting powers just to prove my point.

My dad pulls an absolutely colossal Hera.

"Okay, but that doesn't make things any better for me," Hector says, ignoring our outbursts. "You should have told me. I was devastated after my mom left. And when Kali broke up with me? I didn't know if my heart would ever heal. Do you have any idea how badly I hurt?"

My parents share a look. "We're sorry for that pain, Hector. That was an unintended consequence of keeping secret something that could destroy a lot of lives," Mom says.

"Not good enough, Mom. And what about me? After the Thunderclap?" I ask. My voice is tight and breathy. "You saw how much it hurt me to break up with Hector. And then all this time with Ben! A single moment of truth would have saved us so much heartache."

My mom comes over to me, magicking a chair beside mine. She puts a hand on my back, which, with Hector's hands still on my shoulders, is feeling crowded. "What seems like 'all this time' to you is almost no time at all, even to mortals," Mom says. "Think of how angry you were after your Thunderclap. Were you in a place to listen to us?"

"No," my dad answers for me. I manage to *not* stick my tongue out at him.

"Now think of everything you've been through to fulfill the prophecy. Think of Artemis and her mortal. Think of Ben, who is no doubt wiser for his experiences. Think of the love you feel for Hector in this very moment. Is it not greater for how hard you worked to get here? Can you really be upset by how things turned out?"

I sit up and turn to look at Hector, who's looking down on me with worry on his brow.

"No," I answer.

"Besides," my dad says. "When you've raised hundreds of children, a little star-crossed love is about as surprising as a clear day on Olympus."

Little known fact: Olympians invented free-range parenting.

I'm annoyed and shocked and kind of not shocked, because this feels so right, and, really, I'm over this—all of the drama and the rage and the angst. I've spent too much time feeling sorry for myself and being angry with Fate. Thinking back on these last few months, I'm not sure I would change a thing. This time hasn't been wasted. It's been a gift. It's made me more sure of my calling, more sure of my love than I could ever have been otherwise.

I gaze up at Hector. *My* Hector, and a vision of Elysium enters my mind. Peace, joy, elation.

Heaven.

He beams at me.

Holy Hades, do I ever need to kiss him.

I jump to my feet. "Okay, I get it. You lied, Hector has always loved me, I only ever wanted to be a muse so I could still have an excuse to be around Hector because I've always loved him—"

"What?" Hector stops me. "Even when you were with Ben?"

"Like I could ever stop loving you," I say, my heart expanding. I take his hands, and warm tingles shoot up my arms and through my body, and if I'm not careful, I might accidentally incinerate something else with all this heat. "Now, Mom, Dad. I'm absurdly, stupidly mad at you. Like Old World style. And you may wake up to find a raging minotaur in your room tonight. But I need to talk to Hector. Privately. Now."

Hector is glowing a little—sun God offspring, and all. "Uh, Psyche, Eros, would you excuse us?"

"Shh. They've lost the right to have an opinion about me ever again." I start pulling on Hector, and he follows happily behind me. "Bye Mom. Bye Dad. Don't wait up."

"Don't do anything Aphrodite would do!" Mom yells, laughing.

"No promises!" I yell back.

When we're outside of my house, I flip around so that I'm walking backwards, and Hector's arms are around me, and we're laughing and stumbling and I almost fall over.

Hector growls, catching me mid-stumble. "This isn't working." He grabs my necklace, and when his hands brush against my neck, I shiver. "Cos, you owe us. Port us to the waterfall, now."

Cosmo's voice sounds over us, sounding far too amused. "Fine."

"And give us a heads up the next time our plans are about to be foiled by meddling parents, would you?" Hector says as I try to attack his neck with my mouth. He holds me back.

Then Deya's voice is there. "Have fun, you two."

I grab Hector's chiton in my fists and promise, "We will."

When we vanish and reappear at the waterfall an instant later, the air vibrates and shimmers around us. There's an extra energy here today. The waterfall is creating more mist, almost like it's responding to the mounting tension between us. Soon, the mist surrounds us, clings to us, fills our lungs. My breaths grow more and more shallow until I'm panting. Hector's intensely green eyes go wild, and his gaze drops to my mouth. My lips part. My breath catches. His hands grip my arms, pulling me to him.

And.

We.

Are.

Finally.

Kissing.

Oh my Styx. Kissing Hector is the greatest sensation in the heavens. My hands dive into his hair, playing with his curls. His hands rove over my back, as if he's trying to push out every molecule separating our souls. Our mouths know exactly what to do, when to part, where to meet. Our breath mingles, and it is the sweetest flavor I've ever tasted. We don't fight for bottom lip. We take turns seamlessly. And being able to just grab the muscles in his arms, his back, being able to feel his abs against me. It's heaven. I give his lips a break so I can nibble on his ear, all the while holding him as close as physically possible . . . at least until he starts backing away.

Why is he backing away?

"Kal, hold on," he says with his lips on mine.

"The talking portion of this evening is over, thank you very much." I kiss his neck. "We have entered the kissing portion. No refunds."

His hands on my back don't disagree, but his mouth—that insanely edible mouth that I want back on my mouth—keeps protesting. "Kal." *Kiss.* "Kal." *Kiss.* "Seriously."

I pull back. "What, Hec? What could be more important than this?" I try to kiss him again, and he pinches my mouth before I can. He smirks.

"Okay, that's pretty cute. You have duck lips," he says. Kissing them.

I push his hand away, laughing. "Get off, you nerd. By which I mean, come here."

"Kalixta!"

I jump. "Okay, I get it. You really want to talk. Are-are we okay?"

He pulls me down to the carpet of grass, and plants me on his lap. "Yes, we're okay." To prove it, he kisses my neck, just below my ear, and I'm a puddle of goo. "I just need to ask you something." His eyebrows tug together slightly, and I want to kiss the worry from him. "I want you to tell me why you did it. Why you went to the Oracle, the Fates. Why you challenged my dad, which you are never doing again, by the way."

I chuckle, but I don't disagree. I settle against his chest and take a long, slow breath. "I've been thinking about that a lot since the weekend, but especially since my chat with the Fates earlier." I run a finger up and down his tanned, muscled arm. "Subconsciously, I think I was trying to prove that if I could reverse my arrow, you'd be able to, as well. That would give us the chance to finally see if what we had was real."

Hector's green eyes sparkle with emotion. "Really?" I nod, and he kisses my nose.

"Now it's my turn to ask a question. Why did the arrow never bother you like it bothered me? Why did you embrace the idea of being compelled to love me?"

"That day that my mom announced she was returning to Earth, I was so upset. I thought shooting her with an arrow would solve everything. But that's not the whole reason I went to your house that day. I went because I knew you were the only person who could help me be happy again." He rests his forehead against mine. "But I was scared, too."

"Of what?"

"Of you leaving me like my mom was leaving me. When you stormed through your parents' door—so fierce and protective and worried—and caught me holding that arrow?" He shakes his head. "The love I felt for you in that moment was overpowering. All consuming."

"If only it had been strong enough to keep you from dating Ianira," I tease.

He laughs and kisses the tip of my nose. "I regret nothing," he says. "It made you jealous, and it proved to me the one thing I already knew: I'd never be able to move on from you. Not even Aphrodite's cestus could change that."

I cover my face with my hands. I don't know if I'm crying or laughing or if my mind has been so blown over the last hour that I'm not actually doing either. Hec pulls my hands down from my watery eyes, and he holds my face just inches from his own.

"I love you, Kal. I will always love you."

I wrap my arms around him, pulling him as close as I can. Wishing I could fit him inside my heart, where he's always been.

"I'm sorry for all the pain I caused you, Hec. I never stopped loving you. Not for a second," I admit. "But after the Thunderclap, the thought of you not loving me like I loved you was terrifying. I was too hurt and scared. I stopped believing that real love could exist anywhere anymore, let alone on Mount Olympus. I wasn't ready to trust my own heart, and I wasn't ready to admit that my fate was sealed when we were little brats running around in our whites."

"Fate again, huh?"

"Only the kind I make for myself."

His lips graze mine. "Don't tell me you have another quest to undertake."

I smile and hold him, but I don't respond. Because we both know that my one true quest—the quest for heart—has ended where it should have started: with Hector.

When I lean in to kiss him, it's not with that sense of urgency or desire that I had even twenty minutes ago. It's with love, pure and simple. Our lips touch, and I see into his soul. No, into *our* souls, because I can't tell where his ends and mine begins. We are the stars in a constellation. The trees in a forest. The notes in a chord. We are the river of the heavens meeting the waterfall of the gods.

We are one.

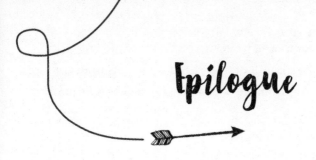

Epilogue

Come on, Deya shouts to my mind. *Hurry up!*

No talking during tests, my mom thinks, pushing Deya out of my head. I finish the last sentence, scan the four hundred and thirty-two page pop quiz for any missing commas, and close the book.

I jump up, hand it to my mom—who winks—and walk out of class with Deya. We rush a little through the gorgeous halls, past paintings and friezes and sculptures of famous lovers that bring tears to my eyes.

"Do not tell me you're getting weepy about all of this again," Deya says, pulling a Hera.

"Hey, you're the one who wanted me to care about my calling again. I blame you."

"Better than blaming the Fates," she says.

We get to the Port in record time, and soon, we're at the O-Ranch, where my dad is waiting. A moment later, my mom appears. "Sorry," she tells my dad. "I got held up by an overeager fifth-year."

I shrug, but pride bursts in my chest. "Where are the guys?" I ask.

"They had to run an errand," Dad says. "Is that what you two are wearing?"

"Oh, whoops," I say, looking in the mirror. We're in mortal dresses—mine a bright blue, Deya's a deep gold—but we've forgotten to wear our mortie faces. In a blink, Deya and I magick out of our glory. The front door opens, and we hear Cosmo and Hector laughing as they come in. When Cosmo sees Deya, he puts a hand over his chest.

"Wow."

Deya glides over to Cosmo and plants a kiss on his cheek. "Wow back at you," she says, ogling Cosmo in his mortie tux. "We really need to rethink the dress code on Olympus." Cosmo blushes.

I'm biting my lip looking Hector over. Holy Hades, the man can wear a suit. And his eyes are practically devouring me.

"You can put those eyes away right now," my dad warns Hector.

"You get no opinions, remember?" I snap playfully. Mostly.

My dad glares, but I remain unsmited and ungrounded. Ha!

"You look beautiful, all of you," Mom says.

"Now stand in front of the fireplace so I can take pictures," Dad says. He pulls an aqua screen from the air and captures image after image of us smiling. "Good! Now let's take some more on the balcony—"

"You have plenty, big brother," Deya says. "We have to get to the school already."

"I think you'll like the ride I've set up," Cosmo says. "Right this way." His limp is more of a hop as he leads us out the front door and down the steps to where a shiny, black limousine awaits us. Deya squeals and jumps in. We all follow.

"Have fun, kids!" Dad shouts.

Fifteen minutes later, we arrive at Ponderosa High. It feels strange being back here. Mr. Gunner told everyone that Deya and I moved back to Greece, but that didn't stop Ben from dropping by the O-Ranch last week with an invitation for us to see his band play. They signed with a major indie label a month ago, and this is their last show before their summer tour.

None of us could resist.

After giving our tickets at the door, we walk into the gym, which has been brilliantly decorated to look like the night sky, courtesy of Zoe and the rest of the decorating committee. The dance is already well on its way (Stupid test. Thanks a lot, Mom.), and students are packed around the room, swaying to the music. The walls look like the tree-lined peaks of a mountain. Constellations hang from the dark ceiling above. And the moon shines its spotlight down on us.

Deya, Cosmo, Hector, and I stand in front of a backdrop that reads "The Stars and More," and get our pictures taken. Then we spot a couple of familiar faces.

"You made it!" Tony Gunner says. "I told you they'd make it."

"Of course they made it," Artemis says. "I told *you* they were going to be late. Which they are."

"And I told you they aren't late until the band starts. And the band has not started. Yet." He snaps, and the moon spotlight beams down on Ben, Paresh, and Shaggy, who are standing on the stage at the front of the gym.

"Hello Ponderosa High!" Shaggy shouts into the microphone. "We are Sasquatch and the Little Feet, and we are here to rock the stars from the sky. You ready?"

The students shout back an emphatic *yes*. Paresh snaps his drumsticks together and the guys start into a peppy song guaranteed to get people moving. I lean against Hector, sighing contentedly.

"I haven't heard this song yet. Is it new?" he asks.

"It must be," I say. I turn my head to smile back at him. "I didn't inspire *all* their songs, you know."

"Just the best ones." He kisses my neck, and folds his arms around my waist.

"Obviously."

His kiss turns into a nibble.

"No making out." Tony interrupts us with a wry grin.

"Not even a little?" Artemis asks with a wink.

A warm blush grows on Tony's cheeks until he's practically shining. Oh, crap.

"Tony, you're shining," I mutter.

"Shoot," he says, concentrating until his inner light turns off. "I still don't have a handle on these immortie powers."

"You're embarrassing yourself." Artemis says. "It's morties, not immorties."

"If anything, I'm embarrassing you, considering your father gave you the responsibility to teach me how to be a god." Tony's words make Artemis bite back a smile that I'm pretty sure would incinerate all of Flagstaff if unleashed. "Besides, that makes no sense. If you call mortals morties, why wouldn't immortals be immorties?"

They bicker and flirt through the next two songs. "Your brother agrees with me, you should know," Tony says at one point.

"No way in Hades does Apollo agree with you."

Cosmo and Deya return from the dance floor. "What are they fighting about now?" Deya asks, looking at Artemis and Tony.

"If Jackie Chan is actually the god Zhenwu," Hector says.

"I could find out—" Cosmo starts.

"Don't," the rest of us say.

He shrugs. "Does anyone else think a Greek god named Tony is kind of funny? Like, 'Hi, I'm Achilles, and this is my friend

Ariadne, and over there are my buddies Daedalus, Prosymnus, Icarus, and Tony.'"

We all look at each other. And burst out laughing.

"It's a good name," Tony says with a glare before turning back to Artemis.

Over their flirting, we hear Ben's voice in the microphone. "I'd like to dedicate this next song to the girl who inspired it in the first place," he says, playing the first few notes of "Lovestruck."

I look at Hector in alarm. Deya leans over. "Um, what?"

"Last August, I walked in on the first day of school and I saw a girl that I never thought I'd see again. She walked down the hall, flipped her red hair in my direction, and I was done for. I started writing this song during the very first class of the day, and I kept at it for months, which probably explains why I got a C." The crowd laughs. "It took me months to get the song perfect, but it took me even longer to admit the truth." He clears his throat, grabs the microphone, and his gaze drops down to the gym floor, where a beautiful redheaded Zoe is clasping her hands together and holding them over her heart. "I love you, Zoe Abrams. This one's for you."

Hector laces his fingers in mine and pulls me out to the dance floor. I rest my cheek against his chest and listen to his heartbeat underscore every beat of Paresh's bass drum. When Ben drops his guitar and sings the final chorus into the microphone, I sing it with him:

> *When you turn from your fate*
> *Give yourself up to luck*
> *That's how it feels*
> *To be lovestruck.*

Hector kisses my head. "That's not *exactly* what it's like."

"Are you saying I'm a bad muse?"

"I'm not *not* saying it."

"Do you want me to smite you?"

"Already smitten, thanks."

"Should I—"

His lips silence mine, and I feel his teasing, wonderful love in every kiss. I laugh as our mouths meet over and over again in the middle of the dance floor, feeling like I'm bursting with excitement and contentment and perfect, all-encompassing joy.

Because that's how it feels to be lovestruck.

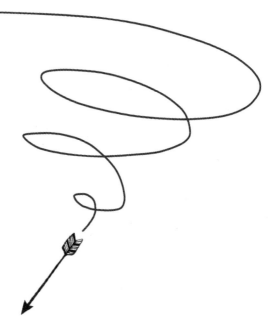

Acknowledgments

They say third time is a charm. Well, let's see if I can make these acknowledgments any less rambling than I'm wont to. But it's just so hard! I have thoughts, y'all! Gushing thoughts that demand to be spilled!

I'm failing already, aren't I?

Moving on.

Readers. Oh, you fabulous readers. Thank you for sticking with me through this wild ride. Thanks to you, I get to keep writing books. I get to live out my dream career. I also have proof that at least some people find me amusing and entertaining, as my family has had their doubts. (Take that, family!) Thank you for loving stories and for loving my stories, in particular.

Dawn Frederick, you goddess divine, you. Thank you for being my guide and advocate and a dream agent. Kelsy Thompson, you continue to be my creative guardian angel. I could have done so much damage to this story if you weren't so cursing good at your job. Your brain belongs on the top tier of Mount Olympus. As always, thanks to everyone at Flux, especially Mari Kesselring, Megan Naidl, McKelle George, and Sarah Taplin for making Kali's story real and a thing of beauty.

The first draft of this story was written in 2013 during National Novel Writing Month, aka NaNoWriMo. (Though I hear some people call that month . . . November? Sounds fake.) The first

17,000 words or so were written in a cabin in the woods where, I am happy to report, I was not brutally murdered. (Thanks for the inspiring, murder-free weekend, Darci Cole!) And Gina Denny, you were the first person I ever talked to about this project and you were spectacularly encouraging. When you invited me to join in on the aforementioned murder-free writer's retreat, you couldn't have known what a huge impact it would have on me. Thanks for your unflagging support, friend.

Hugs and love to my amazingly supportive writing friends: my Storymakers pals and fellow 2017 debuts, Katie Nelson, Emily King, Rosalyn Eves, Caitlin Sangster, and Breeana Shields; the AZ YA writers, especially Abigail, Kelly, Steph and my Flux sister, Amy Trueblood; the Class of 2K17; and the amazing bloggers who support and promote my work, including Krysti at YA and Wine, Sarah at the Clever Reader, and Christy Jane at Book Crushin'. Thank you all.

Emily, Susannah, and Molly—I talked to you about *Lovestruck* almost six years ago, before I even had an agent, and you believed in me. I love you and owe you forever. Molly Tagge, you fabulous harpy, thank you for letting me talk about Kali and Deya and Hector and the lot for weeks on end and for all the brainstorming. The Pygmalion Problem lecture Kali received is thanks to you. PS, this is the best your hair has ever looked. (HA! It works!) Aubrie Baird, thank you for reading this story after I'd shelved it, and thank you even more for loving it. I love your guts.

To my entire Bikman/Cooper-Leavitt and White family, thank you for supporting, championing, and encouraging me. I scored big time in the family department. I love you all.

Elsie, Hugo, and Archer: I love and adore you more than words can express. I am so cursing proud of you and your kindness and courage. I'll hold you forever in the middle of my heart. Dice: Eros and Psyche have nothing on us. For one thing, we have more nicknames and inside jokes in 20 years than they've had in eons. For another, our love story is totally more romantic and swoon-worthy and fated (without being remotely fatalistic, obviously). Also, holy Hades, are you ever hot.

Lastly, to my (profoundly merciful and un-Olympian) God, I express endless gratitude and love for every ounce of inspiration and every blessing I have received.

About the Author

Kate Watson is a young adult writer, wife, and mother of three and the tenth of thirteen children. Originally from Canada, she attended college in the States and holds a BA in Philosophy from Brigham Young University. A lover of travel, speaking in accents, and experiencing new cultures, she has also lived in Israel, Brazil, and the American South, and she now calls Arizona home. *Lovestruck* is her third novel.